DEFENDER HELLHOUND

PROTECTION, INC: DEFENDERS 3

ZOE CHANT

CHAPTER 1

It was amazing how much less time you wasted on the internet when you had only a year to live.

When Natalie took out her phone, she felt no desire—well, very little, anyway—to look up photos of cute puppies. Instead, she used it to double-check the diagram to make sure she'd put on her gear correctly. After all, if she messed that up, she'd have considerably less than a year to live. In fact, she'd have exactly six seconds.

But she'd made no mistakes. In her time as a trapeze artist, she'd learned a great deal about harnesses and buckles, not to mention the value of double-checking them when you intended to leap from a height.

She walked up to the edge of the cliff and looked down. It was a gorgeous view. The early morning light had a translucent quality, making everything seem delicate as glass. Sunrise tinted the clouds the yellow-pink of a ripe peach. The beach below was a golden stripe against the glittering blue-green ocean.

It was so unfair that she had so little time left in this beautiful world.

Natalie shoved that thought aside. Since there was nothing she could do about her situation, she had to focus on not wasting any of the time she did have.

The air was cold and clear, scented with wildflowers and salt. She spread her arms wide, readying to jump.

Someone grabbed her from behind.

Before she could react, her attacker was dragging her away. Whoever he was, he was strong. But she'd been trained in self-defense, and she'd fought a few times in her day. She was startled, but not panicked.

Her left elbow drove straight back, ramming into her attacker's stomach. He let out a pained grunt, and his hold loosened slightly. She stomped on his foot as hard as she could, then kicked backward. Natalie felt his weight shift as he side-stepped, and her foot went through air rather than his kneecap. She took advantage of his distraction to drop down, hoping to use her trained agility and flexible joints to slip from his grip like a watermelon seed.

Triumph flared within her as his arms closed on nothing. Natalie rolled away, catching a quick glimpse of her attacker as she did: a tall man, lean and wiry. Broad-shouldered. He was stronger than her, and had a far longer reach.

She was trapped between him and the cliff's edge. There was no escape.

Natalie looked into his eyes—very dark eyes, wide with some strong emotion—and laughed.

"So long, sucker!" Natalie shouted, and threw herself off the cliff.

He lunged forward with shocking speed, catching her around the waist. But her momentum overcame his strength. They both went over the edge.

Natalie plummeted through the air. It was exhilarating and terrifying—more so because she didn't know if her attacker, who still clung to her, would entangle her parachute, killing them both. But she had no time to check or try to free herself from him. With no other choices, she could only experience the moment of freefall, the rush of adrenaline, the utter clarity of thought:

I'm alive.

This moment, I am alive.

That feeling was why she had come to the cliff in the first place; she was glad the attacker hadn't ruined it for her. She counted down seconds, savoring the experience, then pulled the pilot chute.

The parachute inflated with a jerk. An instant later, she was floating gently down toward the beach—with the man who had attacked her still clinging to her like a limpet. But rather than being afraid, she laughed again, giddy with adrenaline. What a ridiculous predicament!

Her feet touched the wet sand. The parachute settled down behind them.

The man let go of her and stepped back. "You were BASE jumping."

"Yes, of course," Natalie said. "What did you think I was doing?"

"I thought you were throwing yourself off a cliff!"

She could hear the honesty in his voice. Their entire encounter rearranged itself in her mind like the shifting patterns of a kaleidoscope. No longer worried that he meant her harm, she unbuckled her harness and set it atop the parachute, then straightened up. "Were you trying to save my life?"

He gave a deep sigh, rubbing his forehead. "Yes. Did you think I was attacking you?"

"It was a reasonable assumption, considering that you snuck up and grabbed me from behind," she pointed out, then politely added, "But thank you for trying."

"You're welcome." The expression on his face made her stifle another laugh.

"And sorry for elbowing you. And stomping on your foot. And dragging you off a cliff."

He gave her a wry glance, like he was about to smile. He didn't, though. "Don't worry about it. Like you said, it was a reasonable assumption."

For the first time, she had a chance to get a good look at her would-be rescuer. She'd noted before that he was tall and lean, and had discovered for herself the strength in those wiry muscles. Now she saw that he had auburn hair, currently extremely windswept, a handsome angular face with high cheekbones and a strong chin, and dark brown eyes like wells that went deep, deep down. They were eyes that caught her attention, that made her want to look more...

Something about that impulse made her nervous. She broke off eye contact and tried to observe the whole of him objectively. What would she think of him if she was back at the circus, running a roulette table and considering him as a possible mark to be scammed?

I'd decide that he's not a mark, she thought instantly. *He's much too smart. And observant. In fact, if I saw him around, that game would turn into an honest one until he went away, in case he figured out the whole thing and decided to call the cops.*

Natalie wasn't sure exactly what about him had made her think that, but she trusted her judgment. After all, she'd been raised by con artists. If they couldn't make accurate snap judgments about people, they'd try to con the wrong one and end up in jail.

She tried to get more of a read on him, based both on observation and prior experience. Intelligent. Brave. Self-sacrificing. Self-possessed. He didn't seem the slightest bit shaken by having unexpectedly tandem BASE jumped off a cliff. And he knew how to fight. That suggested a military or first responder background... but then again, the same could be said about her, and she was a civilian.

He wore navy pants, a white button-down shirt, a brown jacket, and shoes that looked like they belonged in an office but had soles suitable for running in. The whole ensemble was neither noticeably cheap nor noticeably expensive. It didn't particularly suit him, but it didn't look bad on him, either. If she'd passed him in the street, she'd have guessed "college professor." But that didn't square with the rest, unless your idea of a college professor was Indiana Jones.

And all that time he'd stood there in patient silence, studying her as she was studying him.

"Okay, you got me." She offered him her hand. "I'm Natalie Nash. Who are you?"

He reached out his own. Long fingers, big knuckles, small scars from burns and cuts and scrapes. A handyman? A chef?

Then those long fingers closed around hers, and the crackle of sexual chemistry that passed between them made her stop guessing. She looked up at him, startled, back into those deep dark eyes.

Goddammit.

She'd be dead in a year. The absolute the last thing she needed was to fall in love.

"I'm Ransom," he said. "Ransom Pierce."

Goddammit, she thought again. *Double dammit.*

Natalie yanked her hand from his grip. "You're Merlin's buddy from the Marines! He sicced you on me!"

He looked startled. "No—"

"You're telling me there's more than one tall redhead named *Ransom Pierce?*"

"No, I *am* Merlin's…" He seemed to choke on the word "buddy," and instead said, "I did serve with him in the Marines. And we do work together now. We're both bodyguards in a private security agency—Protection, Inc: Defenders. But he didn't *sic* me on you."

"Okay, so *sic* was a bit of an unfair word," she admitted. "Let me rephrase that. He sent you to find me."

Ransom shook his head. "I came of my own accord. Merlin has no idea I'm here, or that you're in town. All he knows is that you left the circus and you didn't tell anyone why."

Natalie didn't believe that for an instant. "We've never met before, you're buddies with the guy who's practically my brother, and you just happened to turn up here? Why, because you had a psychic vision that I was about to jump off a cliff?"

That wry, *maybe I'm thinking about smiling* look reappeared on his face. "As a matter of fact, yes. That's exactly what happened."

His words had the ring of absolute truth. If he was a liar, he was the best she'd ever encountered. And Natalie, like Merlin, had been raised by expert liars. *Professional* liars, even.

Which reminded her that the woman who'd raised her was a fake psychic, and had taught Natalie how to pretend to have a psychic vision. It was easy. You rolled your eyes, clutched your head, and intoned stuff you'd learned about the person you were conning via basic internet research.

She gave him a fierce grin, enjoying the game. "Okay, Pierce the Psychic. What's my foster mother's secret?"

He pushed back a lock of auburn hair that the wind was blowing into his eyes. "If you mean the woman who runs the crime circus you and Merlin were raised in, I don't need to be psychic to know that. I've met her. Her name is Janet Gold, she has a fake mindreading act under the name of Madame Fortuna, and she turns into a parrot."

Natalie was taken aback. Either Ransom really had met Janet, or Merlin had told him the secret of the Fabulous Flying Chameleons—both its secrets! It not only was a crime circus, but all the performing animals were shifters. But after another moment's thought, Natalie dismissed the idea that Merlin might have blabbed. He thought of Janet as his mom—no "foster" or other caveats about it. He'd die before revealing anything that could harm her.

"How is Janet?" Natalie said hesitantly, feeling guilty that she didn't already know.

"She's fine," Ransom reassured her. "So is everyone else. The circus ran into a bit of a problem, but it's over now."

Natalie was in a quandary. She didn't believe in psychic visions, but he'd found her somehow...

He broke into her thoughts. "Why don't you call Merlin? He can confirm everything I'm saying."

Her hands flew up in an automatic warding-off gesture. "I don't want to call Merlin! Don't tell him you saw me."

"Why? He's worried about you. You must know that. You left the circus without telling anyone why or where you were going."

Natalie gave an uneasy shrug, then a wave of her hand, as if to brush the question aside. He was making her feel guilty, and she hated feeling guilty.

But rather than drop the subject, he pressed forward. "Why don't you want to talk to Merlin?"

"See, now, that is exactly the sort of thing the spirits would tell you if you really were psychic."

Ransom gave a frustrated sigh. "Okay, first of all, there's no spirits involved. Second of all, that's not how it works. I *know* things—a lot of things—but not everything."

He put an odd emphasis on *know*, as if it didn't mean quite the same thing to him as it did to most people. It could almost make her believe… but no, that was ridiculous. He was putting on a truly world-class act, but that was all.

"Right," Natalie said. "That's always the excuse. Drop the psychic act, okay? If you're friends with Janet and Merlin, you should know it's professional courtesy not to scam a scammer."

He rubbed his forehead, but not in a "the spirits are talking to me" way. More in a "this conversation is giving me a headache" way. Then he looked straight into her eyes, pinning her with the force of his dark gaze. "Did you leave the circus because you don't want anyone to know you only have a year to live?"

His words struck her like a gust of strong wind. She actually took a step backwards, right into her parachute. As she started to trip, he grabbed her shoulders, steadying her until she could stand again.

Once again, she felt that jolt of sexual chemistry, but this time it did nothing but add to her roiling emotions and the buzzing hive of thoughts flying around her head. There was no way he could know that. She'd told no one, and she'd given the doctor a false name and a fake insurance card to go with it.

Maybe he really was psychic.

More importantly, he *knew*.

Ransom was the only person in the world who knew that she, Natalie Nash, had only a year to live.

It all hit her so intensely that she slipped from his grasp and sat down hard on the crumpled mound of parachute cloth.

Natalie wasn't sure how long she'd sat there, wrestling with so many feelings that she couldn't even sort them all out, before she realized that she was warmer. A cold breeze had been blowing in from the sea, chilling her without her even noticing it, but it had stopped. She glanced up and saw Ransom crouched on his heels in front of her, shielding her from the wind with his body.

With an awkward abruptness, he said, "I shouldn't have said that."

"Why not? It's the truth." Then, the realization coming just ahead of the words, she added, "I'm glad someone knows. Even if it's someone I don't know, who I'll never see again."

Ransom was giving her the strangest look. As if she was breaking his heart. That couldn't be right. It was only that he had sad-looking eyes. "Why don't you tell Merlin?"

"My God, you're persistent."

He didn't reply, but only made a "go on" gesture.

She could have lied or told him to mind his own business, but the idea of telling him the truth was weirdly tempting. It was also reckless, but being reckless felt good. Having him know her secret felt good. And with this little time left, what else did she have but pursuing what felt good?

"I don't want him to ever find out," she said. "Janet either. Or anyone else at the circus. It would make them so sad. I want everyone who cares about me to believe that I went on with my life, and I'm alive and happy somewhere else." Then, struck by an awful thought, she said, "You haven't told him already, have you?"

He shook his head.

"Good," she said. But *that* didn't feel good. Merlin was her friend, he was right there in Refuge City, and the only way to keep him happy was to never see him again. He was sharp as a tack—if she spoke to him at all, even over the phone, he'd figure out that something was wrong. And now that she and Ransom had settled the question of whether Merlin knew and why she didn't want to see him, her business with Ransom was concluded and she'd never see those sad eyes of his again.

And that made *her* sad.

She had the impulse to grab his hand and say, *"Run away with me."*

Or at least, *"Come have coffee with me."*

She couldn't have a real relationship now, of course. But there was nothing wrong with casual encounters, so long as everyone was on the same page and enjoying themselves. He already knew the most important thing. If he said yes, it would be in the full knowledge that it wouldn't—couldn't—be more than a brief affair.

But there was something about him that was the opposite of casual. If she'd been playing a fake psychic, she'd have felt completely confident in pressing the back of her hand to her forehead, and saying the spirits had told her he'd never had a one-night stand in his life.

And never mind sex, even something as small as having a longer conversation with him felt… dangerous. He was too intriguing. His eyes were too dark. His skin was too warm. He couldn't follow where she was going, and she couldn't stay where he lived. They'd met fifteen minutes ago, and in that time they'd gone off a cliff together and shared her deepest secret. If she let him stick around any longer, who knew what else might happen?

It wasn't even a real question. She already knew where it would go. She was lonely and he had sad eyes, and one thing would lead to another. And that would lead to feelings. And then she'd feel guiltier and guiltier with every moment that passed, counting the hours as they ticked down to the day she'd break his heart. So much for enjoying the time she had left!

As for Ransom, those eyes of his made her think life had kicked him around plenty already. If they got together, maybe her death would be the last straw. Maybe it wouldn't only break his heart, but break *him*.

Natalie shot to her feet, then turned her back on him and began folding the parachute. Without looking over her shoulder, she said, "Nice meeting you! Goodbye."

CHAPTER 2

*R*ansom prided himself on control. Self-control. Taking control of a situation. It was something he'd practiced long before he'd become a Marine, and he was good at it.

But his control had started cracking years ago, and time had only widened and deepened those cracks. The last six months, he'd felt like he was holding himself together with Scotch tape.

In the last ten minutes alone, he'd barged in to rescue Natalie when she didn't need rescuing, and ruined his chances of saving her from otherwise certain death. When she turned her back on him, he felt like he was watching her prepare to jump again, but this time without a parachute.

All his careful planning went out the window, and he blurted out, "No, wait! You don't have to die! I can save you!"

Her small, clever hands ceased their rapid movement. It was like his words had turned her to stone. Then she whipped around, so fast that it sent her hair flying around her face. Her expression was so fierce that he expected her to shout. Instead, she spoke with a quiet intensity that drove every word home.

"I had an accident at the circus." There was no self-pity in her words, only a straightforward recounting of facts. "I touched a live wire, and I got a shock that damaged my heart. I'm sure you've read stuff on the internet about how everything can be cured by magnets or eliminating mold or drinking a tea made from mold or visiting a magical tree in Sardinia, but so has everyone else. Half the reason I'm not telling anyone is that I don't want to spend the last year of my life being pestered to wear healing rocks and give up gluten."

"Every complicated problem has a solution that's easy, simple, and wrong," Ransom said. "That's not what I'm talking about. Also, I think you should eat all the gluten you want."

Unexpectedly, Natalie laughed. She had a lovely laugh, high and clear as her voice. Like a windchime. "Good idea. I'll add it to my list."

"What list?"

"My bucket list. All the things I want to do before I die." She reached for a fanny pack she had clipped to her belt, and took out a folded piece of paper and a pen. Unfolding the paper, she glanced around, presumably looking for a surface to write on, then spotted a flat stone by the cliff edge and headed for it.

He went with her. Since her gaze was on the rock, not on him, he couldn't resist taking the opportunity to observe her.

Be honest, he thought. *To drink her in.*

Natalie wore garnet-red leggings, a black tank top, and black ballet slippers. It had all been chosen for practicality, he was sure, but it showed off her body to perfection.

She was short and slim, with narrow hips and small breasts. When she moved, he could see the strong muscles of her shoulders and arms, her back and legs; unsurprising, as she was a trapeze artist and an acrobat. He'd experienced that strength for himself when she'd fought him. But the overall impression she gave was one of lightness: a small frame, dainty little hands and feet, quick graceful movements. She walked lightly too, as if her feet only touched the ground by her own choice.

Her face was sharp-boned, elfin; her eyes were tilted like a cat's. Her hair was short, tousled by the wind, but he suspected that it always looked that way: it had been exactly as rumpled in his vision of her in the doctor's office as it was right now. But in that vision, she'd been in a green medical gown, sitting under white lights that cast a sickly glare on her skin, dulled her hair, and washed out her eyes.

In reality and in the fragile light of early morning, her rainbow-dyed hair was almost impossibly vivid. Scarlet strands blew in the wind, now making a brilliant pop of color against a wave of gold, now merging with a sunset streak of orange-pink. She brushed a deep blue lock out of her eyes.

Beneath that riot of color, her eyes shone clear and knowing. At last, he could see their color. They were blue, a light gray-blue like a misty morning.

He'd been struck by her beauty in the vision, but that had been nothing compared to seeing the living, breathing, moving woman in real life, close enough to touch. It was like watching a black-and-white film change to Technicolor. And even that was nothing compared to being in her presence, feeling the heat of her body, having the full force of her personality strike him as hard as her elbow had struck his ribcage.

She'd left a mark on him, and in more ways than one. They'd only met a few minutes ago, and already he felt changed.

But he also remembered the terrible knowledge his power had given him when he'd used it to ask if he could save her life:

She *could* be saved... and only he could save her.

He didn't know how he could do it, nor was it at all certain that it would happen. It was only a possibility, and a small one at that.

And along with that possibility came a certainty: if he saved her life, that would somehow cause his team to learn his terrible secret.

At that time, when he'd only ever seen her in a vision, he hadn't been certain he could bring himself to go through with it. Could he really give up everything he had and make everyone he cared about hate him, just for a tiny chance at saving the life of a woman he didn't even know?

But he knew her now. She wasn't "a woman," she was Natalie Nash, who laughed at death and jumped off cliffs and dyed her hair into a living rainbow. He couldn't walk away if there was any chance of saving her, no matter what it would cost him.

The image came to him again, of his shattered pieces being held together with Scotch tape. Natalie was like a whirlwind. Could he save her if it meant shattering himself?

She stopped walking and held the paper to the rock. He quickly moved his gaze from her body to her list. It was written in several different colors of ink, sometimes in pencil, and once with a paintbrush. She had a bold and jagged hand that wasn't easy to read.

BAND LUMP—no, that had to be BASE JUMP—was near the top. As soon as he deciphered it, she struck a line through it.

"Done!" Natalie said triumphantly. She glanced up at him. "Did you enjoy it? What did it feel like to you?"

"The BASE jump, you mean?" As she nodded, the memory of it returned: the sickening horror as they fell, the rush of understanding and relief when she pulled the pilot cord, and the split second of relaxing into the warmth of her body before they touched down and it was all over. But he couldn't remember the sensation of free fall, only his conviction that the last thing he'd ever experience was the knowledge that he'd failed to save her.

"I've parachuted before," he said. "I haven't BASE jumped. I feel like I still haven't. There was too much going on inside my head for me to really experience it. What about you?"

"Oh, it was wonderful." Her eyes shone. Without moving, her entire body seemed to lift. The memory of it alone made her radiant. "Exactly what I'd hoped it would be."

"You weren't distracted by having a mystery attacker literally hanging on to you?"

"Not really. But then again, I'm—I mean, I *was*—a trapeze artist. You have to focus on the moment no matter what else is going on, or you'll fall."

Natalie bent again, scribbling on her list.

"EEL GLUTTON?" he read aloud.

She laughed. "EAT GLUTEN. Like you suggested. Not that I didn't before. But I could always eat more of it. You're right, it's delicious. What's your favorite type?"

"Of gluten?"

She nodded.

He'd never thought of it before, which was unusual for him. Sometimes he felt like he'd thought of everything, a thousand times over. "Fresh-baked bread. What's yours?"

"Cream puffs. Now I'm hungry. Got any gluten stashed in your pockets?"

"I'm afraid not."

"What a shame." She folded the list up again and tucked it away. When she straightened up, a lock of forest-green hair fell across her forehead. Her bright eyes now seemed a light gray-green, like lichen on stone.

Gray, he thought. *Her eyes are gray. They take the color from whatever's nearest to them, or from the light.*

It felt like an important realization. Everything about the meeting felt important, imbued with some deeper significance than was on the surface. Natalie's eyes. Her list. Her rainbow hair. The folded parachute on the wet sand. Himself, standing on the beach beside her, trying to figure out how to convince her to trust in a power she didn't believe in, wielded by a man who wasn't worthy of anyone's trust.

"You were raised by shifters," he said. "So you know there's more to the world than meets the eye."

"I was raised by shifter con artists in an international crime circus," she said. "So I know there's *lots* more to the world than meets the eye. The cards are marked. The bowling pins are glued to tiny springs so they wobble but don't fall over. The woman who asks you to watch her dog while she goes to a job interview is a con artist, and the dog is a shifter."

"Right. I'm a shifter too." He'd intended to mention that only as an introduction to the story that he hoped would convince her. But she interrupted him.

"Oh? What sort?"

Ransom felt like he'd walked straight into a trap. Of course she'd want to know what he was—what he could turn into, he corrected himself, not what he *was*. He swallowed, feeling the dark presence of his beast stir within him. "A hellhound."

"Come on..." Then, looking into his eyes, she said, "Seriously?"

"Yes. I'm not like your friends from the circus. I wasn't born a shifter, I was kidnapped and experimented on. The people who did that didn't only make me a shifter, they gave me other powers too. I see things. I *know* things. That's how I know I might be able to save you."

"Uh-huh." She looked extremely doubtful.

It was only then that Ransom remembered his original plan. He had a very easy way to convince her, and he'd intended to lead with it. But between the shock of finding her at the cliff edge, the bigger shock of the unexpected BASE jump, and the disorienting, overwhelming, unpredictable presence of Natalie herself, it had fallen out of his head. "I had a vision of you, when the doctor told you that you only had a year to live. He warned you that any excitement could strain your heart. He told you to do tai chi and not watch any scary movies."

"Oh!" Natalie's eyes—violet now under a lock of purple hair—opened wide. "Okay. I believe you. I mean, I believe in the visions. Probably. I guess you could have bugged the room."

"Why would I bug the room of a random doctor in the hope of spying on someone I'd never even met?"

She shrugged. "Because a vision told you to?"

"But if I have visions, then I wouldn't need—" He broke off, realizing that she was teasing him. "Very funny."

She grinned. "I try."

"Anyway, that's how I know I might be able to save your life. After I had the vision, I just... *knew* it."

Ransom expected a big reaction, so much so that he was also bracing himself for her disappointment when he explained the rest of it. He wasn't sure exactly what she'd do—laugh for joy, be so overwhelmed by emotion that she'd have to sit down, do a cartwheel—but he knew there'd be *something*.

But there was nothing. Natalie was very still. The only movement was her hair, blowing in the ocean breeze, and the flicker of her lashes as she blinked. For the first time since he'd met her, her face was completely expressionless. He had no idea what she was thinking. Finally, she said, "You *might* be able to."

"Yes. I know I have a chance. I don't know if I'll actually be able to make it happen."

She hadn't looked delighted when he'd said she had a chance, and she didn't look disappointed when he underlined that it was *only* a chance. He didn't understand it. She seemed so in love with life. She should be thrilled to learn that she wasn't doomed after all.

"If you're planning to bite me and give me shifter healing, you need to know that it won't work," she said. "I already tried. Some people just can't become shifters, and I'm one of them."

Shifters did heal better than normal humans, though they were hardly immune to illness and injury. But the thought of making her into a hellhound struck him with a bone-deep horror. What was the point of saving her life only to ruin it? "That wasn't what I meant."

"What, then? What's the treatment you think might work?"

"I don't know. I'm not sure it *is* a treatment. I just know there's something I can do, and it has a chance of working. A small chance. But small is better than none."

Natalie looked deeply unimpressed. He wished he hadn't emphasized how small the chance was. But he couldn't lie to her, especially about her own life.

"Okay," she said at last. "I tell you what. If and when you figure that part out, call and let me know. And thanks for… uh… everything!"

Once again, she turned her back on him. She knelt in the sand and began packing the parachute into the harness.

Ransom was clenching his jaw so hard, it actually hurt. This wasn't how their meeting was supposed to go. All the same, he wasn't giving up. Stepping in front of her, he said, "I'm a bodyguard. Protecting people is my job. Let me protect you."

"I can protect myself," Natalie said. "I even gave you a demo!"

"Not like that. I meant that if I'm with you, whatever it is I can do to save you, I'll have a chance to do it."

She blew out a breath, sending her hair fluttering. He couldn't stop looking at it. There were so many colors, and every time she moved or the wind blew, it changed. Like her eyes. They were pure gray now, like a storm.

"Let me show you something." She took out and unfolded her bucket list. He couldn't read the scribble below BASE JUMP—it looked like RUSTPROOF FEMINIST—but she skipped over it and pointed to the words below that. "See that?"

"TALL MOTEL?" Ransom hazarded.

Natalie snickered. "TAJ MAHAL. Which is in India. My flight is tomorrow morning. So unless you want to follow me there…"

"I'd do that," he heard himself say.

The amusement dropped from her face, replaced by sheer shock. For the first time, he realized, she knew how committed he was.

For the first time, *he* knew how committed he was. Would he really leave everything to follow her, a woman he'd met once in real life and seen once in a vision, just for the smallest chance of saving her life?

In his vision, he'd seen her learn that she was dying, and face the news with a courage that had stunned him. The doctor had told her that any shock—even any strong emotion—could literally kill her. He'd advised her to extend her life as much as possible by living quietly, free of all excitement and stress. She'd told him that wouldn't suit her, and had left to ride a roller coaster!

She had to stay in this world. She *had* to.

Natalie reached out her hand to him. She had such small hands. They looked dainty and fragile, but he'd felt their startling strength. Her nails were clipped very short, and her palms were as callused as if she did manual labor all day. The trapeze looked glamorous from a distance, but it was hard, physical work.

He reached out to her. His hand was trembling. So was hers. In a second, they'd clasp hands, and then his whole life would change.

He felt a heart-stopping jolt as her fingertips brushed his. And then she yanked her hand away like she'd been burned by his touch, leaped backwards, and landed with a very final-sounding thud.

"No!" Her shout made the cliffs echo. Lowering her voice, she said, "No. Look, I get that you *believe* that you can save me. When I was waiting in the doctor's lobby, this woman was telling her friend that going on a macrobiotic diet would save her life, and she absolutely believed it—"

"Drop the stuff about internet miracle cures," he interrupted. "You and I both know that's not what I'm talking about. This is real. Anyway, what do you have to lose?"

Natalie looked at him steadily. The sunlight flickered across her face as clouds scudded in the wind, making her eyes shift from light gray to dark. "More than you know."

What she has to lose is enjoying the last year of her life. The deep growl of his inner hellhound scraped against his mind like sandpaper. *You'd ruin it for her by being there.*

The words hit like a punch to the solar plexus, taking his breath away. As he stood silent, she gave him a wistful smile.

"Good-bye, Ransom." She walked away across the golden sand. Her rainbow hair floated in the breeze, and the rippling waves drowned out the sound of her footsteps.

"You said I could call you if I figured it out," Ransom shouted after her. "I need your phone number!"

Her clear voice floated back to him. "You're the psychic!"

CHAPTER 3

The Rutabaga Festival was a huge disappointment.

Natalie wandered disconsolately through its less-than-teeming crowds, wondering if the problem was it or her. She'd returned the rented parachute and harness, then headed straight out to the festival, so maybe she'd tried to cram too much into one day.

Or maybe rutabagas were an uninspiring vegetable. The History of the Rutabaga stall consisted of nothing but a few posters and a short, unenlightening pamphlet. The rutabaga toss was a basic—not even interestingly rigged—toss stall with rutabagas instead of tennis balls. Even the unintentionally creepy leafy-wigged mascot in a rutabaga costume did little to lighten her gloom.

She tossed her half-eaten skewer of roasted rutabaga chunks into the trash, got herself a cone of rutabaga ice cream, and was dismayed though unsurprised to find that it tasted like rutabaga.

"I don't know what I expected," she murmured aloud as she sent it to join the skewer.

As she spoke, she was struck by the longing to have Ransom with her, to hear her say that and for his face to lighten into that wry almost-a-smile. It was the oddest feeling, as irrational as it was intense. He would seem so incongruous at this ridiculous vegetable festival, which was exactly what made her want to see him there.

"Stop thinking about him," she muttered, drawing a glance from the rutabaga mascot.

She wished Merlin was with her. Now he was a man who would appreciate this sort of thing... though maybe not this exact example of it. A brief grin crossed her face as she imagined him rushing around, trying all the rutabaga fare within a period of ten minutes, concluding that he disliked rutabagas, and dragging her off to a turnip festival instead.

He was so close. They were literally in the same city. All she needed to do was call him, and he'd be there. And she'd be with her best friend, her almost-a-brother, and she'd no longer be alone...

...and, like any good brother, he'd instantly pick up that something was up with her, and he'd hound her until she told him everything. Imagining the look on his face when he found out that she was dying made her feel almost physically ill.

No. What she needed was someone who didn't have all that history with her, who hadn't grown up with her, and who didn't consider her family. Someone who wouldn't cry when he learned her secret, because he already knew it.

A tall lean man with dark brown eyes and red-brown hair, like a spirit of autumn. A man who'd risk his life to save a woman he didn't even know, who'd offer to go to the ends of the earth with her on a moment's notice because he thought he could save her. A man with a little bit of stubble roughening his cheeks and chin. She'd felt it as they struggled together at the cliff's edge, along with the startling softness of his lips as they'd brushed across her wrist...

Natalie shook her head hard, sending her hair flying. She clenched her fists at her sides and told herself, *I don't need Ransom. He is the opposite of what I need. And more importantly, I'm the opposite of what he needs.*

The fact that he'd stuck in her memory, his image so vivid that she could almost feel the ghost of his warmth at her side, was proof that she'd done the right thing in getting the hell away from him. She had a plan for the rest of her life, and she wasn't going to let him mess it up. And she especially wasn't going to let her last action in this world be to mess up *his* life.

It was a lucky thing that soon she'd be eight thousand miles away from him. There was nothing like a lot of distance for removing temptation.

So she didn't feel as enthusiastic now about the Taj Mahal (*the tall motel,* she recalled with another quick grin) as she had when she'd written it down. But once she was actually there, she was sure she'd enjoy it. After all, it was a wonder of the world.

The Rutabaga Festival, she decided, was not even a wonder of the neighborhood. She took out her bucket list and crossed it off. She'd find something else to do for the rest of her day.

A sharp yelp made her head jerk up. It sounded like a puppy—a puppy that was afraid or hurt. Poor thing! Natalie looked around, but saw no dogs other than a few happily trotting along on leashes.

The yelp sounded again, even more scared-sounding. It sounded like it had come from high overhead, but that was impossible. The fair was in a field with scattered trees, and there were no buildings beyond the low food stalls.

She craned her neck anyway. And there, clinging and scrabbling for dear life on a high branch of the tallest tree in the field, was a puppy. A little white husky puppy, fluffy and adorable, stuck up a tree like a cat.

White-hot rage burned through her body as she realized that someone must have put the puppy there. Probably as some kind of sick joke. Or maybe they were filming it, hoping for a viral video. If she caught whoever had done that, she'd give them a viral video—one of her dragging them somewhere high and leaving them there!

The puppy whined, looking down at her with bright blue eyes, and Natalie forgot her fantasies of revenge. She sprang into action.

"You!" She pointed to a woman showing off her homemade quilt in which every square had an embroidered rutabaga. "Grab that quilt and follow me! And you, and you, and you!" Natalie pointed in turn at the nearest three people, making sure to meet their eyes so they couldn't pretend they hadn't heard. "You follow me too! You're going to use the quilt as a net, in case the puppy falls!"

Ignoring the bewildered murmurs, she grabbed the closest two by the wrists (they were a sulky teenage boy and his harassed-looking mother) and hauled them with her. She released them once she got to the base of the tree, hustled them and the others into position holding the quilt outstretched below the puppy, and began to climb the tree.

It wasn't a terribly difficult climb, though there were long stretches with no branches where she had to shimmy up. What made it hard was her fear that she'd frighten or excite the puppy enough to make it lose its grip.

"Hey pal," she murmured as she made her way upward. "Hold still, all right? I'm coming to get you, but you can't move a muscle. Just stay where you are."

The husky puppy gave a piteous whine, but kept still. Natalie's heart pounded as she got closer, reminding her of the doctor's warning to avoid surprises and intense emotions. If she got too scared, it could literally kill her. And then the puppy would fall for sure.

But her heart was only beating faster and harder. That was normal when you were excited. As long as it kept to its current steady rhythm, she'd be fine.

"It's okay," she said softly, unsure if it was to the puppy or herself. Either way, she hoped she wasn't lying. "Everything's going to be all right."

The branch the puppy was on was far too slender to bear her weight, and the poor little thing was too far out on it for her to reach. Natalie frowned, wondering how the hell the horrible person who'd stranded the pup had even gotten it there. *Nobody* was light enough to crawl out on that branch.

Then she realized how it had been done: the branch above it was strong and thick. That puppy-stranding creep must have gotten out on that branch, then lowered the puppy in a basket on a rope.

Natalie didn't have a basket. But she didn't need one. She shimmied upward, wriggled along the branch until she was above the puppy, then locked her ankles around the branch and released her hands, letting herself dangle upside down. She stretched out her arms as far as she could, but she couldn't quite reach…

The little white puppy gave a happy bark and leaped upward, right into her waiting arms.

She caught and cuddled it, dizzy with relief. "You poor thing! Well, you're safe now. Don't you worry, I'll take revenge on whoever put you there if I ever figure out who it was. But first, we have to get back down."

The puppy wriggled excitedly and licked her arms and face. Its fur was incredibly thick and fluffy. Still dangling upside down by her ankles, she considered the route back. She could retrace her climb holding the puppy in one arm, but it would be awfully tedious.

"Don't be scared," Natalie told the puppy. "I promise, this is safe. I've been doing it since I was eleven."

She held the puppy tight with her left arm, leaving her right free, and released her ankles. They plummeted downward, and she heard a chorus of screams from below.

"Oops," she muttered as she caught a branch with her right hand. She'd forgotten that she had an audience. Raising her voice to a shout, she called, "It's okay! I'm a trained professional!"

The puppy barked, as if to say, *"That was fun! Do it again!"*

Natalie obliged, releasing the branch and catching the next one down. She proceeded that way until she got to the last branch. She did a swing all the way around it, just for fun, since the puppy seemed to be enjoying itself. Then she dropped lightly to the ground, planting her feet solidly and without a wobble.

The puppy wriggled delightedly in her arms. The crowd—a much larger one now than the four people she'd grabbed—burst into cheers and applause. Next thing she knew, she was surrounded by a mob of people asking for her autograph and how she'd learned to do that and if she'd be willing to be next year's Rutabaga Queen.

That brought her down to earth. She wasn't going to have a next year. But she smiled and deflected everyone with a fake name and a fake background as a Cirque du Soliel performer, and then turned the questions on them. Apparently the puppy didn't belong to anyone, and no one had seen how it had gotten into the tree.

"I think he's yours," said the woman with the quilt.

"Oh, no," Natalie said. "I can't have a pet. I'm leaving town tomorrow morning."

The puppy gave a gusty sigh, flopped down across her shoes, rolled over on to his back, and began to snore with all four feet in the air, like a dead bug. Natalie, caught between amusement and dismay, noticed that he was a boy.

"Take him with you," said the quilt woman. She bent down, expertly transferred the puppy from Natalie's shoes to the rutabaga quilt, and thrust the bundle into her arms. "There you go. Keep it. A lovely warm bed for your lovely new pup!"

The puppy woke, blinked his blue eyes at her, then lunged forward, his paws going on either side of her neck like he was hugging her, and began licking her face.

"I can't—" Natalie began, and got a very unwelcome French kiss. "Yecch!"

By the time she'd wiped off her face and had the wriggling puppy safely wrapped up, the crowd had dissipated, leaving them alone together.

Natalie gazed down at the puppy. "Guess it's just you and me now, kid."

The puppy conked out again while she called a taxi, and she was able to smuggle him safely into her motel room. Once inside, she left him snoozing on the bed while she took a shower. She'd gotten all sweaty wandering around the Rutabaga Festival, and shimmying up the tree had lodged itchy bits of bark and dead leaves in all the places where you didn't want them.

Standing under the soothing water, Natalie tried to figure out what to do about the puppy. She couldn't legally take him to India, and she didn't want to risk trying to smuggle him onboard a plane. It seemed like her only options were to cancel the trip and keep the puppy, or keep the trip and give the puppy up.

The puppy scratched at the bathroom door, whining sadly.

"I'll be out in a minute!" Natalie called.

She tipped her face up to the water, closing her eyes.

A bark sounded right next to her. She nearly jumped out of her skin, and only her trained acrobat's reflexes kept her from falling over. The puppy had somehow gotten into the bathroom and was standing with his paws on the rim of the bathtub, his white tail wagging madly.

Natalie hurriedly restrained him before he could leap in with her, then scooped him up and carried him at arms-length to the door. She could have sworn she'd shut it, but she must not have closed it completely. Or maybe he'd stood on his hind legs and turned the knob. She'd heard huskies were very intelligent. Either way, he'd evidently pushed it shut behind him after he'd gotten in.

She plopped the puppy back on the bed, closed the door and locked it, and returned to her shower.

He scratched at the door again.

"No!" Natalie called. "You can't come in! I'll be out soon."

The puppy barked, as if in response. Then she heard rapid-fire clicks, like he was madly dashing across the floor, then a thud and a yelp, as if he'd crashed into the wall. This repeated several times. On the third, Natalie burst out laughing. The puppy gave an indignant yip.

"Okay," she said. "You got me."

The Taj Mahal was a wonder of the world, but there was only so long that you could spend looking at a building, no matter how beautiful it was. The puppy had already brought her more happiness than she'd felt in months. Not to mention that the Taj Mahal would be fine without her, while the puppy was a living creature that needed her. If she kept him, they'd make each other happy for a year, and she could make arrangements to get him a good home once her time was up.

Once she made that decision, she felt better. She didn't—she *couldn't*—have human companionship, but at least she'd no longer be all alone.

As Natalie dried herself off and dressed, she realized that a suspicious silence had fallen. Either the puppy had fallen asleep again, or he was up to something.

She opened the door. The puppy was nowhere to be seen. And the room wasn't big. There was nothing in it but the bed, a table and chairs, a closet, and a mini-fridge.

Natalie looked under the bed. No puppy.

She opened the closet. No puppy.

Feeling like a lunatic, she looked inside the mini-fridge. Still no puppy.

Frantic, she rushed to the front door and was about to fling it open when she heard a yelp behind her. She spun around. It seemed to have come from the closet, but there was still no…

A second yelp drew her gaze upward. The closet had a high shelf, well above Natalie's reach or line of sight, but she could now see a fluffy white head sticking over the edge and peering down at her. The puppy let out a nervous whine.

"How in the world did you get up there? You must be some kind of champion jumper…" Her voice trailed off as she remembered how she'd found the pup. Was it possible that he'd put himself in the tree? "Or a champion climber?"

But that made no sense. Dogs couldn't climb trees, the closet had nothing to climb but a bare wall, and while the high shelf was just barely within the possible range of jumping ability, the branch the puppy had been stuck on had not been.

"Little mysteries," Natalie said, smiling. Animals could do the most amazing things…

The puppy jumped. She held up her arms to catch him.

He vanished in mid-air.

Natalie's heart skipped a beat.

The puppy reappeared in the air above the bed and thumped down. He yawned, scratched his ear vigorously with a hind leg, and flopped down, fast asleep.

But Natalie's heart kept on skipping beats. Its normal rhythm was getting more and more irregular, until it felt like a bird with a broken wing flopping around in her chest.

I could die right now, she realized. *Just from the shock of seeing that sweet little puppy teleport.*

Panic rose up within her, but she forced it down. Moving slowly and deliberately, she sat down on the floor, then lay on her side, breathing deeply and rhythmically. One-two-three-four inhale, hold one-two, one-two-three-four exhale, hold one-two. One-two-three-four inhale…

After a few minutes of that, her heart's rhythm returned to normal. Once she was sure she wasn't going to drop dead, she sat on the bed beside the sleeping puppy, stroking his thick fur and thinking about what she'd seen. It had been a shock—the exact sort of shock the doctor had warned her about—but it had come from something real and astonishing, not a hallucination or an optical illusion or a dream.

The puppy could teleport. She'd seen it herself. That had to have been how he'd gotten on the shelf, up the tree, and inside the bathroom.

Rubbing his soft ears, she racked her mind for anything she'd ever heard about teleporting dogs. Janet had sometimes told tales of magical animals. Merlin had loved those, especially the ones about King Arthur's dog Cavall, who could travel seven leagues in the blink of an eye.

"Huh," Natalie said aloud. She'd always assumed that meant Cavall could run incredibly fast, but maybe "in a blink" was the literal truth.

The pup did need a name.

"Cavall?" Natalie asked, nudging him.

He woke up, nipped her finger, then blinked out. He reappeared wedged in the bathroom sink, tummy-up and paddling all four paws in the air.

Cavall seemed maybe a tad too dignified.

He thrashed himself onto his belly, wagging his tail and barking, then blinked on to the floor and began to chase his tail.

Definitely too dignified.

The husky puppy was such a doggy dog, despite his amazing ability. A good doggo, not a figure from legend. But she liked the idea of giving him a circus-related name. He was obviously drawn to high places, just like her. A wire-walker dog, a trapeze dog, a dog fit for the great circus family, the Flying Wallendas...

"Wally?"

She was answered with a joyous yelp.

CHAPTER 4

Ransom watched Natalie walk across the beach until she'd vanished from view. Everything he'd said and done replayed in his mind, as if he was re-watching a scene from a movie and hoping it would come out differently if he re-ran it often enough: hoping that this time, *this time,* they wouldn't go in the basement or the dog wouldn't die or Ingrid Bergman would join the Resistance with Humphrey Bogart instead of getting on that plane.

You'll never see her again, came the low, grinding growl of his hellhound's voice in his mind.

She said I could call her, Ransom silently replied.

He winced at the thought of what it would cost him if he did as she'd teasingly suggested, and used his power to find her phone number. Natalie had no idea, of course, but while some knowledge came to him unbidden, it was far more difficult—and painful—to try to learn a specific thing.

But he didn't need to rely on his power for a question like that. Tirzah, his teammate who did hacking, research, and cybersecurity, could find it for him. He could swear her to secrecy, and not mention that the reason he was looking was that Natalie was in town and he'd seen her.

You'll never see her again, his hellhound repeated. *She'll die because you couldn't convince her to trust you. And that's because you're not worthy of anyone's trust.*

The hellhound's words echoed in his mind as Ransom trudged along the beach, climbed the path up the cliff, and hiked down to where he'd left his car. Every time he thought of something he could do—call her before she got on that plane, stop by her motel room, follow her to India—he ran up against the basic, unsolvable problem of having no way to convince her to let him stay with her, and so doing nothing more than repeating his failure.

When he reached the area where he'd parked off-road, he examined his car from the shadows of the trees. Neither basic observation nor *knowing* warned him of anything, and the fine dust he'd scattered around the car was unmarked by footprints. He got in, feeling somewhat relieved and somewhat regretful. An ambush or a car bomb would have at least provided him with something concrete to fight and a battle he could win.

He drove along the coast, heading toward Refuge City and the Defenders office. As he approached the city, his power began to press upon his mind, throwing him scattered fragments of information he hadn't asked for, didn't want, and couldn't use.

In 1936, a woman named Linda McDonald survived a plane crash that killed ten other people, including her boyfriend. She was the first sole survivor of a plane crash.

A car was crashing right now in Refuge City. All three people in it would survive. The worst injury was to the driver, who had a concussion and a broken ankle.

The woman in the car directly behind him was a professor of medieval literature. One of her students had plagiarized his paper. Her cat had gotten into her closet and was, right now, chewing on her most expensive pair of shoes.

The plants growing on the hillside he was driving past were ragweed, milkweed, pokeweed, pigweed, henbane, sheep sorrel, inkberry, cow parsnip, blue-stemmed goldenrod, seaside goldenrod, mountain phlox, mallow, candle-flame lichen, pincushion moss, common haircap moss, spiky peat moss...

"Stop it," he muttered aloud, pressing his knuckles into his forehead.

It will never stop, growled his hellhound. *And it's all your fault.*

Ransom breathed deeply, letting the flood of information wash over him and past him. Fighting it gave him a headache and focusing on it would distract him until he couldn't do anything else—such as drive. But if he did neither and simply let it happen without getting caught up in it, eventually it would stop.

The flood slowed to a trickle—*it's raining two counties over, the man looking out the window of the building over there is cheating on his wife, Dornberk is a village in Western Slovenia in the municipality of Nova Gorica in the Goritzian region of the Slovenian Littoral*—and stopped.

Ransom, blinking as if he'd just woken up, registered that he was pulling into the Defenders underground parking lot. With wry humor, he thought, *At least it distracted me from rush hour traffic.*

Dali, the office manager, greeted him in the lobby, where she was reviewing a stack of files. "You're here early. Hey—you're tracking in sand!"

She whipped out a broom and handed it to him with a meaningful arch of her eyebrows, adding, "And shake your shoes over the trash can!"

"I remember a time when sand was the least of what was on the floor," Ransom said.

"Yes, and that's why you hired me," Dali pointed out.

It was true. She had transformed the office from a trainwreck studded with booby traps to a professional-looking, pleasant space where everything was easily accessible and easy to find. And where the floors were always clean, except for a few stray hairs from his teammates' magical pets.

As Ransom shook out his shoes and swept up the offending sand, Merlin bounced in from the kitchen with a coffee cup in each hand, a kitten with dragonfly wings perched on his shoulder, and a bright blue bugbear ambling in his wake.

Merlin gave Dali one of the coffee cups, followed by a kiss so enthusiastic that Ransom looked away. It wasn't that it was embarrassing—

Ransom was a man, not a boy still in the cootie stage—it was that their love and delight in each other made the empty places in himself ache. Like there was a black hole inside his chest, and it was sucking him in.

"Hey, Ransom," Merlin said.

Startled, Ransom looked up. Merlin's blue eyes were serious. Intent. Had he somehow found out about Natalie...?

"You'll find your mate someday," Merlin said. "And once you do, you'll know she was worth waiting for."

Why did people underestimate Merlin? Anyone who paid attention would know he was sharp as a tack. Or, in this case, sharp enough to cut.

"I don't have a mate," Ransom said, in a tone intended to end the conversation.

Merlin didn't take the hint. "Sure you do. You shouldn't believe what the wizard-scientists told us—"

Ransom gritted his teeth. It was nice for Merlin that *he* hadn't been traumatized by the experience of being kidnapped and experimented on and made into a shifter, but it had ruined Ransom's life. Talking about it did nothing but bring back painful memories.

"—about them having severed our ability to form the mate bond," Merlin continued blithely. "It obviously didn't work. Pete bonded with Tirzah, and I bonded with Dali. So you can definitely bond with your mate."

Ransom didn't underestimate Merlin, but that didn't mean he never wanted to pitch him out a window. "That's not what I meant. It's irrelevant whether or not I can bond with a mate, because I don't have one."

"Of course you—" Merlin broke off with a yelp. "Ow! Dali, what'd you do that for?"

Dali gave him a bland shrug. "Me? I didn't do anything. Must've been Blue. Ransom, how was the beach?"

Beautiful, he thought. *But not as beautiful as the woman who left me standing on it while she walked away to die alone.*

"It's nice in the morning," he said. "Peaceful."

His teammate Pete came in, also from the kitchen, his muscular body briefly filling the doorframe. "You went for a stroll on the beach in your office shoes?"

His not-officially-a-teammate Carter stepped in through the front door and joined the conversation without missing a beat. "Sea water *destroys* leather. Even a sea breeze is damaging."

"They're not real leather," Ransom said.

Carter himself wore extremely expensive shoes made of real leather, to go with his extremely expensive suit. He bent to inspect Ransom's. "Hmm. Good soles. For the amount you paid for those, you could get much better shoes from an actual designer, so long as you don't hold out for Italian leather. I could recommend—"

"I don't want better shoes," Ransom interrupted. If he took Carter's shoe advice, he'd be a man in inexpensive, boring clothes with exceptionally good taste in shoes—an unusual circumstance that might attract attention. "Is Tirzah here?"

"Yep." Tirzah propelled her wheelchair into the lobby. "Everyone's here. Roland's in the kitchen microwaving… something." She gave a little shudder, which amused Ransom given that Pete was known to eat MREs if he was in a hurry. Or maybe whatever their boss was fixing himself was worse than an MRE.

His power helpfully gave him a flash of the inside of the microwave, which contained a plate of leftover macaroni and cheese topped with half a leftover hot dog. Bun included.

"Ugh," said Ransom involuntarily.

A silence fell. He didn't need his power to know he'd made everyone uncomfortable.

They're thinking of everything they don't want you to know about them, his hellhound growled. *How long will they be able to stand working with someone who could find out all their dirty little secrets?*

Hurriedly, to get them to stop thinking about that, Ransom said, "Tirzah, can I see you in your office? I need some computer help."

"Sure," she said.

But his hellhound wasn't finished with him yet. As Ransom and

Tirzah headed for her office, his hellhound growled, *And that's nothing to how they'll react when they find out about your* other *power.*

That's not my *power,* Ransom said. *That's* your *power.*

It was an argument that made no sense, and his hellhound knew it. Of course he knew it: the hellhound was a part of him, after all. The worst part of him, the part he hated, given a form and a voice. And a dreadful power.

"Ransom?" Tirzah was looking at him quizzically. "What do you need me to do?"

He glanced at her office door, making sure it was closed. He had his explanation all planned out: he was trying to find Natalie because he knew Merlin was worried about her, but he didn't want Tirzah to mention it to Merlin so he wouldn't be disappointed if it turned out that she didn't want to see him.

Ransom couldn't break his promise to Natalie, but he hated to go behind Merlin's back and lie to Tirzah. It wasn't fair to them, and it made Ransom feel like he was betraying their trust.

Because you are, his hellhound growled. *Do you think a good person would get a power like yours?*

Ransom, trying to ignore his hellhound, said, "I need you to track down a phone number."

"Sure," Tirzah said. "Got a name?"

Before Ransom could speak, his hellhound stalked closer within his mind, black as midnight and with eyes of flame. *What sort of man has the power to see the worst moment of a person's life?*

His hellhound's power surged up, showing him a country road at night. Tirzah lay by the side of the road, battered and bleeding and covered in mud, both her legs shattered. But even worse than her injuries was her despair. She was alone in the middle of nowhere, dying, with no help in sight…

Furious, Ransom fought to push the vision away. *Stop it! If she wants me to know, she'll tell me herself!*

But the hellhound didn't relent. Ransom couldn't see anything but Tirzah on that road, tears running down her face as she began to crawl, her legs dragging uselessly behind her…

"I have to go." He stumbled out of the office without waiting for a reply, barely able to see where he was going.

The vision faded as he left Tirzah's presence, leaving his head aching and his heart heavy. Caffeine would help with the headache, but he didn't dare go to the kitchen. If Roland was still there, his hellhound might well decide to use his power again. Ransom had been forced to watch his boss's worst memory before, and he couldn't bear to see it again.

Instead, he hurried through the lobby, nearly colliding with Merlin's bugbear. Blue's tiny dragonfly wings, which were far too small to lift him, buzzed madly as the bugbear turned to lick Ransom's hand.

"Tirzah give you a lead?" Pete asked.

"No, I—I'll ask her later," Ransom said. "I'm going out to get some coffee."

"There's some in the kitchen," said Merlin. "I just made it. From my own stash, so you know it's good."

"I don't want to go in the kitchen," Ransom said. Everyone stared at him. Even the pets. He was trying to think of some reasonable explanation when he suddenly *knew* something was wrong with the machine Carter was tinkering with. "Carter, put that down, right now —not on the rug!"

Carter hurriedly set the little machine on his metal tool tray. A moment after he let go of it, there was a muffled explosion. Sparks flew, and the machine collapsed into a pile of gears and pieces, some of them glowing red-hot.

"Goddammit!" Carter moaned. "I was almost done!"

Since nothing was actually on fire, Ransom took the opportunity to flee. It wouldn't do anything to make his teammates think he was less weird and unfriendly, but it wasn't like he had a choice. At least he'd saved Carter from getting his hands burned.

It was odd how often things he worked on blew up. The man had built a billion-dollar empire off tech, and Ransom had seen for himself how clever his inventions were... when they didn't explode or catch fire. What was especially strange was that Tirzah and Carter could work on identical laptops, doing identical tasks, and only Carter's would short out. It was as if he was under a curse.

Ransom drove around the neighborhood, looking for a coffeeshop he hadn't visited before. He tried not to patronize the same one more than once or twice—he didn't want people to start recognizing him—but luckily, this stretch of Refuge City was full of coffeeshops. They tended to go out of business frequently, especially when they had put more effort into some gimmick than into their coffee, so it was easy for him to only visit each one once without having to drive too far away.

The bits of sky he could see between the skyscrapers were a robin's egg blue, and the sun shone brightly but not too hot. The entire population of Refuge City seemed to be out on the streets, enjoying the weather and taking up all the parking spots. Ransom ended up parking in the first spot he could find. He'd find something if he walked long enough.

He regretted that decision almost as soon as he got out of the car. His hellhound stalked inside his mind, a dark presence with eyes of flame, showing him the worst moments of random passersby, whether they were of bad deeds or trauma or unhappiness.

A man in a business suit walked by talking on his cellphone, and Ransom saw him ducking into a hotel room with a woman who wasn't his wife.

A woman tossed a handful of crumbs to a flock of pigeons, and Ransom saw her hiding an empty bottle of gin under her bed.

A boy jumped his skateboard off the curb, and Ransom saw him silently crying in a school bathroom stall while other boys jeered at him from outside.

Stop it, Ransom told his hellhound. *I don't want to know!*

The world is terrible, growled his hellhound. *I'm just showing you the truth.*

Ransom exerted all his will, forcing his hellhound to submit. The visions stopped, but the effort left him exhausted. His hands were shaking, and his headache had gone from a dull throb to a spike of pain behind his right eye.

Ransom's head hurt so badly that he could barely think. He made himself focus on his original mission: finding a coffee shop.

He didn't have to search long. Three shops down, he spotted a banner.

Grand Opening!
DARKER THAN BLACK
A Murder Mystery Café

The combination of a recent rainstorm and the placement of the awnings had dumped a stream of water over the word MYSTERY, washing it out so the banner seemed to advertise A Murder Café.

It reminded him of Natalie's scribbled bucket list, with TALL MOTEL and RUSTPROOF FEMINIST. He had a feeling Natalie would love to go to a murder café—or even a murder mystery café.

Which reminded him that he'd failed to obtain her phone number. And she was heading for India the next morning. He either had to go back to Tirzah or show up at Natalie's motel and explain that he'd had a psychic vision of her address but not of her phone number. That'd sure help with her confidence in him.

Ransom found himself rubbing at his forehead as if he could erase the pain with his fingers. He decided to put off the decision until he'd had coffee.

When he went inside the café, he found that it had gone all out on the murder mystery theme. The walls were lined with bookshelves filled with murder mysteries, a stuffed raven perched with a balloon in its beak painted with the word "Nevermore," daggers and vials labeled "cyanide" hung on the walls, and the tables were painted with quotes from mysteries. The two close enough to read were emblazoned with Edgar Allan Poe's "It was the beating of his hideous heart!" and Agatha Christie's "You must use your little gray cells, *mon ami*."

An ornate cabinet with a wooden sign reading "The Poison Cabinet" was filled with syrup bottles with labels reading C is for Caramel, H is for Hazelnut, R is for Raspberry, and so forth.

None of this gave him confidence in the quality of their coffee, but all he needed was the caffeine and something warm to hold in his hands, in a cup heavy enough to stop them from shaking.

He walked up to the register, catching in passing a table painted with a Raymond Chandler quote, "It was a blonde. A blonde to make a bishop kick a hole in a stained glass window."

I know a woman with stained glass hair, he thought. *A woman to make a bishop go BASE jumping.*

"Can I help you?" asked the barista. "Hey—I know you!"

Adrenaline surged through his veins as he realized that finally, *finally* his past had caught up with him. This woman had recognized him, and now the house of cards life he'd built for himself would come crashing down. But at least, now that the worst had already happened, he could stop dreading it. It was almost a relief.

"I do, right?" the barista said, a little uncertainly. "Don't you work at Defenders?"

Then he recognized her. She was the barista they'd done a job for, retrieving some stolen property from an ex-boyfriend. "I thought you worked at Starbucks."

"I used to. This place seemed like more fun. Anyway, I really appreciate what you all did for me." The barista glanced behind her, at the older woman making another customer a cappuccino, lowered her voice, and said, "Your drink's on the house!"

Ransom wasn't sure whether she intended to put in her own money or not ring up his drink, but either way, the odds of her getting in trouble seemed high. "Thanks, but no. I like to support new businesses." It was true, in a sense. "A large house coffee, please."

He quickly moved away before she could try to continue the conversation, pretending to examine the pastry case. It continued the mystery theme, with pastries labeled And Then There Were Buns, Whodonuts, and Book 'Em Danish.

Ransom was having *serious* doubts about the coffee.

"Large house coffee," called the barista.

He turned to collect it, then spun back around when he heard a yell. The older woman behind the counter was pointing at the pastry case. "How'd it get in there?!"

A husky puppy was *inside* the pastry case, wagging its tail and licking the whipped cream off a Crime of Passion Fruit Tart. As Ransom stared at it, the puppy plunged its face into the fruit mousse, which seemed to not be to its taste. It jerked back its cream-dabbled muzzle, then turned an interested blue eye to a Death by Chocolate.

"Get that puppy out of there," Ransom said to the older woman. "Chocolate is poisonous to dogs!"

She didn't budge. Her mouth open, she seemed frozen with astonishment.

Ransom vaulted over the counter, banged on the glass to distract the puppy from the chocolate, and unlatched the sliding glass door. He grabbed the puppy just as it made a lunge for the nearest Death by Chocolate.

The puppy gave an indignant yelp, then wriggled around until it was facing him. He found himself gazing into the bluest eyes he'd ever seen, and a face that seemed to be smiling. The puppy's mouth opened, and Ransom tipped his head back just in time to avoid getting licked on the lips. Instead, the puppy began enthusiastically licking his throat.

A freezing cold voice said, "Sir, I'm going to have to ask you to pay for the pastries your dog destroyed."

"It's not my dog," Ransom said.

The older woman gave him a look like she didn't believe that for a moment. "Then I guess it's a stray. In that case, I'll have to take it to the pound."

She reached out for the puppy. Ransom instinctively clutched it to his chest. "No!"

"Then you'll pay for the pastries?"

The absurdity of the situation almost made him laugh. There he was, in a murder mystery café, being blackmailed for pastry money over a dog that had seemingly materialized inside a locked case. But he couldn't bring himself to abandon the puppy. Maybe Tirzah or Merlin would want it.

"Fine," he said, resigned.

"Just so you understand, you're buying the entire case," the woman warned him. "We can't sell pastries that were in the same case as a dog, even if the dog never touched them. It would violate health regulations. Do you want us to box up the ones it didn't touch, or throw them out?"

He would have argued, except that he *knew* that she was correct about the health regulations. Technically speaking, she shouldn't offer them to him, either. But if he didn't pay for them, they'd lose a lot of money. And most of them were untouched.

"Box them up." His office would appreciate them, and they wouldn't go to waste. "Just throw out the ones that actually did get licked or stepped on."

He went around the counter this time, still holding the puppy since he didn't know what else to do with it. As the barista began boxing the pastries, the owner rang him up at a price which, while appalling, wasn't out of line considering that he'd purchased the entire case.

She seemed more kindly disposed to him now that he was actually paying, and said, "It's a cute puppy. Just keep it on a leash next time. I can't figure out how it managed to get inside the case without any of us noticing. And the one time I forgot to latch the door, too!"

Ransom stared at her. The door *had* been latched. Not to mention that he'd been looking into the case seconds before, and there had been no puppy in it. The whole thing was impossible...

...except that he'd personally experienced animals doing impossible things before. Animals like winged kittens, a miniature pegasus, and a bright blue bugbear.

Ransom had to resist the urge to hold the puppy at arms' length to check for very small wings or other not-immediately-obvious unusual features. Instead, he unbuttoned his jacket, then buttoned it up around the puppy, hiding it from view.

The puppy promptly stuck its head out from the collar, panting happily.

"I love your puppy!" It was the voice of a small girl. "Can I pet it?"

The girl's father put his hand on her back. "Sabrina, don't argue if he says no."

The puppy fought hard to escape the jacket, yelping and whining. Ransom hurriedly took it out before it started breathing fire or creating snowballs, and put it down on the floor. Sabrina giggled as the puppy licked her hands.

"She's so sweet," said Sabrina "What's her name?"

Glancing down, Ransom saw that the girl was right: the puppy was indeed a she. "She doesn't have one."

Sabrina stared at him as if he was a lunatic. "Everyone needs a name. Want me to name her for you?"

"Sabrina…" her father sighed.

"Dad and I are reading a book right now, about a girl who lives in the mountains with her grandfather and a herd of goats. She eats lots of grilled cheese sandwiches. I think you should name your puppy after her. Heidi!"

The puppy barked and cocked her head, exactly as it she was responding.

"See?" said Sabrina triumphantly. "She knows her name. Now you try!"

Ransom glanced around for an escape route, but his pastries were still getting boxed up. More importantly, his coffee was behind the counter and out of reach. "Heidi?"

The puppy turned her head to look at him. Probably she responded to anything said in the same tone. "Spot?" The puppy flopped down, ignoring him. "Fluffy? Pepper? Iditarod?" The puppy continued to ignore him. "Heidi?"

She leaped to her feet, tail wagging.

Sabrina's father chuckled. "Guess your new puppy has a name now."

"She's not my…" Ransom began, then decided not to argue. Instead, he looped the giant bag of pastry boxes over one arm, picked up his coffee with one hand and Heidi with the other, and made his escape.

Recalling an unfortunate incident with Blue and six boxes of Girl Scout cookies, he stashed the pastries in the trunk and Heidi in the back seat. She wagged her tail and licked his hand as he checked her for physical oddities, but he found none. Nor did she display any powers. Ransom began to doubt whether there was anything magical about her after all. Well, he'd let Merlin or Tirzah or whoever wanted to adopt her figure that out.

Heidi whined, gazing up at him with those intense blue eyes of hers.

"Sorry, pup," he said, scratching behind her ears. Her fur was incredibly thick and soft. "I can't take you. It's just not in the cards. You'll be happy with Carter or Roland or whoever you'll end up with."

He got in the front seat, but took a long drink of coffee before he started the engine. It was surprisingly not bad, and he did feel better once he'd had some…

Or rather, he realized, he'd started feeling better *before* he'd had any. He wasn't sure exactly when it had happened, but his headache and shakiness had faded away at some point before he'd gotten in the car. That was odd, too. Normally he'd have needed the caffeine, and even then, it would have only taken the edge off.

He sat in the front seat, drinking his coffee and appreciating the absence of pain and the quiet inside his head. If he changed anything, even so small a thing as starting the car, maybe everything would change. And once he got to the office, he'd have to give Heidi away. There was something nice about having her with him, right there in the back seat, as if she was his.

"Hey, girl," he said, stretching out his arm to pat her. He couldn't quite reach. As he started to twist around, she vanished.

Ransom stared at the empty back seat where she had been. A cold nose touched his hand. Heidi sat in the passenger seat, her tail wagging, seeming to grin.

CHAPTER 5

Natalie held her phone, eyeing her flight reservation. The India trip had been her single biggest planned expense, and she doubted that she'd get her money back if she canceled this late. On the other hand, she'd budgeted to spend her entire life savings on her bucket list, so it wouldn't clean her out.

Her finger gave a decisive tap.

A box popped up, asking her if she was sure she wanted to cancel.

Wally also popped up, blinking out of thin air and into her lap. He snuffled at the phone.

"Yes," Natalie said aloud, gently pushing his head out of the way. "I'm sure."

As she once again hit the "cancel" button, Wally gave an excited bark. He began running in circles around the motel room, occasionally popping out of view to reappear somewhere else, still running. This was a much more ambitious technique than he had the coordination for, and sent him tumbling head over heels or crashing into walls or furniture.

Laughing, Natalie said, "Wally! What's gotten into you?"

A second puppy materialized. Natalie stared. Like Wally, it was a husky, and about the same size as him. But while Wally was pure white with only the faintest of pale gray markings, this husky's markings were pitch black against her snowy coat.

The puppies flung themselves on each other, joyously yelping and tussling and blinking in and out to pounce from an unexpected direction. Natalie watched, bewildered and charmed in equal measures.

There was a sharp knock at the door.

"Just a moment!" She lunged for the puppies, thinking to cram them into the bathroom and… she had no idea how to make them *stay* in the bathroom…

"It's Ransom." But he hadn't needed to say so; she'd recognized his voice instantly. He added, "I already know about the puppy."

Natalie opened the door and ushered him in. "It's pup*pies*."

"Oh." He looked down at the cavorting puppies. "I wasn't expecting that."

"No one expects the teleporting puppies."

"I meant that I hadn't realized there were two of them. I found the black and white one in a café. She disappeared when I came up to the motel, and I heard barking, so I knew where she'd gone." He watched them for a moment, not looking anywhere near as happy as a person should while observing a pair of teleporting puppies playing together. "I guess they're both yours, then."

The black-and-white puppy hurled herself at his ankles, set her teeth in his pants and ripped a hole in them, then stood up on her hind legs with her paws at his knees, barking loudly. The next instant, he had an armful of puppy making happy squeaking noises and licking his face.

"No," Natalie said. "Wally's mine. The little darling you're holding is obviously yours. Have you named her yet?"

"Heidi," Ransom said, his voice slightly muffled as he ducked to avoid a kiss on the lips. "But she came here. To be with you."

"*You're* here. She came with *you*." Natalie didn't bother asking how he'd found her motel; the same way he'd found her at the cliff, presumably. "What are you doing here, anyway?"

Ransom deposited Heidi on the floor and held up a gigantic bag with a logo of a gun, a knife, a bottle marked "poison," a pair of handcuffs, a fingerprint, a magnifying glass, and a fedora encircling the words **DARKER THAN BLACK MURDER MYSTERY CAFE.** "I brought you some gluten."

As she watched, incredulous, he began covering the table with pastry boxes stamped with the over-the-top logo and the names of the pastries. To her delight, they were And Then There Were Buns, Whodonuts, Who Bun Its, Book 'Em Danish, Fingerprint Cookies, Crime of Passionfruit Tart, Sinnamon Rolls, and The Butter Did It. As a woman who had spent her entire adult life at a crime circus called The Fabulous Flying Chameleons, she appreciated commitment to a theme.

"You sure know the way into a woman's... stomach." She took out her bucket list, crossed off EAT GLUTEN, and picked up a slice of Key Crime Pie in one hand and a Death by Chocolate in the other. "Go on. Have a seat. Have a terrible pun pastry. Unless you already stuffed yourself in the car."

He shook his head, sat down, and took a Serial Kruller, holding it as gingerly as if it was rigged to explode. It was like eating a pastry was a wholly unfamiliar experience for him. Natalie watched him, fascinated, as he took a bite, chewed, and swallowed.

"How is it?" she asked.

"Good." He sounded surprised.

She gestured at him to go on eating. He did, in the same manner, as if he expected each bite to blow up in his face and was pleasantly surprised each time it didn't, but didn't entirely trust that the next one wouldn't be booby-trapped. She ate both of hers and a Crime Puff in the time it took for him to eat one. Without regular trapeze performances to burn energy, she was less hungry than usual; if she'd performed the night before, she'd have inhaled an entire box in that time.

"Thanks for the gluten," she said. "Did you say you found Heidi in a café? This café?"

Ransom nodded. "Inside the pastry case. Everyone assumed she belonged to me, so I had to pay for all the pastries, because it would have violated health regulations to sell them after that. Oh—I should have warned you—"

"That they've been in close proximity to a puppy?" Natalie waved it off, then pushed the Whodonut he was eyeing into his hand. "Don't worry about it. I grew up in a shifter circus, remember? Merlin and I used to have picnics with tiger cubs and flying squirrel kits."

He took a cautious nibble of the Whodonut. "Yes, I've heard a lot of stories about that from Merlin."

"I bet. Merlin tells great stories." Just saying that made her miss him and his stories with a startling intensity. Ransom was so lucky to work with him. "He must be the life of the office."

"You could say that." Ransom, having apparently satisfied himself that the Whodonut wouldn't explode, took a larger bite. Natalie helped herself to another Crime Puff. They sat in contented silence, eating their pastries and watching the puppies play. Heidi and Wally ran a few more circuits around the room, then flopped down on the rug with Heidi's head on Wally's fuzzy stomach.

"Think they're related?" Natalie asked.

Ransom started to shrug, then said with absolute certainty, "Yes. They're brother and sister. There were only two in the litter."

"Did you just... *know* that?"

"Yes."

He could have been bullshitting her. There was no way to prove or disprove what he'd said. But Natalie was convinced. It wasn't only because he'd proved that he really did have visions—just because something was possible didn't mean it was always true—but because of the careful way he'd eaten the pastries, the anonymous way he dressed, and what he'd assumed when he'd seen her standing at the edge of a cliff.

Cautious man, she thought. *Always expecting the worst.* Bracing *himself for the worst.*

It was the opposite of a con artist's personality. A fake psychic was flamboyant, brazen, and certain that they could fool anyone, so confident in their own skills that it came across as honesty.

"I believe you," she said. "About everything."

His dark eyes met hers, wide and startled. "What convinced you?"

"If you were a great con artist, I wouldn't have doubted you at all. And if you were a bad one, I'd have already caught you with your hand in my wallet."

"Oh." He seemed more wary than relieved. As if the very fact that something had worked out the way he'd wanted it to made him not trust it. But, just like he hadn't hesitated to go over the cliff with her, he didn't let that stop him from pushing forward. "So you'll let me go with you?"

"To India, you mean?" When he nodded, she indicated the puppies. "I canceled my ticket. I decided I wanted Wally more than I wanted to see the Taj Mahal."

"Wally?"

"After the Flying Wallendas. They're a famous family of wire walkers and aerialists."

"I know," said Ransom. She was learning to distinguish his varieties of "I know." This one seemed to only mean that he'd heard of them. "Aren't they mostly famous for falling to their death?"

"Well," Natalie said. "You can't let a little thing like that stop you."

For the first time, she heard him laugh. Just a brief huff of breath, but she'd take it.

"So what's next on your list?" he asked. "After the tall motel?"

And that made *her* laugh. Then she sighed, thinking of all the money she'd lost. "A bunch of other things involving airplanes, unfortunately. That little cutie pie is messing with a lot of my plans. Even for the things I want to do and see in America, I'm nervous about taking a teleporting puppy aboard a plane."

"Understandable. Could you do any of them as a road trip?"

Natalie ran her fingers through her hair. "I'm embarrassed to admit this…"

"Don't be," he said. "I have a friend who had a fear of driving."

"Oh, it's not that," she assured him. It was nice, though, the way he mentioned his friend's phobia. Kind, but not condescending. Pulling out her bucket list, she showed him the relevant line.

"BURN THE HIVE?"

"Please. My writing's not *that* bad."

"I'm going to guess it actually says 'LEARN TO DRIVE,' but that's just because of the context."

"I never got around to it," she explained, ignoring the implication about her handwriting. "We all traveled around in a circus train, so we didn't have cars. Except for the clown car."

A mischievous light glinted in the dark depths of his eyes. "Of course. Well, I know how to drive. If you won't let me be your bodyguard, will you let me be your chauffeur?"

"Bit of a step down, isn't it?"

The light winked out, leaving him utterly serious. "No."

Natalie felt like she'd been skating on a frozen pond, and the ice had cracked beneath her. If she accepted his offer, what would she really be accepting? Heartbreak and loss and grief, false hope that would only make everything hurt so much more than it would have if she'd never hoped at all…

Or, Natalie thought, *I can be an adult, and take the responsibility for keeping it light and professional.*

"To be clear," she said. "You drive, you teach me to drive, and when we stop for the night, we get two rooms."

It was like a wall slammed down between them. The intimacy she'd felt and shied away from vanished, and so did all the restrained emotion she'd sensed in him. Ransom gave a sharp nod. "Understood."

"Good," Natalie said, trying to hide her disappointment. She was the one who'd moved to preemptively crush anything romantic; it shouldn't bother her that he'd agreed.

It *was* good. He was too serious. Too intense. Give him an inch, and they'd both end up a mile deep, and crushed under the weight of it.

Light and professional, she told herself.

She gave him a light, professional smile. "Want to see what's next on my list?"

CHAPTER 6

Ransom told himself that it was unreasonable to be so disappointed. He'd offered to drive her around, and she'd accepted the offer. He'd gotten exactly what he wanted, which was nothing more—nor less—than the opportunity to save her life. As for Natalie, she was being clear and assertive, which were both excellent qualities.

He mentally stomped on the wish that she'd clearly and assertively suggested that they get a room with one bed.

"Of course," he said. "Let's see your list."

"I may need to revamp it. Make it more dog-friendly. Maybe reconsider some items." She pulled out her bucket list and tapped an entry. "This here was a huge disappointment."

"RUSTPROOF FEMINIST?"

She snorted in exaggerated disbelief, though he hadn't been joking. "Very funny. RUTABAGA FESTIVAL."

"Oh, that," Ransom said, nodding. "I saw a flyer for it."

"You don't sound very enthusiastic."

"I don't like rutabagas."

"Neither do I, apparently," Natalie said glumly.

"Then why did you go?"

She held up a slim finger, ticking off the items. "One: I'd never had one before. I wasn't sure exactly what they were, in fact. Apparently they're large turnips."

"A bit sweeter," Ransom said absently. He didn't care for turnips, either.

"Two: I'd heard about American produce festivals, and I thought they sounded like more of a big deal or more fun or something. This had a few food stalls, a stall with pamphlets, and a woman selling rutabaga crafts. Oh, and a mascot. It looked like a leaf monster from a horror movie. That was definitely the best part."

Wally twitched, dreaming, and woke with a startled yip. Natalie petted him. "Apart from finding Wally, of course."

"Oh, was that where you found him? Where was he?"

"Up a tree." She laughed at Ransom's expression, then told him the entire story.

"I wish I'd seen it," he said. "It sounds like you were the highlight of the entire thing."

"Without me and Wally, it'd have been nothing but lowlights." She frowned. "Maybe I'm being mean."

"To the rutabagas?"

"Yes. Poor vegetables, nobody likes them and their festival is tiny and boring."

Amused at her produce obsession, Ransom said, "There's a much bigger one going on this weekend, south of here."

"I can't believe rutabagas inspired even one festival, never mind two!"

"The big one's not for rutabagas, or any vegetable. It's for tomatoes."

"Tomatoes are vegetables."

"Scientifically, they're fruits."

"What? No way."

"A fruit is the part of a plant that contains its seeds. Tomatoes contain the seeds of the tomato plant. Therefore, they're fruits."

Natalie's eyebrows pulled together as she considered the idea.

"That can't be right. If it was true, then green beans would be fruits too. So would bell peppers. And squash. And avocados."

It was fun debating her; she was so quick on the uptake. "They are. All of them. Botanically speaking."

"Well, clearly the botanists were on the losing side of the fruit-vegetable battle, because supermarkets and cookbooks and people in general classify all of those as vegetables. But more importantly, is the tomato festival fun?"

Ransom shrugged. "I've never been to it. It's famous. It's open all year round—I think it's a combined fruit festival and amusement park."

"A vegetable festival slash amusement park." Her eyes were gleaming with a familiar light. He'd first seen it as she'd stood poised on the edge of a cliff. "Is it within driving distance?"

"Sure." It wasn't what he'd have picked for a do-before-you-die list, but then again, he wasn't accompanying her to have a good time. "You like tomatoes?"

"Yeah. But I mostly thought produce festivals sounded fun. A real American thing, you know?"

"Aren't you American?"

"Sure, but I didn't grow up here. The Fabulous Flying Chameleons toured around the world. And before I was with the circus… Well, I was young. I didn't get the chance to do much."

Ransom recalled Merlin's stories about him and Natalie. They all involved the phrase, "Natalie, my best friend since we were eleven." He asked, "Didn't you join the circus when you were eleven?"

"Yeah."

"Fruit and vegetable festivals are family things. The prime time to visit is before you're eleven. Then you're too old, until you become a parent and take your own kids."

"I didn't have a family." Her easy flow of conversation had shut down.

I shouldn't pursue this, he thought. But he wanted to know. That had always been his downfall.

"If you don't want to talk about it, I can drop it," he said.

She gave an impatient hand-wave. "I don't have any forbidden subjects. If you're curious, go ahead and ask. I grew up in group homes. They didn't do festivals. When I was eleven, I ran away to the circus."

Those few sentences covered a whole lot. But he didn't push it. He too had plenty that he didn't want people to know about.

"I read books about stuff normal American kids did," she went on. "State fairs. Sleepovers. Prom. I wouldn't have traded it for the circus, of course. But I was curious. I still am. Look."

Her close-clipped fingernail tapped against her list. With a teasing gleam in her eyes—they looked amber under a lock of golden hair—she said, "Go on. Read me what you think they say."

Ransom could have figured some of the items out, now that she'd given him context. But he obeyed the letter of her request, and read, "QUIZ A HIGH FOOL. SODA BALL. EEL IN A BINDER."

"Soda ball," Natalie repeated, laughing. "Now that sounds like an American thing. After the tomato festival, you attend the soda ball and crown the Root Beer Queen."

"You'd want to go if it existed, wouldn't you?"

"Of course. Anyway, they're actually VISIT A HIGH SCHOOL, GO TO A MALL, and EAT AT A DINER."

Ransom felt an odd pang in his chest, hearing her read out her wishes. They were such ordinary things, but so exotic and desirable to her. He hoped they wouldn't disappoint her. "We could do all that."

"What about you? What's on your bucket list? If there's anything in the vicinity, I'd be happy to come along to yours. Fair's fair."

"I don't have a bucket list."

"It doesn't have to be a literal list," she said. "Just things you've been dying to do—oops, bad choice of words—places you always wanted to visit, but you put it off…"

"I don't have anything like that." Ransom heard how abrupt he sounded, and tried to soften it. "Nothing around here, for sure. I'll meet you here tomorrow morning. Take the pastries you want to eat tonight or bring with us for the road. I'll drop off the rest at the office."

She immediately put the Crime Of Passionfruit Tarts in the bag, saying, "Merlin will love these." A flash of sadness crossed her face, but was quickly replaced by a slightly forced smile as she sorted the pastries, taking out a selection to keep. "See you tomorrow! Heidi too."

"See you." Ransom picked up the pastry bag and whistled to Heidi. "Hey, girl. Time to go ride in the car again."

Heidi cocked her head, then vanished. He had a moment of alarm, then looked out the window and saw her in the front seat of the car.

Natalie stepped forward to look out the window with him."Smart dog."

She was standing so close that he could feel the warmth of her body and breathe in her scent. His senses had sharpened since he'd been made into a shifter; what he smelled wasn't perfume, but a clean, crisp, bright scent like lemon juice and fresh-cut grass, which he knew was hers alone.

He was tempted to linger, but Heidi gave a sharp bark. She could get overheated inside a car with the windows shut. "See you tomorrow."

Ransom had fled Defenders in such a rush, he'd left his laptop in his office. Otherwise he'd have been tempted to call in rather than return to the office. He hoped he'd be able to avoid too many questions about why he was leaving and when he'd be back. He couldn't say he had a new case, though he sort of did, without Roland insisting that he file the proper paperwork. Maybe he could say he was taking some time off.

With a twinge of regret, he decided not to bring Heidi. Everyone would love her, but they'd ask a million questions too, and he didn't want to get quizzed about her when he couldn't tell them about her brother... or her brother's owner.

He stopped at a pet shop and bought Heidi dog food, a bed, a crate that was big enough for two puppies and could fit in a car, a collar, a leash, and some toys, then drove her to his apartment. She behaved beautifully, for the most part, though she refused to stay in the crate, blinking out of it and back to the front seat when he tried to put her in. At least she seemed to understand that it would be a bad idea to teleport out of a moving car. Maybe teleportation came with instincts about using it safely, the same way that dogs knew not to jump off a cliff.

Ransom's current sublet apartment was in a neighborhood that was safe enough to not have anyone trying to break in to steal things, and shady enough that people turned a blind eye to any oddities. His neighbors were neither friendly nor hostile, and that was exactly how he liked it. Especially now that he had a teleporting puppy.

All the same, he carried her into his apartment rather than risking putting her on a leash. There might not be much that would get his neighbors' attention, but he could think of one thing: an empty leash falling to the ground as the puppy at the end of it vanished.

Heidi attacked the dog food with immense enthusiasm once he got her inside, and he took the opportunity to rush to his car and floor it out of there before she decided to follow him. For half the trip, he expected her to appear in the passenger seat, and he only relaxed when she was still a no-show by the time he arrived at Defenders.

He'd hoped that everyone would have left on some errand, but their cars were still in the parking lot. Resigned, he headed up to the lobby. If worst came to worst, he could always grab his laptop, take off, and call Roland after he was safely gone.

Ransom stopped in the doorway when he saw the semi-controlled chaos in the lobby. Spike, Pete's cactus kitten, and Cloud, Dali's dragonfly kitten, flew around in a tight circle, nipping at each other's tails. Dali at her desk, trying to speak on the phone while periodically ducking when the kittens flew low.

Roland was getting a report from Pete. Both men were working hard to focus on the conversation and ignore Blue, who was slowly creeping up on them in what he clearly believed was an extremely stealthy manner, but wasn't given that he was a bright blue bugbear the size of a Saint Bernard with tiny, rapidly buzzing dragonfly wings.

Tirzah and Carter were working side by side on laptops while Batcat perched on her shoulder, chewing on her curly hair. Merlin was talking to Tirzah while twisted into some bizarre acrobat's stretch on the floor, looking totally relaxed even through the pose would have dislocated anyone else's joints.

Except Natalie's, Ransom thought. From what Merlin had said about her, she could do all the same circus tricks he could, and a few he couldn't.

"She's doing it again!" Carter yelled suddenly. Everyone jumped, and Tirzah nearly spilled her coffee mug over her laptop.

"Who's doing what again?" Tirzah asked.

"Fenella Kim," Carter snarled, emphasizing each syllable as if she was some famous villain.

"Never heard of her," said Pete.

Carter rolled his eyes, then turned his laptop around to display an article headlined FENELLA KIM ATTEMPTS HOSTILE TAKEOVER OF HOWE ENTERPRISES. It was accompanied by a photograph of a woman of Carter's age in a white business suit and extremely high black heels, with her black hair in a razor-sharp, asymmetrical cut. Considering how Ransom dressed to avoid notice, he could see instantly how she'd designed every aspect of her appearance to turn heads. She looked fierce: an exceptionally striking corporate shark.

"This is the second time! What has that woman got against me?" Carter demanded to the room at large. After a moment, he added, "Other than that I tried a hostile takeover of her company once. But that was years ago!"

"I think you answered your own question," remarked Roland.

Carter ignored him and began packing his laptop. "I have to go. Do your best to survive without me."

"We'll be fine," Merlin assured him with a bright smile. "After all, you don't even work here."

Carter gave him a blank look, then said, "Right. Right!"

He nearly collided with Ransom as he strode out. Carter glared at him as he caught his balance. "I *don't* even work here, and I'm still here more than you are!"

The door slammed behind him.

"Oh, you're here, Ransom," said Roland. "I didn't see you."

Ransom had, in fact, been deliberately lurking in the doorway, looking for the perfect moment when everyone was so preoccupied that he could get in and out without a fuss. Apparently he'd missed it.

"Hey!" Tirzah spun her chair around. "Are those pastries from the murder café?"

"Murder café?" Pete echoed.

"Murder mystery café," said Merlin, uncoiling himself. "Annabeth works there. You know, the barista whose sofa we returned."

"I know who Annabeth is," Pete grumbled.

Dali hung up the phone and asked, "That's a huge bag. Did you bring them to share? I can get a platter."

Ransom handed her the bag, and she headed for the kitchen with it to a chorus of "Thanks, Ransom," and "Thanks, Dali."

"So, *nothing* on Natalie?" Merlin asked, giving Ransom a start before he realized that he wasn't being addressed. Merlin seemed to be continuing a conversation with Tirzah.

"No, sorry," Tirzah said. "She must not be using her real name. Honestly, Merlin, it sounds to me like she had some personal stuff going on and she'll get back in touch when she's ready. I can't find any indication that she didn't leave of her own accord."

"I know," Merlin said. "But maybe she decided to take a vacation, and *then* she got kidnapped, and now she's being held against her will and no one's trying to rescue her because we all think she's off having a quarter-life crisis or—"

"She hasn't been kidnapped," Ransom said. Everyone stared at him. He dreaded the moment when they'd ask him if he *knew* that, and he'd have to lie. But no one did, and he realized that they wouldn't. They'd assumed it, because how else would he know? That made him feel even more like a liar as he went on, "She's not being held against her will. She left of her own accord."

The relief on Merlin's face made Ransom glad he'd said that much. Then Merlin frowned. "But do you know why she left? And why she's not getting in touch with anyone?"

Roland stepped in, to Ransom's relief. "Merlin, don't ask him that. You wanted to know if your friend was safe, and she is. The rest is her business." To Ransom, he said, "Do not look into that any further."

Hurriedly, more to Ransom than to Roland, Merlin said, "No, no, I wasn't asking that! I just meant if you *already* knew why she left. I wouldn't ask you to look again, on purpose. Don't do that!"

"I won't," Ransom promised, with perfect honesty. He was about to ask if he could speak to Roland in his office when a flash of *knowing* came to him.

Natalie was in danger. The wizard-scientists who had kidnapped him and made him into a shifter were coming after her.

His first impulse was to rush back to the motel to protect her, but a dreadful thought stopped him in his tracks. Ransom was the one who had history with the wizard-scientists, not Natalie. What if she was only in danger because of him? What if returning to her side was what would doom her?

Roland cleared his throat. "Ransom? What's going on?"

"Excuse me." He ran for his office. The faster he followed up on that first vision, the better his chance of getting more information about it. Once inside, he locked the door, then sat down on the floor so if he fell, he wouldn't hit his head.

Before he could do anything more, there was a loud knock at the door. Roland's deep voice said, "What are you doing?"

"I'm working."

There was a brief silence, then Roland said, "Open the door."

What a time for his boss to decide he was needed right now! "I'm busy, Roland. I'll be done in a moment."

"Are you using your power?" Roland's voice nearly shook the walls. "I want to talk to you first!"

Ransom could feel his chance of learning what he needed to know to protect Natalie starting to slip away from him. If he wasted one more minute, it would be lost. He stuck his fingers in his ears, visualized a pair of heavy wooden doors inside his mind, and flung them wide open.

A tide of information knocked him off his feet. It was like having a million TV sets turning on at once, all turned to different stations and all at top volume. He knew so much, he couldn't take in any of it. Knowledge filled his mind and battered at his sanity. It was all he could do to focus on the single question whose answer he needed to know:

Is Natalie safer from the wizard-scientists if I stay with her, or if I stay away from her?

Chasing after that answer was like swimming upstream in a raging river, getting bruised and battered by logs and debris along the way. But at last he had it:

She's safer if you stay with her. Only you can protect her.

He had to fight his way back, clinging tight to his answer, to find the doors in his mind and slam them shut. There was a wrenching jolt, and he found himself in his office on his hands and knees, palms braced on the floor. A splitting headache pulsed behind his eyes.

A loud knock at the door sent a nauseating shock of pain through his head. "Ransom! Open the door!"

Gritting his teeth, Ransom forced himself to his feet. He opened the door and beheld the looming figure of his boss. "What?"

Roland looked him over for a long, disapproving moment. "We need to talk. *Now.*"

The next thing Ransom knew, he was getting frog-marched along the corridor and into Roland's office, where he was forcibly sat down in a chair. Roland closed the door, stood in front of it, then said, "Do you want some coffee? I could get you some from the kitchen."

There was nothing Ransom wanted more than coffee… except to get away. "No. I have to go. We can talk later."

"Sure you don't want any coffee?"

Exasperated, Ransom snapped, "No! What is this?"

"I'm worried about you."

And there it was. "I'm fine."

"You're really not." Roland's tone was kind, but did not invite argument. "Do you even know how many times I've literally picked you up off the ground because you pushed yourself so hard with your power that you passed out?"

"Well, if I was unconscious, I wouldn't know, so…"

"Not funny."

Ransom, who hadn't been joking, decided that anything else he said would only aggravate Roland more. He kept his mouth shut.

Roland changed the subject. Sort of. "Want to tell me what was going on just now?"

"No."

"Or this morning?"

Short of breaking his promise to Natalie, the last thing Ransom wanted was to inform his boss that he'd seen the worst moment of Tirzah's life in a vision. "No."

"Or backstage at the circus, when you wrote down a motel address on your arm right before you collapsed?"

That had been Natalie's motel. Luckily, she hadn't been staying there at the time; it had been the motel she'd booked in advance. Ransom wondered how much time Roland had wasted looking into everyone who was already at the motel before giving up. He was annoyed enough by the prying to hope it was a lot.

"No," said Ransom.

Roland gave an exasperated sigh, then ran his hand over his short, silvering hair. "All right. I'm going to give you some options. One: you don't use your power unless I give you permission. I know some information comes to you whether you want it or not, and that's fine. But no using it to search for anything without my go-ahead. It's too hard on you."

"I don't enjoy it either," Ransom pointed out. "I don't use it unless I absolutely have to."

"You absolutely have to a lot, though. I'd like you to let someone else be the judge of when it's truly necessary."

Ransom instinctively balked at that, but made himself think it through rather than knee-jerk refusing. He'd only found Natalie because he'd decided to chase after that elusive vision of her face, long before he'd had any idea who she was. When he'd pushed hard enough to make himself pass out, he'd gotten the information that maybe he could save her. And just now, he'd learned how to protect her. Would Roland have authorized any of that?

"It's my power," Ransom said. "I can't hand it over like a set of car keys."

Roland folded his arms across his broad chest. "Option two: I want you to talk to someone about whatever it is that's going on with you."

Tempted as he was to pretend he didn't know what Roland meant, Ransom asked, "Who?"

"Anyone! Me, one of your teammates, someone from the west coast team, a therapist…"

"If I tell a therapist I turn into a hellhound and I have visions, they'll get a completely wrong idea about what my problems really are."

"No. They won't." Roland slid a piece of paper across the desk. "Here's the names and phone numbers of three therapists. One of them is in Refuge City, and the other two will work over video. They'll keep everything confidential, including from me, and they won't think you're delusional."

"What makes you think that?"

Triumphantly, Roland replied, "Because one's a coyote, one's a raccoon, and one's a pegasus."

Ransom had to appreciate the masterly way his boss had maneuvered him into asking that question, so he could provide that response. But he knew enough about therapy to know that it only worked if you were honest and forthcoming. And he couldn't trust in confidentiality. Even the best-meaning people were human, and could slip up. Not to mention that rooms could be bugged and session notes could be stolen or hacked.

He slid the paper back across the desk. "Sorry. It's just not for me."

The entire atmosphere of the room shifted, as if a bright sky had gone overcast. Roland's tone was distinctly ominous as he said, "I've only got one option left, and you're not going to like it."

Ransom couldn't imagine that he'd like it less than the other two. "Go on."

"Take a leave of absence. Get your head together however you want to do it: walk the Appalachian trail, live in a Zen monastery, stay home and watch Netflix, anything. We'll welcome you back... when you're ready to try one of the other options."

Ransom had imagined plenty of versions of this conversation, but he hadn't expected to just be cut loose.

It was inevitable, growled his hellhound. *Actually, they put up with you for a lot longer than I'd expected.*

Roland gave a deep sigh. "I'm not firing you. I *want* you here. We all do. But I've been watching you self-destructing before my eyes ever since we started, and I don't know what to do about it because you won't even tell me what's going on. So I'm done with watching. Get help and stop hurting yourself, or go away until you're ready to."

Go away, repeated his hellhound. *Go away.*

A chill struck through to Ransom's bones. He heard its flat coldness in his voice as he said, "If I walk out the door under those conditions, I'm not coming back."

Roland stood up. He was as tall as Ransom, but broader. Bigger. But his presence wasn't only a matter of size. When he chose, and sometimes when he seemed to not even be trying, he commanded attention. Ransom had carefully observed him do it, to see if he could learn how to do the opposite and vanish, but had eventually concluded that it was an indefinable personality trait and not something that could be taught.

Roland started to speak, but his voice was drowned out by the hellhound's snarl as it surged forward, ripping and clawing its way to the front.

Images flashed before Ransom's inner eye:

Roland bleeding on the ground while a woman stood over him, swinging a tree branch at a pair of black-clad men. Ransom could feel his terror that she'd get herself killed, and his fury and shame at his own inability to protect her.

Roland in an underground laboratory, his chest bandaged, learning that the woman had died. Pressure in his wrist as he nearly broke the handcuff chaining him to the bed, a hot wetness across his chest as his wound opened up and another in his eyes as tears flowed, shouting, "What was her name? She died for me—at least I should know her name!"

Ransom came back to himself with an unpleasant jolt. Roland was gripping him by the shoulders, looking worried and angry. "What was that?"

There was stinging liquid in his eyes. Ransom thought for a moment that it was tears, then realized that it was sweat. He was shaking so badly that he wasn't sure he could stand if Roland let go of him. "Nothing."

"Don't give me that!"

"Nothing I want to talk about," Ransom corrected himself. Roland was angry at being stonewalled; fine. That was better than being shocked and horrified and betrayed if he knew what Ransom had seen.

Just go, growled his hellhound.

Ransom stepped away, bracing one hand on the doorframe to keep himself upright, then walked out.

He had to concentrate hard to stop himself from staggering like a drunk. He made it to his office, grabbed his laptop, and took a quick look around to see if there was anything else he wanted. Pete had family photos on his desk, Merlin had plastic dinosaurs, Tirzah had cookie jars, Carter had tools, Dali had boxes of homemade candy, Roland had potted plants that he traded out for new ones when they inevitably wilted and died. Ransom had nothing. They could give his office to someone else, and they wouldn't even need to clean it out.

He wanted to make a quick, unnoticed getaway, but whether by accident or design, everyone was in his way. They were all talking, but he couldn't distinguish what they were saying. He was too drained by his vision to fight his hellhound, and the black beast responded by shoving quick flashes of everyone's worst moments at him:

Pete as a cave bear, raging and out of control.

Tirzah at the side of the road, her hair matted with blood and mud.

Dali opening her eyes in a hospital bed, bewildered and afraid.

Merlin as a little boy at the dinner table, watching his parents talk to each other and ignore him.

He didn't only see their pain, he felt it. Their fear and confusion and sadness and despair and loneliness and rage was a weight on his back. He had to get away before it crushed him.

Someone grabbed his arm, but he shook them off. He made it down the stairs and to the parking lot, then into his car. His hellhound sank back down into the darkness of his mind. The visions faded away, leaving him with a headache so intense that it made him feel shaky and sick.

His knuckles turned white as he gripped the steering wheel, willing himself to drive safely. Much as he couldn't bring himself to care for his own sake if he crashed, there were other drivers on the road. He had to protect Natalie. He had Heidi in his apartment.

A whine sounded from the passenger seat. Ransom glanced over, and saw Heidi sitting beside him. He was so disoriented that he wasn't sure if she was real or a vision until she laid her head down on his thigh and nuzzled his side.

Her touch grounded him. He blinked hard, forcing himself to concentrate. Probably he should have taken a cab, but he couldn't stop now when Heidi was with him. Ransom drove on pure instinct, unable to focus beyond not driving into anything or running any red lights, until he found himself in a parking lot. He hoped it was the motel's, but darkness was closing in on his vision.

He brought the car to a jerky stop, then sat in the driver's seat for some time before remembering to put it in park and turn off the engine.

You have to get out, he told himself. *You need to warn Natalie. And the car will get too hot for Heidi.*

But he couldn't make himself move.

Until someone opened the door.

CHAPTER 7

It wasn't unusual for Natalie to feel restless. Normally she'd have dealt with it by practicing the trapeze or acrobatics, or looking around until she found someone who wanted help practicing their own act, or finding Merlin and asking him if he wanted to do something. But she didn't have a trapeze, the motel room was too small for acrobatics, and she'd never see the circus or Merlin again.

She'd gone out after Ransom had left to buy dog food and a leash, so in theory she could take Wally for a walk. But in reality, he was fast asleep. She could go for a walk by herself, but she wasn't sure it was safe to leave Wally alone given that he could teleport.

Natalie got down on the floor and did some stretches, then got up and tried to read a book, then lay down and petted Wally, then stood up and paced. Having that ticking clock at the back of her mind should have made her more focused, but it also introduced the element of "If I only have a year to live, is this a good use of my time?"

It made so many ordinary moments incredibly fraught. When she only had so many books left to read, it was hard to concentrate on any given one because that little voice in her head kept asking, "Are you enjoying this one enough that you'd be okay with it being the last book you ever read?" If she was hungry, she'd get caught up in wondering if she should skip the fast food joint and find somewhere really good, only to spend hours searching for a worthy restaurant and then being disappointed in it, when she could have eaten a burger in fifteen minutes and then gotten on with her life.

"I need to raise the proportion of bucket list moments to ordinary moments," she told Wally. He twitched in his sleep, scrabbled briefly with his paws, then lay still again. Natalie decided to take that as agreement.

"I only have to get through today and tonight," she went on. It was great to have someone to talk to, even if it was a puppy who didn't understand a word and also was asleep. "Then it'll be all bucket list. Even the downtime, because one of my items is 'road trip' and that includes every bit of the road trip. Even the—"

A black-and-white shape materialized beside her. Natalie jumped, startled, then relaxed as she recognized Heidi.

"Came to visit your brother?" Natalie asked with a grin. She hoped Ransom wasn't going to worry that she was lost. Though presumably if he did, he could use his psychic powers to figure out where—

Heidi barked, jumped off the bed and ran to the door, then looked back and barked again.

Natalie had no idea why Heidi wanted her to follow, but it was clear that she did. And Natalie was more than willing. She hurried to the door and flung it open. She only realized that she'd expected to see Ransom when she felt her own disappointment at the sight of nothing but a half-empty parking lot.

Heidi ran out, making a beeline for a car parked across two spaces. It was a dusty, dull red Honda like many others, but Natalie recognized it as Ransom's. She'd run enough cons involving recognizing cars that she'd automatically memorized his license plate. She should have been glad to see it, but instead she felt uneasy. Taking up two spaces was inconsiderate and rude, and also attracted attention. It didn't seem like him.

Natalie ran after Heidi. Her heart lurched when she saw Ransom slumped over the steering wheel.

She yanked open the door.

He gasped, jerking awake, and grabbed her hand. "You're all right. I was on time."

Her relief that he was alive and conscious was immediately replaced by concern. He looked terrible, pale and sweating, with bruise-dark smudges under his eyes. Her first thought was that he'd been in an accident, but she didn't see any blood and the car wasn't visibly damaged. But a seemingly minor impact could have big effects. He could have whiplash or internal injuries or had a blow to his head…

Heidi materialized in the passenger seat. She nuzzled him, whining, and he laid his other hand on her head.

"Ransom?" Natalie asked. "What's the matter with you?"

"My power. It gives me migraines if I use it too much."

"Oh, thank God. I mean, sorry, I've heard migraines are awful. I thought you'd crashed your car, even though it's obviously not damaged, but you looked so bad…"

Ransom closed his eyes briefly. He took a deep breath, visibly gathering his strength, then opened them. "Never mind me. They know where you are."

"What?" She had no idea what he was talking about, but his tone made her skin prickle. Heidi gave an urgent whine. "Who knows where I am?"

"Enemies," he said tersely. "We have to get out of here. Get Wally. And your clothes. Hurry."

The prickle became a tattoo of icy needles, making her shiver. "Did you have a vision?"

He nodded.

"Do I need to warn everyone? Evacuate the motel?"

"No. They're only after you."

The needles became a freezing rain. "I'll call a cab."

"We can't risk a stranger getting caught up in this. I'll drive." He absolutely did not look like he could drive. Natalie's doubt must have been visible in her face, because he said, "If you have any coffee… Caffeine helps."

"I'll get some. I'll be right back." She hesitated, reluctant to pull her hand from his grip. It was so tight that it felt desperate, and she hated to leave him like this. And, though he didn't seem in any shape to protect anyone, she irrationally felt safer with him than alone. "Ransom... You need to let go of me."

He glanced down, looking at his hand like it didn't belong to him, then released his grip. Natalie bolted for her room, her heart pounding. She had no idea what was going on, but if Ransom thought she was in danger, she *absolutely* believed that she was. He looked like he'd driven through Hell itself to rescue her.

Wally woke up with a snort when she came in. Her nerves apparently infected him. He rushed around, barking and tripping her up, as she flung everything into her suitcase, then grabbed the bag of pastries that she'd stuffed into the mini-fridge. She was used to packing in a hurry, and had left most of her stuff in her suitcase anyway; it took two minutes, tops.

She didn't have any coffee ready, but there was a pot in the motel lobby. Grabbing her suitcase and the pastries and whistling to Wally, she bolted into the lobby. The coffee pot was empty, but there was a jar of instant coffee on the table beside it.

Natalie snatched up the jar, dropped her key and a handful of crumpled dollar bills on the desk of the startled clerk, and fled back to the car with Wally at her heels. She tossed the suitcase into the back seat, deposited the pastries more gently, shooed Wally in, and climbed into the passenger seat. Heidi refused to move, making Natalie hold her in her lap.

Ransom was sitting up, both hands clenched on the steering wheel, his face white as paper. This close, she could see tiny droplets of sweat sparkling on his coppery eyelashes.

"No coffee, sorry. But I got this," Natalie said, holding up the jar.

"Thanks. I can brew some at home."

"If you just need the caffeine, you can chew on instant crystals. We used to do that at the circus, if we were traveling and didn't have running water. They don't taste good, but they get the job done. Here..."

A measuring spoon came with the jar, buried in the coffee. She fished it out and filled it. Ransom let go of the steering wheel with one hand—he seemed to be using the other hand to brace himself so he wouldn't collapse again—and reached for it. His hand was shaking so badly that she cupped hers around his, helping him tip the instant crystals into his mouth.

He chewed, made a face, and swallowed. "Ugh. Let me have another."

"Yeah, I know that feeling."

After three spoonfuls, his hand stopped shaking. He started the car and pulled out of the parking lot. The car moved jerkily, but she didn't worry that he would crash it. Natalie could almost feel the intensity of his concentration. Heidi squirmed around in her lap, then laid her head down on his thigh. Natalie glanced at Ransom, wondering if that would distract him, but he didn't seem bothered. In fact, the car moved a little more smoothly.

Natalie wished *she* could do something to help. Heidi's touch had steadied him, but Heidi was a dog. Human touch was so much more… complicated. Fraught. But if she'd been trying to do a difficult task while in danger and in pain, she was certain she'd feel a lot better if he was touching her.

They stopped at a red light. Before the light could change or she could lose her nerve, she blurted out, "Can I put my arm around your shoulders?"

He glanced at her like he couldn't believe his own ears. Just as her face began to burn with embarrassment, he swallowed and nodded.

She leaned over and put her arm around him. The locked tension in his shoulders was shocking—they felt like they'd been carved from stone. But they softened slightly under her touch, and she felt as much as heard him give a sigh of relief. The light changed to green, and the car moved forward—for the first time, without a lurch.

So softly that she wouldn't have heard it if her face hadn't been so close to his, he said, "That's better."

She squeezed his shoulder, willing him her strength as he threaded his way through a warren of narrow streets in a rundown neighborhood. He parked on the street near an apartment building like many others on the street, worn and anonymous, the sort of building you'd never give a second glance. When he turned off the engine, the lack of sound and vibration was startling

Ransom closed his eyes briefly, winced, then opened them. "We're safe now. They didn't track us."

Natalie realized that she'd been clenching her jaw for the entire trip when it finally relaxed. "You said 'enemies,' but who are they? Why are they after me?"

"They're... It's complicated..."

He looked and sounded so exhausted that she broke in, "You know what, never mind. Explain later, okay?"

"I will. If you could take the keys...? I don't think I could get a key in a lock just now." Ransom sounded apologetic, as if he was imposing on her rather than having saved her life.

"Of course. Here, let me help you out."

She unsnapped his seatbelt and put her arms around him. His shirt was soaked through with sweat, but he was shivering, his skin cool verging on cold. If he hadn't already told her it was a migraine, she'd have thought he was in shock.

"Come on," she said. "Lean on me."

Once he was out of the car, she put his arm over her shoulders, then grabbed the suitcase and pastries. Heidi and Wally followed them. She had thought it would be difficult to get him inside—she was strong, but he was much taller than her—but he could bear more of his own weight than she'd expected. He wasn't weak so much as disoriented, and needed guidance rather than support.

Natalie expected a bunch of nosy neighbors, but the few people who were around ignored them. It should have been a relief, but she instead felt indignant on Ransom's behalf. Why weren't his neighbors concerned that he was obviously sick or hurt, and with some woman they'd never seen before? If she'd shown up at the circus barely able to walk and being led by some strange man, everyone would have descended on them at once to make sure she was all right and find out who he was.

She opened his apartment and kicked the door shut behind them.

He winced, and she felt immediately guilty, realizing that the noise had hurt him.

It was a tiny one-bedroom apartment with an open kitchen off the living room. The living room wasn't just uncluttered, it was barren. It had a beautiful polished hardwood floor, but no furniture, no pictures on the walls, and no knickknacks. Aside from some brand new puppy toys on the floor, the one concession to anything personal was a small fold-up bookcase crammed full of books.

She could see a bed through a half-open door. Natalie put down the suitcase and pastries, and steered him to the bedroom. It was as impersonal as the living room: a dresser, a bed, a table with a reading lamp, and nothing else.

The bed was as small as the one in her motel room. She pulled back the covers and helped him lie down. She was annoyed to see that it was too short for him, forcing him to pull up his legs so his feet wouldn't dangle over the edge. It must be horrible for him to be in so much pain and unable to even stretch out properly.

"Why's your bed so small?"

"It's a sublet." He was still shivering, though the room was warm.

"Do you have a doctor?" she asked, but was unsurprised when he said no. Shifters would only go to a shifter doctor for fear of discovery, and not all cities had one. "Can I call someone else for you?"

"No. I'm used to this."

"Hell of a thing to be used to," Natalie said before she could stop herself.

Ransom gave her a startled glance, as if no one had ever put it that way before. "It's not dangerous. I'll be fine tomorrow."

Heidi appeared on the bed beside him, curling into the space between his shoulder and neck. Natalie saw him relax a little as she began to lick his face.

She bent to take off his shoes, but he reached out a hand to stop her. "You don't have to do that."

"What, you think it's beneath my dignity? Don't be ridiculous."

"No," he said uncertainly, having obviously thought exactly that.

She took off his shoes and socks, then belatedly added, "Unless you *wanted* them on? I could put them back on…? Just the socks…?"

Despite his obvious pain, his lips moved into that almost-a-smile. "No. Thanks."

His bare feet made her aware of how uncomfortable he had to be in the rest of his clothes: his belt buckle, his cold wet shirt.

"I'm going to take off your shirt, okay?" she asked. "It's freezing cold. You could get pneumonia."

"I can do it." Ransom fumbled with the tiny buttons, his hands shaky and uncoordinated, until she laid her hand over his.

"Let me. You brought me pastries, I can take off your shirt." She realized what that sounded like as soon as she said it, and felt her face grow warm. "I mean…"

The almost-a-smile returned. "Thanks."

She undid the buttons and draped the shirt over the back of the chair, wondering how he normally managed. Did he have a significant other? A roommate who'd recently moved out? Or could he usually fend for himself, and this migraine was much worse than usual?

Everything she'd observed pointed to *none* of those possibilities being true. He hadn't responded to the chemistry between them like he was already in a relationship, and he seemed the type who'd rather live in the smallest, crummiest apartment alone than deal with roommate issues in a better one. And he wasn't acting like he'd never been this sick before, either.

"Who usually helps you do this?" she asked.

"No one." After a moment, he added, "I just sleep in what I'm wearing."

Natalie was appalled by that idea, then reminded herself that he was a shifter. They were much tougher than humans. He wouldn't actually get pneumonia if he slept in a cold wet shirt. On second thought, it was still appalling. He might not be harmed by it, but that didn't mean it wouldn't be miserable.

"I'll take off your belt," she said brusquely, wishing she hadn't said that thing about the pastries. Awkward!

"Thank you," he said simply, and the awkwardness vanished.

Natalie pulled the covers up over him. Wally jumped up on the bed and curled up at his feet.

"Have you already taken your meds?" she asked. "Or can I get them for you?"

"It's not a normal migraine. Meds don't help." The strain on him was audible in his voice, and the deep lines carved into his face. She'd thought she'd hurt him when she'd kicked him in the shins and stomped on his foot, but now she realized that his pain tolerance was much too high for those blows to have done more than simply register: *this* was what pain looked like on him.

"I could get a cold cloth for your forehead," she offered. "Or actual coffee, if you have a coffee maker. Or more instant crystals. Or I could shut up, turn off the lights, and go away. Seriously, if that's what you need, tell me. It won't hurt my feelings."

"Don't go." Ransom lifted his hand, reaching out to her as if he thought she was about to bolt for the door.

On impulse, she caught his hand and held it. "I won't."

His fingers curled around hers, gripping as tightly as if he'd caught her in midair as he hung from a trapeze. She thought of him suffering alone with no one to help him or even stay with him, and she wasn't surprised that now, with his defenses torn down by pain, he was hanging on to her like he thought she'd change her mind and leave him if he let go.

"I'm not going anywhere." She sat down on the bed, kicked off her shoes, and pulled up her feet, still holding his hand. Maybe that convinced him, because he relaxed and closed his eyes.

The room was quiet, with a mid-afternoon stillness that made her think of long summer days. Motes of dust flowed in the air, visible in the shafts of sunlight. Ransom's hand slowly warmed in hers. She laid the back of her hand on his forehead, and found that the chill had left his skin.

Natalie leaned back against the headboard and cupped his hand in both of hers. He didn't stir. His breathing had evened out, and he seemed deeply asleep. He had big hands, especially compared to hers, with long fingers. His nails were clipped short, and he had patches of thickened skin on his palms in the same places that she did. She'd gotten hers from holding the bar of the trapeze. Maybe he'd gotten his from lifting weights.

The lines had faded from his face as he slept, making her realize that he was younger than she'd thought. She'd guessed he was ten or fifteen years older than her, but she now revised that about five. Had being a Marine aged him that much? It hadn't done that to Merlin.

The more she saw of Ransom, the more mysterious he seemed. Why was he so determined to save her life? Why was he dealing with everything alone when he was friends with Merlin, who had the biggest heart in the world and would happily help him out? What exactly was a hellhound?

But in another sense, she already knew a lot about him. She knew he was willing to risk his life for her, because she'd seen him do it. Twice. She knew he was the sort of man who'd rescue a puppy, and the sort of man that puppies loved. She knew he'd pay for a bunch of pastries that weren't his responsibility, just so a café wouldn't lose money.

And though she didn't know that the books in the living room were his, she bet they were. Whoever he was subletting from seemed to have taken their personal possessions with them, and the bookcase was folding, easily portable, and didn't match the rest of the furniture. If Natalie hadn't still been holding his hand, she'd have been tempted to sneak into the living room and take a look at them, to see if they offered any clues.

Ransom's hands clenched, the one at his side tightening into a fist. His eyes didn't open, but he mumbled something she couldn't catch. He sounded agitated, and his eyelashes fluttered. In the bar of sunlight that shone across his face, they looked like tiny curved flames.

"It's okay," Natalie said softly. She stroked his sweat-stiffened hair, then rubbed his shoulders. She felt the release of tension there first, as the rock-hard muscles softened and gave under her hands, then saw it when his clenched fist opened. But his other hand still held tight to hers.

It was strange to be so close to him—to *feel* so close to him—while knowing so little about his history. He'd said he'd been kidnapped and experimented on, made into a shifter and given psychic powers. Was that why using his power hurt him?

Natalie suddenly remembered her teasing suggestion to use his power to figure out her phone number, and her entire body burned with shame. But though she'd joked about that, not knowing what it cost him, he *had* used his power for her. He'd paid a terrible price to learn that she was in danger, and endured so much to rescue her. And he'd asked for nothing in return—he didn't even seem to expect thanks.

Ransom inhaled sharply, his muscles tensing, and mumbled, "No… Don't go there…"

She rubbed his back, whispering, "It's all right. Everything's all right."

He sat bolt upright, his eyes flying open. But he looked past her —*through* her—yelling, "No! Look out!"

And he pitched forward into her arms.

CHAPTER 8

*R*ansom awoke sitting up, his heart pounding and his face buried in someone's shoulder. Natalie was holding him. He knew it before he opened his eyes, even before he remembered where he was and how he'd gotten there. They'd clung together once before, in mid-air, and he'd never forget the shape of her body as long as he lived, nor the bright sharp scent of her.

Her soft hair tickled his cheek, and her warm arms were around him. It had been so long since anyone had touched him for more than a second or two, and most of that had been professional or impersonal or violent—a medic taking his pulse, a clerk passing him change, an enemy snatching for his gun. Only his teammates had touched him with kindness, and he hadn't been able to bear it for more than a moment before he'd pulled away. He'd been too afraid of what they might learn about him, or too guilty over what they didn't know.

But Natalie held him tight, and he had no desire to push her away. Her small strong hands rubbed his back, kneading at the painful knots in his muscles, and he could feel her warm breath on his face as she murmured, "It's all right, it's all right. You were having a nightmare…"

At that word, he remembered that he'd had a vision. That was what had woken him up. He jerked upright, pulling away from her without meaning to, mentally snatching at the memory even as it faded away. "Wait! I saw… I know…"

And it was gone. There was nothing left but the knowledge that something had existed once, like the hollow in a forest floor where a tree had once stood. "I lost it."

"Lost what?"

Pain pulsed behind his eyes, making it hurt to even try to focus. "I saw something…" But now that he was awake, he was less certain of that. "Maybe. I can't remember now."

"I think you were dreaming," she said gently.

"No. I can tell the difference." He slumped back, leaning against the headboard. She was sitting beside him, so close that he could feel the warmth of her body, but she didn't try to hold him again. Of course not. She'd only been trying to rouse him from what she believed was a nightmare. And now that they were no longer touching, he longed for her with a hunger as sharp as pain.

If she didn't move away, *now,* he might not be able to resist reaching out to her. And she'd already told him she didn't want that. She'd specifically said she wanted separate rooms, and here he was, literally in bed with her.

A groan escaped his lips.

"Is there anything I can do?" she asked. "Coffee?"

He hated to make her fetch and carry for him, but he had to get her off the bed. And once he got some more caffeine into him, he could pull himself together—at least enough to get out of bed himself. "Yes, please. There's a coffee maker in the kitchen."

"Sure." She moved across the hardwood floors as gracefully as a snow leopard padding over ice. Her bare feet were small, high-arched, and looked very pale against the dark wood. The apartment was so small that he could see her out the bedroom door, through the living room, and in the open kitchen as she ran water into his coffee maker.

Heidi cuddled up and nuzzled him, giving an uncertain whine. He stroked her ears. "I'm all right. Don't worry."

The weight across his feet shifted, and he saw for the first time that Wally was curled up on them. The puppy blinked his blue eyes, then went back to sleep.

"They love you," Natalie remarked over her shoulder. "I think they know you're sick."

He glanced at Heidi, and saw her gazing at him with a pure and unmistakable adoration that he'd done nothing to earn. Ransom petted her, and she shoved her head into his hand, demanding that he keep going.

His hand moving automatically over her soft fur, he said, "Once I have some more coffee, I'll get out of bed. Make it up with clean sheets for you. I'll take the floor."

Natalie turned, coffee pot in hand. The late afternoon sunlight came in through the window and made all the warm colors in her hair glow like a sunset. "What? No, you won't!"

"There's only one bed. I can't keep it."

"Of course you can." She dumped coffee into the filter, straight from the can. "How's that?"

"Fine," Ransom said, then realized that was ambiguous. "I mean, fine, that's plenty, and no, I can't keep the bed. There's no sofa—there's nowhere else for you to sleep."

Shooting him a horrified look, she said, "All the more reason for you to keep the bed. I'm only sorry it's so short. You must be subletting from someone my size."

"I guess so." He never kept his sublets for more than a month or two anyway, so he didn't fuss about the furniture. "She's a dancer, I think."

"That explains the living room. It's her practice space. Anyway, it's fine. I'm small. There's room." Her eyes—gold-touched blue in the sunlight—gazed into his, then she laughed. "Don't look like that. We don't need to share. If anyone sleeps on the floor, it can be me."

Ransom hadn't been alarmed at the idea of sharing a bed with Natalie. He'd wanted it. He'd wanted it way, way too much. And that was what had alarmed him. Even if nothing actually happened—and nothing would, he felt too ill and he'd never do anything she didn't want—it wouldn't really be nothing. It would be touch and intimacy and closeness, which he didn't deserve and couldn't have, least of all from her. Getting a taste of them would only make it hurt more when he lost them forever the next morning.

"Cream and sugar?" Natalie asked.

"If there is any. I might be out."

She investigated the cupboards and fridge, but found that he was indeed out of sugar and the last of the milk had gone bad. Moving as often he did, it was easier to get everything to go. At least that meant he had some paper cups. Natalie frowned over his coffee.

"Black is fine," he said.

"Ah!" She took a Crime Puff out of the pastry box, put the rest of the pastries in the fridge, scraped some of the whipped cream off the Crime Puff, and stirred it into the coffee.

"Excellent out of the box thinking," he remarked.

"I've always been good at improvisation." She held out the cup, not releasing it until she could see that he could hold it. Their fingers touched for a moment, and then she let go, turning away to busy herself with the coffee implements.

Ransom drank slowly, putting off the moment when he'd have to get up and put a door between them. Once she saw that he could stand on his own feet, she'd realize that he didn't need to be monitored.

The caffeine eased his headache, but as his clarity of thought returned, so did the memory of his fight with Roland. He wished it had gone differently, but he didn't see how it could be undone now. The team (and Carter) had been as close as he'd ever come to having friends, and now he'd never see any of them again.

"Coffee's not working?" Natalie asked.

"No, it is. I only…" Ransom fished for an excuse, then wondered why he was even bothering. Without the Defenders, he felt completely adrift. He'd save Natalie, if he could, and send her back to her life. After that, he supposed it didn't matter what happened to him. At least now he didn't need to worry that saving her life would mean his teammates would learn his secret. They weren't his teammates anymore.

She was watching him, her head cocked, her streaky gold-crimson-violet hair falling across her forehead. Waiting for an answer.

"I got fired," he admitted. "It doesn't affect what I'm doing with you, though. That was never something I was doing for work."

"Fired? From Merlin's team? Why?"

He hesitated, not wanting her to think less of him. In a sense, it didn't matter. Nothing would ever happen between them other than this one job. But it had been hard to get her to agree to let him stay with her, and he didn't want to say anything that might make him seem unstable or dangerous or otherwise not a man she ought to have around.

"He wanted me to get permission from him before I used my power," Ransom said. It was true, at least, if incomplete.

He watched her eyes flicker—he could practically see the wheels spinning in her mind—as she put the pieces together. "Oh. Huh. I guess I can see why…"

"He was trying to protect me," Ransom said. "But I have to make my own choices."

"I get it. Believe me, I get it. It's why I had to leave the circus. I couldn't waste my last year in hospitals, getting treatments that even the doctors admitted wouldn't really help. But Janet would have tried to make me, on the off chance they were wrong. What I'm doing now—she'd see it as giving up. I see it as *living*."

Her admission made him understand her better, though it didn't completely surprise him. He'd never quite believed that not wanting the people who loved her to be sad was the entire reason she'd run away from them.

"I understand," Ransom said.

She smiled, a little wistfully. "You know, I really believe you do. We're lucky."

"Lucky?"

"To find another person who understands."

Ransom had never in his life thought himself lucky. But now, sitting with an aching head on a bed too small for him, he knew that he was *incredibly* lucky to have found her. "You're right. We are."

She tilted her head, letting sky-blue and moss-green strands of hair fall across her forehead. "Not to change the subject, but who exactly is after me?"

He'd put off telling her, at first because he wasn't sure he could explain it coherently, and then because it would mean he'd have to talk about things that he didn't even like to think about. But she deserved to know.

"It's kind of a long story," he said. "Mind if I have some more coffee first?"

"Of course!" She took his cup, poured him more coffee, stirred in more whipped cream, and absently ate the rest of the Crime Puff. He liked watching her eat. There was so much enjoyment in it. She ate quickly, as if someone might snatch it away from her at any moment, but she savored every bite.

Swallowing, she said, "Want one? Or another pastry? There's nothing else in your fridge."

"No," he began. His headaches always left him feeling sick to his stomach; he couldn't eat anything till the last of the pain was gone. But even as he said it, he realized that while his head did still ache, though not as badly as before, he didn't feel nauseated. In fact, he was hungry. "I mean, yes. Please."

"Got a favorite?"

"You pick one for me."

She brought him a Crime of Passion Fruit Tart. He slowly began to eat. The mousse was creamy and light, more tangy than sweet, and the crust was crisp and buttery. He glanced up and caught her watching him with an intent, pleased expression, like a cat watching a long-awaited mouse begin to emerge from a hole.

She gave him a somewhat embarrassed smile. "Caught me staring. Sorry. It's just that you eat like you haven't had anything good in ages."

He stopped eating, surprised.

"No, go on. I don't mean you were gobbling or anything. I meant..." She twirled a lock of buttercup yellow hair around a finger. Her eyes were dark blue in the fading light, and he felt like they could see straight into his heart. "Every time I've seen you enjoy yourself, you always look surprised, too. If I was trying to con you… Well, I wouldn't, you'd see through it, but *if*… I wouldn't pretend you'd inherited money or could get rich quick. I'd say you owed taxes or had broken some law. See, you seem like you've been having such a hard time for so long that you've not only stopped expecting anything good, you wouldn't believe it if someone told you."

She *did* understand him. So much so that it was almost scary. She wasn't a shifter and didn't have powers, and yet she saw as much as he did with nothing to work with but her eyes and her quick, clever mind.

"You're right. It has to do with what I need to tell you." He took a deep breath. In order to inform her that she was in danger from the wizard-scientists, he had to tell her who they were. He'd never told that story to anyone, and there were parts that he intended no one, including Natalie—especially Natalie—to ever know. But he had to gear himself up to tell her even the censored version.

"I was a Marine." That wasn't the beginning of the story, but it was the only safe place to start. "I was on a fire team with Merlin and Pete Valdez—Pete's in Defenders now too—and another guy, Ethan McNeil."

"Merlin told me a bit about them. You too."

"What'd he say about me?"

"That you were smart and you knew a lot and you were a lot of fun to talk to when you were willing to talk, which you mostly weren't. That you were a crack shot. And that you were so good at spotting ambushes and booby traps that he wondered for a while if you were a shifter and were doing it with enhanced senses. He tried dropping some hints so you'd know he knew about shifters already and it was safe for you to tell him if you were, but you always looked at him like you thought he was talking nonsense."

Ransom hadn't had any idea that Merlin had paid that much attention to him, let alone that he'd suspected him of secretly being a shifter. He thought back to some of Merlin's odder remarks, and saw them in a whole new light. "He went on and on once about people having secrets about themselves that weren't bad, but could get them into trouble. I thought he was either working himself up to coming out to me or was trying to tell me it was safe for me to come out to him."

"Oops," said Natalie, grinning. "What did you say?"

"I told him I wasn't, but my uncle and my best friend in high school and a bunch of other people I knew were, and it made no difference to me. And also, that he'd be surprised how many Marines were too, now that they wouldn't kick you out for it. He gave me the weirdest look, then he cracked up and said he wasn't either. And that was the last of those sorts of conversations with him."

Natalie burst out laughing. "Merlin must have been so confused for a second, wondering why you knew so many shifters when you weren't one yourself."

"Not to mention the Marines having official policies on whether they were allowed to serve," Ransom said, smiling. Then he remembered something he needed to clear up before he told her his story. "Hey—Is there *any* chance you'll talk to Merlin again? Because there's some things I could tell you about him, but I think he'd much rather tell you himself."

Natalie's expression sobered, her eyes darkening as she cast her gaze downward in thought. When she looked up, her eyes were still dark. "I don't know. Don't tell me his secrets, though. Even if we never talk, I feel like I shouldn't know things about him that he wouldn't want me to hear from someone else. Just tell me one thing. Is he all right?"

"He's fine. It's nothing bad." And then he couldn't put it off any longer. "We were ambushed on patrol. Shot with knockout darts. Ethan got away, but Pete and Merlin and I were captured. I woke up alone, in an underground military base. It was…" He swallowed, his throat dry.

Natalie got up and brought him more coffee. "You sure you want to tell me about this?"

"Yes. You need to know." He drank, then went on, his voice carefully controlled. "There was a black ops agency called Apex that experimented on people. It made them into shifters and gave them powers. Some of the bodyguards at Protection, Inc., the west coast branch of Defenders, were their experimental subjects. They thought they'd destroyed Apex, but they hadn't, exactly. It had been taken over by a different group: the wizard-scientists. They're shifters who blend magic and science. They claim to descend from the days of King Arthur."

Natalie blinked at this, but didn't seem disbelieving. "That sounds like something out of Janet's stories."

"That's exactly what they are. Her stories are real." He took another sip of coffee. It was bitter; Natalie had forgotten to put in the whipped cream. "The wizard-scientists were the ones who captured us. They changed me. Made me a hellhound. Gave me powers. In their lab, I was seeing so much, all at once… I knew so much, and I couldn't filter any of it out…"

Ransom took a deep breath, then another. Keeping it under control. "I don't remember that much of what happened. I was really out of it. I kept seeing danger and trying to warn my teammates, but I couldn't tell what it was or when it would happen. I only know exactly what went down because they told me afterward. Ethan had met up with one of the Protection, Inc. bodyguards, and the entire team came to the rescue. Plus Carter."

"Who's Carter?"

"Another one of the Apex experimental subjects, back from before the wizard-scientists got involved. He didn't join the Protection, Inc. team. He didn't join our team either, exactly. He sort of… freelances with us. Anyway, they rescued us. Roland too—he was in the Army, but he got kidnapped at the same time as us. Now he's our boss. While we were running around the base, we released a bunch of magical creatures the wizard-scientists had captured. I think that's where Wally and Heidi come from."

The puppies looked up, hearing their names, and Heidi began licking Ransom's hand. It was amazing how much better that made him feel.

"We fought the wizard-scientists and blew up their base. But some of them escaped. They've been coming after my teammates ever since, one by one."

Natalie's eyebrows pulled together. They were golden brown, which he supposed must be her natural hair color. Like a beach in late afternoon. It was a pretty color, but the rainbow suited her better. "Were you all experimented on, then?"

"Yes."

"Merlin too?" Natalie had the strangest tone, as if she couldn't tell whether to be hopeful or afraid. "I know I said I don't want to know, but... Maybe if you don't tell me all the details...?"

Ransom carefully thought through the minefield of what to say about Merlin, given what Natalie wanted and what Merlin would want. It was so tiring, especially since he also had to conceal how he felt about it.

Or did he?

Lucky to have someone who understands, she'd said. Maybe this could be one secret he didn't have to keep.

"They made him a shifter, and they gave him powers," Ransom said. "I won't tell you what they are or what he turns into—that's what he'll want to show you. And he really is fine. He loves his shift form, and he loves his power. I'm happy for him—I hate seeing him sad or upset—but I'm jealous, too. It was like he pulled a diamond out of a toxic waste dump. But for me..."

She brushed her fingers across his forehead, ruffling his hairline. Everywhere she touched stopped hurting, as if she had healing in her fingertips. If she could touch him everywhere, all at once, maybe then he'd feel all right.

"You drew the short straw," Natalie said. "Hey, remember when I said we were lucky? I'll tell you another way we understand each other. I love Merlin, but I'm jealous of him too sometimes."

"You are? Why?"

She made a sound like a laugh, but there was no happiness in it. "Well, now I have a new reason. He's a shifter, and I always wanted to be one. When we were kids in the circus, we both wanted to shift, but Janet warned us to never ask another shifter to bite us. She said it was too risky. It might make us a shifter or it might kill us, and there was no way to know which would happen."

"Merlin never tried," Ransom said. He didn't *know* it, he just knew it. Merlin loved life too much to risk it on a chance like that.

"No. I asked him, and he said it would break his mother's heart if he got himself killed trying to do something she'd specifically warned him against. I didn't tell him I'd already tried—tricked one of the flying squirrel kits into nipping my finger while we were playing. She didn't even notice." Natalie sighed. "Turned out that sometimes you don't die *or* shift. You just stay the same person you always were."

"You wanted to be a flying squirrel that much?"

"Not a squirrel specifically. I wanted to fly, and we only had three types of flying shifters. Janet would never agree to do it, and I couldn't think of any way to get one of the sparrows to peck me hard enough to draw blood without them noticing. So flying squirrel it was."

Ransom noticed that she hadn't answered his original question. "But you didn't know Merlin was a shifter till a minute ago. Why were you jealous of him before that?"

"He was the circus golden boy, you know. He got adopted by its leader under dramatic circumstances. I was kind of a tagger-on—I only got in because he asked them to let me. They took me in, but I never had the kind of relationship with anyone that Merlin has with his mom. Don't get me wrong, I loved the circus, but… not like he did. I know he did way more agonizing over leaving than I ever did." She frowned, seeming to search for words. Finally, she said. "He belonged there. I'm not sure I've ever belonged anywhere."

"Me neither. Especially not now. The way they changed me, in that lab… I feel like I'm not even living in the same world as everyone else. I see things… I know things… And it hurts. All of it."

He stopped talking, surprised at himself for saying so much. Natalie's hand stole into his, and she squeezed it.

Lucky, he thought again. And he knew that it was true.

"Today I *knew* that you were in danger from the wizard-scientists," he said. "That's why I had to get you away from the motel. They knew where you were."

"The wizard-scientists?" She sounded baffled, not frightened. "What would they want with me?"

"I don't know. I thought maybe they'd hurt you while they were trying to get to me, just because you were nearby. That's why I pushed my power so hard today. The question I asked was whether you were safer with me or without me. The answer is with me."

Natalie, who had tensed up as soon as he'd mentioned the question, relaxed at the answer. He supposed even someone as brave as her wouldn't want to face danger alone. "Are we safe here? Do they know where we are?"

Her question triggered a memory. He rocked back with a gasp as it flooded his mind, then rushed to reassure her. "I'm fine. I just remembered the vision I had this morning. It was of them trying to get to you. A blonde woman and a big man. I didn't recognize them. They were breaking into your motel room. But it was empty. The blonde woman was the boss. She said they weren't going to try an immediate pursuit because…" He closed his eyes, trying to recall more, then opened them. "That's all I remember."

"No immediate pursuit, that's good," said Natalie. "And now you know what they look like. If they do come back, maybe you can spot them before they spot you."

"I can do better than that. I can…" He hesitated. This skirted too close to what he intended to never reveal. Finally, he said, "I usually know when I'm in immediate danger."

Natalie nodded, as if that made perfect sense. But of course it would, to her. All she knew about his powers was what he told her.

"Or you could stay at our safehouse," he said, though he felt sure she'd refuse. "It doesn't matter that I got fired. The whole team could protect—"

"Nope." She smiled. "You knew I'd say that."

"Didn't even need my powers."

She took his hand in both of hers. Looking down, he saw that he'd crushed the paper coffee cup in his clenched fist. She opened his hand, taking it from him, and dropped it on the floor. Then she held his hand between her palms. When she spoke, her tone was even warmer than her skin. "You endured all that pain for me."

"Don't worry about it. It's better now."

"And you told me a story that you obviously would have rather not, because you thought I needed to know."

Honestly, he said, "It wasn't as hard to talk about as I thought it would be."

Because you didn't tell her the crucial parts, growled his hellhound. *You didn't tell her the truth about you. But she'll find out. And then she'll be so horrified that she'll run off to die alone instead of spending one more second with you.*

That sandpaper growl scraped across his mind, setting off his migraine again. He flinched, his hand pulling out of her grasp.

Natalie, who had started to lean in close, jerked back. "Sorry. Sorry. You need to rest. Lie down."

He lay back down, once again dizzy and sick with pain.

Lowering her voice to a near-whisper, she said, "Does it hurt to hear me talk? Would you rather it was quiet?"

Sound did hurt, normally. But her voice didn't jangle inside his head. It was like a clear cool stream, soothing his pain. "No. And no. Tell me more about your bucket list. What did you do before the BAND LUMP?"

She pulled a face at him, then said, "Well, growing up in a traveling crime circus full of shifters, I'd already been to a bunch of places and done a bunch of things that normal people might put on a bucket list. I grew up swimming with seals, for instance. Shifters, but still. But I'd never swum with dolphins—shifters or real ones—so that was number one."

Natalie told him all about her trip to swim with dolphins in phosphorescent waters, painting a vivid picture of the playful dolphins, the beauty of the sea and the night, and the ease and freedom and pleasure of swimming beneath the moon. He felt transported, as if he was swimming by her side.

By the time she was finished, the room had grown dark. He could see the glimmer of her hair, but not its colors. His eyelids were heavy, and his whole body ached with exhaustion. If he didn't get up now, he never would. He wasn't sure he could stand, but he said, "You should take the bed."

He felt more than saw it when she lay down beside him. The breath that formed her words touched his cheek as she said, "I can sleep here with you, or I can take the floor. That's it. Those are your options."

Ransom wanted to tell her he'd take the floor himself. But with her actually lying next to him, he couldn't bring himself to object. The bed was so narrow, it forced them to lie close together. She had fitted herself into the space his body didn't occupy, like water flowing into a cup. Her silky hair touched his face and throat, and her bare skin brushed against his, feather-light and burning hot. He swallowed, and knew she felt the movement.

"No one's taking the floor," he said.

"I knew you'd come round." There was a tremble of laughter in her voice, like the shimmer of sun on water.

She stretched, shifting her weight, and almost fell out of bed. He flung his arm around her, catching her, then pulled her in closer. She didn't resist. His breath stopped. Natalie was in his arms, warm and alive, her scent filling the air. He could feel every breath she took. He could feel her heart beating.

She touched his head. "Does it still hurt?"

"A bit."

She rubbed his temples, very gently. "Does this help?"

He nodded. It did, but he wouldn't have told her to stop even if it had made the pain worse. His entire body came alive to her touch, prickling and tingling, as if it had been asleep for years and was only now waking up. He hadn't realized how lonely he'd been, how much he'd longed for someone to touch him, until she was there with him, so close that you couldn't have slipped a sheet of paper between them.

There was nothing he wanted more than to keep quiet and let it continue. But he had to know. "Why are you doing this?"

"Because I want to."

"You told me we'd have separate rooms," he said. "I mean…"

"We will. In the motels. This is only for tonight."

Of course. He was in pain, and she felt sorry for him, and she was a kind person. That was all. Ransom was at once disappointed and relieved. He couldn't help wanting more, but "more" wasn't for someone like him. If she had meant this as anything beyond kindness, he'd have to tell her…

Everything, growled his hellhound. *You'd have to tell her what you've done. You'd have to tell her who you are. You'd have to tell her about me.*

"Ransom?" Natalie asked, her fingers stopping their gentle circular motion. "Are you all right?"

He prepared himself to fight his hellhound, if it tried to show him her worst moment, but the beast sank back down.

"Yes. Don't stop."

She resumed, but he was no longer relaxed. Instead, a wild, desperate, impossible hope flared up within him. He wasn't worthy of a woman like Natalie. And if she knew who and what he was, she'd never accept him. But what if he could *become* worthy of her?

He knew the method of destroying one's inner animal, but he hadn't yet gotten up the nerve to try it. If he killed his hellhound, he'd lose the inner voice that wouldn't stop tearing him down, and he'd lose the "worst moment" power that was nothing more than a curse. He'd also lose the ability to shift, but he wouldn't miss it—not when the only form he could become was that of the beast he hated.

There's a reason you haven't tried it, his hellhound snarled. *You can't kill me without killing yourself.*

CHAPTER 9

Natalie awoke with a sense of contentment that she hadn't felt in a very long time. Normally she woke wide awake and sprang out of bed, rushing to greet the day. But this morning she was in no hurry. She had things to do, sure, but maybe the first one was to enjoy being held in strong and loving arms…

With that, she came wide awake, remembering where she was and who she was with. She and Ransom were crammed into the Natalie-sized bed with their arms wrapped around each other. Her head was nestled into his shoulder and his cheek was pressed against her hair. Even their legs were entangled. Heidi and Wally were sound asleep, flopped on top of Natalie's ankles and Ransom's knees.

Ransom's feet dangled over the edge of the bed. He was breathing deeply, still asleep, but his arms tightened their grip around her, as if he'd sensed some shift in her and wanted to keep her close.

Her bucket list did not include "Cuddle with the man who collapsed in a motel parking lot with a psychic vision-induced migraine that he deliberately gave himself saving you from rampaging wizard-scientists." But she had to confess to herself that she was enjoying it more than some of the supposed peak experiences she'd tried. It had been so long since anyone had touched her, beyond a brush of fingers as money or motel keys were exchanged.

When she thought back to the last time she'd been embraced by a man, she first had to run through a bunch of pleasant but extremely platonic hugs and trapeze catches to even get to the last time she'd dated anyone. He'd been a bartender in Japan she'd met when the Fabulous Flying Chameleons had played in Tokyo. Hayao… or had it been Hayato… had been a nice guy and they'd had fun exploring the city for the month the circus had stayed there.

Before that, when the circus had played in Paris, she'd met a guy who set off fireworks at parties. He'd asked her if she'd like to be French kissed in France, and she'd laughed and agreed. His name was… had it been Pascal? Pierre? Patrice?

Philippe or whatever his name was had been very romantic. So had Hatsuo (if that was his name). They'd given her champagne and red roses (Paul-Louis), and sake and red tulips (Haruki), and taken her to to exclusive underground clubs (Harutaka) and strolls along the Seine (Paul-Michel). She could remember all the places they'd gone and the fun they'd had. But she couldn't recall what their arms had felt like around hers, or the texture of their hair, or whether she'd been sad when they'd said good-bye.

When Natalie had stroked Ransom's hair, it had been damp with sweat, and the moisture had made it curl more than it normally did. Locks had curled around her fingers, wrapping around them and then snapping back into place when she pushed her hand through. When his hair was dry, the sun struck glints of copper and bronze against a darker background. Wet, it was nearly black. She couldn't imagine ever forgetting its smooth resilience, or the way he'd turned his head into her touch.

Natalie lifted her head, ever so slightly, so she could get a glimpse what his hair looked like now. The movement woke him. His copper eyelashes fluttered, and his dark eyes looked directly into hers.

For the first time, she saw him smile. It was a bright, warm, sweet smile, touched with a natural sensuality that made her hot all over. It transformed him.

This is how he's supposed to be, she thought. *Now I'm really seeing him.*

All her resolve to keep things light and professional, all her carefully thought-out reasons to not get involved, and every shred of her self-control went right out the window. The only reason she didn't lean over and kiss him that instant was that she wanted to look at that smile for a moment longer.

Ransom touched her hair, very lightly, but even that sent a jolt of electricity from her head and along her spine and all the way down to her toes. "Good morning. Thank you for taking care of me."

His voice was different, too. There was an ease to it that hadn't been there before, and a slight morning huskiness that made the sexual electricity already circulating along her nerves take some extra stops in some very sensitive places.

Natalie gulped. Her thoughts had scattered like leaves in the wind. She lay still, waiting for him to kiss her.

In a single easy movement, he swung his legs over the edge of the bed. He scooped up his discarded shirt, padded barefoot and steady to the bathroom, and closed the door behind him. A moment later, she heard the shower running.

What? Natalie thought.

Heidi stretched, barked, and vanished. Wally wriggled his way up the bed and licked Natalie's face.

At least I got a kiss from someone, she thought.

Had she hallucinated all that sexual chemistry and intimacy and how good it had felt to touch each other?

Then she remembered what she'd said last night: that it was only for one night and they'd have separate rooms from then on. She'd blurted it out as her last-ditch attempt to stick with the light-and-professional thing, but obviously Ransom had taken it to heart.

She wished she'd never said anything about the two rooms. All her reasons for not wanting to get involved were still true, but her resolve had gone right out the window the moment she'd woken up with his arms around her. She'd felt so comfortable and steady and protected, as if she had all the time in the world to lie with him and be happy. As if she had a future.

Which she didn't, of course, no matter what *he* believed.

Just as she started wondering if she needed to take Wally outside, he disappeared. A few minutes later, both he and Heidi reappeared. They seemed perfectly content rather than whining at the door, so Natalie decided they must have taken themselves outside.

"Very convenient," she informed them. "It makes up for all the ways that teleporting puppies are very inconvenient."

Of course, it wasn't convenient for whoever stepped in it, since no one had been there to pick up after them. Natalie resolved to watch the sidewalk when she left the apartment.

She went into the kitchen and fed the pups, then started another pot of coffee. The bathroom door opened with a creak. Glancing back, she saw Ransom rinsing his shirt in the sink, wet-haired and clad in nothing but a towel wrapped around his hips. His lean musculature looked like something you'd see in a museum, if you got really turned on by marble statues.

Light and professional, she thought. *What the hell was I thinking?*

"I'd ask you how you're feeling, but I can tell the answer's 'better,'" she said.

"The answer's '*a lot* better.' Fine, even. And this time I mean it." He wrung out the shirt, then began to dry it with a blow-dryer he produced from under the sink.

"So you know that old traveler's trick."

"I didn't know it was a trick. The washer-dryer's been broken ever since I moved in." He unplugged the hair dryer and took it out of the bathroom, then plugged it in beside the coffee maker. "Shower's all yours."

She hesitated, imagining herself saying, *"About last night..."* But he had his back turned and clearly wasn't expecting either an intense discussion or a declaration of... what, exactly? "I think you're incredibly hot, let's have sex?" "I like you a lot and I want to know you better?" All that seemed so casual, and that was the opposite of the way she felt. But when she only had a year, she couldn't possibly do anything other than casual.

Putting off the decision, she grabbed some clothes from her suitcase and fled to the bathroom.

Once she was in the shower, everything felt so much more complicated than it had been when she'd woken up. Was he holding back because he thought she'd already said no, or because he'd taken a clear-eyed look at their non-existent future and decided to steer clear? Did he even have the same sorts of feelings she did?

She let the shower run and run, but by the time it ran cold, she still had no idea what she wanted to say.

I'll play it by ear, she decided, and immediately felt less stressed. She'd go with her instincts and do what she wanted to do in the moment, just like she always did.

When she emerged from the bathroom, Ransom had gotten dressed, apparently in enough of a hurry that he hadn't completely dried off; his shirt was slightly damp and clinging to his muscles. He looked a lot more dangerous and less professorial that way. Natalie would have loved to have seen him in a regular tight T-shirt. Or a trapeze artist's skin-tight leotard. Or naked. She'd felt for herself that he had an impressive pair of legs hiding beneath those loose-fitting pants.

She splashed cold water over her face until she felt confident that those thoughts weren't hovering in a visible cloud over her head, then joined him in the kitchen. He'd poured out coffee for her—from the color, he'd doctored it with a Crime Puff—and set out the last of the pastries on paper plates.

He gestured to the only chair. "Take it."

She made a little hop, and sat herself down on the counter, legs dangling. "You take it. I prefer to perch."

"Like a parakeet. No, like a rainbow lorikeet."

Natalie had never been to Australia, but she'd seen the colorful birds in a zoo. "I'm flattered. Have you been to Australia?"

He shook his head. "I've only seen photos. You've got even more colors, though."

They finished off the pastries as they chatted about Australia and lorikeets and chairs vs. counters. She'd expected the "about last night" to hang over them, but it didn't. Instead, she felt strangely relaxed. Ransom seemed relaxed, too.

The night before hadn't dispelled the sexual tension—if anything, it had intensified it—but it wasn't *tense*. Not so much sexual tension as sexual intensity. She was very aware of his body, his movements, of when he looked at her and when he looked away, but it didn't give her that jittery "will we/won't we" feeling. Which was odd, too, considering that she had no idea whether they would or wouldn't.

She couldn't help hoping for "would."

When they finished their breakfast, she packed her little roller suitcase. It took her less than a minute, as all she had to do was put in her toothbrush and dirty clothes.

Ransom experimentally lifted it. "It's so light."

"Not much room in a circus train. You don't get a chance to accumulate stuff. Half my outfits were costumes anyway, so I left them. My books are on an e-reader."

"Mine too."

Natalie felt obscurely disappointed. "Oh… The bookcase belongs to the dancer?"

"I should've said, *most* of my library is on an e-reader," he said. "The bookcase is the part that isn't."

She headed over to inspect his books. She was instantly enchanted by their sheer variety, from horror paperbacks like *The Face That Must Die* to serious nonfiction like *The How and Why of Military Failure* to elegant antiques like *The Conference of the Birds* to handbooks like *Shrubs and Trees of the Southwest Uplands* to textbooks with incomprehensible titles like *Stereochemistry of Organic Compounds*.

"I haven't even heard of most of these," Natalie said. "And I read a lot. Kudos."

"These books all only exist on paper. So they're pretty obscure."

She spotted the word 'circus' on a faded spine, and crouched down to get a closer look. It was *British Circus Life* by Lady Eleanor Smith. Next to *Satan's Circus*, also by Lady Eleanor Smith. Delighted, she asked, "Mind if I browse?"

"Not at all," Ransom said. "I have to pack a bag anyway. It'll just take a minute."

"Sure."

He went into the bedroom and closed the door. Natalie, paging through *Satan's Circus*, wouldn't have thought anything of it if she hadn't happened to hear the sound that followed, which was the soft click of a lock.

Satan's Circus forgotten in her hands, she stared at the closed door. Why would he lock the door on her? It couldn't be habit, because he lived alone. And she'd already spent the night in his bedroom.

She remembered that he hadn't gotten dressed until she was busy showering. She hadn't thought anything of it at the time—obviously they weren't at the "get naked together" stage—but now that seemed even odder. He could have told her he was getting dressed, and she wouldn't have come in.

What was he hiding?

CHAPTER 10

Ransom had no idea if Natalie would recognize tincture of shiftsilver, but even if she didn't, he had no intention of risking her seeing it. The vial of shimmering silver liquid was bound to provoke questions, and he'd promised himself that he wouldn't lie to her.

When he opened the drawer, he could see it glimmering. He'd shoved a pair of pants over it when he'd gotten dressed that morning, but they hadn't covered it completely. He thanked his lucky stars he'd remembered to wait till she was in the shower before opening the drawer.

He took a deep breath. Maybe he should leave it where it was. He could always use it later. But he'd rather have it and not need it than need it and not have it. He removed the vial, wrapped it carefully in a shirt, and crammed it into the bottom of his duffel bag.

You won't have the nerve to try it, jeered his hellhound. *You'll never be rid of me.*

Ransom packed quickly, trying not to think too hard about the vial that could destroy his hellhound… or kill him trying.

A few minutes later, he unlocked and opened the door, and found Natalie sitting on the floor, twisted into a painful-looking pretzel that she clearly found perfectly comfortable, engrossed in *Houdini's Escapes and Magic: Prepared from Houdini's Private Notebooks.*

Ransom, who never loaned any of his precious out of print books to anyone, saw how reverently she turned the pages and found himself saying, "You can borrow it if you like."

"Can I? I promise to be careful with it."

"I know." He watched her tuck it away, thought how fun it would be to discuss books with her, and said, "You can borrow any of mine."

She pounced with an eagerness that made him smile. He leaned over to see what she picked out, enjoying her pleasure in looking over his collection.

"You've got good taste," she remarked as she pulled out a horror novel whose cover depicted a zombie skeleton rabbit climbing out of a magician's hat.

"I think you're the first person who's ever looked at *Abracadabra* and said that."

"Only the coolest people are interested in stage magic," she replied, tucking the book beside *Houdini's Escapes and Magic.* "Also, I love horror. The trashier, the better. So there's another point to you. Are you a chemist? You have a lot of chemistry books."

He thought guiltily of the tincture of shiftsilver, which he'd used his old skills to make, and even more guiltily of his actual career in biochemistry. "Not anymore."

"Pick something out for me. Something you think I'll enjoy."

That was easy; he'd already been thinking of recommending it to her, the instant she'd mentioned trashy horror. "Since you missed prom... Have a *Prom Dress.*"

She pounced delightedly on the novel, whose cover showed a teenage girl confronted by a glowing prom dress hanging in a closet. "Did you miss prom too? Did you wish you'd gone with a girl in a haunted prom dress?"

"I collect 80s horror," he said, dodging the question. "That's from the Point Horror line. See, I also have *The Babysitter, Trick or Treat, Party Line...*"

"You *definitely* missed prom," Natalie said, laughing. She laid *Prom*

Dress atop *Abracadabra*, then added *Trick or Treat*. "Now pick another. Something less on-the-nose."

Acutely aware of her gaze, he looked over his bookcase. He considered books with dogs and books about road trips, then ruled those out, along with books about circuses, as too on-the-nose. Then he saw one which didn't have anything to do with Natalie's life, but which he was certain she'd enjoy. "Here you go. *Modesty Blaise*. She's kind of a female James Bond."

"Might be a *little* on-the-nose," she replied. "I always wanted to be a secret agent."

"I didn't know that. I'm a psychic, not a telepath."

"I love that I'm about to go on a road trip with a man who has to make that distinction," she remarked, and packed the books with a level of care that might have even gone beyond what he would have done himself.

They shooed the puppies into their crate and headed for the car rental. Natalie was bent over, wiggling her fingers at the puppies in the carrier, when the salesman came out. To Ransom, he said, "I have a nice black Honda Civic. Or if you'd prefer a larger car, I have a brand-new gray Ford Fusion."

A brand new car would attract more attention. And Natalie might be more comfortable learning to drive a smaller car. Ransom was about to say he'd take the Honda when she straightened up.

The salesman took one look at her, his gaze lingering on her hair, and said, "Actually… Forget what I just said. I have the perfect car for you."

"What is it?" Natalie asked.

The salesman actually winked. "Let me show it to you."

Ransom and Natalie glanced at each other as they followed the salesman to the parking lot, Ransom lugging the puppy carrier.

"Is this how car rentals usually work?" Natalie asked.

"No, never." It was so unusual, in fact, that his normal level of caution was raised to something approaching paranoia. Ransom made sure that his body was between her and the salesman, then handed her the carrier so he could shield the pups too.

"Oof," Natalie muttered. The puppies weren't heavy individually, but they were together, and so was the sturdy carrier.

"Sorry," Ransom said quietly, his attention still fixed on the salesman. "I'll explain later."

The salesman, oblivious to their conversation, led them around a corner and flung out his hand. "There! That's your car! Isn't she a beauty?"

Natalie exhaled a long, delighted breath as they beheld the most attention-attracting car Ransom had ever seen. It was a cherry-red Mustang convertible, sleek and sporty and riding low.

To Natalie, the salesman said, "The moment I saw you, I knew that was the car for you." Barely glancing at Ransom, he said, "You two." Back to Natalie, he went on, "Imagine riding in that car, your hair blowing in the wind. Ever driven a Mustang before?"

"No, never," said Natalie, sliding a wicked glance at Ransom.

"You won't believe how fast and smooth she is. And responsive! She stops and starts on a dime. And look at this!" The salesman opened the passenger door. The Mustang symbol of the rearing horse was cast on the garage floor in light.

"Ooh," said Natalie.

"You're going to love this car. Shall we take her for a spin?"

Ransom felt like a heel, breaking up the swiftly developing love affair between Natalie and the Mustang convertible, but he had to stop it before it went any farther. "We wanted something discreet, remember? This car is going to attract the attention of every cop on the road. We'll pay for it twice over in tickets."

"Not if you drive sensibly," said the salesman—to Ransom, not Natalie. "Which I'm sure you do!"

"I do, but..."

"Go on, give her a try," urged the salesman. "Which of you would like to go first?"

"He would," Natalie said, sticking the puppy carrier in the back seat. She climbed into the passenger seat and buckled up. "Come on! I want to feel the wind in my hair!"

With no other alternative, Ransom took the keys. They included a silver key ornament in the shape of a rearing mustang. He started the car, then gently pressed down on the gas. The car leaped forward.

"Whee!" squealed Natalie.

Heidi gave a startled yelp.

Ransom, hurriedly lessening the pressure, muttered, "This car isn't responsive, it's practically telepathic."

"I love it. Take it outside!"

Ransom could see the salesman in the rear view mirror. He had to at least make the pretense of a test drive. Leaving the parking lot, he began driving down a city street. Natalie's hair blew back in the wind, sparkling and glittering in the sun like a dragon's treasure heap of precious gems.

"It does suit you," he admitted. "But it really will attract attention. And I don't mean from police at speeding traps."

"From the wizard-scientists? If they're as powerful as you say, a cool car shouldn't make a difference in them noticing us, right?"

Ransom hesitated. He hadn't been thinking of the wizard-scientists, exactly.

She pounced like a cat. "And they already know who you are. And where you work! Being generally inconspicuous won't help with that."

He didn't want her wondering why, in that case, he was trying to be generally inconspicuous. "You're right. And it does drive beautifully."

He swung the car back into the parking lot and stopped on a dime.

"Well?" said the salesman.

"I love it," said Natalie.

"We'll take it," said Ransom.

As they pulled out, he said, "There's a short way to get to Tomato Land, and a long way. The long way is more scenic—it runs along the ocean. The short way is basically fields and cows."

"Do you even need to ask?" Natalie inquired, grinning.

"Scenic it is."

He had driven on that highway before, though not that exact route. But driving alone in a rental car selected specifically for being boring was nothing like driving in a sports car with the top rolled down, with

Natalie beside him and a pair of teleporting puppies in the back seat. Sunlight glimmered on the blue-green water. He could smell sea brine and wildflowers and the scent of his own shampoo in her hair. He'd never even noticed that it had a smell before, but it did, woodsy and clean.

"What are you going to do when we're done with my trip?" she asked.

It was hard to imagine a life without his team *and* without Natalie. Without the Marines, too. And before he'd had the Marines... well, he couldn't go back to *that*.

The silence stretched out, and she said, "Would you go back to the Defenders, if you could? If your boss dropped the idea of trying to control how you used your power?"

Roland would have to drop some other things, too. And after the way Ransom had left, he couldn't imagine them taking him back. But she'd said *if*, so he said, "Hypothetically... yes."

"I bet Merlin would put in a word for you with your boss, if you asked him." She grinned. "Maybe even if you didn't ask."

Ransom shrugged. Merlin would put in a word for anyone in need. He was that kind of guy. And Roland would know that. Merlin's word, should it materialize, wouldn't carry any weight.

"He told me about Pete already, from when they were Marines," she went on. "Merlin said he wasn't sure if Pete liked him, but he was incredibly brave and had a big heart."

"That's true. And Pete does like him. He just gets exasperated sometimes."

"He sounds like the kind of guy who might also put in a word for you."

"Maybe." But he doubted it. Pete's power had allowed him to get into Ransom's mind. Pete had claimed he hadn't seen any of his secrets, but had only gotten a general impression of what it felt like to be him. Since Pete hadn't immediately attacked him, the no-secrets part had to be true. But even a general impression seemed unlikely to make Pete want him back.

"And there's one other guy, right? The freelancer, Carter. What's he like? You said he'd been experimented on by Apex, the guys before the wizard-scientists. What does he shift into?"

"I don't know."

Natalie looked disappointed. "Oh—you must really not know each other, then."

"No, it's not that." He knew where she was going with all this, and he was tempted to ask her to drop it. But that could backfire. Better to simply answer her questions and move on.

"Carter was born a snow leopard shifter, but Apex did something to him. He can still shift, but not into a snow leopard. He won't say what it is, and none of us have seen it."

"Don't you know, though?" Hurriedly, she added, "I don't mean that you'd deliberately spy on him, but you said you can't control your power, so I thought it might've just shown you."

"It hasn't. There's something odd about Carter, or about what they did to him. A kind of… interference. My power doesn't pick up on him at all. He's like a blank spot."

"But are you close?"

He knew what question she was asking—would Carter intervene on his behalf—but he replied to the literal one. They had the same answer, anyway. "Carter's been asked to join the team a bunch of times, and he's never agreed. He keeps us all at arms' distance, and he's been very clear about wanting things to stay that way."

To fend off further questions, he added, "I'll figure out Defenders after the trip is over. While we're on the road trip, I want to focus on the road trip."

As he'd expected, this struck her as completely reasonable. With a smile, she said, "Good idea. I promise not to bug you about it till we're back in Refuge City."

They swung around a curve, and she gasped in delight. Paragliders were drifting in the air above the ocean, dangling from their single crescent wings. The sky was very blue, without a cloud, and the bright colors of their gliders stood out like fragments of a rainbow.

"Have you done that yet?" Ransom asked.

"I have—it was on my list—but nowhere near this pretty. Maybe we could make a big circle and do it at the very end of our trip. Make sure we go out on a high note."

Ransom, who had been about to suggest that they try it after Tomato Land, felt a pang in his chest. *Go out on a high note* felt so final. Why was she so convinced that she couldn't be saved?

Because her only chance is you, growled his hellhound.

That idea haunted him for the entire rest of the drive, coming back to him at odd moments whenever he managed to forget it. He didn't want to believe it, but he didn't have a better explanation. Trying to keep his thoughts quiet enough that the hellhound wouldn't jump in, he told himself that he'd beat the odds, regardless of what she believed.

As they drove, Natalie kept squirming around in her seat, pulling up her feet and wriggling into a more "comfortable" position that looked like she'd tied herself into a knot. Her hair sparkled like living rubies and emeralds, sapphires and garnets, peridots and aquamarines. She noticed that he was getting a sunburn and rubbed sunscreen into the back of his neck with cool, slippery fingers, so he wouldn't have to stop to do it himself. When the puppies got bored and teleported out of their crate, she scooped them up and secured them in her lap without missing a beat.

She loved stage magic and puppies and trashy horror novels. She cared about him losing his job when she was at risk of losing her *life*. She'd held him in her arms when he'd been sick and in pain.

He had to save her.

CHAPTER 11

"Tomato Land may not live up to your expectations," Ransom warned her. "If it's Rustproof Feminist Take Two, we can always ditch it and take the pups to the beach instead."

"We should definitely take the pups to the beach *also*." Natalie paused to untangle herself from Wally's leash, then to untangle his leash from Heidi's leash. To Ransom's relief, they had shown no inclination to randomly teleport when they'd taken the pups on a test walk in a deserted industrial area before continuing on to Tomato Land. "But this is the *famous* vegetable festival! It must be good."

"Some people are famous for being famous."

"Yes, but those are people," Natalie pointed out. "These are tomatoes."

Ransom stepped neatly over Heidi's attempt to clothesline him. "I'm just saying. You grew up in a circus, so a few basic carnival games aren't going to impress you. Don't be too disappointed if it's nothing but a pizza stand, a bored mascot in a red shirt, a booth hawking mass-produced tomato keychains, and…"

His voice trailed off as they turned the corner and came face to face with a carnival ride. It was a gondola pirate ship shaped like a giant knife, swinging in and out of a slot cut into a wall shaped like a giant tomato. Every time the knife-ship "sliced" the tomato, a fountain of red water sprayed out and drenched the cheering, squealing riders.

He stopped dead in his tracks. The ride was so over the top, so absurd, and so utterly committed to the tomato theme that it ran right over the edge of tacky and landed in fabulous.

"Yes?" Natalie said. "You were saying? Something about how boring and ordinary and disappointing Tomato Land would be?"

"I take it all back. Also, I hope you're not attached to that outfit, because I know you're not passing up the chance to ride a tomato knife."

"I hope *you're* not too attached, because I'm not passing up the chance to make you ride it with me."

Ransom had never in his life imagined riding a tomato knife and getting drenched in fake tomato juice. If he had, he'd have thought it sounded like torture: the absolute worst of the large category of supposedly fun things that made him feel trapped and miserable and like something was wrong with him for not enjoying himself. But when he thought of doing it with Natalie, it didn't sound horrible at all. It sounded… fun.

She grabbed his hand. His fingers closed around hers, a little harder than he'd intended, at the jolt of sexual chemistry. There it was, still. Every time they touched, it startled him all over again, making his breath catch and his heart beat faster. And it wasn't just him; he'd heard her sudden inhale and felt her tightened grip. What would it be like if they ever actually kissed, let alone made love?

"Come on." Her voice came out breathless, and he saw her throat move as she swallowed. "Let's get tickets."

Ransom paid for them both, quickly so it would be done before she could object.

"Hey!" Natalie protested. "You're bodyguarding me. *I* should be paying *you*."

"You can buy me a tomato."

The clerk stamped their hands with a plump red tomato ink stamp. "Enjoy Tomato Land!"

"Let's save the tomato knife for last," Ransom suggested. "It won't be much fun walking around in wet clothes."

"Good idea. It can be the grand finale."

They stepped into Tomato Land. It was hot and crowded and noisy and dusty, full of tomato-themed carnival games, souvenir booths, and kid-sized inflatable green tomato worms that tipped over and then bounced back up when punched. Kids were everywhere, punching the worms and wearing tomato beanies and sucking tomato-shaped lollipops and running around yelling. As Ransom had predicted, the attendees were mostly families with children aged eleven or younger, plus some bored teenagers who'd clearly been dragged along and some teenagers pretending to be bored while secretly enjoying themselves.

There were also a few teenage couples who'd come by themselves, a scattering of old people, and plenty of leashed dogs. Ransom could only cross his fingers that Wally and Heidi wouldn't get excited enough to teleport, but they seemed content to sniff around.

In his entire adult life, Ransom had never set foot anywhere that was less the sort of place he'd ever expected to be. He hadn't particularly enjoyed his childhood, and had never wanted to recreate it. But like the idea of riding the tomato knife, it felt different when he had Natalie at his side. She spun around, her rainbow hair flying around her face, as she tried to take in all the sights at once. Her cheeks were flushed pink, her eyes were sparkling, and her happiness was contagious.

"I don't know where to start," she said. "The climbing wall is cute, with the tomato vine holds, but way too easy. Should we get our picture taken with The World's Largest Tomato? Check out the craft booths?"

"I could throw tomatoes to win you a prize," Ransom suggested.

She glanced at the stall, then gave a scornful sniff. "Way, *way* too easy. They didn't even bother to rig it."

"How about—"

A hideous monster stepped out from behind a booth. It was a giant scarlet head with bulging eyes and huge green lips puckered up in a kiss, topped with a fuzzy mass of what looked like mold. It had no body, only a pair of human legs in a mini-skirt and high heels, both the exact same green as the mold ball.

Ransom recoiled. Natalie let out a strangled shriek. Heidi and Wally erupted into ferocious barking and lunged at the eldritch horror. Wally smacked into the head and bounced off, but Heidi managed to nip it. There was a pop like a bursting balloon, and the scarlet head deflated.

Natalie grabbed Wally and Ransom grabbed Heidi as the creature pulled off the mold blob, revealing the head of a young woman.

"I'm so sorry," gasped Natalie.

"I'll reimburse you for the costume," said Ransom.

"No need," said the young woman cheerfully. "We'll slap another patch on and reinflate it. For some reason, dogs don't seem to take to the Tomato Land mascot costume. It must be the smell of rubber."

She poked at the green kissy lips, which were now drooping over her waist. They wobbled in an unpleasantly realistic manner, as if they were going to lunge in for a kiss. Wally tried to flee through Ransom's chest, scrabbling frantically, while Heidi made an equally determined effort to attack.

"Right," said Natalie. "The smell of rubber. That must be it. Sorry again!"

She and Ransom hurried away, then ducked behind a stall. There they put down the puppies and burst out laughing. He couldn't remember the last time he'd laughed like that. Every time he started winding down, he'd remember Wally's desperate attempt to escape the lips and start up again.

"The thing over her head!" Natalie gasped. "Were those supposed to be leaves? It looked like fungus!"

"The high heels were what got me. The perfect shade of mildew!"

Natalie wiped her eyes. "Well, I call that an excellent start to the day. What next?"

"How about there?" Ransom pointed at a tomato-shaped tent.

She read its sign aloud. "'The History of the Tomato?' Really? Won't that be boring?"

For the first time in his life, Ransom was grateful to his parents and his schools for dragging him to produce festivals. Without that prior knowledge, Natalie would have been deprived forever of The History of the Tomato.

"Let's try it. I have a feeling you'll enjoy it."

"You're just hoping to nerd it over me if they explain that it's a fruit," she said, but followed him inside.

The interior of the tent contained several attendants in tomato-shaped beanies guiding a line to an ominous-looking staircase leading underground.

"What is that, a converted storm cellar?" Natalie asked.

"I think it's actually a converted bomb shelter," Ransom said.

"In case of flying tomatoes," she said with a snicker.

An attendant said, "He's right. It was built during the Cold War. The History of the Tomato will tell you all about the impact of the tomato on that terrifying time."

"Impact of the tomato," Ransom whispered when the attendant turned away. "Interesting choice of phrase."

"Does it need an entire exhibit to say 'splat?'" Natalie whispered.

Downstairs, the bomb shelter was cool and cavernous, made of reinforced concrete and steel. Ransom had been wondering why the History of the Tomato required the bomb shelter rather than the tent above, but he understood once his eyes adjusted to the dimness. He'd expected dioramas or a short film. He had not expected a circular track with tomato-shaped carriages, or that when he and Natalie took their seats on the soft red cushions, they'd be squeezed quite so close together.

"*Now* I get it," she said. "This is the Tunnel of Love. I mean the Tomato of Love."

Ransom could actually feel her heart beating. Every time she took a breath, he felt that too. When he tried to whistle to the pups, he ran out of air halfway through. They jumped up anyway and sat panting on his feet.

The lights went down and a tinny recorded voice announced, "Welcome to the History of the Tomato, Earth's mightiest crop!"

"Mightiest?" whispered Natalie.

"Note how they're dodging whether it's a fruit or a vegetable," said Ransom.

The carriage lurched forward. A spotlight came up on a diorama of Eve in the Garden of Eden, eyeing a tomato vine. An animatronic serpent poked its head out and hissed as Eve's arm jerked mechanically toward the tomato.

The recorded voice announced, "The tomato was once known as the Love Apple. Some believe that it was not an apple, but a tomato, which was the forbidden Fruit of Knowledge."

"Who believes that?" whispered Natalie as their carriage rolled forward.

"I don't know, but they're right that it's a fruit."

"They are not. You don't put fruit on a pizza."

"Ham and pineapple," whispered Ransom.

"That doesn't count. It's not a real pizza."

"Pizza isn't defined by its toppings."

They fell silent when lights rose on a diorama of cavemen staring down at a tomato. As a tinny recorded voice said, "UGG!" the main caveman brought down his club, stopping just short of a real tomato resting on a rock.

"Some believe that the tomato was the first plant cultivated by man," announced the voice.

"Who's that some?" whispered Natalie.

"Blaming it all on 'some' allows for a whole lot, doesn't it?" whispered Ransom.

She began to shake with silent laughter at the next exhibit, in which Christopher Columbus waved a map reading HERE LIE TOMATOES, and was in near hysterics by the one which depicted Paul Revere brandishing a tomato and suggested that *some* believed a tomato tax was a key cause of the American Revolution. Ransom managed to hold out until they got to the diorama in which Betsy Ross dyed an American flag with a tomato, and then he too began to laugh.

Once he started, he couldn't stop. Neither could Natalie. They clutched at each other, laughing hysterically, as the puppies set up a chorus of yips and other riders shushed them and the tinny voice proclaimed that *some* believe that non-polluting fuel may be extracted from that humble yet magnificent plant, the titanic—

"Sir? Ma'am? I'm going to have to ask you to leave." A stern attendant was frowning over them, shining a flashlight that illuminated his tomato beanie.

They scrambled out of the carriage, taking the puppies with them. Still laughing, they staggered up the stairs and out of the tomato dome, and sank down on a bench painted with a cheerful pizza motif.

Ransom's sides ached. He had actual tear tracks on his face. His voice cracked as he said, "The Apollo astronauts survived on freeze-dried tomatoes!"

"A Russian fad for ketchup ended the Cold War," gasped Natalie.

"The titanic tomato!"

"The tremendous tomato!"

"The tantalizing tomato!" He gulped for air, then wiped tears from his eyes.

Natalie gave a happy sigh as she wiped her own eyes. "That was amazing. Thank you so much for making sure I didn't miss it. Are they always like that?"

"More or less. I remember one that claimed that without artichokes, there would be no America. But this was the best I've ever seen."

She nodded. "I feel like anything after this will be an anticlimax."

Ransom spotted people lining up at a sign reading TOMATO THROWING PERFORMANCE. 1 DAY ONLY. 10 THROWERS. 10,000 TOMATOES.

"I don't," he said.

The next thing he knew, he was once again wedged in close with Natalie. But this time, he was also wedged in with a huge crowd, all facing a completely white enclosure with three high walls and a floor, but no ceiling. There was stadium seating, but it had been completely filled by the time they arrived, so they hunkered down on the grass, holding the puppies in their arms.

Crouched down, Natalie seemed barely bigger than the two children on her other side.

The little girl turned adoring eyes to her. "I like your hair."

"Thank you," said Natalie. "I like your shoes."

The girl glanced down at her shoes, tapped one on the ground to make it flash, then indicated the little boy. "I'm six. He's four. How old... wait... are you a grown-up?"

"Yes," Natalie said regretfully.

The girl looked disappointed. "Oh."

"She's young at heart," Ransom put in.

The little girl gave him a look of utter scorn, then turned away, bored.

"I guess I deserved that," said Ransom.

The ten tomato throwers stepped onstage, along with four assistants with buckets of tomatoes. The assistants were in street clothes, the throwers in pure white and safety goggles. The throwers and assistants murmured to each other and walked around, trying to get the assistants, their buckets, and the throwers positioned in exactly the right places. Backstage, more crew members moved more tomato baskets into place.

"I've never seen an audience this riveted by twelve people wandering around a stage," Natalie murmured.

"The great acting teacher, Stanislavsky, created Method Acting when he saw how fascinated audiences were by real things happening onstage, even ordinary things like someone frying an egg," said Ransom. "The stage focuses attention on human behavior and makes the ordinary seem extraordinary."

"It helps if you're waiting for tomatoes to start flying."

A thrower made a sudden and unexpected lunge for a basket, seized a large tomato, and hurled it across the stage, splattering the man across from her. With that, chaos broke loose.

Tomatoes flew back and forth, squashing against the white walls and floor and clothes. Within minutes, everything was dyed red: walls, floor, skin, hair, clothes. Safety goggles were knocked off by high-velocity tomatoes. Teams formed among the throwers, then turned on each other and broke up.

An errant tomato flew into the audience, straight for Natalie. Ransom lunged forward, caught it neatly, and threw it back, scoring a direct hit on the thrower.

"Bravo!" shouted Natalie.

Encouraged by this, some throwers began deliberately throwing tomatoes into the audience. Most of them were caught and thrown back—the onstage throwers were careful to throw gently, as there were children in the audience—but a few splatted into audience members. Another hurtled toward Ransom, but before he could catch it, Heidi vanished from his lap, appeared in mid-air, and batted it aside with her nose.

The little girl tugged at her mother's hand. "Mommy! The rainbow hair grown-up's boyfriend's puppy can fly!"

Between Heidi teleporting in public and being seen doing it, and getting called Natalie's boyfriend, Ransom was struck absolutely dumb.

The girl's mother chuckled. "Huskies can jump very high. I had one when I was your age."

"I saw her," the girl said obstinately. "She flew *up*."

Natalie gave them both a bright smile. "She's a *magic* puppy. Don't tell, it's a secret."

Satisfied, the girl said, "I knew it."

Her mother winked at Natalie, who winked back. Ransom's heart rate slowly returned to normal.

Onstage, the tomato throwing was still going strong. The floor was covered in an ever-deepening layer of crushed tomatoes, making the throwers slip, slide, and sometimes fall in a spray of salsa. One thrower slid on his knees to catch a tomato as if he was sliding into home.

The scent made Ransom feel as if he was inside a vat of spaghetti sauce. Natalie's hair glowed all shades of crimson and burgundy and orange and red-gold in the tomato-tinged light.

The backstage crew rushed back and forth, pouring new tomatoes into baskets. One of them was hit right in the face—whether accidentally or on purpose, Ransom couldn't tell. The backstage crew began vengefully tossing tomatoes at the throwers. The throwers onstage began randomly chucking tomatoes back over the wall. So many tomatoes accumulated on the floor that some throwers lay down on it and began doing the backstroke. The throwers onstage turned on the assistants and attacked them with tomatoes.

At last, visibly exhausted, the throwers collapsed to the floor, still flinging tomatoes from kneeling positions.

Ransom had never experienced such utter, inspired, delightful madness in his life. It was absurd and hilarious, and it made him feel good about a world in which someone got the idea to throw 10,000 tomatoes, and then actually made it happen.

The throwers staggered to their feet, dripping, and took a bow. The audience cheered and clapped.

Natalie's clear, mischievous voice rose up above the applause, shouting "Encore! Encore!"

The throwers began scooping up tomato pulp from the floor and hurling it in all directions. The audience fled for their lives.

Ransom and Natalie fetched up near a waterpark where gleeful kids in swimming suits rocketed down a slide shaped like a curling vine and splashed into a pool of red-dyed water.

"Boring," said Natalie. "Ordinary. A huge disappointment."

Ransom laughed. He couldn't remember when he'd last felt so free and easy. His hellhound hadn't said a word since he'd set foot in Tomato Land, and his information powers had left him alone as well. It was probably only an exceptionally pleasant turn of chance, but if it turned out that all his powers were deactivated by tomatoes, he'd fill up his apartment with vines.

CHAPTER 12

Natalie's expectations of Tomato Land had been high, despite Ransom's warning, but it had far surpassed them. And so had Ransom himself. She'd hoped to see him happy, but she'd never dreamed that she'd see him literally laugh until he cried. He looked so different now than when she'd first seen him. His eyes were bright, there was color in his cheeks, and the sun lit his hair until the individual strands glittered like sparks.

She took his hand, relishing the delicious shock of contact and its promise that maybe later there'd be more than just hand-holding. "I'm starving. Let's eat."

They stepped through an archway that had real tomato vines twining over it, with green and red cherry tomatoes dangling amidst the lush foliage. It led to a set of food booths which were familiar in one sense—her circus also had food stalls—but these were entirely tomato-themed. Stalls sold tomato soup, tomato salad, tomato pie, eggs poached in tomato sauce, and fried green tomatoes. The pizza stall advertised ABSOLUTELY NO WHITE PIZZA. DON'T LIKE TOMATO SAUCE? WHAT ARE YOU EVEN DOING HERE?

"Remember my offer to buy you a tomato? By that, I meant 'buy you lunch,'" said Natalie. "Because that is clearly the same thing around here."

"I'll bite. So to speak. I want what he's having." Ransom indicated a man with an open-faced sandwich topped with a thick slice of the biggest tomato she had ever seen. "Other than that, surprise me."

That was all the permission she needed. She left the puppies with him and darted from stall to stall, buying everything that looked good, seemed especially American and therefore exotically tempting, and anything she thought Ransom might appreciate. She wanted to see that look on his face, the wide-eyed surprise at how good something was and that he was enjoying it. Though she'd seen it a lot that day, she never got tired of it.

But there was another look she hadn't seen yet, which she wanted to see even more. She hoped that if she got him enough good things, maybe someday he'd stop being surprised.

She returned to him carefully balancing a tray shaped and painted to look like a tomato.

Ransom was sitting at a wooden table (round and painted to look like a tomato), in a chair (same), under a canopy (same) where families sat around eating entirely red meals. He'd apparently stopped at a stall himself while she was getting lunch, because beneath the table, the puppies gnawed on rawhide discs. They were not dyed red, but she felt certain that the shape was meant to represent a tomato.

"They missed a trick," Ransom said, examining the paper plates. "The plates aren't red."

"Not at all. The plates are white to make the tomatoes show up better."

She'd gotten herself the same sandwich he had, a giant slice of salted and peppered tomato over mozzarella. And also fried green tomatoes, tomato pie, and a pair of bloody Marys adorned with a forest of celery, a slice of candied bacon, and a skewer of ripe, roasted, and pickled cherry tomatoes.

Natalie lifted her glass. "To that rightfully celebrated vegetable, the tomato."

"To the mighty tomato, that rightfully celebrated fruit."

"To the know-it-all sitting across the tomato from me." She tried to glare, but couldn't help grinning. "A man with unusual taste in books—unusually good taste—who drives like a dream and BASE jumps without a blink."

"Oh, you like my driving?" And there was that look she'd been waiting for: surprised by happiness. For some reason, it made her eyes sting as if she was about to cry. As she blinked hard, he raised his own glass. "To the woman with rainbow hair and every-color eyes, who finds the joy in everything and fears nothing."

They touched glasses and drank. The bloody Mary was ice cold and spiked with tabasco, refreshing and eye-opening. They shared the fried green tomatoes, with a crisp cornmeal coating over their juicy interiors, and the homey tomato pie. The sandwich was both light and hearty, like a steak salad, leaving her contented without feeling weighed down.

"That's the first time in my life that I've had a three-course meal made almost entirely out of fruit," remarked Ransom. "Four-course, if you count the bloody Mary."

"You should, it's basically a deli case in a plastic glass. But actually, there's five courses." With a flourish, she set a small styrofoam cooler on the tomato table. "And I'm not even going to fight you over the 'fruit' thing, because the last one is a dessert and eating a dessert made out of vegetables is just plain wrong."

"I won't argue with that. Roland brought homemade zucchini cake to the office once. We fed it to Blue when his back was turned, so we wouldn't hurt his feelings. What is it, tomato sorbet?"

"Nope." Natalie opened the cooler and lifted out their dessert. It had been so expensive that she'd only bought one to share, especially since there was every chance that it would be inedible.

They stared at the dessert in awe. It was a tomato, complete with stem and leaf. A very beautiful, peeled, juicy-looking, glistening tomato, sitting in a pool of wine-red caramel. Beside it was a scoop of cream-colored ice cream, exactly the size of the tomato, surrounded by crushed pistachios.

"What is it?" Ransom asked. "I mean, obviously a tomato—even if I couldn't see that, I'd know from context—but…"

"It's a caramelized tomato stuffed with twelve flavors, and star anise ice cream. Apparently it's a dish from a restaurant that's famous in Australia, which says something about how hard they had to look to find a tomato dessert."

"What are the twelve flavors?"

"No idea. Let's find out."

They each took a spoon and dug in. Natalie had expected it to be weird, and it was, a little. But weird in a good way. Weird like Tomato Land was weird. Weird like her hair and his books.

"Lemon," said Ransom. "Pistachio."

"Vanilla," added Natalie. "Almond."

They considered the tomato, and both took another bite.

"Apple, definitely," said Ransom. "And I think… orange?"

"And blueberries." She ran her tongue over her teeth. "Pepper! Just a tiny bit of it."

"Cloves," said Ransom after a moment. "And cinnamon. That's what's giving it that almost apple-pie feeling."

"That's ten. Does the tomato itself count as a flavor?"

"I'm not sure. Does caramel?"

There was very little of the tomato left now, barely enough to share. Ransom drew a neat line with his spoon, dividing the final bite. "Last chance."

Their spoons touched as they scooped up their shares.

"Mint!" Natalie exclaimed triumphantly.

"And pineapple," said Ransom.

They'd been leaning across the table to share the dessert, but now that it was gone, they didn't sit back. The air felt electric, as if there was a current running between them. Neither of them moved, but she knew he was going to kiss her.

I wonder if that's what it feels like when he knows *things,* she thought. *No, can't be. It hurts him. This feels wonderful. Like the moment you jump off the platform holding the trampoline, in the split second before gravity takes hold. Free fall.*

He kissed her. Or maybe she kissed him. Probably they'd moved simultaneously, like hands reaching out to catch in mid-air. The jolt when their hands touched was nothing to what it felt like when their lips touched. She'd never felt anything like it before. That one kiss set a fire that curled through her entire body and made all thought go up in smoke. It was the most glorious and thrilling moment of her life.

Her heart skipped a beat.

Not in the romantic way. In the awful, terrifying way that had sent her to the doctor in the first place, for the series of tests that would change her life. There was a steady rhythm to a heartbeat, an unvarying pulse of all-is-well, all-is-well. You don't notice it until it breaks up into a series of stutters that spell out nothing you want to know.

He jerked his head back. "Natalie? What's wrong?"

"Nothing."

But that jagged no-rhythm was still going. She thought wildly of running to the bathroom to breathe inside a stall, then returning to claim indigestion or the start of her period—some bodily TMI that would stop him from inquiring more.

Stress yourself more, while this is going on, and you'll never even make it there, she thought. *Or you'll drop dead when you close the door behind you.*

With a cold, detached resolve, knowing she'd never again find that passion and joy she'd felt in the first instant of their kiss, she pushed back her chair and sat down on the ground.

"Natalie!"

She'd have explained, but she couldn't speak and breathe at the same time. She lay down on her side right there on the dusty ground, breathing deeply and rhythmically. One-two-three-four inhale, hold one-two, one-two-three-four exhale, hold one-two. One-two-three-four inhale…

Distantly, she was aware of strong hands lifting her, slowly and gently so as not to break her rhythm. Her head was in Ransom's lap, and he was holding her, breathing with her, his hand curled around hers.

Very quietly, he said, "Do you want an ambulance? Squeeze my hand once for yes and twice for no."

She squeezed twice, grateful to him for giving her a way to make her wishes known that wouldn't affect what she needed to do, and more grateful that he cared what her wishes were.

"She doesn't need a doctor," he said, calmly but with an underlying edge of tension, his voice pitched to carry to onlookers. "I know this looks scary, but it's not dangerous. It's an inherited condition, like epilepsy. Please don't crowd around, you'll embarrass her…"

Natalie wasn't tracking time, but it felt like it took longer than usual before her heartbeat returned to normal. When her vision cleared, she saw Wally lying beside her and licking her face, Heidi curled up beside her and nuzzling her throat, and Ransom looking down at her with a tenderness in his dark eyes that she could only perceive as love.

His arms tightened around her. "Can I carry you now?"

For an instant, she let herself relax into his warmth and strength and caring. There was nothing she wanted more than to let him lift her up and carry her home, safe and protected and loved.

Home. Where had that word come from? She'd never had a home, not a real one. Home was a place where you always belonged and never had to leave. The circus had been the closest she'd ever come to that, but she'd had to leave that too.

As for safety, that word applied to her even less. She trusted Ransom to protect her from the wizard-scientists, if they ever tried to come for her again, but he couldn't protect her from her own failing body. Nobody could. She'd come this far and crammed in this much living into her short life by having no illusions. She wasn't going to start conning herself now.

"No," Natalie said. "I want to walk."

"Are you sure?"

"Yes."

She sat up, slowly so the blood didn't rush to her head, and then stood. He supported her as she did, lending her the strength she needed. She stood blinking in the sunlight, then put on a bright smile for him and the rather large crowd that was lurking and fiddling with stray tomato-shaped things and pretending not to watch.

"Sorry," she said, pitching her voice to carry. "I forgot to take my meds this morning. Let's go back to the hotel and get them."

"Good idea." Ransom offered her his arm, but she gave him a quick head-shake. The dizziness had faded, her heart beat steadily within her chest, and she was afraid that if she laid hands on him now, she might not have the strength to let him go.

They headed out of the food court, the puppies trotting at their heels with none of their usual exuberance. She paused when they reached a dunking booth where you could throw a tomato to hit a target and drop a local celebrity volunteer into a vat of tomato sauce.

"I really do feel fine now," she said. "We don't need to go."

Ransom gave her a long, considering look. "Would it still be fun?"

As usual, he'd cut right to the heart of things. She had never felt in a less fun mood in her entire life. "Probably not. But it's so depressing if I have to leave and never come back because of *this*."

"You can come back. We were going to swing back this way anyway, remember? To go paragliding. We can take an extra day for Tomato Land 2: The Reckoning."

She was startled into a laugh. "You're right. Let's do that."

But as they continued to walk, not even the thought of Return to Tomato Land could console her. How perfect everything was otherwise made her feel even worse. She was in a ridiculous, hilarious, marvelous, extremely American, and absolutely bucket-worthy place, with a pair of teleporting puppies and a man who was not only extremely sexy, but also brilliant, funny, brave, and kind. The one kiss they'd shared had been the sweetest and most joyous moment of her entire life, something she'd trade her entire bucket list to experience again.

And it had almost killed her.

CHAPTER 13

You'll never come back, growled his hellhound.

No. Ransom caught himself shaking his head, as if they were speaking aloud. *No. I'm going to save her. If I have to sacrifice my own life to do it, I will.*

That's too easy, his hellhound snarled. *That won't be how it works. Whatever your chance is, you'll ruin it, like you ruin everything you touch.*

With Natalie walking silent and sad at his side, Ransom wanted to comfort her. But he didn't know what to say. And without the distraction of conversation, his hellhound began shoving people's worst moments at him.

A young father walked by, bouncing his squealing toddler daughter atop his shoulders. Ransom saw him dressed in black at a funeral, a baby cradled in his arms. His grief was overwhelming, unbearable…

Ransom looked away, desperately searching for something else. Something happy. The glitter of a gold wedding ring caught his eye, and he saw a woman reaching upward to cup her wife's head for a kiss. They were middle-aged, unglamorous, and looked very much in love.

And then his hellhound pounced, and he saw the one whose ring glittered in the sun barehanded and in dirty clothes, crouched on a sidewalk and shaking a cup with nothing in it but a few quarters. Hunger gnawed at her belly, and despair gnawed at her heart. Ransom tried to tear himself away, but his vision shifted to her wife as a teenager, opening the door and finding a grim-faced man in a military uniform. Before he even opened his mouth, she knew her father was dead...

"Ransom?" Natalie was looking at him quizzically. "Are you all right?"

Her question hit him like a punch to the gut. She was the one whose life was in danger, she was the one whose heart had nearly stopped, and *she* was worried about *him*.

She's too good for you, snarled his hellhound. *You don't deserve her.*

He couldn't argue with that. And he didn't want to make her worry about him when she had so much to deal with herself.

The sandpaper rasp of his hellhound's growl filled his mind. *You mean, you're afraid she'll be horrified if you told her what you really are. And you'd be right.*

"Seriously," she said. "Are you getting a migraine?"

"No."

"Then what? I know something's up. You can't con a con artist."

She was so small, so delicate-looking, but there was a startling strength in her. Like a steel wire stretched from pole to pole, thin but able to support the weight of a tightrope walker. He could hear in her tone that she wasn't going to leave it alone.

Don't tell her. His hellhound sounded almost... afraid. *She'll hate you. She'll leave you. Imagine the look in her eyes of horror and disgust...*

Ransom looked into her eyes. They were a clear pure blue, like the sky above. He wanted to take her into his arms and hold her close, so much so that not doing it physically hurt. He'd never in his life longed for anything so much as he longed to kiss her, both to comfort her and to once again experience that joy and passion and intimacy that had set him aflame, body and heart and mind.

But that was something they could never do again.

How could you have been so selfish and thoughtless? growled his hellhound. *You knew her doctor warned her against strong emotions and excitement. You almost killed her!*

I know, Ransom replied. His guilt was a physical pain, twisting in his gut. *And I won't follow it up by lying to her.*

Before he could second-guess himself or his hellhound could browbeat him into silence, he said, "I have two powers. Most of us who were experimented on by the wizard-scientists do. One belongs to our human self, and one to our beast. The knowing, the visions—that's my human power. I told you I can't control it very well. It turns on of its accord. My hellhound's is… a different sort of information, and I have the same problem with it."

"And it hurts too?" she asked. He nodded, but before he could say more, she burst out, "I hate those wizard-scientists for doing this to you! I hope they do attack us again, then I'll get a chance to kick them a few times on your behalf!"

It was the last thing he'd expected her to say. Her anger on his behalf touched him so deeply, he felt on the verge of tears. But he pushed past them, determined to be honest. "The physical pain isn't the bad part—well, it's the less bad part. My hellhound's power is to see the worst moment of a person's life. And not only see it, but experience it as if it was happening to me. Their grief or loneliness or guilt or pain…"

Her eyes were wide, her mouth open. She was horrified. Of course.

Forcing the words out past the cold and rising tide of misery within him, he said, "If you don't want to get in a car with me, I can call a cab. Or I could have one of my teammates pick you up—it wouldn't have to be Merlin, and he wouldn't have to know about it. I could talk to Tirzah, she's good at secrets—"

Natalie threw her arms around him. It was so unexpected that he froze, unsure what was going on, until she squeezed him tight and he realized that she was hugging him. He'd told her something terrible, something that ought to horrify her, and *that* was her response?

"Oh, Ransom." Her voice was muffled; her face was pressed into his shoulder. "That must be so awful for you. To see all that pain—to *feel* all that pain—and not even be able to help, because it's already over."

Cautiously, barely able to believe his ears, he put his arms around her. They stood locked in an embrace, giving each other the strength that neither of them had alone. He bent his head, touching his forehead to hers; that was as close to a kiss as he dared. Her hair was feathery to the touch, and her lemony scent had a faint overtone of tomato.

"Aren't you afraid?" he asked.

"Afraid of what?" She sounded genuinely puzzled, not putting on a show of bravado. "Oh! You mean that you'd see my worst moment? *Have* you seen it?"

"No." It was strange, now that he thought of it. He'd dreaded having her worst moment forced on him, and he'd thought that would make his hellhound jump at the chance to do it. But even now that he was thinking of it, nothing happened. His beast was nothing more than a lurking presence in the back of his mind. "At least, not unless that doctor's visit was it."

"Who knows. I've had lots of bad moments. None of them are secrets, really. If you happen to see one of them, well…" She shrugged. He could feel the entire movement as it rubbed her body against his.

He closed his eyes briefly, struggling to control his desire. A single kiss had almost stopped her heart. They could never do that again; never do more than hold each other, like they were doing now. It felt like he was tearing his own body apart, but he forced himself to step away.

"I have to," he said. "I'm sorry."

There was both hurt and understanding in her gaze, now a smoky gray in the darkening light. "Yeah. I know."

When they got in the car, he kept the top rolled up. It was getting cold. At the motel, he said, "I know you wanted separate rooms, but…"

"But that was before the best kiss I ever had," she said.

"It was my best, too."

They both sighed, in such perfect unison that Natalie gave a rueful chuckle.

"What a screwed-up world," he said.

"Could be worse." She ruffled his hair. The touch of her fingers made him gulp for air. "I'm so glad we met, and that could've never happened. Or we could not be able to touch at all. Imagine if I was Rogue from the X-Men, and I couldn't touch you without stealing your power and knocking you unconscious."

"True. And I love that you thought of Rogue."

"I love that *you* know who she is. She's the best."

"So," he said. "One room, two beds?"

"If you can stand it, I can stand it."

He thought of the shimmering vial buried deep within his duffel bag, and set a mental reminder to himself to never completely unpack. "I can stand it. And I'm glad you're with me, too."

Inside the motel lobby, a bored clerk glanced at the pups and pointed to a sign saying that a maximum of two dogs or cats could stay in a room so long as they didn't weigh 150 pounds combined.

"I think we're good," she said.

On their way out, Ransom said, "Imagine two cats weighing 150 pounds combined."

"I don't have to imagine it. I grew up with tigers."

The motel room was distinctly no-frills, much like the one she had stayed at in Refuge City, with a pair of narrow beds close together in the small room. By what seemed to be mutual accord, neither of them brought up any of the serious topics they could have talked about. Instead, they unpacked the puppy beds and toys and food and set them out, and sat on their own beds and watched Heidi and Wally chase each other around, blinking in and out to evade or attack. It was impossible to watch and not have your heart lifted.

"Too bad we can't put this on YouTube," Natalie remarked. "Biggest viral hit ever."

When the pups wore themselves out and flopped into a fluffy heap on the floor, she took out the books she'd borrowed, touching their covers with anticipatory delight. Glancing up, she said, "Hey… Want to trade?"

Puzzled, he said, "I brought an e-reader."

"Want a new one?" Natalie took hers from her purse and offered it to him. "You let me see your library—want to see mine?"

"Of course!" He took her Kindle and turned it on. It was a device identical to millions and millions of others, but the books downloaded to it made it unique. They would show him what she was interested in and what she enjoyed, much as his bookcase had told her something about him. It was a very intimate possession to loan out—a gesture of trust, even.

He was soon engrossed in her library. It was hard to tell if she had everything Stephen King had ever written, because her books weren't sorted in any way, but it sure looked like it. Not to mention a whole lot of other books whose covers featured vampires, living skeletons, and giant ants. There was even one with a fanged skeleton riding a giant ant.

In addition to horror and stage magic, she also seemed fond of old children's books—boarding school stories, dog stories, and horse stories—and romance. The lack of organization made for some hilarious juxtapositions on the screen, with a tentacled horror on the left seeming to reach toward the kissing couple on the right.

"Found anything interesting?" Natalie asked. Teasingly, she said, "Stretch yourself—read about a lonely widow and the hunky drifter who saves her ranch and warms her bed!"

If he had to read about other people having sex, he'd lose his mind. "Do you have anything on here that was a favorite book of yours when you were a girl?"

"Lots." She stretched her lithe body across the space between their beds and rapidly flipped through her Kindle. She stopped on a cover with a pair of pink ballet shoes. "Here you go."

She returned to her bed. A quick glance showed that she had selected *Modesty Blaise* for her own night's reading. Ransom settled back with *Ballet Shoes*. He never reneged on an offer, and he wanted to get a window into what Natalie had loved as a girl. Though he wasn't sure exactly what he'd learn. It seemed obvious that she would have been interested in a book about girls performing onstage.

When he looked up, he found that night had fallen. Natalie was still engrossed in *Modesty Blaise*, holding it close to her face and squinting in the dimming light. She glanced up when he clicked on the bedside lights.

"What's Modesty up to?" Ransom asked.

"She just rescued Willie from Gabriel's gang. I love her. She's badass." Mischief twinkled in her eyes as she said, "What do you think of *Ballet Shoes*? Or are you giving up?"

"Of course not. I finished it. It's short. And I liked it. It was a lot less… fluffy pink tutus… than I expected. The personalities of the sisters were so vivid. Your favorite sister is Posy, right?"

"Of course," said Natalie. "But not because she's the one who performs in a leotard."

"No. Posy's incredibly determined. She knows what she wants, and she goes after it, no matter what anyone else thinks. That's very you."

"Your favorite is Petrova, right? Smart, interested in science, cares more about her work than getting applauded, fits in even less than Posy."

"You got it," Ransom admitted. "I identify."

"What did you read when you were a boy?"

"Nonfiction, mostly. Some science fiction. When I was a little kid, I was really into dog stories."

"Did you ever have a dog?"

"No. My mother was allergic." Ransom leaned over to scratch Heidi's ears. She gazed up at him with the utter adoration that the dogs in the stories always had, and which he'd eventually decided was a fictional device to make kids buy books. But no. Heidi loved him, absolutely and unconditionally. He could feel it. "I'd forgotten about the dog books. I didn't keep reading them after I was ten or so. Now I remember why I loved them."

"I never forgot the things I loved as a kid," said Natalie. "You should download some of those dog books. Read them again with Heidi at your feet."

"Only the ones where the dog doesn't die."

"I hated the books where the dog dies!"

"And the ones where the kid has to give away the dog at the end. They were so depressing."

They lay in their separate beds, side by side, talking about the books they loved and the books they hated and the books they'd never been able to find again because all they remembered was something like, "The cover was green and the villain falls into a well at the end."

The hours flew by until they caught themselves yawning at the same time. One by one, they shut themselves in the bathroom and got into pajamas, and then returned to bed.

"Good night, Natalie."

"Good night, Ransom."

They turned off the lights. But though he was tired, he lay wide awake, listening to her soft breathing. He could imagine the length of her slim body so vividly that it was almost as if they lay in the same bed; whenever he moved, he was jarred by touching empty space.

His mind wouldn't turn off, wouldn't even slow. He worried about Natalie, longed for Natalie, and wondered how she really felt about him. He tried not to, but he couldn't help torturing himself by imagining what she'd do if she found out his last, worst secret.

In the brief breaks between thinking about her, he thought about his team and how he'd never see them again. He kept uselessly replaying his confrontation with Roland and rewriting it so that it came out differently, only to know that it had already happened and could never be changed.

His power began to creep in, pushing useless information on him. *A type of Vietnamese folk painting on paper made from bark of the rhamnoneuron balansae tree uses powdered egg shells and charred bamboo leaves for white and black paint. The motel clerk was, right now, watching a rerun of Top Chef, season nine, episode six, eleven minutes and thirty-two seconds in... thirty-three seconds... thirty-four seconds...*

"Ransom?" Natalie's voice was the barest whisper, but it cut through the churning storm inside his mind.

"I'm awake," he whispered back; he didn't need to worry about waking her up, but it felt wrong to break the hush in the room. "Are you all right?"

"Yeah. But I can't sleep."

"Me neither." He wanted to reach out to her, but was immediately swamped by a million reasons why he shouldn't do it, along with details of a road being built in Canada and the scientific names of several types of butterflies and—

Ransom stretched out his hand across the space between their beds. It was barely visible in the darkness, a shadow amongst shadows. But he saw movement, and then warm slim fingers wrapped around his.

At first he was only aware of how much he cared about her, how much he wanted her, how frustrating it was to only touch like this, and how wonderful it was to touch her at all. Then he realized that his power had turned off. His mind was quiet, and even the rush of his own thoughts had stilled.

"That's better," murmured Natalie. "Don't let go."

"Don't let go of me, either."

They didn't.

CHAPTER 14

The time that followed was the happiest and most heartbreaking, the most wonderful and most frustrating of Natalie's life.

She and Ransom found a deserted section of the beach, where she built a sand circus and he built an amazingly sturdy driftwood castle to which she added a moat stocked with sand crabs. Wally played chicken with the waves, standing with his paws braced in the sand and barking at them, then teleporting back to dry sand a second before they came crashing down. Heidi preferred to attack the waves, rushing them headlong and cunningly teleporting behind them, only to be annoyed anew every time she got a nose full of salt water.

Ransom taught her to drive, patiently coaching her as she drove the Mustang around empty parking lots. Sometimes she caught his knuckles going white when she stepped too hard on the gas and nearly achieved escape velocity, but he never said a word.

She achieved GO TO A MALL, dragging him to eat Cinnabons and watch her pop in and out of dressing rooms, modeling outfits. Neither of them could finish even a single Cinnabon—apparently her tolerance for sugar maxed out at half of one—and the clothes modeling turned out to be an exercise in sexual frustration.

Natalie began to resort to more and more frumpy, baggy, unflattering outfits in an effort to drag her mind away from the image of yanking him into the dressing room with her so she could unbuckle his pants while he took off her blouse and—at that point she had to press her hot forehead against the cool wall and think very firmly of the least sexy things she could imagine, like cold mashed potatoes and being chased by an angry swan.

When she finally emerged, back in her original clothes, she found Ransom gone. He eventually returned with his shirt damp and his hair wet, explaining unconvincingly that a water fountain had splashed him. Natalie was pretty sure that, lacking a cold shower, he'd done the best he could manage with a bathroom sink.

She crossed off EAT AT A DINER multiple times, since she enjoyed the first one so much. Hamburgers and Coke and French fries and all types of pie, jukeboxes and friendly waitresses and bottomless cups of coffee—it was always a delight, especially with Ransom across from her, looking incrementally less surprised every time he tried a slice of pie and found it good.

The waitresses kept commenting on how sweet they were, the way they held hands across the table. Ransom always flinched when they said it, so subtly that they never noticed: a tiny flicker of the eyelids and a fractional tightening of his grip. It gave her a prickle at the back of her eyes, which she drove away by thinking of how not-sweet she'd like to be with him, which then forced her get up and do what she'd begun thinking of as the Ransom Maneuver: dunking her entire head in the bathroom sink with the cold water on full blast.

With all the extra hair-washing she was doing, her dye began to fade. She got out her rubber gloves and tubes of dye, brought a chair into the bathroom so she could sit over the sink and face the mirror, then called Ransom in to help her with the back.

"How often do you do this?" he asked.

"Every three months at a salon, and I touch it up myself every other week." She had to laugh at his surprise. "What, did you think it grew like this?"

"It's hard to remember that it's dye. It seems so natural on you. When did you start?"

"I tried out a couple colors when I joined the circus. Red, black, blonde. None of them suited me, any more than my real color does."

"What is the real color?"

"Dust." She shivered, thinking of dust swirling around her ankles. Sterile, powdery dust, in which nothing could grow…

In the mirror, she saw Ransom's dark eyes, the color of rich fertile earth, seeming to look straight into her soul.

"Did you see something, right now?" she asked. "I mean, with your power."

He shook his head. "I was wondering if you were remembering something."

Relieved, she said, "Right! When I started dyeing my hair. Janet gave me a trip to a fancy salon for my thirteenth birthday. The hairdresser had skin the color of ebony and hair the color of sunshine. It looked so gorgeous on her, I told her I wanted to color my hair, I didn't want it to look natural, and to do whatever she thought suited me. I said, 'Go wild. Seriously.' She looked at Janet, and Janet nodded. And the next thing I knew, I had beautiful rainbow hair. For the first time in my life, I looked the way I felt inside."

"You're making me want to dye my hair."

"You could. I've got everything you need right here."

He smiled, a little wistfully, and shook his head. "I don't think I could get that feeling from my hair, no matter what I did to it."

"Well, your hair's perfect for you already. It'd be a shame for you to change it. All those shades of red and brown…" She reached backward and tugged on a lock. It was silky but resilient, holding its wave. She traced it down to his scalp, and watched his eyes close and his open hands curl into fists.

"I don't…" His voice cracked. "I don't think I should help you with the dye. If me touching your hair feels anything like you touching mine…"

The memory of her heart fluttering like a trapped bird made her pull her hand away. "Right. You're right."

She turned back to the mirror, squeezing out dabs of brilliant dye and streaking them through her hair, highlighting some locks and leaving others alone to fade to pastel.

In the mirror, Ransom watched her, his gaze hungry. When she used a hand mirror to dye the back, he said, "You never needed me."

There was a bitter edge to his words that made her wonder if they had a double meaning. True, she didn't *need* him. She'd never *needed* anybody. She'd survive, for better or for worse, but she'd survive...

She corrected herself: she'd *believed* she'd survive.

"I *wanted* you to help. But no, I don't *need* you. I can do it myself, I always have. Don't watch, I want to surprise you." Her voice came out louder and sharper than she'd intended. It had to, to drown out her own thoughts.

He went out, and she closed the bathroom door. She had to wait for an hour for the dye to sink in, and she hadn't brought a book or her Kindle. She hadn't intended to spend that time sitting alone in the bathroom because she was afraid that she'd start to cry if she saw him and let herself think about everything she could never have. But here she was, stuck inside, without anything to distract her from the thoughts she didn't want to have.

"I'm going to slide something under the door," Ransom said from outside.

Bewildered, she watched as a flat black thing slid under the door. It was halfway in before she recognized her own Kindle case.

"Thanks," she called back. "Set a timer for an hour, will you?"

"Got it."

He'd not only thought to give her the Kindle, he'd warned her in advance so she wouldn't be dangerously startled by a black thing sliding under the door.

He'd jumped off a cliff for her.

He'd given himself the world's worst migraine for her.

He'd let her drag him to diners and malls and amusement parks, and he hadn't been embarrassed to have fun at them too.

He'd never made her feel inferior for her lack of formal education, even though she'd never even gone to high school and he had a degree in biochemistry and read textbooks for fun.

He'd never tried to stop her from making her own decisions.

He'd held her hand all night when she couldn't sleep.

When all they could do was hold hands, she'd learned every inch of his: every nail, every callus, every knuckle, every line on his palm. When all they could do was look, she'd memorized his autumn-colored hair and his broad shoulders and his sad eyes.

He loved Heidi and Wally, and they adored him.

He shared his books.

He'd not only read *Ballet Shoes*, not only enjoyed it, and not only admitted that he enjoyed it, he even had a favorite sister.

I love him.

The thought filled her first with joy, and then with terror, and finally with a frustrated anger at herself. How could she let herself fall in love now, when they couldn't even kiss without risking her life? What could love do for either of them now, other than breaking their hearts?

She could never tell him how she really felt.

Natalie had never learned to walk the tightrope, but she knew what it felt like now: balancing on a wire above an abyss, taking careful step after careful step, and smiling all the while.

CHAPTER 15

You said the wrong thing, growled his hellhound. *You always say the wrong thing. You've ruined everything.*

No, I haven't. Ransom threw images to his hellhound of Natalie reaching for his hand, Natalie enthusiastically recommending books, Natalie watching him eat when she thought he wasn't looking and smiling, always smiling. *She's just taking a time-out.*

Sure enough, once she was done waiting and showering and blow-drying, she threw open the bathroom door, ran to the window, and held her head in the sunlight. "What do you think?"

The sun made her newly-dyed hair glow like light itself. There were bold streaks of color against soft pastels, individual strands dyed to blend together like a pointillist painting, parts that made him think of sunsets and parts that made him think of oceans and parts that made him think of graffiti. But none of it clashed any more than a rainbow or a butterfly clashes. And while her hair drew his eye, so did the rest of her: her ever-changing eyes, her strong chin, her lithe body, her clever hands. Everything about her was all of a piece, unique and unusual and beautiful and perfect.

"You look like an Impressionist painting," he said. "Not just your hair. All of you."

"Thanks, that's the best compliment. Especially with colors like these, you want to wear them. They shouldn't wear you."

"They most definitely don't."

She smiled brightly. Maybe a little too brightly. He couldn't put his finger on exactly what it was, but something about her felt too… shiny. Brittle, like a spun sugar shell. A fragile shell, but still one meant to keep him at a distance.

He recalled her past as a con artist, and how she'd once said that she'd never try to con him because he'd see through it.

He was about to ask her when his hellhound cut in, growling, *Do you really want to know?*

With a cold chill, Ransom realized that maybe he didn't. What had knowing things ever gotten him, other than migraines and losing his team and seeing over and over and over again that the truth always hurts? He could push her to tell him what was going on, but what was she likely to say?

His hellhound supplied some answers:

I'm worried that you're getting too intense about me. Don't. I'm just lonely. I'm not really into you, Ransom.

I know we've been flirting but it's only for fun, so don't get any ideas it's anything more than that.

I don't need you. Don't act like I do.

His beast was right. Ransom didn't want to know.

"I was thinking about how to pick what to do next," Natalie said. He could hear that candy-shell brittleness in her voice, and see it in her movement as she spun around to take out her bucket list. "Close your eyes and touch it. We'll do whatever the finger picks."

I don't want to know, he thought. And he closed his eyes and reached out.

"QUIZ A HIGH FOOL," he read. "I remember that one."

She rolled her eyes. "It's VISIT A HIGH SCHOOL. I never got to attend one, you know."

"I did, and I wouldn't use the phrase 'got to.' For me it was definitely 'had to.' In fact, my actual high school isn't that far from here."

His power, helpful for once, informed him that it was 297.3 miles away. "About a five-hour drive."

"Would you want to visit your own school, though? If it's got a lot of bad memories…"

"It's just a building," Ransom said dismissively. He'd endured so much, what were a few bad memories of high school? He'd barely notice the sting. "If you want to go when it's in session, we'll have to do a guided tour. They won't let in a pair of random adults. We could pretend we're parents who want to check it out for our kid."

She sat on the bed, frowning. "I hadn't thought of that. I hate guided tours. Can't we disguise ourselves as students?"

"You could. I'd never pass. It's either an official tour, or we sneak in after hours, when everyone's gone."

The brittle shell fell away as an absolutely sincere delight lit up her face. "Ooh, let's do that. That sounds much more fun. And you know the building, so you can show me around."

"You're on."

Natalie took the first half of the drive, her longest so far. Though she tended to go terrifyingly fast, especially around curves, her quick reflexes made up for it. If her driving was a bit too nervewracking for Ransom to completely relax, he did love watching how much fun she was having.

The drive to his hometown wasn't a road he'd ever taken before, but once they reached the town itself, he recognized almost everything. It was startling how little it had changed.

"There's the library," he said. "My home away from home. I used to catch the bus after school straight to it, and stay there until the last bus back."

"I'm jealous. I never had enough books until I finally got my Kindle. I couldn't check anything out of a library, because we never stayed in one town long enough for me to get a card."

"And there's the alley where the guys used to hang out and drink beer they'd swiped from their parents' refrigerators."

"Guys including you?"

Ransom couldn't help making a face. "I didn't want to be there, and they wouldn't have wanted me, so it all worked out."

The motel they checked into was a new one, he thought, though he'd never seen the inside of any hotel while he'd lived in the town. All motels were beginning to seem the same to him.

When night fell, he took the wheel and drove Natalie and the puppies to his old high school. She gave a baffled look at the football field. "Where's the school?"

"Who cares about school? Football's the important thing. Football and cheerleading and partying and getting drunk and throwing up in the alley."

Dryly, she said, "Sounds like exactly your scene. I can see why you loved it so much."

He had to chuckle. "Come on. I'll show you the actual school."

They parked several blocks away, then headed to the back, pretending to be innocent dog-walkers while actually checking the security cameras and alarm systems.

"There's some gaps in the camera coverage," he said. "I can show you where they are, but the alarm system is harder to deal with. The only access point I can see, you'd have to dangle from a tree branch by your feet to get to it. I think we'll have to come back with some specialized equipment to deactivate it from a distance."

"I can dangle from a tree branch by my feet," said Natalie. "And I've had lots of experience turning off alarm systems."

"Oh. Then let's go for it."

They let the puppies off their leashes—they'd taught them to heel by then—and he led her to the edge of the zone the cameras covered. Standing in the shadows, he pointed out the areas where the cameras didn't quite reach.

"It's narrow," he warned her. "If you even let your elbows stick out too much, they'll get in the frame."

She smiled. "I have perfect control over my elbows."

With that, she ran lightly to the fence, her footsteps silent in her soft-soled black ballet slippers. She was dressed all in black, as was he, with a black baseball cap jammed over her head to conceal her hair.

While still several yards from the fence, she leaped into the air. Her body seemed to float in slow motion, arcing toward the fence until she caught it with both hands and her feet as well, landing so lightly that the chain links barely shook. It was an astonishing feat of athleticism, strength, and precision… and one which was also incredibly beautiful to watch.

Natalie had caught the fence in a standing position, and she climbed it with so much ease that she seemed to be walking in place. Ransom blinked once, and she was standing on top of the fence, her hands loose at her sides, as casually as if she was on the sidewalk. He didn't even see her muscles tense before she was once again flying through the air, hands outstretched to catch the branch of a tree inside the school grounds.

She caught the branch, pulled herself up, then walked along the narrow branch until she was as close as she could get to the alarm. Natalie examined the branch, tested its strength, moved one inch over, and stuffed her baseball cap down the front of her tight black tank top. Then she dropped with a speed that made him gasp until she caught herself an instant later, dangling upside down with her ankles locked around the branch.

She could barely reach the alarm, and was forced to work entirely with the tips of her fingers. But they moved deftly and confidently. Even someone who had no idea what she was doing would have been able to tell that she was good at it. Only a few minutes later, she bent at the waist, reached upward, pulled herself back up on to the branch, left the baseball cap hanging from a stub, climbed down the tree, and walked to the fence.

The moonlight made her skin shine like a pearl, and bleached her hair to intricate streaks and strands of darkness and light. She crouched down and whistled softly. Wally vanished and reappeared beside her. Heidi cocked her head at Ransom and gave an inquisitive whine.

"Go on," he said. "Go to Natalie."

Heidi too vanished, reappearing beside her brother. And then Ransom ran for the fence.

CHAPTER 16

Ransom climbed the fence with the muscular grace of a panther. With his larger frame, it was much harder for him to squeeze himself into the narrow space where the camera's gaze didn't reach, but he managed it, executing the difficult turn at the fence top with ease. Seconds later, he was inside, walking up to her in his black clothes like a shadow, feet silent as paws.

She'd thought "panther," but his other form was canine, not feline. Was a hellhound more like a dog, or more like a wolf? And what made it hellish, anyway? Its existence seemed like such a painful topic for him that she'd never asked.

"Welcome to Ellisville High," he said. "Home of the Cavemen."

"What?"

He indicated the side of the building, which was graced with an absolutely hideous mural of a pack of heavy-browed, jaw-jutting, matted-haired cavemen waving clubs.

"Why?" asked Natalie.

"It's our mascot and the name of our football team. There's a cave nearby where supposedly William Whipple spent a night sheltering from a thunderstorm—"

"Who?"

"He signed the Declaration of Independence. Anyway, the whole cave thing never happened. It's an urban legend. But it's called Whipple's Cave, and Ellisville isn't famous for anything else, so we got to be the Cavemen. And by the way, you would not believe how seriously everyone took them."

They had been walking around the building, but when she glanced back over her shoulder, the mural was every bit as much of a monstrosity as it had been when seen head-on.

"It's not that I think you're making it up," she said. "It's just that it's hard to believe."

"Yeah. I felt that way too." Ransom stopped at a door. "How are you at picking locks? Merlin taught me, but it takes me forever."

"The same person who taught Merlin taught me, and I'm pretty fast. Shall I take the lock, and you take the alarm?"

He stepped aside to let her at it. She took out her lockpicks out of her bra, which was where she stashed small items that she'd like to still have in the event that she got arrested, searched, and locked up. It had happened a couple times.

Natalie got to work, occasionally glancing over at Ransom as he disabled the security alarm. He had such utter concentration when he worked, with his long fingers moving as gracefully and confidently as a magician's, but he also had an aura of alertness. She had no doubt that should anyone try to sneak up on them, he'd have them facedown on the ground and be patting them down before she'd even noticed they were there.

They finished almost at the same moment. Ransom opened the door for her, then closed it behind them. They'd brought flashlights, but dim safety lights were on, illuminating a long corridor.

Heidi and Wally stuck their noses in, then backed away, sneezing indignantly.

"Ugh!" said Natalie. "What's that smell?"

"We called it the Ellisville Reek. It's equal parts chlorine, sweat, hot dogs, and Axe body spray."

"Uuuuuggggggghhhh."

"Regretting this already?"

"Not a chance." She stepped inside. With some coaxing, the puppies followed, their nails clicking on the linoleum. "Lead on. Pretend I'm the new girl you're showing around."

To her amusement, he threw himself into the role. "That's the school counselor's office. His name's Wayne, but we call him Wayne the Weasel. Don't ever tell him anything. He says it's confidential, but it isn't. And that's the principal's office. At least, we think we have a principal. No one's ever seen her. Maybe she doesn't exist."

"Why is Room 113 next to Room 9?"

"Oh, right. The room numbers aren't sequential. My theory is that it's to keep us subtly disoriented, so we'll be less likely to revolt."

There were Cavemen posters, football posters, and cheerleading posters everywhere. The only break from the football theme were the posters warning students not to do drugs and not to drink and drive.

In her "new girl" persona, Natalie said, "I'm really into gymnastics. Can you do that here without being a cheerleader?"

"No, sorry. Cheerleading is it here as far as gymnastics are concerned."

"Hmm," she said, pretending to think it over. "That might be okay. Do you know any of the cheerleaders? Date any of them?"

He smothered a snort of disbelief. "No. I'm not the kind of guy cheerleaders date. And you're not the cheerleading type. I know in some schools the cheerleaders are athletes, but here they wave pompoms for the football players and do the occasional backflip. Also, I hear the other girls say they're mean."

She could see him as a teenager now: tall and lanky, hunched over to avoid attention, observing everything and drawing his cynical conclusions. She couldn't think of anyone who'd fit in less in this setting, not even her.

"Your hair," he added. "I hate to break it to you, but 'unnatural colors' aren't allowed."

"Well, that sucks."

"Sorry. I think it looks great."

"Thanks." Natalie heaved a sigh. "Let's see… I love to read. How's the library?"

"Small. I'll show you." He led her to a door that she had thought was a closet, but when she peeked through the glassed-in rectangular insert, she saw that it was in fact a library… a library crammed into a closet. Also, it had more DVDs than books.

Forgetting her role, she burst out, "This is terrible! Ransom, I'm so sorry I dragged you here. I should have asked you first."

"No, it's my fault. I shouldn't have taken you. I know the sort of high school experience you were thinking of—prom and beach parties and making friends and putting on plays—and some people do have it. Some people even have it here, at Ellisville High. It's just that I didn't."

"It sounds like I wouldn't have either."

"No. You like to read and do gymnastics and dye your hair unnatural colors and play with puppies and go to produce festivals. Every single one of those things was weird or uncool or childish here. And that would be that. It wouldn't matter if you were the prettiest girl or the best athlete in the entire school—which you would have been, both of those—or the bravest or kindest or smartest. Which you also would have been. But no one would have cared." After a moment, he added, "Except me."

She took his hand. It was only when love surged up inside her, filling her heart and soul and body, that she remembered her determination to keep her distance. But when his fingers closed around hers, she found herself unable to let go.

"Anyway," he said at last. "Ellisville High isn't what you were looking for. I should've found a school that was, and taken you there."

"No." She squeezed his hand. "I wanted to know what it would've been like if I'd gone to high school. And now I know. I would've hated it."

"But Ellisville High isn't… I don't want to say it's not typical, because it's definitely typical of a specific sort of high school experience. But you might have gone to a better one."

She shook her head. "If I hadn't run away and joined the circus, I would've stayed in the group home. And let me tell you, based on the elementary schools I went to, my high school would not have been good. It might've had less football, but it would've had more metal detectors. And I still wouldn't have fit in. I didn't at the group home. Did you fit in when you were ten?"

"No. I was always different."

"Me too." Without thought, she leaned her head against his shoulder. His arm slipped around her waist, so immediately that she knew he too had moved out of instinct and desire, not conscious intent. The Ellisville Reek was driven out by his natural scent, something woodsy and smoky and masculine.

"Didn't you fit in at the circus?" he asked.

Natalie hoped she hadn't actually flinched at that question. But Ransom didn't move, so she guessed her reaction was only on the inside. She scrambled to find a response that would be honest but also change the subject. "I did. I loved the circus. It was everything before the circus that was unhappy—my teenage years were way better than yours. Do you have *any* happy high school memories?"

"Yes, actually. There was one high school event that was a real highlight. I'll show you where it happened." As he led her through the dim, smelly corridors, he said, "My junior year, there was a football game that was a big deal for… some reason I forget. They called us into an assembly, and told us that except for the football players and cheerleaders, all our PE sessions for the next month would be devoted to teaching the entire student body to march in formation to spell out GO CAVEMEN and then make the shape of a caveman."

Natalie burst out laughing. "Come on."

"I'm serious," he protested. "I said, 'I refuse to participate in this idiotic exercise in ant-like conformity.' Only no one heard me, because they were all busy cheering. Except for the guy next to me, Johnny Trevisano, who whispered, 'I have an idea for getting out of this. Stay after the assembly.' The only reason I even knew his name was that he was the only out gay guy in the entire school."

"Good for him."

Ransom nodded. "I'd always respected him for that—in our school, being different in any way took courage. So I stuck around. Once we were alone, Johnny said, 'The cheerleaders don't have to march because they have to cheerlead. I think we can get out of the march if we propose doing our own thing. I've been teaching myself to juggle, but I can't learn any two-person techniques because I don't have another person. Want to do a two-man juggling act with me?'

I said, 'I don't know how to juggle.'

'No problem,' he said. 'I'll teach you.'

I said, 'What if I suck?'

Johnny said, 'No one who wins medals shooting is going to suck at juggling.'"

"Wait a sec," Natalie broke in. "You won medals shooting?"

Ransom looked mildly surprised. "Oh—I guess I never mentioned that. I was a state champion at high-power rifle. It wasn't through school. I think Johnny must've known because it was in the local paper a couple times."

"And that wasn't considered cool?"

"Nope. At least, not when it was me doing it."

They ducked under a drooping GO CAVEMEN banner and went out a door. To her immense relief, it was an exit. She gulped in the cool night air as they headed toward the football field, which sent up a much more pleasant scent of wet grass.

"Johnny got permission for our act, and while everyone else marched around the football field in the shape of a caveman, he and I practiced juggling in his backyard. It was a lot of fun. No one was watching us and we were a pair of teenage boys, so we got wilder and wilder. We juggled knives. We juggled flaming torches. We juggled chainsaws."

"I wish I could've seen it. Too bad I can't juggle."

"I could teach you."

"Really?" Natalie asked eagerly. "Yes, please!"

"You're on. Anyway, the day of the big game, we brought in all our equipment in duffel bags, which luckily no one checked. Half the audience was laughing at us before we even started, and the other half wasn't paying any attention. And then we did our act. Torches and chainsaws and all."

He grinned at her, his eyes bright. "You would've loved it. Not just because it was good. It was like the sort of high school story you were looking for. First the audience stopped laughing, then they started paying attention, and at the end they cheered. Afterward, Johnny got popular. He started a gay and straight alliance club, and he ended up taking a boyfriend to the prom. They didn't get elected prom kings, but no one dumped pig's blood over them either, so... happy ending."

"What about you?"

"We stayed friends. After high school, he moved to the west coast. He's a professional magician now. Performs at the Magic Castle. He's not a superstar, but he makes a good living and he's very respected by other magicians. He's married. Not to his prom date, to a guy he met in LA. I haven't met him, but he sounds pretty great from the way Johnny talks about him."

Natalie nudged him. "I'm very happy for Johnny, but what about *you?* How was your prom?"

"I didn't go. Johnny told me about it afterward. Our juggling act was a high point for me because I made a friend, and I had so much fun learning to juggle and then actually doing it. But Johnny saw that moment where everyone cheered us as a chance to change his social status. He followed up on it and went to parties and so forth. I didn't. I didn't want to hang out with people I didn't even like."

"Did they at least stop bullying you?"

"I wasn't ever bullied, really. Mostly, I was ignored. Anyway, the next year I qualified to do online courses at a two-year college, which meant I could skip most of the school day. My senior year, I was barely there. I skipped prom *and* graduation. They mailed me my certificate. See, I didn't want to be popular, not at a place I couldn't stand. I wanted to be somewhere else."

They stood in silence while the puppies snuffled around in the grass. The night sky spread out overhead, vast and dark and empty.

"Let's go back," said Ransom.

And then Natalie got an idea. "Wait."

CHAPTER 17

"Remember when I was the new girl and you were showing me Ellisville High?" Natalie asked. "You're the new boy now, and I'm going to show *you* around."

"Okay…" Ransom said doubtfully, but he stepped back into his teenage shoes. He could recall it all too well: his bad skin and height that made him painfully self-conscious, his carrot-colored hair that hadn't darkened till college, his acute lack of comfort inside his own skin.

Natalie, however, was nothing if not comfortable within her skin. She rumpled her hair, then gave him a smile that had never been directed at him when he'd been a teenager, the nervy, flirty smile of a girl who sees a boy for the first time and likes what she sees. "Hi! I'm Natalie Nash. Welcome to Sweetwater High, home of the Huskies! Our mascot, unsurprisingly, is the Siberian husky. How do you feel about huskies?"

Amused and trying not to look at the pups, who presumably did not exist in the game, he said, "They're objectively the world's best dogs. And I love dogs."

"You're in luck!" Indicating Heidi and Wally, she said, "These little darlings here are our in-school therapy dogs. If you're feeling down or for any other reason, you can always cuddle or play with them. You don't need to ask permission, and no one will tell your parents."

"That sounds like it would improve the high school experience by about a thousand percent."

"It does," Natalie assured him. "Of course, if you want to speak to an actual counselor, we have a human one, Wayne. We call him Wayne the Wombat, because like a wombat, he makes you smile."

In the interest of staying in character, he suppressed the laughter welling up inside of him. Natalie was going all-out, and he loved her inventive twisting of everything terrible about Ellisville High into something good. "What's that smell in the air?"

"We call it the Sweetwater Scent," she replied without missing a beat. "We all have our theories, but I think it's a mix of soft puppy fur, fresh-baked bread from the bread-baking classes that supply our cafeteria, herbs from the garden that also supplies the cafeteria, and our cafeteria chefs' famous tomato sauce."

"You can learn to bake bread here?"

"Absolutely. Sweetwater High may be a science and performing arts magnet school, but it also has great cooking and English classes. And don't be put off that it doesn't have any competitive team sports —we have world-class shooting, juggling, gymnastics, and trapeze. Swimming, too. Our pool gives our school its name."

She pointed across the football field. "See that beautiful natural lake? It's crystal clear, fed by mountain streams. A little chilly, but so refreshing in the summer. And if you prefer more intellectual pursuits, we have a complete laboratory for science fair projects. Also a book club, which meets in our enormous library."

"What about prom? Do you have that?"

"Not exactly. We have morp instead—it's prom spelled backwards. It's like prom, but minus the social pressure and expense and conformity. We all pitch in, show up, and have a good time. You can dress up if you want to, and not if you don't want to. No elections, no kings or queens. It's a party where you can do whatever you want, whether it's to dance or have pizza or go outside and look at the stars."

Ransom put his arm around her. "Just so you know, I'm having a perfect morp."

Dropping her teenage persona, Natalie said, "I wish I'd met you earlier."

"Me too. Even Ellisville High, home of the Cavemen, would have been bearable if you'd been around."

"I didn't mean in high school. I meant a year ago. But hey… here we are now." She melted into his arms. Her soft breasts and slim body moved against him, and his own body responded against his will. He heard a sound escape his lips, something between a growl and a moan. Natalie tilted her head back, eyes half-closed, lips parted, as if she was inviting him to kiss her. It took every ounce of self-control he had not to.

"Go on," she murmured.

She *was* inviting him to.

One of his fists clenched with the effort of holding himself back, and the other trembled like a stretched wire as he stroked her silken hair. "I wish we could too. But you know we can't. We should probably step away now."

"I don't care any more." Her eyes opened all the way, reflecting the black night sky. "I've tried and tried to keep my distance, and it's not working. To hell with it. Let's seize the day. I'm crossing out the rest of my bucket list and writing KISS RANSOM at the top."

She locked her fingers behind his head and pulled him down to her waiting lips. Stunned and tempted, he didn't resist until he felt the sweetest, lightest brush of her lips on his.

Ransom wrenched away.

"Hey!" Natalie exclaimed. "Get back here. Don't you want to?"

"Of course I want to!" His voice came out louder than he'd intended to, raw and ragged. He forced it down before he went on. "I've never wanted anything more in my life. But remember Tomato Land. We have to wait."

"Wait for what?" There was an unsettlingly harsh edge to her voice.

"For it to be safe. For you to be cured."

"Cured!" Natalie nearly spat the word out. "Get real, Ransom. There is no cure. There's only now. This is our chance. Come on. Take it with me."

They faced each other across the grass with only air between them. It would be the easiest thing in the world to take one step forward, and sweep her into his arms.

He took a step back and folded his arms across his chest. "No."

She stared at him, incredulous and hurt. "No?"

His hellhound's growl filled his mind. *You rejected her. She'll never forgive you. She'll never touch you again. You've ruined everything.*

"It could kill you!" Ransom heard himself shouting, trying to drown out his hellhound. "Why don't you believe that I can save you?"

"Because if you could have, you would have by now!"

Because you failed, growled his hellhound. *You think you're so smart, but you can't solve the most important problem of your life. You're a failure and she knows it. You're not good enough for her.*

"I could bite you!" The moment the words escaped Ransom's lips, he wanted to take them back. Sure, shifters healed faster and better, but there was no guarantee that being one would actually cure her. And more importantly, there was the reason why he'd never offered before: he'd be putting a hellhound inside of her. What good would it do to save her life if he ruined it?

But if she was this desperate, he had to at least offer her the choice. Even though it would mean telling her what his own hellhound was, so she'd know what the choice meant.

"I already tried that," she said. "It didn't work."

"I know, but that was with a normal shifter. I'm a mythic shifter. It might make a difference." He swallowed, trying to gear himself up to telling her the rest.

But she was already speaking. "I tried more than once."

"What?"

"I had that idea too. And I knew some mythic shifters. One of them was a ruby dragon who'd come to see one of our performances. After I got my diagnosis, I contacted her. I didn't tell her why. I just said I wanted to fly, and I knew it was safe for me because I'd already been bitten by a flying squirrel and nothing happened. I talked her into it. But nothing happened. Again."

Natalie swallowed. Her voice came out thick with suppressed tears when she said, "It was such a disappointment. I'd gotten my hopes up, and then… Well, anyway, thanks for the offer. But I already know it won't work."

See, growled his hellhound. *It's hopeless. You were her last chance, and you let her down. You've failed her. You're not worthy of her. You can't save her. She'll die and it'll be your fault.*

Ransom felt as if he was drowning in darkness. His hellhound went on and on, its sandpaper voice a litany of accusations he couldn't deny. Natalie stood with her arms folded in a mirror of his, her lips trembling. Disappointed in him. Everything was falling to pieces. *He* was falling to pieces.

A furry head butted his ankle. Automatically, he scooped up Heidi and held her to his chest. She wriggled around, planted her paws on his shoulder, and licked his face. Past Heidi's furry black-and-white head, he saw Natalie cuddling Wally.

"Forget about it." Her voice was flat, her eyes black. He couldn't read anything in her expression. "Let's go back to the deal we had at the beginning, okay? I do my list, and you stick around and protect me from the wizard-scientists. Are we still good with that?"

What wizard-scientists? jeered his hellhound. *We haven't seen hair nor hide of them. The only thing she needs protection from is the one thing you can't help her with.*

At that instant, Ransom made his decision. He tried not to think about it, to keep his hellhound from catching on, but kept his wordless resolve in his heart, unbreakable as steel.

"Yeah," he said. "We're good."

They retraced their steps and escaped Ellisville High, which he hoped to avoid for the rest of his life. Back at the hotel room, they changed in the bathroom one by one, then got in bed and turned out the lights. Neither of them attempted to read, nor did they hold hands. But they did say goodnight. There was still that much left between them.

Ransom lay in bed, silent and motionless, waiting and listening and trying not to think. He focused on the sound of Natalie's breathing as if he was meditating, excluding everything else from his mind. When its evenness told him she was asleep, he still waited until he heard the slow, deep breaths of stage four sleep, the deepest kind. She wouldn't wake up now unless he shook her awake.

Still keeping his mind on her breathing and his intent buried deep inside him, he got up, padded silently to his duffel bag, and felt around inside it until his fingers closed around the vial of tincture of shiftsilver.

And then there was no concealing what he meant to do. His hellhound snarled at him, accusing him of everything under the sun.

It won't work.

I'm the only special thing about you—you'll destroy the one thing that makes you unique.

You're a failure.

Everything is hopeless, and so is this.

But his hellhound's reaction only made Ransom more determined. Now that he knew for sure that he couldn't help Natalie by biting her, he had no more use for his hellhound. It was the worst part of him, the darkness and guilt and shame and fear and self-hatred inside of him. It made him unworthy of Natalie. It cut him down and ate away at his confidence, and that made him less likely to be able to save her if he ever did get the chance.

He had to destroy it.

Ransom went into the bathroom, closed and locked the door, and sat down on the bathmat, wedging himself in between the bathtub and the sink. As his hellhound raged and snarled within him, he drew up a single drop, capped the vial, and set it down inside the bathtub. He didn't know how fast the stuff worked, and he didn't want to risk spilling the vial or waking Natalie with a crash.

His heart was pounding and his skin prickled with a cold sweat, but his hands were absolutely steady. Tilting his head back, he squeezed a drop of liquid silver onto his tongue. It tasted metallic and burned going down, but like whiskey rather than the fire or acid he'd been braced for. Maybe this wouldn't be as hard as he had—

The bathroom vanished. Cold stone was beneath his bare feet. He was in a vast, dim room like a huge dungeon. Its edges vanished into darkness. Shivering, he wrapped his arms around himself, and found that he was wearing lightweight scrubs and a white lab coat. He tried to rip off the coat, but it was sewn or glued to the scrubs. It wouldn't come free.

He stopped wrestling with the coat when a movement caught his eye. Something big and inhuman within the darkness, coming toward him.

First he saw a pair of flames within the darkness, hot and red as the pits of Hell. As the thing came closer, he saw the white gleam of fangs. The flames resolved into eyes. The hound stalked closer, big as a pony, black as coal, fiery-eyed and wreathed in smoke.

Ransom had never seen his hellhound before. He'd caught glimpses of it within the darkness of his own mind, but that was nothing compared to seeing it looming over him.

That thing is a part of me, he thought with a horror that chilled him down to the soul. *And if I want to get rid of it, I have to kill it with my bare hands.*

"Come on!" Ransom shouted. His voice didn't echo, but sounded flat and small in the huge space. "If you hate me so much, come and kill me if you can!"

The hellhound sprang.

CHAPTER 18

Something's wrong.

Natalie sat bolt upright in bed, abruptly wide awake, filled with the knowledge that something terrible was happening.

Ransom's in danger.

She didn't know how she knew, but she was certain.

"Ransom?"

There was no answer. The motel room was dark, and she couldn't see if he was in his bed. She flipped on the light. His bed was empty, but a line of light shone at the bottom of the closed bathroom door. Heidi was nowhere to be seen, but Wally was awake, his blue eyes fixed on the bathroom door. As she watched, he vanished.

She scrambled out of bed, ran to the bathroom door, and gave it a sharp knock. "Ransom?"

There was no reply. She tried the knob, but it was locked.

Wally reappeared at her side, followed by Heidi. Natalie's growing alarm sharpened to fear when she saw a smear of blood on the white fur of Heidi's muzzle. Natalie parted the fur, looking for the injury, but there was none. It wasn't the puppy's blood.

"Ransom!" She banged on the door with her fist. Nothing.

Heidi vanished again, while Wally began to whine and scratch at the door. He could easily get inside if he wanted to, so Natalie was sure he was trying to tell her where to go.

"I know." She gave the door a shove, then a kick. It shook, but didn't give way. Ransom was undoubtedly strong enough to kick it in, but it was too sturdy for her.

There was no keyhole, so she couldn't use her lockpicks. She fetched a credit card instead, slid it into the crack, and began maneuvering it against the latch. Out of the corner of her eye, she saw Wally vanish again. Inside the bathroom, she could hear the puppies whining and barking, but absolutely nothing else.

The precise and delicate work of opening the door was all in her fingers, leaving her mind free to spin out scenarios of what the hell was going on inside.

He's having such a bad migraine that he can't even speak. (Didn't account for the blood.)

He tripped in the dark, hit his head, and knocked himself out. (Ransom, who moved like a panther, was about as unlikely to be unable to catch himself as Natalie herself. Also, the light was on.)

He overused his powers and passed out. (Why would he do that? Because she'd driven him to desperation with her disbelief?)

The latch popped back. Natalie yanked the door open.

There was blood everywhere. On his shirt, on his face, on the edge of the bathtub. He'd somehow wedged himself between the bathtub and the sink, with his long legs stretched out across the floor. His face was very pale, and his eyes were closed.

For a panicked instant, she had no idea where to even start. She couldn't call 911, she didn't know where the blood was coming from, she couldn't tell if he was even breathing—

There. She'd start there. Natalie grabbed his pajama top by the collar and ripped it open. Little buttons flew everywhere. His muscular chest was slightly stained with blood, but there was no wound that she could see. Nor could she see any movement.

Her own heart lurched.

"Not now!" Her voice rose up, shrill and echoing.

By sheer force of will, she made herself draw in a deep breath, then another. *Calm, calm, calm.* She couldn't help him if she passed out herself.

Her heart steadied. She laid her head against his chest, feeling and listening. There was an agonizing pause, and then she heard a heartbeat. Pause. Another. Then a breath, so faint and shallow that she almost missed it. Heartbeat. Pause. Heartbeat. Breath.

That was wrong. That was all wrong. He was alive, but something was horribly wrong and she had no idea what it was and no one she could call for help.

Terror again threatened to overwhelm her, but she forced it back. Closing her eyes, she visualized her panic as a mob of tiny spiky creatures, waving their matchstick arms and screeching at her. She imagined dropping a huge, thick carpet over them, squishing them to the floor and muffling their cries. There. The panic was still there, but stifled and shoved to the back of her mind where it wouldn't stop *her* heart.

She opened her eyes. Ransom was unconscious and bloody, Heidi was pawing at him and howling, Wally was barking in a corner, and someone in the room next door was banging on the wall.

"Be quiet," Natalie whispered fiercely. "Heidi, Wally, shush!"

The puppies quieted down, and the other motel occupant stopped pounding on the wall. Good. Now at least she wouldn't have someone banging down their door. She stood up, looking around the bathroom for some clue to what the hell had happened, broken glass or—

There was a tiny vial in the bathtub, almost full of a silvery liquid. She picked it up. The silvery color was familiar. She could swear she'd seen it before, but the only silver liquid she knew of was mercury, and it didn't look like that. Maybe she'd seen it when it wasn't liquid...?

At that, she knew what it was. She'd seen it at the circus—they had some handcuffs embossed with shiftsilver, for dealing with unfriendly criminal shifters, like robbers. Touching shiftsilver forced your inner animal down into the depths of your mind, so deep that you couldn't shift. But drinking tincture of shiftsilver forced you down along with it.

Natalie had never seen it in its liquid form or known anyone who'd actually used it. But she'd heard that it was sometimes used as a last-resort remedy for shifters who'd somehow lost the ability to shift, to allow them to get back in touch with their inner animal.

She'd never seen Ransom shift. For an instant, everything seemed to make sense: he couldn't shift, and he'd gotten so desperate that he'd tried an incredibly dangerous cure. She could understand that...

...but no, that made no sense. He'd offered to cure *her* with a bite, and that would only work in his hellhound form. And she'd told him it wouldn't help anyway, so he couldn't have done this in the hope of saving her.

Whatever his reasons were, something had obviously gone terribly wrong. Setting aside that mystery, she wet a washcloth and sponged off his face. It looked like he'd been in a fight. His nose was bleeding—that was where the blood had come from—and there was a blackening bruise on one cheekbone.

He made a very soft sound, just a slightly deeper inhale. Heidi barked sharply.

"Ransom?"

He didn't stir. But a patch of skin over his ribs turned red. Horrified, Natalie realized that it was a bruise. What was *happening* to him?

The panic under the carpet began to screech and thrash, but she threw another mental blanket over it. She needed to think.

He was trapped inside himself with his inner hellhound. There was no antidote to tincture of shiftsilver, which was one of the reasons it was so dangerous. But Ransom wasn't careless. He was thoughtful, cautious, and smart. He'd planned to do this, so he'd have calculated the exact dosage he needed and not a drop more. It might be possible to just... wake him up.

Natalie turned the shower on to cold, full blast, and stepped in. Air hissed through her teeth with the shock of it—it felt maybe two degrees above freezing.

"Good," she muttered, and dragged Ransom in with her.

She kept his head turned so he wouldn't breathe in any water, but the rest of him was drenched instantly. She was shivering already, but he didn't stir. Her heart sank.

"Come on," she murmured, her voice barely inaudible to her own ears against the hammering water. "Come on, Ransom. Wake up."

Heidi jumped into the shower, followed by Wally. Both dogs seemed unaffected by the cold, though Natalie's teeth were starting to chatter. They nosed at Ransom, but he didn't respond to them any more than he'd responded to her. The bruise across his ribs darkened and spread.

"Come back. I love you. Come back to me." She bent down and kissed his cold lips, water running down her face like tears.

Ransom awoke, gasping and clutching at her. They held each other tight, wet hair mingling and wet skin pressed together, until he said, "You're shivering."

"You too."

But it was another minute or so before either of them could let go of each other for long enough to turn off the shower. When they did, the sudden silence felt deafening.

A trickle of red traced along the bottom of the tub and swirled down the drain. Natalie watched it, puzzled. Ransom's nose had stopped bleeding, and everything else she'd seen had been bruises. Then she saw Heidi frantically licking his ankle and whining apologetically.

"I think Heidi bit you," Natalie said. "She was trying really hard to wake you up."

Ransom rubbed her ears until she stopped whining. "Good girl. You did what you had to do."

"Do you have a first aid kit?"

He nodded. "In my duffel bag."

She fetched the entire bag. "I'll bandage it after you get dressed. You're freezing. Yell when you're ready."

She grabbed a towel for herself and retreated from the bathroom, then bolted back in, catching a startled Ransom taking off his shirt. Natalie snatched up the vial of shiftsilver and went out, shutting the door behind her. She dried herself off and dressed in under thirty seconds, a skill she had learned from making quick-changes at the circus, then stashed the tiny vial in her bra along with her lockpicks.

Wally appeared on her bed, shook himself all over her and it, then curled up at its foot. She wiped the doggy shower water off her face.

"Natalie?" Ransom called from the bathroom.

"Coming!"

But he came out himself, in a dry set of black pajamas and not even limping, and sat down on the edge of his bed, across from her. Heidi followed him, but had the grace to shake off in the middle of the room instead, sending droplets all over the TV. Then she jumped on to Ransom's bed, also curling up at the foot.

He stroked her, then pushed up his pajama leg to reveal a pair of band-aids on his ankle. "She really didn't do much damage." The color had come back to his face, but the bruises remained. He looked exhausted. Worse, he looked defeated. But he lifted his head to look Natalie in the eyes, and said, "I apologize. I had no intention of putting you through… *that*. I thought you'd sleep through the whole thing."

"I know you didn't do it on purpose." She heard how stiff she sounded, but decided to move on rather than back. "Listen, I took the vial of shiftsilver. I know what it is, but only in theory. I've never seen it before, or known anyone who's used it. What exactly were you trying to do with it?"

"If you know what it is…" he began, sounding puzzled, then shrugged as if it wasn't worth pressing the point. "I was trying to kill my hellhound, of course. But I—"

"You WHAT?" Natalie burst out. "You can do that? *Why* would you do that?"

He gingerly touched his bruised cheekbone, then dropped his hand. "I think we're not operating out of the same knowledge set. Let's get on the same page. Stop me if I say something you didn't know or don't think is right. This is tincture of shiftsilver…"

"Yes."

"In solid form it stops shifters from transforming into their animal. In liquid form, it enables you to go inside yourself and confront your inner beast…"

"Yes."

"And fight it."

"What? No!"

"If you can kill it, then you lose the ability to shift and any other powers that went with it, and it never speaks to you again. If it kills you, then you die."

Natalie hadn't been angry at him until that moment, but that touched her off like a match tossed into bone-dry weeds. "And then I wake up in the morning and find you dead in the bathroom?"

He flinched. "I wasn't intending to die."

That only fed the flames. Her voice rose and rose until it was a full-fledged yell. "But you knew you could! And you nearly did! I'm pretty sure you were getting your ass handed to you when Heidi bit you and I kissed you!"

A loud bang made them both jump. The room vibrated, and a book fell off the table. From the next room over, a man yelled, "Keep it down in there!"

"Sorry!" Natalie shouted.

"We will!" Ransom called. Then, pitching his voice low, he said, "You're right. I *was* losing. You and Heidi saved my life… but I still have my hellhound."

He looked and sounded so bleak that Natalie got up, lay on his bed, and tried to pull him down beside her. Resisting, he said, "You don't want to do that."

"I'm not going to do anything dangerous. I promise. The kiss was just because…" She stopped before she could say, *"I love you."* Instead, she said, "Because I care about you and I thought you were dying and I panicked."

He cupped her cheek in one hand. It sent a tingle down her spine, making her shiver. "Natalie. You don't have to apologize for that. I only wish I'd been more… present… for it. But that wasn't what I meant. I'm going to tell you everything. All my secrets. I was wrong to keep them from you. But once you know who—*what*—I am, I don't think you'll want to be in bed with me."

He made it sound so ominous, as if he was about to rip off his human mask and show her a monster.

"I don't believe that," she said. "No one who loves puppies and has a favorite *Ballet Shoes* sister can be *that* bad."

"Some serial killers are very well-read," Ransom said glumly.

"Puppies though? Are there any who love puppies?" When he gave a doubtful shrug, she added, "Also, are you a serial killer?"

"No, but..." While he paused, seeming to struggle to speak, she recalled the moment when she'd seen him sleeping and realized that he was much younger than she'd thought. But now the lines in his bruised face had deepened, and his eyes held a hundred years of weariness and guilt. Finally, he said, "I was responsible for something that killed a lot of people."

"You mean, when you were a Marine? You didn't spot a bomb or an ambush, and you feel like it was your fault that people died?"

Ransom was slowly shaking his head. For the first time, Natalie felt a chill. She'd been so sure that whatever he felt guilty about couldn't be as bad as he was imagining, but now she wondered.

"This was before I became a Marine," he said. "And it's so much worse than you're imagining."

CHAPTER 19

RANSOM'S STORY

My father was a Marine. When I was a little boy, he'd want to play catch, and I'd want to read. When I was a teenager, he'd want to play pickup basketball, and I'd want to work on a science project. That's why I got into competitive shooting, so I could do one thing he'd appreciate. And he did appreciate it. Only he thought I ought to join the Marines and be a sniper, and that was about the last thing I wanted to do. We didn't get in fights about it—he knew better than to try to force me to be someone I wasn't—but it was always in the back of my mind that I wasn't the son he wanted.

I went to college and majored in biochemistry, and I co-authored a few papers with some of my professors. I was getting job offers before I even graduated—from pharmaceutical companies, from the Department of Defense, you name it. I could have taken a cushy job in a big company and made lots of money making tiny improvements to existing medications, or worked on weapons with the military. But neither of those were what I wanted. I wanted to do something useful, and I wanted to do something new.

I thought I was in luck when I got an offer to do both at once. It was from a man who had a start-up working on a very unusual project, a process to enhance intuition. We have lots of medications to treat mental illness, and of course there's drugs that make you high. But we don't have much intended to make the mind work *better*.

I was approached by the CEO, a man named Jager. He was a biochemist himself, which was unusual—but then, this was a small start-up with a big budget. Think of Steve Jobs creating Apple computers in his garage, only with chemistry and in an actual lab.

We worked on the enhanced intuition project for years before we were ready to do human testing. That's very strictly regulated for safety and consent. And because the purpose of our process was so unusual, we couldn't get permission to try it on humans.

The process was Jager's idea, but I was the one who'd made the conceptual breakthrough that we thought would make it actually work. I was so sure it was my life's work. I imagined how many lives it would save if we could give doctors that extra edge of intuition to know which patient was about to have a crisis, or soldiers to spot the hidden bomb, or firefighters to know that the roof was about to collapse. But if we couldn't test it, that would be the end of it all.

One night Jager and I were working late after everyone else had left. We were talking about how we couldn't let everything go down the drain because of regulations. He said we should apply again, but say it was for something more normal, like lowering blood pressure, and secretly test the subjects for effects on intuition. I said that was illegal and unethical and out of the question. I suggested testing it on ourselves.

Jager wouldn't go for it. He said it wouldn't be a valid experiment, since it was only two of us and there wouldn't be any control group and we might just imagine that our intuition was better. And that was all true. But I wanted to try it anyway.

I asked him if he had any better ideas. He said he did. But everything he suggested doing was totally unethical – all sorts of variations on experimenting on people who didn't know what they'd be getting themselves into. Over the years we'd been working together, I'd gotten the impression that there was something a bit cold and sketchy about him. But it was nothing I could ever put my finger on. Everything I actually saw him do, he did by the book. And I was so invested in the intuition project, it didn't even occur to me to leave because of some vague bad feeling.

How's that for irony?

It was Friday night. Jager told me we should go home, get a good night's rest, clear our heads, and check back in on Monday. And he left. It didn't occur to me then, but now, I think he was afraid of trying it himself. He must have understood the risks better than I did—which makes it even worse that he was the one who wanted to give it to people without their informed consent.

But I still didn't get it. I thought he was proposing all those unethical experiments because he didn't see a better alternative, and if I gave him one, he'd drop it. Also… I really wanted to try the process. I thought it would work. But I couldn't know until we tried it on a human subject. And I really, really wanted to *know*.

That night, I ran the process on myself.

I was very careful. I used the lowest possible dosage and setting. But I was still flying blind. It was targeted specifically to the human brain and didn't affect animals, so we only had theories on what it would do to a person. I figured either it would work or it would have no effect at all, and I'd just be very tired and disappointed by Saturday morning.

Halfway through, I started feeling… strange. Disconnected. Dizzy. I was seeing movement out of the corner of my eyes and hearing sounds I couldn't identify. I'd be sure something terrible was happening somewhere, but I had no idea where or what it was. My head ached. My joints ached. I started running a fever. I felt worse and worse. At one point I decided I had to call Jager because I wasn't sure I could finish it on my own, but I couldn't figure out how. I looked at my own cell phone and I had no idea what it was.

Jager found me on Monday morning. I had a bad feeling about him, but at that point I was having bad feelings about everything. I felt like the fluorescent lights were watching me and the air was toxic and there was always someone behind me. I knew it wasn't real, but that helped less than you'd imagine. So when he told me I shouldn't go to a hospital because any medication they gave me might interact badly with the process, that sounded reasonable to me.

He got me into his car and said he was taking me home. I was lying down in the back seat with my arm over my face. The light hurt my eyes. Everything touching me—the seat, the seatbelt, my own clothes—felt… wrong. Alien.

All of a sudden, I *knew* something. I yelled, "STOP!"

He slammed on the brakes. I think it was mostly out of reflex. If I hadn't been belted in, I'd have ended up on the floor.

Jager said, "Ransom, what—"

And then I heard him gasp. I grabbed on to the back of his seat and hauled myself up so I could see the road. A tennis ball was bouncing across it. A second later, a dog came bolting straight into the road, right in front of our car. There were bushes blocking our view of its front yard, so it seemed to come out of nowhere. At the speed we'd been going and given where the dog ran out, if I hadn't made us stop, we'd have hit it.

The dog picked up the tennis ball and ran back into its yard.

Jager said, "It works."

I was in such bad shape, I couldn't even reply. But I remember how proud and happy I was. I thought, *This is the greatest moment of my life.*

That kept me going for the next six months, which is how long it took me to recover. Jager took me to my own apartment and called in someone to take care of me. He said it was a friend who was a paramedic, but I think he was a guy criminals called to treat them because doctors have to report bullet wounds. For all I know, he was a veterinarian.

I'm not sure exactly how long the vet or whoever he was stayed in my apartment. Maybe a couple weeks. After that, I felt better physically and I could take care of myself, more or less. But when I tried to sleep, I'd wake up every half hour or so, sure that something bad was happening somewhere. Probably it was, but that was useless because there was no actual information to go with it. It happened when I was awake, too. I was exhausted all the time.

But I knew there was a purpose to it. At first I couldn't write—my hand-eye coordination was shot—so I asked Jager to get me a tape recorder so I could take notes on my symptoms and progress. He went straight out and bought me one. Once I could type again, I used my laptop.

Jager came in almost every day. We'd do experiments on me in the apartment. He'd roll dice and I'd try to guess what had come up, that sort of thing. To this day, I can't stand hearing dice click together.

Sometimes he'd drive me around and see if I could pick up on anything going on. I definitely had gotten enhanced intuition, and what it mostly seemed to do was alert me a few seconds before something dangerous was going to happen. The closer the danger was to me, the more specific the alerts were. If someone else was in danger a mile away, I'd just get that non-specific feeling. We figured that one out by driving me near an emergency room.

At first I tried to focus on getting more information about what the danger was if it was farther away, but I got nowhere with that. So I started teaching myself to ignore those alerts. Gradually, they began to fade away.

In all this time, I'd assumed that any further actual experiments were on hold while we studied me and worked on refining the process to reduce the side effects. And then we'd publish a paper about the process and its effect on me, and see if we could get permission to use informed human subjects then. I figured we could get some volunteers from the military or firefighters or even war correspondents—people whose lives were dangerous enough already that they'd think it was worth the risk and potentially being out of work for six months.

But when I told Jager I was ready to go back to the lab, I got a sort of generalized bad feeling. It was so different from the immediate danger alerts that I didn't recognize it. I thought maybe I was anxious about going back to work, which didn't make sense because I wanted to.

He said, "I've got a surprise for you."

And then he told me what he'd been doing in those six months. It turned out that he'd never had any intention of submitting a paper on me so we could continue working on the process legally. Instead, he'd gotten a lot of shady contacts together so he could do experiments completely underground, on people no one would believe if they turned up claiming to have been paid to try a blood pressure drug that actually made them sick for months and then gave them an extrasensory danger sense.

I was so shocked that I didn't say a word. He went on and on, telling me how cleverly he'd planned it all and how once he had the process working perfectly, then he'd take it to his "contacts in the government."

To this day, I don't know whether the bad feeling about Jager that I got at the beginning of the conversation was my enhanced intuition or the regular intuition I'd had all along, but ignored. And I also don't know which caused the feeling I got after he'd told me his plan, which was that I should pretend to go along with it because it would be dangerous if he knew I thought he was a sociopath.

Either way, I kept nodding like I agreed. Even when he was telling me what a genius I was to help create the process that he planned to use on people without their consent. Even when he said that I'd been very conservative when I'd used it on myself, and that was why my intuition was so low-level.

"Just imagine what might happen at higher doses," he said.

I could imagine, all right. It was true that I might have gotten a stronger, more precise danger sense. But it also might have caused permanent damage or killed me.

I nodded and agreed. Yes, I was very excited. Yes, I couldn't wait to start. Yes, I'd love to look over his plans.

As soon as he left, I packed my laptop, checked into a hotel, and contacted the Office for Human Research Protections. I told them the entire story, filed a formal complaint, and gave them Jager's plans as proof.

For a supposed genius, I can be a real idiot.

You can see where this is going, right? He conned me, and I fell for it. The plans were fake. They had details that could be checked out, and every single one was disproven. Meanwhile, he'd already spread it around that I'd tried to take credit for his work, and I'd left the lab threatening to ruin him. The whole time I was at home, recovering from the process and thinking we were working on an important experiment, he was busy undermining me.

He'd gotten everything he needed from me, the first human subject. And when he was done with me, he did exactly what he'd told me he'd do to his next human subjects: make sure no one would ever believe anything I said about him.

My danger sense went off every time I even *thought* about him. I was sure he really did mean to do exactly what he'd told me, and it was only the details that were wrong. I couldn't let him.

I reported him to the police. I reported him to the FBI. I contacted everyone I knew in the scientific community and warned them about him. And then, to make sure it would hit the news, I sued him for stealing my idea.

I knew no one would believe me, but I was hoping to draw so much attention to him that he wouldn't be able to go ahead with his plans. Finally, he shut down the intuition enhancement project.

My plan worked, but it cost me my reputation and my career. Everyone in the scientific community thought I was a backstabber and a lunatic. I lost the lawsuit, and I was ordered to pay for Jager's court costs. After that, I had no money and I couldn't get hired to wash test tubes. Even my parents thought I'd had a breakdown caused by overwork.

I knew I'd done the right thing, but that's cold comfort when you're unemployed, broke, and the *best* anyone thinks of you is that you temporarily lost your mind.

It turned out that when I got stressed, it was harder to screen out my danger sense. Any time anyone was about to have a heart attack or crash their car or get lost, I'd suddenly get a gallon of adrenaline dumped into my bloodstream, along with the feeling that something terrible was happening and I had to go save someone, right now. Except I had no idea what was happening or who was in danger or where they were. It was like the world's most useless superpower.

But that was only because the danger was too far away. If I had a job where *I* was in danger, my enhanced intuition might be useful in exactly the way I'd intended when I started the project.

So I joined the Marines. I wanted to make my father proud, and I thought that once they saw me shoot, they wouldn't dig too closely into the rest of my background.

You won't be surprised to hear that I didn't fit in. But I'd been right: I was useful.

I already told you how I got kidnapped and changed, but I left out some key details. When my fire team was ambushed by the wizard-scientists, my danger sense went off a second before. I had just enough time to shove my nearest teammate, Ethan, into a river before I was hit with a tranquilizer dart.

I woke up strapped to a hospital bed, with doctors and technicians working on an apparatus I recognized. It was the intuition enhancement process, but different. More complex, but also more streamlined. If mine and Jager's was 1.0, this was something like 10.0. And the other thing I saw was a doctor filling a syringe with one of the drugs we used for the process, at a dose twenty times what I'd given to myself the first time.

One of the techs said, "He's awake. Give him more sedative."

I was so panicked at the thought of getting an overdose of that stuff that I blurted out the only thing I could think of that might stop them, which was, "I've already done the process!"

A woman came forward. She wore a white doctor's coat embroidered with symbols in black. Scientific symbols and magic symbols. I learned later that it meant she was a wizard-scientist, but I'd never heard of them then. Even later than that, we encountered her again, so I know now that her name was Morgana.

She said, "We know. That's why we're so curious to see what will happen when we put you through it again."

"It'll kill me, at that dosage," I said.

Morgana shook her head. "We've improved the process a great deal since you left the project. There was a conceptual breakthrough on the level of the one you had to create it. Ours allows us to enhance the subjects' healing abilities and endurance, which enables them to survive much higher dosages. Well. Mostly they survive."

I said, "So Jager's been working on this all along?"

She waved her hand dismissively, and said, "He *was* working on it. After you betrayed him, he took the process to the government. They saw more possibilities in it than he ever had. It was one of them, a shifter, who had that conceptual breakthrough."

And then she told me all about shifters, and how making the human subjects into them was what allowed them to survive the process. I thought it was some weird mind game, but I played along. I was hoping that if she talked long enough, I'd figure out how to escape. I figured Pete and Merlin were trapped along with me, and whatever was really going on, I had to get to them before they got put through the process.

But I couldn't budge. The straps were incredibly strong. And my danger sense was going off like a fire alarm inside my head. It made it hard to think.

Meanwhile, Morgana was monologing away. She said at one point how much she enjoyed having a subject who understood the technical side of things, not to mention having been present at the very beginning. She gave me the entire history of what happened after I left. The more she talked, the more convinced I was that she was telling the truth. And afterward, I found out that it *was* all true.

Jager had partnered with government black ops to create an agency devoted to the intuition enhancement process. They called it Apex.

They used unwilling human subjects—people they literally kidnapped—to test the process. A lot of them died. The survivors, who had powers that went way beyond enhanced intuition, were forced to work for them as spies and assassins. But some of them had fought back, destroying Apex bases and freeing the captives. Jager had been killed in one of those battles, blown up along with his base.

The whole time she'd been talking, I'd been planning to go after Jager and kill him. When I heard he was already dead, it was like the floor dropped out from under me. I realized that I'd been plotting revenge on him to distract myself from my own guilt.

I'd created the process that had been used to kill all these innocent people, and ruin others' lives. I'd known Jager had planned to do something just like what he did do, but I never followed up after I learned that he'd supposedly ended the project. I went and joined the Marines, when I should have been monitoring him and tracking his movements.

Everything, all of it, was my fault.

I barely heard the rest of what Morgana was saying—how the wizard-scientists had taken over from Apex, and had their own master plan that involved me and my fire team. I was drowning in guilt like I'd fallen in a well of it and breathed it into my lungs.

She could tell I wasn't really listening. She snapped her fingers, and one of her techs turned into this huge black hound with fiery eyes. It leaned over me and opened its jaws. I guess I couldn't have fought anyway, but I didn't even try.

The last thing I remember thinking was, *I deserve this.*

I woke up in a cell with a collar around my neck. It had a shift-silver disc on it, which kept me from shifting and kept my hellhound from speaking to me, though I didn't know that at the time.

Think of my intuition power as a dripping faucet. One drop of information at a time. What I woke up to was a firehose. I was getting flooded with information, so much that I couldn't think for myself, couldn't pick out any individual pieces, and couldn't block it out. I felt like I was losing myself.

I didn't rescue anyone. I just sat there, fighting just to hold my ground, fighting to stay *me,* until my teammates and some bodyguards from Protection, Inc. came and rescued me. They say I helped them in the fight they had to get out of the lab, but I barely remember that. Mostly, I remember what happened when they got my collar off. That was when my hellhound started talking to me.

CHAPTER 20

Ransom fell silent. His eyes were more than sad, they were haunted. The bruises on his face had darkened, making him look like he'd lost a fight, and his posture was one of utter defeat. Natalie longed to comfort him, but he'd flinched every time she'd reached out to him. At first she'd thought he didn't want to be touched, but now she wondered if he thought he didn't deserve it.

She wanted to throw her arms around him and tell him none of it was his fault. But he hadn't yet finished his story. And she knew him well enough now to be sure that until he'd told her everything, he'd think that one last bit of information would be the one thing she could never forgive.

It felt cruel to push him to talk about what seemed to be the most painful part of all. But she thought of the blisters and bruises she'd gotten learning to be an acrobat, and of a surgeon's scalpel. Sometimes you had to endure some pain to get what you needed. And if there was one thing Ransom could do, it was endure.

"Ransom?" she prompted him. "What did your hellhound say?"

He looked away, unable to meet her eyes. When he finally spoke, his voice was barely audible. "He said it was my fault. He said I killed all those people. He said I was worthless, and a failure, and there was nothing in the world but pain. He spies on the worst moments of people's lives, and he makes me watch."

"Ransom..."

He didn't seem to hear her, but went on, his voice rising. "The Protection, Inc. team came to rescue us from the lab. Three of them were Apex subjects. My hellhound showed me the worst moments of their lives—being tortured, being forced to kill, watching their friends die, knowing they'd been turned into monsters—and it was all my fault. My process did that to them. *I* did that to them. Carter was kidnapped and imprisoned for a year. His inner animal—a part of his self—was destroyed. Pete's power was out of control. Whenever he touched anyone, it physically hurt him. And Roland... When they captured him, a woman tried to defend him. They took her too. And the process—my process—*killed* her!"

He glanced around, then lowered his voice. "Roland puts up a strong front, but that broke him inside. He walks around like a widower who was married for thirty years, grieving for a woman whose name he doesn't know. I did that to him. And every day at work, my hellhound reminds me."

Natalie's heart broke for the victims of the experiments, the living and the dead, and for all that pain and guilt Ransom had been enduring every day, silent and alone. She was so full of emotion, she couldn't find words for it.

After a long silence, he went on, "Your shift form is a part of you. It can't be anything you're not. If my hellhound is a monster, it's because I'm a monster. It's my dark side—the part of me that hates me—the part of me I hate—the part of me that hates myself. That's why I tried to kill it. But I couldn't. It's stronger than I am. I was wrong to imagine I could ever be with you. Now that you know what I am, of course you wouldn't want—"

"Hey!" Natalie spoke loudly enough to cut him off. He glanced up, startled. "That's it, right? Every single secret you've been keeping? Is that all of it?"

He nodded. With the faintest glimmer of dark humor, he said, "Seems like that's plenty."

"Right. Well, let me tell you the secret *I've* been keeping. I love you."

His dark eyes widened, his lips parted, and then he blinked a few times, slowly. He looked more like he'd been hit over the head than like he'd heard a declaration of love. Finally, he said, "What?"

"I love you," she repeated. "I'm in love with you. Ever since you slid my Kindle under the bathroom door. And absolutely nothing you've told me tonight has changed that. What does your hellhound have to say about that, huh?"

"Uh… 'She doesn't mean it… You heard that wrong… She'll have second thoughts tomorrow…'"

"I do mean it, you didn't hear it wrong, and I won't have any second thoughts. I had all my second thoughts already. They're what kept me from telling you till now. And none of them were about you not being good enough. Or anything about you, really. They were about me. Not me as a person, but my limited time. I thought it would break our hearts. And it will. But now you know. I must be on my five thousand and eighty-ninth thought by now, and it's this: I love you." She grinned fiercely. "What's your hellhound have to say about *that?*"

"Nothing," he said, after a moment. "I think you scared him off."

At last, their eyes met with no barriers between them: no fear, no doubt, no guilt, no shame. She knew what he felt without him having to say a word.

"I love you," he said. "But you knew that already, didn't you?"

Natalie nodded. She'd always known, she supposed; she'd only conned herself into believing anything different.

The room around them and the bed beneath them seemed to fade away, until nothing was left in the world but the two of them. The air was hot and still, holding them suspended as if in amber.

She was utterly focused on Ransom, catching and savoring the smallest details. His still-damp hair was drying in waves and curls. If she watched closely enough, she could see individual strands coming free, sparkling copper or glittering bronze where the light caught them.

The tendons at the back of his hands stood out and the muscles of his forearms bulged as if he was lifting some heavy weight, though he held himself absolutely still. If she was seeing him for the first time now, she wouldn't think his eyes were sad. She'd think they were hot... passionate... *hungry.*

She could feel the beating of her own heart, quick and hard with desire, but it didn't frighten her. She didn't care if she dropped dead immediately after ripping his clothes off and having sex up against the wall, as long as she got to finish it first.

Ransom jumped off the bed. "Excuse me."

He ran to the bathroom. Not even bothering to slam the door, he went straight to the sink, turned the cold water on, and stuck his head under the tap.

Natalie lay back with a groan. "You're being sensible, aren't you?"

"Yes," he said, walking back in. "Bathroom's all yours."

Sighing, she got up and splashed her own face. The truth was, cold water didn't do much. It was mostly a signal of intent to oneself, a promise not to act on impulse. Self-restraint had never been her strong suit. But she thought of Ransom, and how difficult their situation was for him as well as her, and the flash of gut-wrenching terror in his eyes when she'd had to lie down in the dust at Tomato Land. He'd been through so much already. She couldn't put him through any more pain.

When she returned to the bedroom, she found that he had managed a quick-change act of his own. His feet were still bare, but he'd switched out his pajamas for pants and a shirt. As he finished buttoning it, all the way up to the collar, she remarked, "Button-down shirts: the modern chastity belt."

He gave a wry smile. "Think you'd be all right lying down with me?"

She climbed on to his bed and they lay down together, holding each other close. The sexual awareness of each other was still there, but there were other feelings as well, friendship and comfort and intimacy and tenderness. And most of all, love. Their shared love was like a cord binding them, silken but unbreakable.

His arms were strong around her, his body heat warming her down to her bones. The jittery urgency to go, do, hurry before it's too late, which had driven her ever since she'd learned that she had limited time, began to melt away. For the first time that night—for the first time that trip—maybe for the first time since she'd seen that doctor—Natalie relaxed.

"About what you told me," she said. "The enhanced intuition project. Jager. Apex. The wizard-scientists. You didn't experiment on anyone but yourself. You didn't kidnap anyone. You didn't kill anyone. You didn't even know any of that was happening. Exactly how is any of that your fault?"

She felt his body tense and his breathing catch. "I was responsible for the original process. It was Jager's idea, but he couldn't get it to work. I did that. None of it would have happened if it wasn't for me."

"You had no idea anyone was going to use it like that. That's like saying that the guy who invented gunpowder so he could kill a deer and feed his family is responsible for everyone who's ever been shot to death."

"Gunpowder wasn't invented for hunting. It was originally used for fireworks. It wasn't until the tenth century in China that the first weapons…" He broke off, seeing her grin. "Okay, point taken. But—"

"But nothing! Ransom, you didn't do anything wrong. You burned down your entire career trying to stop Jager. It's not your fault he was too sneaky for you. If a soldier was killed trying to defend his position, and it got overrun anyway, would you say it was his fault?"

"No, but that's different. That soldier did everything he could. I didn't. I assumed I'd fixed things, and then I stopped looking."

She gave a frustrated sigh. It was so obvious to her, but she couldn't get him to see it. If it had been her…

Dust swirling around her ankles.

Ashes falling from the sky.

If you rub them between your fingers, they're the same dry powder, like flour…

"Natalie? Are you all right?"

"Of course!" The brightness in her voice was tinny, false. A kind of lie. She'd never lied to him. So why did it feel like she was lying now?

Why were some stories so hard to tell? The facts weren't a secret. It was something else... the feelings behind the facts?

Natalie couldn't help shying away from that train of thought. Finally, she said, "Ransom, can I tell you a story?"

"Of course."

She'd already told him what her childhood was like, more or less. And this particular story was so relevant to his situation. But the words didn't come, and she didn't know why. Then she remembered their play-acting at Ellisville High, and said, "Could I tell it as a kind of hypothetical story? Not about me, about a hypothetical girl?"

He smoothed back her tumbled hair from her face. His long fingers were so gentle, she had the irrational desire to cry. "Of course."

She took a deep breath, and then the words came. "Once upon a time, there was a little orphan girl. For whatever reasons, this orphan girl hadn't ever found a permanent home. When the story starts, she was ten years old, which is much too old to be a desirable adoption prospect. Parents want a baby or a toddler, who they figure won't have been too damaged for them to fix."

"That is so wrong!" Ransom burst out. "No one's too damaged to deserve love."

Natalie felt her eyebrows rise. "Yes, exactly, Ransom. Don't forget you said that. Anyway, this orphan girl was living at a group home when some foster parents showed up. They had a big, happy family of foster kids, living in a big, beautiful house in the country. They showed her photos. And let me tell you, the photos looked great. Well, this orphan girl knew she was a troublemaker—she'd been told that often enough—and she knew this was her last chance—she'd been told that too. So she promised herself that she'd be good, and she promised those foster parents that too. So they took her away to their big, beautiful house."

"What was it, really?"

"A big, beautiful house." She sighed. "And the foster kids were only allowed in one wing of it, which needless to say was not one-tenth as nice. They weren't even allowed into the rest of it. Our 'parents' ate steak with the money meant to support us, and we ate cereal with powdered milk. At the time I assumed the social workers were in on the scam, but who knows, maybe they were overworked and didn't have time. Whatever. They never checked up on us."

"Unbelievable," he muttered. "I mean, I believe it, it's just terrible."

"Now, that orphan girl didn't think of telling the authorities. Literally: it never occurred to her. So she waited till the parents were out on a dinner date and the kids were unsupervised. The rest of the house was locked up tight, but you learn things in group homes. That orphan girl promised the rest of the kids she'd take the blame. And they all went outside, and she broke into the big, beautiful house and set it on fire."

"Good for you!" Ransom blurted out. "Uh... her. Good for her."

"Right. She felt pretty good about it. Especially when she broke into their garage and set their second car on fire too. Her only regret was that their other car was at the fancy restaurant they were eating at. Well, the social workers came and asked her why she did it, but she never even considered telling them the truth. It didn't occur to her that they didn't already know, or that if they didn't know, that they'd care."

"Oh, Natalie." Ransom's arms closed tight around her.

She blinked back a stinging in her eyes, and went on, "So she said she liked playing with matches. Luckily for that girl, she was only ten so there weren't any real consequences. She was sent to a group home for troubled kids, which by then she was very familiar with, and knew she would never, ever have a real home."

"Nat—"

She hurried on. "She didn't follow up on the foster parents, to see if they were ever investigated or if they got a new house and kept on stealing money meant for kids."

"You were *ten*."

"I'm not ten now." With that, the stinging faded away. Now she was on safer ground, back to the only reason she'd been able to tell that story: to convince Ransom to set down his burden of guilt. "I could have checked on them at any time. But I never did. It never even occurred to me that I could, until right now. If they went on running their scam, am I responsible?"

"Of course not!"

She didn't reply, hoping his own words would sink in.

"You're *not* responsible," he repeated. "You don't think you are, do you?"

"No," she said honestly. "I don't. So why do you?"

"Well—I was an adult—"

"I'm an adult now."

Ransom neither argued nor agreed. Instead, he laid his cheek against hers and said, "You were so brave. And smart. And strong. You took all the responsibility. I wish someone had seen who you really were, and gotten you the home you deserved."

"Merlin did. And really, I couldn't possibly have done better than a crime circus for shifters."

"True… How old were you when your parents died?"

"I was young. I don't remember them." Again, she felt on thin ice. The facts were one thing, but with the love that bound them, she could tell that he was about to ask about feelings. She changed the subject. "What do you think now? About Apex… the intuition project… Your hellhound?"

His reply was completely unexpected, but so *Ransom* that it almost made her laugh. "I think I should have actually researched what tincture of shiftsilver does. I found out about it when I asked my power how I could get rid of my hellhound. There's a lesson in there about the perils of asking the wrong questions. What's it normally used for?"

"It's supposed to get you in touch with your inner animal. If you were unable to shift for so long that you lost the ability to do it, a drop of tincture of shiftsilver will send you down deep inside yourself, to find your animal and bring it back to the surface. Or if you're having trouble controlling your shift, you can use it to talk to your animal on a deeper level. I don't know much about it, actually. But I do know that you're not supposed to use it to try to *kill* your animal!"

"Yeah." He gingerly touched his side. "I wanted so much for that part of me to be gone."

Natalie thought back to his story. "You were blaming yourself for everything *before* you got bitten. Would killing your hellhound even do anything?"

"It would let me stop seeing everyone's worst moments." He tilted his head back, gazing up at the ceiling. "But you're right that it didn't put those thoughts in my head. I always had them. Since I was a teenager, at least. Ellisville High was objectively terrible, but even at Sweetwater, I might've needed those therapy puppies."

"You ever do any real therapy?"

He shook his head. "When I was a teenager, my option was Wayne the Weasel. In college and with the intuition enhancement project, I focused on work and used that as a distraction. In the Marines, there's a lot of 'real men handle things themselves' still going around. Afterward... Oh. One last secret. I'd forgotten about this one. Roland didn't just tell me to ask permission before I used my power. My other option was to talk to someone. He tried to give me the names of some shifter therapists. I walked out on him."

"What do you think now?"

A familiar bitterness returned to his voice as he said, "Doesn't matter if I said yes now. Now that I've told you everything, I couldn't keep on hiding it from them if I tried to go back. And I couldn't take it if they found out that I'm the one who invented the thing that ruined their lives."

She wanted to say that Merlin wouldn't blame him, but the words never reached her lips. Natalie too couldn't ever see Merlin again, because there was something she couldn't hide from him that she wanted him to never find out. How could she argue without shining a spotlight on her own decision?

Ransom sat up. "Can you give me back the tincture of shiftsilver, please?"

Suspiciously, she asked, "What for?"

But his gaze was clear and calm, not haunted and desperate. "I want to talk to my hellhound."

CHAPTER 21

There was nothing Ransom wanted more than to stay where he was, holding Natalie in his arms and basking in the love that they shared. He'd imagined that seeing her face when she learned of his guilt would be the worst moment of his life, but she hadn't blamed him or left him or stopped loving him. Instead, she'd held him closer, told him she loved him, and given him some badly needed perspective.

He couldn't shake off the last six months of his life like Heidi shook water out of her fur, but for once, having a lot to think about made him feel better rather than worse.

He only wished he could do the same for Natalie. Her story had broken his heart, but though she'd accepted his touch, she'd steered hard away from his attempts at getting her to talk to him the way he'd talked to her. He could only hope that, like the boys in books who tamed wolves and foxes and skittish stray dogs, if he was patient and proved himself worthy of her trust, eventually she'd come to him.

And to be worthy of her trust, he had to deal with his hellhound. One way or another.

"The vial's in your bra, right?" he asked. "Because you're clutching your breast like you think someone's going to steal it."

She let go with a flicker of a smile, but even that quickly faded. "I don't think you should do this. It's too dangerous. You could die."

"Have you ever heard of anyone dying from using tincture of shift-silver to try to talk to their animal?"

"No, but you already pissed yours off!"

"I know," he admitted. "But it's something I have to do. And this time I won't try it alone."

Her hands were trembling as she lifted out the vial. "If it looks like it's going badly, back in the tub you go."

"If it does, feel free." He unscrewed the vial, extracted a single drop, and recapped it.

She replaced the vial in her bra. "Lie down."

"Good idea." He lay down, dropper in hand, and looked up at her. He couldn't take her with him into the cold and dark, though she'd be brave enough to go, so he tried to capture her image as she was now: rainbow hair tangled, opal-gray eyes both worried and trusting, lemon-sharp scent rising off her warm skin.

She took his free hand and held it tight. He could feel the strength of her dainty-looking hands, which could bear the weight of her own body and more. "I won't let go."

"I'll come back to you," he promised, and put the drop on his tongue.

Once again, he felt the whiskey heat sliding down his throat. Once again, he found himself in that cold and shadowy realm.

But it wasn't quite the same this time. Ransom no longer wore scrubs and a lab coat, but a button-down shirt and pants. And his hellhound was already there, lurking in the shadows, only barely visible as a vast and looming shape. The twin flames of its eyes blazed like wildfires within the darkness.

"Hello," Ransom said.

The hellhound snarled, but came no closer.

It took all of Ransom's courage, but he sat down cross-legged on the floor. He'd be a sitting duck if the hellhound attacked him, but it was a position that was non-threatening without being one of surrender. He opened his hands, showing that they were empty.

Pitching his voice low and soothing, he said, "I read books about dogs when I was a boy. Boys with hunting hounds. Boys with huskies. Boys with terriers and retrievers and greyhounds. They all said a dog doesn't care if you're cool or rich or good at sports. A dog will love you just because you're you. I guess I wanted that."

The hellhound came a step closer. The smoke that surrounded it drifted over Ransom. He expected it to smell like sulphur and gunsmoke, but the scent was of wood smoke. If he hadn't know what it came from, he'd have felt very confident in guessing that it was from a campfire.

"I've been thinking about your power. You say it shows how terrible the world is. But I remember those women I saw at Tomato Land, the married couple. One of them used to be homeless. One of them lost her father. But when I saw them, they were happy and in love. Is your power really about how bad things can get? Or is it about how far we can come?"

The hellhound took another step closer.

"I love Natalie," Ransom said. "I want to be worthy of her. I don't ever want her to wake up and find me like she did. I'm not going to beat myself up about it, but it was wrong. I'm not going to do it again."

The hellhound gave an uncertain whine.

Ransom kept his voice soft. Gentle. The hellhound was a part of him. It felt strange to be gentle with himself. "Come here. I promise not to hurt you."

The hellhound laid his head in Ransom's lap. Ransom stroked his head and ears and shoulders. The hellhound's fur was short and sleek, as velvety as a puppy's.

The first time Ransom had left that inner realm, the transition had been abrupt and violent. One moment he'd been struggling on the ground with his hellhound's fangs at his throat, and the next instant he'd been drenched in freezing water. This time, the scene dissolved like a dream on a lazy Sunday morning, the hellhound's soft fur becoming Natalie's soft skin.

Ransom opened his eyes, and looked into Natalie's.

I know her now, said his hellhound. His voice was still a growl, but one with a distinctly different tone. It used to sound like a dog throwing himself against a fence in an attempt to rip out someone's throat. Now it sounded like Heidi or Wally having a friendly tussle over a ball. *She's our mate.*

Ransom had never believed in mates. He knew that shifters believed that they could recognize the person with whom they were completely compatible, the person they would love forever until death did them part. But people believed in all sorts of things. Throw a rock into the stands at a football game, and you were likely to hit someone who believed that gluten was made out of aliens.

So when the wizard-scientists had told him and his team that they'd destroyed their ability to recognize and bond with their mates, Ransom had assumed it was nothing more than an attempt to damage their morale. And when Pete and Merlin had said they'd managed to bond with their mates anyway, he'd figured that was just shifter-speak for falling in love.

But now Ransom knew the truth, with an understanding that went far deeper than anything his power of knowing could tell him. Mates were real. Natalie was his, and he was hers. He'd loved her already; this didn't make him love her more, because that would be impossible. What he knew now was that neither of them would ever fall out of love.

After all the time he'd spent believing that he was broken and the entire world was untrustworthy, he'd finally found something unbreakable.

"I love you," he said.

Natalie was bending anxiously over him, her rainbow hair shadowing her face, her changing eyes a pure dark gray. She'd never let go of his hand. "I love you too. Are you all right? Did it work?"

He nodded. "My hellhound says we're mates."

Inside his mind, his hellhound watched with fiery eyes. He was still dark and dangerous, but Ransom no longer feared him. He was a guard dog, a loyal hound, his fierce instincts now turned to protecting the ones Ransom loved.

Natalie gasped aloud. "What? I thought we couldn't be. Shifters recognize their mates on first sight."

"The wizard-scientists did something to stop that. But my hellhound recognizes you now. *I* recognize you now."

Her lips were parted, pink and kissable. The desire to take that kiss he knew she wanted as much as he did, to sweep her into his arms and claim her as his own, was so overpowering that he scrambled off the bed, barely managing to avoid the sleeping puppies, and stumbled backward until he hit a wall.

Natalie let out a piercing shriek of frustration. "This is making me crazy!"

"Me too." Ransom pressed his palms against the wall. "Me too."

The person in the room next to them banged on the wall. A male voice boomed out, "SHUT UP, YOU TWO! YOU'RE MAKING *ME* CRAZY!"

"Sorry!" Ransom and Natalie called. Their voices were as united as their bodies couldn't be.

Patience, said his hellhound in that deep rumble of a voice. *You are mates. You cannot be parted forever.*

Got any ideas? Ransom returned.

His hellhound cocked his head in a canine shrug, and repeated, *Patience.*

Ransom passed on the exchange to Natalie, who rubbed her forehead. "Right. Patience. The thing I have so much of. Your hellhound's really changed, though. That's great. What did you do?"

"I petted him." When he saw Natalie's disbelieving expression, he couldn't help laughing. "Seriously." He told her the whole story, then added, "I don't want to sound like everything's sunshine and daisies…"

"If you did, I'd be worried that you'd been replaced by a pod person."

"I do feel a *little* sunshine and daisies. But it's more like I'm not drowning anymore. There's solid earth under my feet now, and I can go forward. With you."

He held out his hand. She got up and walked slowly toward him, clasped his hand, and put her other arm around him, burying her face in his chest. They stood there in silence until he felt the hot wetness of her tears seep through his shirt.

"Natalie?"

"Sorry," she mumbled, the words stifled and barely understandable. "Sorry. I'm happy for you."

He didn't need enhanced intuition to know that wasn't why she was silently crying. Holding her close, he said, "There's nothing to be sorry about. Just tell me what's really going on."

She lifted her head. Tears were streaming down her face, faster than she could swipe them away. "Goddammit! I never do that."

"Don't worry about it. Just talk to me."

Natalie pulled away from him, went to the bathroom, and splashed her face. When she came out, her eyes were dry of tears, but the sparkle that normally animated them was gone. With a chill, he realized that he'd seen that blank, flat stare many times before, when he'd caught a glance in the mirror. She sat down on her own bed, and held up her hand when he started to sit beside her. Instead, he sat across from her, and kept his hands to himself.

"I promised myself I wouldn't let you get close," she said. "I was afraid it would break you if you fell in love with me. Now you're telling me we're mates and you can walk forward if you walk with me. What's going to happen to you at the end of the year?"

"Nothing. Because nothing's going to happen to you."

She scoffed angrily. "How can you keep believing that?"

Unexpectedly, his hellhound spoke. *Why doesn't she?*

Ransom had wondered that before, but had always been distracted by answers that were easy, simple, and wrong, like *because I'm not trustworthy* or *because I'm a failure*. But Natalie had never thought badly of him, she'd never disbelieved him or lacked faith in him, and she knew that his power was real. So why had she so consistently disbelieved in the possibility of him saving her?

"Why don't you believe me?" Ransom asked.

"If you could save me, you would've by now."

"That's not a valid argument. I might as well have said, before I met you, 'If I was going to meet my mate, I would have by now.' You're too smart to believe that."

She gave an uneasy shrug. "You said yourself it was only a small chance."

"Do you believe there's even a small chance?"

"No," she admitted.

"Why?"

She flung out her hands. "What does it matter?"

It matters, growled his hellhound. The beast was as relentless as always, but Ransom could tell that the hellhound wasn't attacking her the way he'd once attacked Ransom. He might be ruthless and hard, but he was a part of Ransom, and Ransom would never harm the woman he loved.

"I think it matters," Ransom said. "I'm not telling you to believe something you don't. I only want to know why."

"Can't you use your power?" Natalie muttered, then hurriedly said, "I'm not serious!"

But her tone had been pleading, not sarcastic. As if she'd blurted out something that she really did want.

"Which one?" he asked.

The dull look vanished from her eyes. Now she looked half-eager, half-terrified. Like someone psyching themselves up for freefall, except that Natalie had never been afraid to jump.

"If you want me to, I will," he said.

"I can't ask you to. Just because I'm too… too… I don't even know." She ran her hands through her hair, leaving it a wild mass of many colors. "I don't want you to hurt yourself on my behalf."

My power won't hurt you, said his hellhound. *Not anymore.*

Ransom repeated that, adding, "If that's the one you meant."

She gave a single jerk of her head. "I'm too scared to talk about it. I'm too scared to *think* about it. But I don't mind if you know. So go ahead, if it won't hurt you. Take a look."

"You realize I won't just see it," he warned her. "I'll know your thoughts, your emotions…"

She made a sound halfway between a laugh and a sob. "That's the point. Do it, Ransom. Do it now, before I lose my nerve."

The truth was, he too was afraid. Whatever the worst moment of her life had been, it had to be worse than everything she'd already told him: losing her parents, living in group homes, having the prospect of a family dangled before her only to be snatched away. He almost didn't want to know.

But whatever it was, she'd been living with it. Whatever it was, it had put that wild look in her eyes and that jangling edge in her voice. If she was forced to bear it, then sharing it was the least he could do.

Ransom closed his eyes and asked his hellhound to show him her worst moment.

He saw Natalie as a skinny little girl in a faded dress, her light brown hair in braids. Dust swirled around her ankles as she jumped out of a car and ran toward a mansion. He could feel her joy and excitement as she thought how it looked exactly like the photos, the big, beautiful house she'd be living in with her new family.

Puzzled, he thought, *But she already told me about this.*

The couple that got out of the car pulled her back before she could reach the steps. They told her coldly that she wouldn't be going into that part of the house, ever. None of the children were allowed in. They had their own space with their own door.

Ransom forced back his fury as he watched them open another door and show her a cramped room with nothing but bare-bones cots, like Marine barracks minus the charm and livability. He couldn't get distracted by his own emotions; he needed to focus on hers.

It's all a lie, Natalie thought. *A con. And I was stupid enough to fall for it. Of course I'll never have a family. Of course I'll never have a life like girls in books. I should know better by now. If I hadn't believed them, and I'd just expected to be moved to a different group home, then I wouldn't care now.*

Her anger and disappointment and sadness filled her until she felt like it would rip her apart from the inside out. Frantic, desperate to end the pain she was in, she sought refuge in an ice-cold numbness. Natalie sat down on a cot, a little girl filled with a determination that would shame most adults, and made a vow to herself.

The next time someone promises me something too good to be true, I won't believe it. Adults say kids forget everything when they grow up, so I swear now, I won't forget this. I won't forget how much it hurts when you believe promises because you want them to be true. I won't forget how much it hurts when you believe in happy ever after. I swear this, now and forever: I'll never believe again.

CHAPTER 22

Natalie knew exactly what Ransom had seen—and experienced—when he opened his eyes. He'd said it wouldn't hurt him, but it had. Migraines weren't the only kind of pain.

"I'm sorry—" she began.

He pulled her into his arms and held her tight. She turned her face into his shoulder and breathed in his scent. Its clean masculinity was both a maddening temptation and a comfort. She wanted him so much, it hurt. But at least she had his touch, his presence, and his love. Wanting more than she could have was a recipe for heartbreak.

At least now he understood that.

"I wish I could go back in time and get you a big, beautiful house and a loving family. But since I can't, I'm really tempted to look up those foster parents of yours right now, so I can toss them off a cliff." A beat later, he added. "Without a parachute."

"I figured. People like that don't deserve nice things like BASE jumping."

"You do, though." He laid his head down atop hers. "You deserve everything."

He sounded so sad that she said, "I got a lot, you know. I got the circus. I got Merlin. I got to be a target girl and an acrobat and a trapeze artist. I've BASE jumped. I've seen the world. I've gone to Tomato Land. And I've got you, even if it's only for a little while."

"Don't be so sure of that."

Natalie sighed. "I just want to enjoy the time I have, and not break my heart asking for more. I don't want be believe, and then be disappointed."

Ransom lifted his head. His eyes had the intensity that had caught her attention the first time she'd seen him, like a fire burning dark instead of light. "Did you believe in the circus?"

"It took me a while. I kept dreaming that the circus was a dream, and I was waking up at the group home. Or in the house I burned down." Slowly, she said, "It's always felt a bit like a beautiful dream. When I got the diagnosis, I remember thinking, 'Of course. I knew something like this would happen.'"

"What do you mean?"

"The diagnosis was the part that made everything feel real: I really did have this wonderful life, but I wasn't going to have it for very long." She touched a lock of Ransom's hair, rubbing it between her fingers. It was so soft, and smelled a little like woodsmoke. "I found a man who's brilliant and sexy and kind and brave and passionate and honest and reads cool books. A man I love, who loves me back. And we can't have sex or even kiss, and I'll only have you for a year. But that's what makes it real. If I could have you for a lifetime, in every way, it'd be too good to be true."

The dark fire in his eyes seemed to blaze up. If she hadn't trusted him so deeply, she'd have flinched back. "What would it mean to you if we could have everything? If we could kiss and make love and be what we are now, for a lifetime?"

The force of his will made her imagine it. Her and Ransom and the puppies, in a big beautiful house. Having sex in the shower, the couch, the bed, the floor, up against the wall. Waking up in the morning with their naked limbs entangled, and kissing before their eyes were quite open yet. Having all of that, with no expiration date, like normal people did. A happy ending that lasted a lifetime.

She imagined herself believing it. And then she imagined how she'd feel when it turned out that it was only a beautiful dream.

The pain that knifed through her heart made her reflexively jerk away from Ransom. "I can't believe in that! You shouldn't either. It'll only break your heart."

The blaze in his eyes was undimmed. "If it breaks, it breaks."

Natalie swallowed, then whispered, "Okay."

"Come back here." His tone was gentle, not commanding. She returned to his arms, and then lay back down on his bed. The pale light of dawn was starting to come through the windows. Ransom followed her gaze to it. "I feel like we've lived a lifetime in one night."

"Me too." In his arms, she felt a sense of fragile peace, like an opening flower. "I want to go home."

"To the circus?"

"Go back, I meant. Back to Refuge City. I could stay at your apartment. We could just… live."

"Sounds good to me. The apartment's tiny, though, and the sublet is nearly up. We could pick out a new one together. Not another sublet, an apartment of our own."

On a one-year lease, she thought. But she didn't say it. Ransom believed what he believed, and she had to accept that. "I'd love to pick out an apartment with you. How come you always had sublets?"

"Same reason I switch out rental cars and phones, and try not to attract attention. I was afraid someone who'd been kidnapped by Apex, or one of their loved ones, would come after me."

"And try to kill you?"

"Yeah, probably, but that wasn't the part that scared me. My worst nightmare was someone who *didn't* want to kill me—someone who wanted to accuse me, face-to-face. That seemed worse than an assassin." She felt his chest move with a ragged breath. "It still does."

Natalie, who knew all about fearing things more than death, didn't argue. "We could get a bigger sublet."

"No, no. I can't drag you into that kind of life. If someone does track me down, I'll have to face it. I gave up on fading into the background when we rented the Mustang, anyway."

Mischievously, she said, "Does that mean I can dye your hair purple?"

"Nope."

"What about taking you clothes shopping?"

She was amused to see a slightly panicked look cross his face. "What were you thinking of?"

"Bondage gear. A spandex trapeze leotard. A black leather jacket. Anything but your 'professor who shops at K-Mart' look." Then, graciously, she said, "Unless you actually like that."

"Not especially." Then, after a moment, he said, "Would you like to see me in a black leather jacket?"

She grinned. "We are *definitely* going shopping."

They dozed off for a few hours before the puppies woke them up with barking demands to be fed and entertained. They fed the pups, then went to the motel lobby and paid for the man in the room next door, leaving a note of apology with the clerk. Natalie wrote the first one, but Ransom claimed that it looked like "ME AGONIZE FOR BEING SO NOSY" and wrote a new one himself.

Then they had breakfast at an outdoor café, where they planned their trip back.

"I'd still like to hit Tomato Land again," Natalie said.

"And paraglide?"

"And paraglide. They're both on the way back anyway." She seized his wrist. "And now... we're going shopping."

One mall and three shops later, she decided that she should have put WATCH RANSOM MODEL CLOTHES on her list. It was definitely a bucket list-worthy experience, even though it did require a few trips to the restroom for cold water to the face.

When they checked out of the motel, carrying their bags toward the car with Wally and Heidi at their heels, she took yet another moment to drink him in. Black boots, black jeans, white T-shirt, and black leather jacket; the only color was his red-brown hair. The jeans showed off his legs and the shirt showed off his chest and the jacket brought it all into focus. He looked strong and tough and a little bit dangerous: the kind of man your mother might warn you about.

He caught her eyeing him. "No more professor?"

"Professor Indiana Jones, maybe."

He looked pleased, but said, "I'd need a fedora."

"Not a whip?"

"I already nixed the bondage gear."

She laughed and slid behind the wheel. The wind blew back her hair and the car practically purred under her hands. Ransom kept his arm around her shoulders and Wally sat in his lap with his head on her thigh, while Heidi curled up at his feet.

She had so much, it seemed greedy to want more. Greedy, and reckless, and dangerous. But she did.

By the time they arrived at Tomato Land, it was about to close for the day. They went to the nearby beach instead, the one with the paragliders. The next morning, they'd visit Tomato Land and go paragliding; the morning after, they'd head back to Refuge City.

It was near sunset, with a chilly wind blowing in from the ocean. The puppies weren't bothered, but the few people who'd been on the beach when they arrived soon packed up and left. Natalie shivered. Ransom took off his leather jacket and draped it around her shoulders.

The title of an old movie came to her mind: *An Officer and a Gentleman*. That was Ransom. Though technically speaking, he'd been an enlisted man in the Marines, not literally an—

"Get down!" He flung himself on top of her, crushing her into the sand, then grabbed her and rolled.

A black dart buried itself in the sand an inch from her shoulder. It stuck there, quivering.

Natalie had never seen that sort of dart before, but she remembered the description from Ransom's story. They'd been ambushed by the wizard-scientists.

Her heart skipped a beat.

CHAPTER 23

Ransom shielded Natalie with his body as he scanned the area, his gun steady in his hand. He could feel her muscles take on a smooth tension like a hunting cat's, ready for action.

And he felt it when she froze, the steady rhythm of her breathing breaking into jagged gasps. "Sorry—my heart—"

In all his years of combat, no bomb or gunshot had ever sent a such a shock of terror into him as her soft words. But he kept his voice calm and reassuring as he said. "Do your breathing. Don't worry about anything else. I'll protect you."

A male voice shouted, "Throw your gun into the ocean!"

No, Ransom thought. *It can't be. He's dead and gone.*

But he knew that voice, much as he wanted to deny it. And he had no choice but to obey—not when any sort of fighting in the vicinity could distract Natalie from her breathing.

He tossed his gun into the waves, then examined her. She lay on her side with her eyes closed, her expression one of fierce concentration as she breathed in a slow, deep rhythm. He sat down cross-legged and cradled her head in his lap, stroking her wind-tangled hair.

She's survived this before, he told himself. *She'll survive again if I can buy her enough time.*

Wally blinked in and cuddled up to her, licking her hands. A moment later Heidi appeared, wet and smelling of brine. She shook herself, spattering Ransom with salt water. She planted her paws in the sand and growled, though, low and ominous, her gaze fixed on a boulder.

"Come on out, Jager," Ransom shouted. "I know it's you!"

Jager stepped out from behind the boulder and walked up to them with a quick, familiar stride.

"I should have known better than to believe you were really dead," said Ransom. "You're like a cockroach crawling out from under the rubble."

"I asked Morgana to tell you that," said Jager. "It would have been very disruptive to have you pursuing me at that time."

Insults were obviously going to get Ransom nowhere. "What do you want?"

Jager eyed him with the same dispassionate interest he'd had when they'd worked together in the lab, or when he'd come to Ransom's apartment to see if his enhanced intuition could predict the roll of dice, or when he'd proposed experimenting on human beings without their consent.

"I want you to work with me again," Jager replied. His voice was even, calm, slightly flat. "We're doing very exciting research which I know you'd find fascinating and challenging—"

"On people you kidnapped?" Ransom had to fight to keep his own voice from rising to a shout. He couldn't disturb Natalie. "How many of them have you killed with your *fascinating* research? How many lives have you ruined with your *exciting* experiments?"

Jager's gaze was tolerant, but slightly contemptuous. "Don't be so emotional. It gets in the way of rational thought. Anyway, if that was a real question and not a rhetorical one, of course you'll have access to our mortality data."

Mortality data, Ransom thought. Real people Jager had killed with his experiments, turned into numbers and percentages on a computer screen.

Ransom had thrown away his gun, but that didn't mean he was

helpless. Jager was far too cautious to have walked out alone with no one covering him, but maybe if Ransom moved fast enough...

Don't do it, growled his hellhound. *Stall. Protect your mate.*

Ransom took a deep breath, pacing it to Natalie's. His hellhound was right. It was too dangerous to fight back right now. And he had a perfect opportunity to learn exactly what Jager was up to.

He called back memories of his own past self, that intense young man burying himself in work to avoid facing his inner demons. Trying to sound like the Ransom-who-had-been, he said, "That *would* be interesting. How are you working now? On your own? With the wizard-scientists?"

"With them, for now. But I want to re-start Apex. With you. The wizard-scientists have a fascinating depth of knowledge, but their goals have nothing to do with science."

"What *are* their goals?"

Jager gave a dismissive shrug. "Rule the world, bring back the glory days of the golden age, garbage like that. I don't have any interest in that stuff. I only want to design the weapons—I don't care about the war. So to speak."

Natalie continued her deep breathing, her eyes closed, but beneath Ransom's fingers, her pulse had returned to its steady rhythm. He supposed she too was stalling for time. But time to do what? If he fought Jager, would that be enough stress to stop her heart?

"How much do you know about Apex's first breakthrough program?" Jager asked. "Ultimate Predator 1.0."

Way too much, Ransom thought. He knew three people who'd been put through it, all of them against their will. Two of them had been forced to become assassins, and had been so deeply traumatized that it had taken them years to even begin to recover.

He took a deep breath, controlling his voice. His face. His body. Everything. "It gave people powers. I assume it grew out of the enhanced intuition project."

Jager nodded. "But we took it so much farther than that. What else do you know about it?"

"It killed the majority of the subjects. And that was even when it was administered after turning them into shifters, so they'd be stronger and have better healing abilities. I don't know what the mortality rate was before you started doing that."

"Upwards of ninety percent. Go on."

"It required regular, ongoing treatments. If those weren't kept up, the reaction typically killed the subject." He hesitated, wondering if he should pretend not to know the loophole, but couldn't see any benefit to that. Jager had to have researched him enough to know that the west coast team of Protection, Inc. included three former Apex subjects. "That wears off after a few years, though."

"That's correct. It wasn't an intended effect, though it had its uses."

Uses, Ransom thought. *Like having a time bomb implanted in your heart, so you couldn't run away.*

"2.0 didn't have that. We decided the shortcomings outweighed the benefits. But after observing the wizard-scientists' continuing experiments, I re-thought that. The version used on you and your team—let's call it 3.0—had a number of bugs as well. How's your power working for you?"

Much as it went against Ransom's grain to let an enemy know his weakness, he suspected that not only did Jager probably know plenty already, but he'd be better off letting his former co-worker underestimate him. "It isn't. I use it once, and I'm out of commission for the next day or so."

"And your other power?" Jager spoke casually, but Ransom wasn't fooled. The only person who knew he *had* another power was Natalie. Jager was just fishing.

Ransom shook his head. "That's it. We didn't all get two powers. My boss—my ex-boss—didn't either. He can control fire as a phoenix, but he doesn't have a power as a man. What's all this about, anyway?"

For the first time, Jager smiled. It wasn't a pleasant expression. "It's about how I can make sure you won't promise the world, and then betray me the second I turn my back. It's about that woman you've got an inexplicable but convenient emotional attachment to. Convenient to me, that is." Raising his voice, he said, "Sit up, Nash or whatever you're calling yourself nowadays. I know you're faking it."

Natalie sat up. Sand was crusted down one side of her pale face, and her lips were pressed into a thin and bloodless line. "How do I come in? A test subject for Ultimate Predator 2.0, so I can be a hostage who can never run away?"

Ransom's stomach lurched. He'd had the same thought, but hearing it from her lips made it seem even more horrifyingly plausible.

Jager seemed taken aback, as if he hadn't expected her to be that quick on the uptake. With a flash of anger, he snapped, "No! You're forgetting the loophole. I don't want to get two years' work out of him, then have him run away with you when the need for treatments wears off."

Natalie's expression didn't change, but he felt her give him the tiniest nudge with her elbow. Didn't Jager know she only had a year to live? Had he assumed she'd fainted from shock? It seemed likely that he didn't know, now that Ransom thought about it. Natalie hadn't told anyone.

"Ultimate Predator 2.5," said Jager. "Designed for exactly this sort of situation. The need for booster treatments never wears off. She'll be bound to Apex for life. And so will you. Cross me or run away, and she dies in agony."

Ransom didn't speak, but Heidi seemed to pick up on his rage and horror. She snarled, baring her teeth at Jager.

"Heidi!" Ransom grabbed her by the collar. She might be able to teleport, but she was still just a puppy. Heidi subsided, returning to her low growl.

"What's in it for me?" Natalie asked.

Jager eyed her as if it had been Heidi who had spoken. Dismissively, he said, "This isn't about you. Ransom, what do you say?"

"This is absolutely about me," Natalie said. "Ultimate Predator means I get powers, right? I want more than being held hostage to compensate me for, well, being held hostage. Otherwise I might decide life in captivity isn't worth it, and use my powers on you."

As she spoke, Ransom caught her gaze flicker toward where they'd parked their car, then back to him. He felt sure she was signaling to him that they could fight, then make a run for the car. But what would all that excitement do to her?

"Go on," Natalie said. "Make me an offer."

"I don't have to bargain with *you*, you ignorant little con artist," Jager snapped.

"Oh yes you do," she returned. "I know Ransom's the one you really want, but if I take off and that kills me, then you have nothing to blackmail him with. So if you're going to bargain, you better bargain with *me*."

As she continued baiting Jager into arguing, Ransom thought fast. Her heart condition seemed to be set off by either sexual excitement or sudden shocks. Maybe some running and fighting would be fine, so long as she was prepared for it and knew it was coming. But what if it wasn't? Could she survive two stresses on her heart in quick succession?

It wasn't a risk he was willing to take without having all the information. He needed to *know*.

Then know, growled his hellhound.

Ransom set aside his roiling emotions to evaluate his chances of getting that piece of information without Jager noticing what he was doing, and then being able to fight afterward with what was very likely to be the worst migraine of his life.

I can do it, he decided. He only needed to fight and then get to the car. Once he was in it, Natalie could drive. If they were pursued, he could tell her to call his team. They were good, honorable people, and regardless of what they thought of him, they'd protect her with their lives. She could even call Roland and ask him to leave Merlin out of it.

"Aren't powers enough for you?" Jager demanded.

"Not if they mean being a hostage for life," Natalie retorted. "If I'm going to be a prisoner, I want the world's most luxurious prison."

Ransom lowered his head. He didn't dare close his eyes, but he let them drift out of focus until all he saw was a shimmering, sand-colored blur. He visualized the big double doors within his mind. All the information in the world lay outside those doors. He could find the answer he needed.

Will trying to escape now harm Natalie's heart?

Bracing himself for the pain and the whirlwind, he opened the doors. The flood of information poured over him. But this time his hellhound was at his side, bracing him. Shielding him. And sniffing.

There, barked his hellhound. *That one!*

Ransom snatched it up and slammed the door.

And then he was back on the beach, jaw clenched and heart hammering. Jager and Natalie were still arguing; apparently Ransom had only been gone for a few seconds.

His head ached, but the pain was dull and manageable, not the agony he'd expected. He could easily fight or drive or even read a book. He was tired, but like he'd had a sleepless night, not like he was going to pass out at any second.

More importantly, he had his answer.

Trying to escape now would be safe for Natalie's heart. She'd still be in danger from whatever Jager could throw at them, but she wouldn't be sabotaged by her own body. She was prepared for a fight, and so it wouldn't shock her.

He just hoped she'd be prepared for *this.*

Ransom reached into himself, seeking his hellhound.

He'd never before been able to wear that body without a sickening sense of horror and revulsion at the dark beast within him. But now, in the nanosecond before he sprang at Jager, he felt nothing but relief that he had such a big, strong, fierce form to call upon. Even if he was shot in mid-spring, he'd still crash down on his enemy, hopefully giving Natalie time to escape.

His jaws gaped wide as he leaped, his fiery eyes fixed on his enemy. As a hellhound, the world was tinted scarlet, but he could still see clearly.

The instant before his fangs would have closed on Jager's throat, his enemy vanished.

CHAPTER 24

Natalie had expected Ransom to shift. He'd thrown away his gun, and Jager was deliberately standing too far away for a human to reach him without giving him time to react. She'd grown up among shifters, and she'd seen people become lions and tigers and bears (also white rats, flying squirrels, and calico cats) in the blink of an eye. She just hoped that she was right to assume that he wanted her to run for the car the instant he became a hellhound. Whatever a hellhound was.

But she hadn't expected the beast he became. She'd heard "hound," and thought "dog." But the hellhound was no more a dog than a dragon was a lizard.

He was the size of a pony, but long and lean-bodied, halfway between a Weimaraner and a wolf. His fur was blacker than engine oil or black paint or a moonless night, so black that he seemed like a hound-shaped hole in the world. His eyes were like windows into Hell itself. Smoke wreathed his body, curling around him and dissipating, unaffected by the ocean breeze. Even more eerily, it didn't seem to come from anywhere. It was just... *there.*

Natalie saw all of that in a single, indelible glimpse. The next instant, the hellhound leaped. She had a second of fierce joy, imagining him taking down Jager. Then the great black hound crashed down to the beach and tumbled head over heels. For a terrifying instant, she thought he'd been shot. Then she realized that Jager was gone.

A black dart hit the beach beside one of Ransom's massive front paws.

"Darts!" Natalie shouted. She flung herself to the side and rolled. Another dart barely missed her.

The puppies disappeared. That was a relief. They must have gone somewhere safe.

Ransom became a man again. He bolted toward her, then abruptly dove to the side. A dart thudded into the sand where he had been. He started to scramble to his feet, then ducked. Another dart missed him. She realized that he had to be using his enhanced intuition.

"I'll carry you," he called.

"No need!" She leaped, curling into a ball and spinning over and over until she landed upright on the sand, only to once again catapult herself into the air. He could avoid being hit by knowing when and where the darts were fired; she could do the same by making herself an impossible target.

When she managed a glance behind her, she saw that Ransom was still running, but behind her, slowed by his need to dodge. She'd get to safety first…and that meant she'd need to rescue him.

She varied her movements, sometimes cartwheeling, sometimes diving, always moving, always unpredictable. Her blood sang with the thrill of almost-flying, of her control over her own body, and with the knowledge of danger. Would she be struck by a dart? Would the excitement make her heart stop?

She saw the Mustang parked up ahead, with Heidi and Wally barking urgently from the back seat. Natalie snatched the key from her pocket as she again landed on her feet. She stopped tumbling and ran, hitting the button to roll down the top as she went.

When she hit the point where the sand ended and the parking lot began, she made her final leap. She'd made this move before, but never over so far a distance. If she missed by a fraction of an inch, she could break her kneecaps. If she missed by more, she could break her back.

Her aim was true. She landed with a jolting thud in the driver's seat.

Natalie started the engine and stepped on the gas, swinging the Mustang to the edge of the beach and putting it between Ransom and whoever was shooting at him. She slowed enough for him to wrench open the door and jump into the passenger seat, then floored it out of the parking lot and onto the highway, leaving their enemies behind.

She hoped.

He reached across her and buckled her seatbelt.

"Thanks," she gasped. "Do yours too."

He did. A moment later, Heidi and Wally appeared in his lap.

"Is anyone following us?" Natalie asked. She didn't dare take her gaze off the road.

Ransom was already twisting in his seat to scan behind them. "Not that I can tell. But apparently Jager can teleport. And I didn't see where he went when he disappeared. Did you?"

"No."

"You didn't have any problem when I shifted. Was it because you were expecting it?"

"Yeah. I figured you would."

"So you can handle adrenaline, but not surprises."

"Right…" She saw what he was getting at. "Oh. I should start expecting to get shot at any second now, right? And for Jager to suddenly appear."

"Also for any kind of weird shifters to attack. One of the wizard-scientists turned into a four-headed dragon."

"Seriously?"

"Yeah. Also, since the wizard-scientists are involved, expect some kind of magical attack."

"Like what?"

Ransom spread his hands. "Could be anything. Just… expect the unexpected."

That seemed daunting. On the other hand, she hadn't been raised in a crime circus of shifters for nothing. Not to mention that her entire childhood had been the opposite of stable.

"Expect the unexpected," she murmured to herself. "Jager suddenly appearing. Four-headed dragons. Magic. Darts. Bigfoot. Ransom becoming a hellhound. Anything."

A tomato-shaped sign loomed ahead. She briefly thought of losing any possible pursuit by ducking into Tomato Land and blending into the crowd, then remembered that it was closed for the night.

"Look out!" Ransom shouted.

Natalie had taken her gaze off the road to look at the sign. It was only for an instant, but when she looked back, Jager was standing in the middle of the road, aiming a gun directly at the car.

She swerved. The car spun out, fishtailing. She fought for control, all the while bracing for the impact of a gunshot. She had a brief moment of terror, and an even briefer moment of relief when she saw that Ransom was clutching the puppies tight to his chest.

There was a sudden hard jolt. The puppies yelped, and Natalie was flung forward. Her seatbelt caught her before she could hit the steering wheel. Then she was dangling somehow. She couldn't make sense of her tilted perspective.

"It's all right." Ransom's calm voice settled her fear, even while her confusion remained. "We went into a ditch."

Once he'd explained what had happened, everything she saw made sense. The car was tipped forward, with the front end in a sandy ditch and the rear wheels off the ground. Both she and Ransom had been caught by their seatbelts and were suspended by them. He was still clutching the puppies. None of them seemed to have been hurt. Even the Mustang didn't seem badly damaged, but it was very thoroughly stuck.

"Where's Jager?" She looked all around, but she saw nothing but the side of the road, the highway, the mountains, and the sea. And the sign for Tomato Land, of course. They were lucky she hadn't hit that. "I don't see him anywhere."

Ransom tried to look past the squirming puppies he held. "He must have teleported again. I don't see him, and I'm not getting any 'immediate danger' signals."

Heidi gave a sharp bark and vanished, reappearing outside the car.

"Go, Wally," Natalie said. "Go to your sister."

Wally appeared beside Heidi.

"Don't move," Ransom said. "I'll get out, and then I'll get you out."

"Actually…" Natalie slithered out of the seatbelt and landed lightly on her feet beside the car. "Here. Put your hands on my shoulders, and your left foot right here…"

He followed her instructions. When she unsnapped his seatbelt, he was able to jump to the ground. "I forgot. This is much more your kind of thing."

"I can't believe you forgot already that I jumped into the driver's seat. Or were you too busy dodging darts to catch that?"

"No, no, I saw it. I only wish I hadn't been dodging darts, so I could have enjoyed the entire thing. You were amazing."

"So were you. You were so quick, and brave, and I finally got to see your hellhound! Wow, was that not what I'd expected."

"What had you expected?"

She shrugged. "A greyhound with little red devil horns?"

Ransom gave a startled laugh. "What did you think of the real thing?"

"It was awesome. In the old sense of the word. I felt awed. It was like seeing a wild tiger in the jungle. It's a predator that could kill you in a second if it decided to, but it's beautiful, too. Breathtaking. Only the hellhound was more than that. It was… unearthly."

"But it didn't shock you."

"No."

"Or scare you?"

She took his hand. "Ransom, it was *you*. There's nothing about you that scares me or horrifies me or repulses me."

The sun had gone down, leaving only a fading blue-gray light. She could see him swallow, and a shine in his eyes that might have been tears.

"Thank you. I wish…" His voice cracked, and he swallowed again. "I wish you could believe in yourself like that."

She wasn't sure what he meant. There was nothing about herself that she found frightening or horrifying or repulsive. But he kept on looking at her with those sad eyes of his—with those eyes that, for a while, hadn't been sad at all—then sighed and looked away.

He spotted something on the ground and stooped to pick it up. It took her a moment to recognize it as part of a cell phone. "You don't still have yours, do you?"

She shook her head. "I lost my purse at the beach."

"We have to get to somewhere safe… Safer, anyway. We're completely exposed here."

"Tomato Land," said Natalie. When he turned to stare at her, she said, "I'm serious. It's big, it has lots of hiding places, and between us, we could break into any of them."

His incredulous expression shifted to agreement. "You're right. We'd have a much better chance in there. And if Jager doesn't show up again, we can wait till morning and then borrow someone's phone when they open."

They walked the short distance alongside the highway, then cut across the Tomato Land parking lot. There didn't seem to be any real security beyond a chain link fence. They climbed the fence, and the puppies teleported through.

Tomato Land was a very different place after hours. The light was rapidly dimming, and the buildings were only vague, dark shapes. They looked ominous, like haunted houses. The vines twining over the entrance looked like snakes.

Expect anything, Natalie reminded herself. *Jager. Giant opossums with twelve heads. Purple toads with devil horns. Flying—*

A set of floodlights came on. Natalie was startled, but not shocked; Ransom's hand leaped to his hip, then dropped when he found no gun.

"I think they're on a timer," she said.

"Well—that's good. It'll be harder for anyone to sneak up on us."

Natalie wasn't so sure. The floodlights were harsh and white, casting pools of light that only deepened the shadows around them. If anything, they made what she could see of the deserted Tomato Land even eerier. The knife-shaped Viking ship hung motionless, like a sword some giant might stoop to snatch up at any moment, and the tomato vine water slide looked like an immense cobra rearing up over a well of darkness.

Expect the giant snake slide to come to life, she told herself. *Expect that tentacle-shaped shadow to suddenly grab your ankle.*

A hand touched her shoulder, and she let out a strangled shriek.

Ransom yanked his hand back like he'd been burned. "Sorry!"

Natalie giggled, a little hysterically. "No, I'm sorry. I was trying to expect anything, and I think I overdid it."

She was about to explain what she meant, but he said, "Did you feel like everything was alive and watching you?"

"Was that what the enhanced intuition was like when you first got it?"

He nodded. "Tomato Land after dark is giving me a bit of the same feeling. I'm trying not to let it get to me."

"I can't believe we survived a car crash and a teleporting enemy and getting shot at, and we're getting creeped out by a water slide."

He gave her a wry smile. "Are you regretting every horror novel you've ever read? Because I sure am."

"No, I'm not," she said firmly, averting her eyes from a gently bobbing blow-up tomato worm. It was moving in the breeze, that was all, not of its own accord. "Because now I know what not to do in a creepy amusement park at night."

"Don't go into the basement," said Ransom.

"Don't eat the candy," said Natalie.

"Don't investigate the weird noise."

"Don't strip down to your underwear to investigate the weird noise."

"And whatever you do…" Ransom paused, and they both finished, "Don't go near the clown!"

They laughed, and her tension eased. As they ventured farther into Tomato Land, she remained alert but didn't jump at every moving shadow. Ransom moved with the cool competence that she suspected was a holdover from the Marines, wary but not hypervigilant.

"Where do you think would be a good place to hunker down?" she asked.

"The bomb shelter would be the most defensible," he began.

"Ransom, no. That hits 'don't go in the basement' *and* 'don't lock yourself in with the creepy animatronics that are definitely going to come to life and grab you.'"

He chuckled. "I was going to say, 'but too easy to get trapped in.' One of the stalls would probably be best. Let's check them out."

They stepped out of the pool of light they were standing in and into the shadowy area of the stalls. Natalie went ahead of him to inspect the locks.

"Get back!" Ransom shouted. "Back to the light!"

Startled, she whirled around. He snatched up Heidi, who was snuffling around at his feet. And that was all that either of them had time to do.

The shadow they stood in rose up from the ground. It covered her feet and legs, tight and clinging and cold and utterly unyielding, pinning her where she stood. Ransom too was caught, trapped in shadow from the waist down.

"Ransom, shift! Your hellhound might be strong enough to—"

But he was shaking his head. "I can't even hear him, let alone reach him. This stuff seems to stop powers from working."

"It's not touching Heidi," Natalie said.

Quickly, Ransom ordered, "Heidi! Go somewhere safe!"

She vanished. But Wally had all four paws mired in shadow. He stood there struggling and yelping frantically, unable to teleport away.

"It's all right, Wally," Natalie called, feeling like the world's biggest liar.

She couldn't reach him, but he calmed down at the sound of her voice. At least, he stopped yelping and started whining. Ransom was too far away to touch either of them, and she didn't see Heidi anywhere.

"This has to be the wizard-scientists. Or it could be Jager, I guess.

But the Ultimate Predator powers aren't usually this..." He made a vague gesture.

"Trashy horror novel?"

Ransom managed a smile. "Yes. Exactly."

A woman stepped out of the shadows. She looked about Natalie's age, with long blonde hair and pale eyes, wearing a white coat embroidered with black symbols. It was open at the front, revealing what looked like a bodysuit but was darker than any cloth could be, dark as the fur of Ransom's hellhound. With a shudder, Natalie realized that it was probably made of shadows.

"Ultimate Predator powers aren't this *powerful*," said the woman. Then she turned her back on Natalie and addressed Ransom. "Greetings, Dark Knight. My name is Elayne."

"My name is Ransom."

"Not for long. I have an offer for you. An offer… and a new name. Better than that, a new identity." Elayne looked him over with a sharpness that unnerved Natalie. It was an expression that she'd often seen on Ransom's own face, when he was talking about something that interested him and that he knew a lot about.

He was silent, watching her with equal intentness.

Just studying his enemy, Natalie told herself. *Figuring her out, so he can rescue us all.*

"I know how you've wished you could erase your past," Elayne went on. "I knew how you've wanted to get rid of parts of yourself. I can give that to you. I can take away everything about you that you hate, everything that causes you pain, and give you something new."

"Really." His voice was flat.

He's stalling, Natalie told herself. *He's inviting her to talk so he can gather information.*

She wanted to believe that. She *had* to believe that. After everything that they'd gone through together, after the new relationship he'd forged with his hellhound and himself, surely he wouldn't throw it all away in order to exist without pain.

But a voice within herself, dark as the shadows that bound her, said, *Wouldn't he?*

And then, *Isn't that what you've been doing?*

She shied away from that thought. There was no time for it, anyway. Elayne was speaking again.

"I can take away your pain," Elayne said. "I can silence your hellhound."

His head jerked up sharply. "What makes you think I'd want that?"

"Your hellhound is you. And I know all about you. I've studied you like a textbook or a book of spells. Everything you've done speaks of how much you hate yourself. So I can guess at what sort of things your hellhound says to you. Join me, and you'll never hear its voice again."

"You can really do that?" Ransom's face and voice were open and raw, like they'd been when he'd told Natalie about his hellhound, or about the enhanced intuition project, or high school. Or that he loved her.

He's conning her, Natalie thought fiercely. *He's using real feelings for a false purpose, to make himself sound convincing. It's a classic trick.*

She tried not to think that he'd never been able to do that before.

"Yes, I can," Elayne assured him. "And I can do more. Every bit of pain you feel, I can take away. I know your powers don't work right. I know they hurt you. I can fix that. I know there's been a sadness in you, all your life. I can take it away. I know you lie awake at night tortured by guilt. I can take that away too. Everything that hurts you will be gone. You can't imagine how free you'll feel without it."

Elayne sounded so honest. So *reasonable*. Natalie had never hated anyone so much in her life, not even the fake foster parents with the big, beautiful house.

But Ransom didn't look like he hated her. He looked at Elayne the way Natalie must have looked at the fake foster parents when they'd promised her a family and a home.

Natalie longed to shout at him not to listen. She wanted to tell him that Elayne was a liar, like the fake parents. If Elayne really could take away his pain, she wouldn't do it in any way that he'd want. It would be like when he'd tried to destroy his hellhound, only worse. She'd cut away his pain and his self along with it, leaving him an empty shell.

Natalie wanted to tell him that so much that she had to bite her lip to keep herself silent. The sharp coppery taste of blood was her reminder to herself to trust him. If he was conning Elayne, he had a plan and she had to play along. Ransom was smart—Ransom was *brilliant*—and if he wanted her to chime in now, he'd have found some way to signal to her.

"What about Jager?" Ransom asked abruptly. "He talked to me, too."

Elayne nodded. "Yes, Jager and I made a deal. We both want you, so we decided that the only fair thing was to allow you to choose. He made you an offer, but from the way you arrived here, it seems like your answer was no. So now it's my turn."

"Jager didn't *offer* me anything. He threatened me. You're the only one making an actual offer. And I have to say… it's tempting. If I take it, what do I have to do for you?"

Natalie recognized the greedy gleam in Elayne's eyes. Ransom *was* playing her. Elayne was a mark, and he had her on the hook. The eagerness in her voice was unmistakable as she said, "You didn't ask what I'd do with your pain, or how I'd take it from you. I can wall it away from you, so you don't feel it yourself but can project it into others. It will become your weapon that will drop your enemies—our enemies—in their tracks. All I ask of you is that you join us. You will be the first of our Dark Knights, and your name will be Despair."

He was silent for a long time. Then he said, "I accept. Get rid of this stuff."

He waved a hand at the shadows, encompassing Natalie and Wally as if they were completely unimportant.

Elayne's greedy gleam intensified, but it was joined by a cunning that Natalie didn't like at all. "Excellent. There's just one little thing we need to settle before our deal can be sealed. It's the matter of your guttersnipe girlfriend and the gone dogs. Where's the other one, by the way?"

Ransom's gaze flickered to Natalie, and she knew, with as much certainty as he felt when he *knew*, that her time to speak had come.

"Heidi's gone, like you said," Natalie told Elayne.

"That's what they're called, Natalie. They're 'gone dogs.' Gone, like 'not there.'" Ransom's voice practically dripped with condescension. If that didn't convince Elayne that he didn't care about Natalie, nothing would. To Elayne, he said, "I don't know where the other one went. It takes off and comes back all the time. It'll be back. What were you doing with the magical animals, anyway?"

"You'll learn that and much more when you become Despair," replied Elayne. "First, I want proof of your commitment."

"Sure." He made an awkward movement, as if he was trying to walk away, then glanced down at himself. Apologetically, he said, "Er, I'm still stuck."

Elayne started to raise her hand, then caught herself.

Dammit, Natalie thought. *That was so close!*

Elayne made a complex series of gestures with both hands. "There. You can walk now. Move slowly, or you'll lose your balance."

Ransom cautiously lifted one foot. The shadows stretched between his sole and the ground, as if he was stuck in black tar. He gave a shudder that Natalie was certain wasn't part of the act.

"Proof of commitment," repeated Elayne. "Don't harm the gone dog; I have plans for it. Kill the woman."

Natalie bit down on her lip again, suppressing her shock. *Expect anything. Anything!*

She didn't know what Ransom intended to do, but the shadows caught him before he could do it. All she saw was him making a quick movement, then falling to his knees. The shadows rippled around him in a way that she couldn't help interpreting as eagerness. Or worse, hunger.

"Don't try to trick me," said Elayne. Her voice was as cold and inhuman as the shadows. "My offer still stands. I can take away your guilt. I can even take away the memory. It'll hurt, but only for a short while. And then you'll never hurt again."

He struggled fiercely, but to no avail. The shadows rose around him, oozing up to catch his hands and lock them against his sides. Natalie could do nothing but watch helplessly as he sank down, sweating and gasping and mired in darkness.

"I thought as much," said Elayne. "You really do care about her. What an unfortunate complication. That's why I went to the motel where she was staying, before you went on your little trip. I was going to remove her from the equation. But you got ahead of me. It took us this long to track you down."

Remove me from the equation, Natalie thought with a shudder. Ransom really had saved her life.

Elayne went on, "She's your mate, isn't she?"

"Yes." Ransom's voice was hoarse, but his gaze was calm. "I'd die before I'd hurt her. And if you try to hurt her, I'll fight to the death to save her, and then I'll be dead and of no use to you."

"I'd prefer you dead than of no use to me," said Elayne sharply. "As you've no doubt figured out, I can't alter your emotions if you fight me. I need you to surrender control and let me do it."

"Never," said Ransom.

With an eerie false cheer, Elayne said, "Never say never."

She raised her hand, and the shadows rose to swallow Natalie. They oozed up her body, slick and cold, until she too had her hands trapped. She could do nothing but watch as Elayne strode across them. They dimpled beneath her feet, as if she was a water strider skating across a pond.

"Don't touch her!" Ransom shouted. "I'll do whatever you want!"

Elayne paused. She was so close that Natalie could have raised a hand and slapped her, if her hands weren't trapped.

"Ransom, don't!" Natalie called back. Tears slid down her cheeks, hot as the shadows were cold, as she said, "It doesn't matter! I'm dying anyway. Don't throw away your own life!"

"I'll do it!" Ransom yelled. "Elayne! I accept!"

"No, don't, don't!" shouted Natalie. "Don't you dare!"

Elayne clapped her hands sharply. "If you don't both stop yelling, I'll gag you with shadows."

Natalie closed her mouth so quickly that her teeth snapped together. Ransom's face was white against the darkness that trapped him.

"Luckily for me, I'm not alone," said Elayne. "And I brought someone who can help me determine the truth. Costello!"

Another woman walked out from between a pair of tomato-shaped tents. Costello wore a black shirt and pants—made of cloth, not shadows—and looked tough but in an ordinary way, like a security guard or a soldier. She edged around the shadows that Elayne was controlling until she could look at Ransom straight-on from about six feet away.

"Now answer me again," said Elayne. "Do you accept my offer?"

"If you don't harm Natalie, yes," he said.

"He's lying," said Costello.

"I'm not," said Ransom. "She's wrong."

Elayne shot an annoyed look at him. "She can't be wrong. It's one of her Ultimate Predator powers. One last chance. If you agree to let me into your mind, will you use the opportunity to try to attack me or escape with your mate?"

"No," said Ransom.

"Lying again," said Costello.

"That woman is playing some kind of game with you, Elayne," said Ransom. "Maybe *she* wants to be the Dark Knight."

Natalie kept her expression blank, but inwardly, she cheered him on. It probably wouldn't work, but it was a good try.

Elayne gave an exasperated sigh, then reached into her coat pocket and removed a syringe filled with a cloudy liquid. Natalie jerked backward, or tried to; the shadows clung tight, holding her still.

Natalie spat in Elayne's face.

Elayne let out a shriek of shock and fury. The shadows holding Natalie felt less tight. She put all the strength she had into leaping free. For a second, she thought she'd succeeded. Then she fell over, caught around the ankles and wrists. At the same moment, Ransom lunged forward, but also went sprawling.

But in the midst of her fear and anger, Natalie saw something that gladdened her heart. The shadows had left Wally to surge up around the humans.

"Go!" Natalie yelled. "Go to Heidi!"

Elayne whipped around, but she was too late. Wally had vanished.

Lying on the ground, trapped in clammy shadows like quicksand, unable to touch each other or fight back, Natalie and Ransom looked at each other and took comfort in their shared relief.

"What a good doggo," she said.

"You saved him," said Ransom. "You nearly saved all of us."

A sharp, small pain like a bee sting stabbed Natalie's upper arm. Elayne straightened up, the empty syringe in her hand.

A fear even colder than the shadows clenched around Natalie's heart. "What was that?"

"For you?" Elayne's lip curled. "Death. Unless your mate takes my offer."

"Poison?" asked Ransom. He could do nothing to fight back, but if Natalie had been Elayne, she'd have run. The chill in his voice and eyes reminded her that in the Marines, he'd been a sniper.

"Adrenaline," said Elayne. "Altered with a little chemistry and a little magic. The effect is slower, but more intense. For a normal person, it would be unpleasant but not dangerous: like a severe panic attack. For someone with a heart condition, no amount of deep breathing and calming thoughts can save them."

Natalie clamped down on her panic. For all she knew, the syringe had been filled with colored water and Elayne was just messing with her.

But she could feel her heart speeding up.

Elayne snapped her fingers. Two men and a woman came out, all in black pants and shirts like Costello. Of the men, one was big as a pro wrestler, and one was normal-tough like Costello. The woman was skinny, even wispy, and didn't look at all like a fighter.

"Norris, get him in shiftsilver cuffs," said Elayne to the big man. "Regular for her. I'll clear a path."

Elayne gestured, and the shadows oozed aside, allowing her people to get to Ransom and Natalie. She gestured again, and the cold, clinging shadows withdrew from their wrists... but not their hands. Natalie ground her teeth in frustration as Norris cuffed Ransom and Costello cuffed her.

Only then did Elayne gesture to make all her shadows vanish. She staggered, panting, and Costello grabbed her shoulder.

"I'm fine," snapped Elayne, shaking him off. But she stealthily leaned against a stall.

Natalie would have been glad to see that Elayne could only control her shadows for so long, and that doing so drained her. But she had other things to worry about. Her heart was pounding, and she felt short of breath. A cold sweat was making her clothes stick to her body. And hard as she tried to stay calm and breathe deeply, she was terrified.

"Chain them up in the bomb shelter," said Elayne. She put a walkie-talkie in Ransom's hand. "You have half an hour or so to wrestle with your conscience. If you can honestly tell me that you'll join me, hit the button to call in. Costello will come down and make sure you're telling the truth. If you are, I'll give your mate the antidote. And I'll give her something else too: a cure."

"Liar! There is no cure!" Natalie's voice came out breathless and shrill, not forceful like she'd intended.

"I can command shadows," said Elayne, still addressing Ransom. "I can take away your pain and your memories. You think I can't fix her heart?"

"How?" said Ransom.

"Magic," said Elayne. "And science. I could give you all the details, but it would take more time than she has. Think about it."

The next thing Natalie knew, she and Ransom were being dragged into the History of the Tomato tent, then down the stairs. She wanted to kick Elayne's minions in the shins, but with their hands cuffed, a fall down the stairs could break her neck. Or worse, Ransom's.

Dim emergency lights illuminated the carriages and animatronic figures. Costello and Norris shoved Ransom and Natalie to the ground, then used two more pairs of handcuffs to lock them to the tomato carriage track by their ankles. They were taking no chances on getting jumped. Then they went back up the stairs and slammed the door, leaving Ransom and Natalie alone on the floor.

They strained toward each other, but they were too far away to touch. Natalie subsided, dizzy from the effort.

"About your heart—" Ransom began.

"Don't even think of taking her offer! She'd use you to kill innocent people. And I don't believe she has a cure, anyway."

"That's not what I meant." He was trying his hardest to sound calm, but she could hear the fear and anger beneath it, like an undercurrent. "I love you, and I'm not going to let you die."

She knew he wanted her to promise that she wouldn't. But she couldn't let her last words be a lie. "I love you."

He looked at her like he'd heard her thoughts, and wanted to argue with her. Then he shook his head. "I'm going to use my power to find out how to save you. Lie still and breathe. It'll only take a minute or so."

He closed his eyes. But Natalie didn't lie still. He'd already tried to use his power that way, and it hadn't worked. It wasn't going to be any different now. But she refused to die until she could save him.

If she'd had her legs free, she'd have already been out of the handcuffs. All she'd have needed to do was push her legs up and back through the ring of her arms until her cuffed hands were in front of her body, remove her lockpicks from the secret pocket inside her bra, and open the cuffs.

With one ankle locked to the track, it was more difficult. It was especially more difficult when her heart was staggering like a drunk, she couldn't get enough air into her lungs, and that damn adrenaline-induced panic kept threatening to overwhelm her. But Ransom wasn't close enough to reach the lockpicks. She was the only one who could save him.

"Houdini would be out by now," Natalie muttered to herself as she worked one leg back between her arms.

She twisted her body until her shoulder threatened to come out of its socket, and managed to extract the lockpicks with her left hand. Of course it had to be the left. But she'd practiced working with her off-hand, and though it wasn't easy, she managed to get her own cuffs open.

After that, it was quick work to unlock her foot, then go to Ransom and unlock him. As she opened the cuff around his ankle, his eyes opened. There were creases of pain around them, and they looked sadder than ever.

"You didn't get anything?"

His bleak expression was the answer. "I could try again—"

"How many times have you tried asking that question?"

"A couple," he muttered, which she supposed was code for "I laid myself out in excruciating pain repeatedly, and always for nothing." Then he glanced down. "You got us loose." A desperate light burned in his eyes. "Forget my power. Let me bite you. It *might* work. It's a small chance, but—"

That again. The same small chance, the same *might* that he'd been talking about from the very beginning.

This is going to break his heart, she thought. Hoping and then being disappointed was the worst pain in the world.

But he'd never give up until he saw for himself that it wouldn't work. If she let him try, once he saw that it had failed, then he could turn his attention to escape. Natalie couldn't let him die because she was too stubborn to say yes.

"Do it," she said.

He got up and stepped back. The room filled with the smell of woodsmoke, and the great hound loomed over her. He bent down—she could feel the heat of his fiery eyes—and bit her at the junction of the neck and the shoulder.

Then Ransom was back, lifting her into his arms. "I thought I should get it as close to your brain and heart as I could, in case that makes it work faster. It should only take a minute or so. It doesn't hurt too badly, does it?"

"No." A cold numbness had spread through her body. She'd barely felt his teeth go in. She couldn't feel the heat of his arms, either. All she could feel was her heart, fluttering more and more weakly within her chest, and the painful laboring of her lungs.

He held her close, his cheek pressed to hers, while they waited. Finally, he said, "Do you feel anything?"

She shook her head.

"This has to work!" Ransom shouted. His eyes were wild, his calm shattered. "It has to!"

The agony in his voice tore at her heart. If only she could live for him. If only she could bring herself back the way she'd brought him back, with a kiss...

The memory of that kiss was more vivid in her mind than anything happening in the present. The freezing water, the cold of his lips, the faint taste that must have been shiftsilver, metallic and burning...

Natalie fumbled inside her bra. Her fingers touched the vial of shiftsilver, but couldn't grasp it.

"Help me," she whispered, but couldn't go on.

She could barely hear her own voice. But at least she wouldn't need to explain her idea to Ransom. As soon as he saw what she had, he'd immediately know what she was thinking: if a bite alone couldn't change her, maybe the shiftsilver could send her deep enough to find her inner hellhound and draw it out.

The darkness had closed in on her. She couldn't see him, but she felt his hands over hers as he took the vial from her, opened it, and held it to her lips. She swallowed. It tasted like metal and burned going down.

And then she was somewhere else. Natalie blinked into the bright afternoon sunlight. Dust swirled around her ankles, powdery as flour.

She looked down at herself, half-expecting to see a child's body. But no, she was her adult self... but dressed in that same faded dress she'd worn as a child. She touched her hair and found the short tousled cut she always had. Suspicious, she pulled a lock into view. It was her natural shade, the yellow-brown of dust.

Slowly, she raised her head, certain of what she'd see. And there it was. The big, beautiful house. Natalie shuddered. She'd rather walk into Elayne's shadows than go back inside that house, but she somehow knew that her hellhound was in it.

There was no point delaying. Her body was dying, and she had to move fast if she was going to save herself. Natalie ran headlong at the house.

Abruptly, she was inside. In the basement, a room where the kids had sometimes been sent to fetch things. It was dark, with the shelves of stuff barely visible.

"Hello?" Natalie called.

What do you want? The voice was a low growl that was nonetheless distinctly female.

"You. I want you."

An impatient snort echoed in the darkness. *What do you* want?

"I want to live."

What will you give?

"Uh… My love?"

An even more impatient snort. *What will you risk?*

This wasn't how she had expected the encounter to go, and she could feel the seconds ticking away. Ransom had only had to pet his hellhound, not play the world's most nervewracking game of Twenty Questions.

"My life?"

A long, unnerving growl made the jars on the shelves rattle. *Your life. The life you refuse to believe can be saved.*

"But I do believe it! I let Ransom bite me. And here I am."

That reply was met with silence. Apparently her hellhound was sulking.

Natalie thought frantically. What was she doing wrong? Was she supposed to go into the darkness and pet her hellhound? Apart from the shelves around her, she couldn't see a thing. For all she knew, there was no floor, except for the bit she was standing on. A single step forward might send her plunging into a bottomless pit.

Whatever she did, she had to do it fast. Ransom must be losing his mind, sitting in the darkness with her limp body. He'd be so disappointed if he couldn't save her, after he'd been reckless enough to keep on hoping…

"Oh," Natalie whispered. *"That's* what you want."

The growl that rattled the shelves sounded encouraging. Or maybe challenging.

What her hellhound wanted from her was hope. To save her own life—to save Ransom from falling back into despair—to have any chance of having a life with him—Natalie had to do the one thing that terrified her. She had to believe in the possibility that she might live. And not only for a little while longer, but for an entire lifetime.

She had to believe that she might have everything she'd ever wanted, and that believing in it wouldn't mean it would immediately be snatched away.

She had to hope so hard that being disappointed would feel worse than dying. And if she *was* disappointed, she couldn't just die and be done with it all. She'd have to endure that pain, get up, and hope again.

Natalie thought of Ransom, waiting for her in the dark. And she closed her eyes and stepped forward, hoping to touch soft fur.

CHAPTER 25

Ransom cradled Natalie in his arms. She was so cold, and he could barely feel her breathing. He'd bitten her, but nothing had happened. He'd helped her with her brilliant idea to drink tincture of shiftsilver, but *still* nothing had happened.

A bark cut through the silence. Wally appeared beside them, a ball of white in the dimness. He whined urgently as he nuzzled Natalie, but she didn't stir.

Just a small chance of saving her, Ransom thought. *That's all I ever had.*

The darkness of despair tugged at him, like an undertow dragging him into a cold and empty sea. It was dreadful, but also tempting. If he gave in to it, at least the endless, excruciating struggle would be over.

She is our mate, his hellhound growled. *Fight for her!*

Ransom had no idea how he was supposed to do that. He'd already done everything he could. But his hellhound's words steadied him, as if he'd been thrashing around in the water, and then felt sand beneath his feet. Natalie needed him, even if he didn't know what to do to help her. He couldn't give up.

"Find your hound," he whispered in her ear. "She's there, somewhere. You can find her. Reach out to her, Natalie. Reach out. I'm with you. I love you. You can do this…"

He kissed her chilly lips. A tear ran down his cheek, hot as shiftsilver, and splashed on her icy skin.

Natalie gasped. Her limp body abruptly came to life as she clutched at him. He held her tight as her skin warmed against his, feeling the rhythmic pulse of her heart. When she looked up, her eyes held the same irrepressible spark he'd always loved, but there was something new in them too. Behind the glitter and the razzle-dazzle, there was a strength and steadiness he'd never seen before.

"Come on," she said, her voice husky with desire. "Don't stop there."

He didn't have to ask if it was safe. She was breathing easily, she was warm in his arms, she'd gone deep within herself and come back again. With the same instinct that told him that she was his mate, he knew that she'd never ask him to do anything that could hurt her.

He'd spent so much time longing to kiss her and imagining kissing her and remembering their one kiss before its disastrous end. But actually doing it put all of that to shame. Their mouths met in a blaze of heat and passion. He didn't know how long it lasted, but it felt like an eternity of bliss. Heat surged through his body, making him feel like he'd been the one to come back to life. When the kiss finally ended, they still held each other tight, as if they'd never truly let go.

"I'm going to live," she said.

The hope he felt was as piercing as pain. "You're healed? Completely?"

"I'm definitely not dying right now. Beyond that…" She shrugged. "Who knows. I'll probably have to see a doctor to find out for sure. But once we get out of this, I'll do it. I won't give up rollercoasters and horror movies, but if they want me to take pills, I'll take them. I want to have a life. With you."

Ransom swallowed, so overwhelmed with relief that he couldn't speak.

She touched his cheek, tracing the path of his tear. "You saved me. You always knew you could, and you were right."

Remembering his own meeting with his hellhound, he said, "You must have saved yourself, too."

"I was in the dark—I never even saw my hound. She wouldn't let me near her until I was willing to believe I could have a future. I had to take a leap of faith to reach her. Literally." Natalie's gaze took on a distant look. "She's me, right? The part of myself I buried so deep, a flying squirrel and a dragon couldn't pull it out. She's my hope."

"Hope." Ransom's voice came out rough and choked. "I'm glad you found it."

Wally gave a sharp yip. Natalie stroked him. "Hey, Wally. I have a hellhound in me now. Can you sense her?"

He barked, sniffed all around Natalie, then sneezed. She giggled, then sobered. "Where do you think Heidi is?"

"I told her to fetch your purse, so we could have your phone. But if she knew what that meant or if it was easy for her to get to, she'd be back by now." He tried not to worry about her. She could teleport; she was safer than any of them.

"I could ask Wally," Natalie said doubtfully. "Though I'm not sure he knows what it means either."

"I think the magical animals have a special bond with their owners," Ransom said. "I've seen them do some very unusual things to help out. Try picturing him bringing your purse to you when you ask him."

Natalie stared intently into Wally's eyes, and said, "Wally, fetch me my purse."

He rolled over and paddled his legs in the air. Natalie scratched his belly, making his legs paddle faster. He wagged his tail and yipped happily.

"Okay, let me stop distracting him…" She stopped scratching him. He paddled his legs even faster, with a distinctly hopeful air. "Wally. Fetch my purse!"

Wally flopped down on his side and drooled on her foot.

"Fetch!" Natalie commanded.

He vanished. Natalie grabbed Ransom's hand. "He's doing it!"

Wally reappeared with a rubber tomato in his mouth, dropped it at Natalie's feet, and wagged his tail.

"This is not giving me high hopes for where Heidi went," said Ransom.

"Maybe I should just send him away, so he's safe. I'm pretty sure he knows 'go to Heidi.'" The instant she said that, he vanished. They waited, but he didn't return. "Why do I think neither of them is anywhere near my purse right now?"

"They're probably inside a pastry case," Ransom said.

"Hopefully not eating any chocolate. Well—we know they can find us. I guess they'll come back when it's all over."

She stood up and stretched. Her ease and comfort with her own body had returned, along with her usual grace. Despite their desperate situation, seeing her well and strong again filled him with a deep and resounding joy.

"Want to practice turning into your hellhound before we break out?"

Her face scrunched up quizzically. "Um, how do I do that?"

He'd never had any difficulty with that, himself; if anything, he'd had to hold his hellhound back. "You picture your hellhound, and you let it—her—come forward."

Natalie closed her eyes. After a minute or so, she opened them, frowning. "I know she's there, but I can't get her to come out."

"It's okay. She'll come out when you need her. At least, that's how it seemed to work for my teammates."

"I don't want to rely on that. Let's scrounge up some weapons." She ran to the nearest animatronic figure, an astronaut holding a pouch of red powder, and tugged at his hand.

"You're going to throw dehydrated tomato powder in their faces?"

"I was going to rip off his arm and hit them over the head with it, but it's attached pretty tightly," she replied. "Come on, let's see if any of them have any dangerous props."

"Good idea."

They made a quick inspection of the animatronic figures. Natalie was briefly excited by the caveman's club, but it turned out to be painted styrofoam. The cowboy's pistol, unsurprisingly, was a toy. But his whip was real. Ransom pulled it out and gave it an experimental crack. It echoed in the cavernous space like a gunshot.

"Indiana Jones," said Natalie, grinning. "Keep it."

He stuck it in his belt, then rummaged through the props on the remaining figures. Nothing seemed particularly promising. The Viking broadsword was painted plywood. Marie Curie's beaker of radium was plastic with an LED that made it glow. Then he checked the California frontiersman who was taking a break from panning for gold to refresh himself with a tomato. "The river rocks are real. Small, but I think they'd be pretty distracting if you got one thrown in your face."

"Oh, I can do better than that." She went to the cowboy, confiscated his neckerchief, and folded it deftly.

"Is that a slingshot?"

"Uh-huh. I used to be pretty good with one. I'd hide in the rigging and try to bean Fausto with a peanut when he was a flying squirrel." She strapped the pirate's gunpowder pouch around her slim waist, then filled it with as many river rocks as it would hold. "There. I'm ready."

She stood small and fearless in the dim light, armed with nothing but a handful of rocks and an uncooperative inner hellhound.

That's my mate, he thought with pride.

They were imprisoned, outgunned, and outnumbered, but he'd never been so happy in his entire life. He bent and stole a quick kiss, which she returned with interest.

"Just wait till we're alone and not locked up by evil scientists," Natalie muttered. "I am going to ride you like I'm that cowboy and you're the bucking bronco."

The image of that briefly drove all other thoughts from his mind. "We're going to make up for so much lost time… But first, we have to get out. Let me use my power to see what it looks like outside."

He closed his eyes and visualized the doors in his mind. But when he tried to open them, they felt incredibly heavy. He struggled to push them open, but even with the aid of his hellhound, they wouldn't budge.

You are tiring yourself out, warned his hellhound. *You must save some strength to fight.*

Ransom opened his eyes. He was sweating, his head aching and heart pounding, breathing like he'd run a mile at an all-out sprint. "I didn't get anything. I used my power too often today already. I could've pushed harder, but..."

Natalie shook her head. "Don't. I'd rather have you able to fight whatever we find outside than know exactly what's there but be too worn out to fight it."

"Yeah, same here." He forced his breathing back under control, wiped the sweat out of his eyes, and said, "Whoever's out there, we'll hit them hard, take them by surprise, then run. Our car's disabled, but they have to have parked somewhere. You run to the parking lot and hotwire whatever you see. I'll hold them off."

"Then we drive out of here like a bat out of hell! I mean, like a pair of hellhounds out of hell!"

Hand in hand, they crept softly up the stairs. Natalie took out her lockpicks and began working on the lock while Ransom stood guard. He had the whip in his belt, but doubted that he'd use it once he was out in the open and had enough room to become a hellhound.

The door gave a soft click.

"Stay out of the shadows," he whispered.

"You too," she murmured back.

He waved her to the side. She flattened herself against the wall as he flung the door open. He was already shifting as he lunged through the doorway. With his red-tinted vision, he had a split second to see that the entrance was guarded by Costello the human lie-detector and the big man, Norris. They were too far apart for him to be able to bowl them both over in a single jump; he had to pick one. Ransom leaped at Norris.

He slammed into what felt like a metal wall and bounced off. Dazed, he scrambled to his feet and blinked bewilderedly at an immense armored...

…fish.

It was massive, the size and bulk of a bus, and the head alone was taller than he was. Its fins splayed out on the ground, blocking his way.

A Dunkleosteus, Ransom's power helpfully informed him. *An extinct armored fish from the Late Devonian period.*

The Dunkleosteus that Norris had become used its huge fins to flop forward. It was awkward on land, but so big that Ransom had to again scramble backward to avoid it as its gaping, beak-like jaws snapped at him.

"Roll!" Natalie yelled.

Ransom rolled, and a creature thudded down where he had been. It was the size of a bear but bipedal, with a row of spines down its hairy back. The thing turned an eerily reptilian face toward him. Its jaws opened and a long black tongue shot out, unrolling at lightning speed. Ransom shifted back to human form, and the tongue shot over his head.

Chupacabra, his power told him. *Goat-sucker. It's Costello's shift form. The tongue can drain your blood.*

Snatching his whip from his belt, Ransom lashed out at the chupacabra. It leaped out of the way, shockingly quick, and landed in front of him. The thing was too far away for him to punch, and too close for him to use the whip. As he flipped the whip around, intending to hit it with the handle, the thing opened its jaws again. He knew he wouldn't have time to evade its tongue this time.

A rock slammed into the goat-sucker's head. It slumped to the ground, its tongue hanging out of its mouth like a length of slimy black rope.

"Come on!" Natalie shouted, fitting another rock into her slingshot.

The Dunkleosteus vanished, becoming a man again. But at least they didn't have to worry about Norris pursuing in his human form. He was gasping, having been unable to breathe on land as an armored fish.

Ransom and Natalie ran through Tomato Land, trying to stay out of the shadows. They bolted through the food court, dodging around the tables, and passed the stalls. Natalie started to veer toward the gates when Ransom's enhanced intuition blared a danger warning. He had no time to speak, but grabbed her by the forearm and yanked her aside.

For a second, he worried that he'd hurt her, but her trained agility and quick reflexes allowed her to go with his movement and turn it into a jump. She seemed to float, light as a feather. He guided more than pulled her behind a stall. An instant later, an inhuman screech rose up.

"What the hell was that?" Natalie muttered.

"A harpy," Ransom said, as the knowledge came into his head. "It's Elayne's shift form. My power's been telling me who and what everything is. Nice that it's being helpful for once."

She glanced around uneasily. "That's a sort of bird-woman, right? We need to get somewhere with a roof, or she'll come down on our heads."

"I know. I wish I hadn't lost my gun." Other than the bomb shelter, Tomato Land was notably lacking in sturdy roofs. "I think our original plan is still best. You go for the cars. I'll protect you as a hellhound. If the harpy tries to dive-bomb us, you duck and I'll jump and bite it."

"Like a dog catching a frisbee."

"I was imagining something a bit more ferocious and terrifying, but sure."

Ransom shifted. The world took on a fiery glow. He was about to stalk out when Natalie petted him.

"Your fur's like black velvet," she said. "I wish you could see yourself. You're magnificent."

Despite everything she'd said, a part of Ransom was stunned that Natalie not only didn't fear his hellhound, but found beauty in it.

Of course she does, said the hellhound, sounding distinctly smug. *Hellhounds are magnificent.*

Ransom remembered then that Natalie was a hellhound herself.

He couldn't wait to see her in that form. Nothing she could become could be anything other than beautiful.

He nuzzled her, then jerked his muzzle to the side. They could skirt around the wall, then climb the fence and cut across to the parking lot.

Together they ran for the fence. Though each of his strides covered the same ground as six of hers, she didn't have trouble keeping up. All his senses were alert for danger, but with every stride, he exulted. They were so close! They were almost—

A wall of black stone rose up before them, emerging from the earth itself and rising above their heads even as they stared.

Ransom skidded to a halt, while Natalie caught herself more gracefully. He started to turn, but walls were coming up on every side. In the blink of an eye, they were trapped within a stone circle that rose ten feet above their heads.

The triumphant screech of the harpy resounded through the air. It was followed by another cry, this one deeper and more masculine. Natalie looked at Ransom.

He shifted back to human form to say, "A gargoyle. They have powers over stone. He's the one who raised the walls. And they can fly."

"Great," muttered Natalie. "Okay, I'll be ready with the slingshot, and you be ready to catch the frisbee."

He shifted back to being a hellhound, crouching to leap. Beside him, Natalie stood ready with her improvised slingshot. She was so small and brave, his heart ached with love for her.

The gargoyle flew into view, swooping and diving, far too high for Ransom to jump at him. It had membraneous wings and a strangely distorted body, and looked as if it had been roughly chiseled from obsidian. Natalie raised her slingshot, then dropped it with a yelp. It shattered at her feet—it had turned to glassy black stone.

Then their other enemy flew overhead. It was the harpy. She was smaller than the gargoyle but much quicker, darting about and changing direction with dizzying speed. She looked something like

Elayne and something like a huge hawk, with strangely metallic feathers.

His intuition screamed a warning at him. He let out a low growl.

"It's okay," Natalie said, stroking his fur. "You can protect me. Just grab them when they come in low."

Elayne shrieked, high and piercing and filled with malice. Her wing whipped down, and feathers shot out. They whistled through the air, glinting like metal. Ransom lunged to shield Natalie with his body. The feathers struck him in the chest and side, stabbing into him like darts.

He howled, more from rage than pain. The harpy was far above him. She could kill him at her leisure, and then there would be no one to protect Natalie. Though he knew it was hopeless, he tensed to leap.

"No!" Natalie shouted. "You'll hurt yourself! I love you, Ransom, I have to protect you…"

Her yell became a howl as she shifted.

Ransom stared at her, stunned. Her hound was as tall as his, but lighter, slimmer, long-legged and narrow-bodied as a greyhound. Her sleek fur was white as clouds on a summer day. White-feathered wings sprang from her back, broad and powerful as a swan's. Her eyes, like his, were windows to some other place. But while his opened to a raging fire, hers showed the night sky with all its twinkling stars.

His power told him that she was a Gabriel Hound. And his heart told him that it was the power of her love for him that had finally allowed her to shift.

The Gabriel Hound that Natalie had become leaped into the air, caught a wind current, and flew.

CHAPTER 26

Ahhh, said Natalie's inner Gabriel Hound. *That's better.*

The moment Natalie shifted, she knew why she hadn't been able to before. She'd been so sure of her own form that she'd tried to become a hellhound. But that wasn't what she was. It was only when she'd stopped thinking about what she'd become, and only longed to protect the man she loved, that she could take on her true form.

Her wings spread out, her powerful hindquarters tensed, and she sprang into the air. An instant later, she was out of the stone prison, glorying in the freedom of the sky. She realized then that her longing for flight, her skill at tumbling and trapeze, even her ability to be spun on a wheel and not get motion sickness, had all expressed an aspect of her innate self. She flew because it was her nature to fly.

Harpy above!

Her inner Gabriel Hound's warning allowed Natalie to veer to the side. The harpy dropped down, barely missing her. It screeched in fury and whipped its wing at her, sending metallic feathers whistling through the air. Natalie beat her wings furiously, soaring upward, and evaded the feather-darts.

The gargoyle slammed into her, clawing at her with its taloned hands. She tried to bite it, but the angle was wrong and it was too quick. It clung to her while she snapped furiously, her jaws always closing on air. She couldn't get to it with her paws, either. Her fur was giving her some protection from its talons—it was fluffy like a husky's, with a thick inner layer—but she couldn't get the gargoyle off her.

Out of the corner of her eye, she saw the harpy Elayne diving down. Not toward Natalie—back down into the stone cylinder where Ransom was trapped. He'd already been wounded protecting her, and inside the stone trap the gargoyle had made, he could neither fight nor evade the harpy's attack.

Natalie pawed and bit, but she couldn't shake off the gargoyle. It clung to her like a sloth. Desperate to protect Ransom, heedless of her own safety, she folded her wings and dropped from the sky like a stone.

The gargoyle screeched, flapping its own wings to slow their descent. At the last moment before they hit the ground, it shifted back to human form and tried to force her to take the brunt of the fall. Natalie shifted as well and escaped his grip, tucking and rolling, protecting her head. It was a hard fall, but she didn't feel any bones breaking.

Just bruised all over, she thought. *I must have hit every pebble in Tomato Land.*

The man who had been a gargoyle hadn't been so lucky. He'd hit his head and was out cold. She staggered to her feet and watched the stone cyclinder he had created breaking up. It fell into little pieces that bounced and rolled like safety glass at a car crash, then dissolved into dust.

The harpy screeched angrily, then veered away and vanished into the night.

Natalie rushed to Ransom's side. He was still a hellhound, his fur wet in patches where the darts had struck. His great head turned to her, and she looked straight into his hellfire eyes before he became a man again. The darts fell to the ground with a pair of disturbingly solid clunks, and he winced and put his hand to his chest.

She reached out to try to stop the bleeding with her hands, but he shook his head. "Not here. We have to climb over the fence—Oh."

She followed his gaze. The shadows along the fence were alive and writhing, animated by the power of the unseen Elayne.

Natalie looked around frantically. The living shadows were in front of them, oozing and roiling along the entire length of the fence. The only other way out would require turning around and running all the way across Tomato Land. That not only seemed like an extremely unwise thing to do while Ransom was hurt and bleeding, but it would also involve going straight back to where they'd last seen the chupacabra and the Dunkleosteus. It was also extremely shadowy.

Ransom nudged her, jerking his head upward. She followed his gaze. The knife-shaped pirate ship loomed above them, lit by a huge bright spotlight. It would be visible from the freeway, which presumably was the intent. "No shadows there."

They scrambled up the stairs, on to the platform, and into the ship. Once they were in it, they sank down on one of the bench-seats. They were still vulnerable to an attack from above, but at least they'd see it coming.

"I finally got you on the tomato knife," she said.

"You were amazing," he said, touching her cheek. "So beautiful and fierce."

"Don't look at me, look out for enemies."

"I can multi-task," Ransom said, but he tilted his head back to watch the sky. She hoped it was the effect of the fluorescent light, but his face looked very pale.

"Where's your Swiss Army knife? I need to cut off your shirt."

"Forget about that. The gargoyle's out cold and you're a match for the harpy. You need to fly out of here and—"

"What? I'm not leaving you!"

"—and get help," he continued, without pausing. "It's probably too late for anyone to be at the office, so you should go to Roland's house. He can call everyone else, then come himself. He can get here fastest, because he can fly. He's at—"

"Ransom. I'm not leaving you."

"You have to. We're completely outnumbered, and that's not even counting Jager. I burned out my power and I don't have a gun. Elayne's blocked the way out, and—"

Natalie kissed him, partly to make him stop talking and partly because she loved him so much. It was brief, but it ran fire through her veins. "I'm not abandoning you."

"It wouldn't be abandoning me. It'd be getting reinforcements."

"I don't care what you call it. I'm not leaving you alone. That's off the table. Now are you going to sit here bleeding and arguing, or are you going to let me patch you up so we can both survive?"

After a moment, Ransom said, "My Swiss Army knife's in my hip pocket."

Natalie took it out, then helped him take off his leather jacket; he winced when he tried to move his left arm. Beneath the jacket, the left side of his T-shirt was soaked in blood from collar to hem. She cut it off, then began slicing up the right side of his shirt to make bandages.

"I don't think the feathers went in very deep," he said. "Maybe an inch or two."

"That's plenty deep enough!"

"I mean, it's not like I got stabbed."

"You absolutely got stabbed," she said, bandaging his shoulder. "There's no length requirement. You get punctured with a sharp object, you got stabbed."

"You wouldn't say 'I got stabbed with a pin,'" he objected.

"I might. Depends on the circumstances. Also, while we're talking definitions, tomatoes are vegetables."

"They're fruits." He breathed deeply, but didn't flinch as she pressed a pad of T-shirt cloth into his side and secured it with more strips of cloth. As she helped him back into his leather jacket and zipped it up, he said, "You fell hard. Are *you* hurt?"

"A bit bruised."

"You're shivering." He put his arms around her.

She gratefully leaned into his warmth, but her thoughts raced ahead. His wounds might not be knife-deep, but they'd bled a lot.

Would her makeshift bandages hold if he had to run or fight? And where should they even run to? They were surrounded.

Fly.

Natalie was still unused to hearing a voice in her head, but she didn't twitch. It was new, but it felt natural. The voice was low but still feminine, with a gravelly, growly undertone. A whiskey-and-cigarettes voice. And yet Natalie could hear that it was a version of her own voice.

I can't leave him, she told the Gabriel Hound in her head.

Her Gabriel Hound gave a snort that reminded her of Wally. *Of course not. Fly your mate to safety.*

"My Gabriel Hound says you could ride me," Natalie said.

Ransom looked deeply dubious. "Wouldn't I be too heavy? She's not that big."

Neither is your human form, said the Gabriel Hound. *But it's stronger than it looks.*

Natalie repeated that, adding, "Remember how she needed me to take a leap of faith? I think it's our turn again."

"I trust you. And her." He paused for a moment, then added, "So does my hellhound. Let's get out of here."

Natalie reached inward, seeking her Gabriel Hound. This time shifting was as easy and natural as doing a cartwheel. Wings blossomed from her shoulders.

Despite their urgency, she loved seeing Ransom's expression of wonder and awe as he gazed at her other form. Then he swung a long leg over her back and settled in behind her wings.

Then it was Natalie's moment to doubt. The Gabriel Hound was much more lightly built than the hellhound, and Ransom was tall.

Leap of faith, she reminded herself, and spread her wings.

She flapped hard, lifted a couple inches off the floor, then thumped back down.

Uh-oh, Natalie thought.

Ransom started to swing his leg off her, but Natalie, driven by the sharp negative of her inner hound, swung her head around, nipped the edge of his leather jacket, and sat him back down.

"Okay," he said. "But…"

Let's try it without having to do a lift-off, suggested her Gabriel Hound.

How do we do that? Natalie asked, though she had an uneasy idea that she knew.

The Gabriel Hound's starry eyes moved to the bow of the pirate ship, and the thirty foot drop to the ground.

We jump.

CHAPTER 27

It was an ordinary late night at the Defenders office. Everyone was either working on a case or catching up on old work or hanging around to get a share of the pizza Carter and Tirzah had ordered, and they'd all gravitated to the lobby to eat it.

Eat the pizza, Merlin's inner raptor demanded. *Eat it ALL!*

Without conscious intent, Merlin's hand stretched out to the last slice of hot sausage and wildflower honey pizza.

"Hey!" Carter exclaimed. "That's *my* pizza. If any of the rest of you had said you wanted it, we could have ordered more of it, but no, you all said it sounded gross—"

"I didn't," said Merlin.

"—and 'You get it if you want it, Carter,' and then you ate more of it than I did!"

Merlin withdrew his hand. "Sorry. Raptor acting up. You can have it."

"I don't want it now that you've touched it," Carter said grouchily. "Blue was licking your hands a second ago."

Roland reached over both of their shoulders and helped himself to the slice. "I don't mind."

Carter's howl of outrage made Blue jump to his feet and start barking, his tiny dragonfly wings buzzing madly.

Tirzah laughed. "You're such a troll, Roland."

"Troll as in internet, or troll as in hungry creature that lives under a bridge?" Roland asked, then ate half the slice in one bite.

"Both," said Carter, glaring.

Dali cleared her throat. "Since the hot sausage drizzled with wildflower honey was clearly the popular favorite, shall I order another one?"

"Yes," said Roland, swallowing. "Thank you."

Pete returned from the kitchen with Spike and Batcat clinging to his shoulders, and a can of root beer in his hand. He passed the can to Tirzah, then demanded, "Merlin, did you eat all the sausage pizza?"

Volunteer to go downstairs and collect it when it arrives, his raptor suggested. *Then eat it ALL!*

You're not helping, Merlin returned.

Out of the corner of his eye, he spotted Blue stealthily bellying up to the untouched Hawaiian pizza. Merlin snatched it away, petted his bugbear in apology, then passed it to Tirzah, who was the nearest person to him who wasn't busy ordering another pizza.

"This has ham on it. I don't eat ham." Tirzah passed it to Pete.

"I know, I was just getting it away from—" Merlin began.

"Pineapple doesn't belong on pizza." Pete passed it to Carter.

"I'd never order that abomination." Carter passed it to Roland.

Roland considered it, then said, "I think I'll hold out for Carter's special gourmet sausage." Glancing at Merlin, he asked, "Is Blue allowed to eat pizza?"

"No," said Merlin. It wasn't entirely true, but he certainly wasn't allowed to eat an entire pizza by himself, and when no one else wanted it, that was what one bite would lead to.

Dali hung up the phone, and Roland passed the Hawaiian pizza to her. Cloud, who was sprawled over the lobby counter, spat in disgust.

"No, thanks." She glanced around the room. "Why'd you guys put it on the list if nobody likes it?"

Everyone looked at each other. It was like all the light went out of the room.

"It's Ransom's favorite," Pete said.

It was an ordinary late night at the Defenders office, except it wasn't. Ransom wasn't there, and his absence was like a black hole in the room, an invisible but ever-present force. And like a magic spell, the mention of his name opened the floodgates.

"I shouldn't have let him walk away like that," Merlin said.

"Oh, Merlin," Dali said, putting her arm around him. "You tried to stop him. You grabbed him by the arm, but he shook you off."

"I *let* him shake me off," Merlin corrected her. "My raptor was yelling, 'Grab him, sit on him, don't let him get away!' I should've listened."

"I should've bugged his car," Tirzah said glumly. "I actually thought about it. I was worried that he'd overuse his power and collapse somewhere and we wouldn't know where he was."

"He'd have noticed," said Pete. "I caught him checking his car for bugs once."

"I should've bugged his laptop," said Tirzah. "He wouldn't have noticed that."

"He left his laptop at his apartment," said Carter. Everyone turned to stare at him. Defensively, he said, "I came back to the office, and he was gone and you were all freaking out! I was worried. I mean, I was curious."

"Curious enough to search his apartment?" Pete asked. "How'd you even know where it is? He sure never told me."

"Or me," said Merlin.

Carter made a vague gesture toward his own laptop.

"Oh," said Dali. "You hacked him."

"Not very effectively," said Carter. "I found his apartment, but he's gone and the trail ends there."

Stake it out, suggested Merlin's inner raptor. *If he comes back,* then *you can sit on him.*

Merlin would have gone for it, but he didn't think Ransom had any intention of returning to his apartment. He'd have left it behind for good, like he'd left his team.

Like Natalie had left the circus, without explanation or goodbye or forwarding address.

Merlin knew it wasn't personal. Ransom had been deeply unhappy and had obviously been running away from something when Merlin had known him in the Marines, and that was *before* he'd been experimented on and given a shift form he hated for some reason Merlin didn't understand and a power he hated for very obvious reasons. As for Natalie, Merlin had no idea why she'd left, but it had been of her own free will, and certainly had nothing to do with him.

But he couldn't help feeling that even if he hadn't been the problem, he ought to have been more of a solution. He'd written to Natalie, but maybe not often enough. He'd assumed she knew that she was his best friend and his practically-sister, and that he'd do anything for her if she ever needed a hand. But maybe she didn't know it. Maybe he should have explicitly said so. And had there been some hint in her letters to him that he'd overlooked, some clue about something wrong that he still hadn't figured out even though he'd re-read them a hundred times by now in search of it?

As for Ransom, Merlin should have reached out to him more. He should have pushed harder to get his teammate to talk to him. He should have—

Roland, who had been very silent up till then, said, "This is on me. I pushed him too hard. And now he's gone."

He looked so bleak that the team jumped in with a chorus of "You meant well" and "You told him he could come back" and (from Merlin) "Honestly, Roland, I tried a bunch of times to get through to him, but he's so—"

Tirzah's phone went off with a ringtone Merlin hadn't heard before, the opening chords of "Born to Run." Her voice rose high and excited as she snatched it up. "That's my Ransom alarm! Quick, Pete, pass me my laptop!"

As Pete handed her the computer, Dali said, "Your Ransom alarm?"

"Mmm-hmm. I installed an alarm on his door, so I'd be alerted if he came back." Defensively, she said, "But I didn't break into his apartment and search it!"

Peering over her shoulder at her laptop, Roland said drily, "No, you just broke in and installed a hidden camera."

"No-oo-ooo," Tirzah said, squirming. "I didn't go inside. I got Batcat to stick it on the outside of one of his windows. In case he needed help. Like in case he got dragged back by wizard-scientists. Or something."

Now everyone was watching over her shoulder. The camera had been stuck on the window at an odd angle, so the view was sharply tilted, showing more of the walls than anything else. It was also very dim, lit only by streetlights outside. Merlin's eyes ached as he strained them, waiting for Ransom—or someone else—to step into frame.

An extremely adorable black and white husky puppy trotted into view.

"Awww," said Merlin, delighted. "Ransom has a puppy!"

The puppy sniffed the wall, then disappeared. Literally.

"Stupid glitchy camera," Tirzah muttered. "I *told* Batcat not to chew on it, but..."

"Hang on," Carter said sharply. "Look at the timestamps."

Another puppy, an equally adorable white fluffball, appeared in the view. It didn't walk on. It was just suddenly there.

"Did that puppy...?" Dali began.

The white puppy was joined by the black-and-white puppy, which was also just suddenly there.

Merlin felt his face crack with a grin. "Ransom has magical puppies! Look how darling they are!"

"You're right," said Tirzah. "The camera never stopped filming. The puppies teleported."

"But where's Ransom?" asked Roland.

The two puppies sniffed and licked each other, then sat back, raised their muzzles high, and began to howl. Their piercing wails were audible even to the camera stuck to the outside of a closed window, and must have been earsplitting from inside. But no one stepped into the frame to comfort them.

Blue woke up with a start and also began to howl. Batcat and Spike flapped their wings and yowled, and Cloud began flying in circles close to the ceiling.

"The pets don't act like that unless something's wrong," said Dali. "Maybe Ransom sent them to alert us."

"Shouldn't he have sent them here, then?" Carter asked.

Merlin shook his head. "I don't think he could. They've never been here. And, well, he's Ransom. He easily could've known his apartment was being monitored."

"Maybe he didn't," Tirzah said quietly. "Maybe he sent them somewhere safe."

That idea gave Merlin an unpleasant feeling in the pit of his stomach. The way Ransom had looked when Merlin had last seen him, Tirzah's theory seemed a lot more plausible than that Ransom would ever ask them for help.

"They're wearing collars," said Carter. "I could put trackers on them, and then all we'd need to do is get them to go back to where Ransom is."

Roland stood up. "Let's do it. And hurry. The way those pups are howling, they might not wait much longer before they go back to him."

Carter made a dash for the tech room, calling over his shoulder, "I'll get the trackers!"

"And my comms equipment!" Tirzah shouted.

"And weapons," said Roland. "If Ransom's in trouble, we won't have a chance to stop back here."

Yes, very good, said Merlin's raptor. *Rescue the puppies, rescue our teammate. Adventures in the middle of the night!*

Merlin leaned over to give Dali a quick kiss. "Save a slice of pizza for me."

"Actually..." Dali said slowly. "I'll come along for this one."

Merlin gave her a startled glance. Though Dali was a Navy veteran and he'd seen for herself how well she could fight, she was the office manager, not a bodyguard.

"You might need someone to puppy-sit while you fight," she said, her eyebrows arching playfully. Then she admitted, "This is going to sound silly, but I feel bad for not knowing Ransom liked Hawaiian pizza. It makes me feel like I missed something about him—maybe something that would have made a difference. I don't want to miss this chance."

"It doesn't sound silly at all. I feel the same way."

The rest of the team returned, loaded down with equipment. Carter was last, having stopped to collect his long black coat. By the time he arrived, everyone was waiting at the door with their kittens perched on their shoulders. Blue scratched himself, sending up a cloud of bright blue fur to settle on Carter's coat.

Carter turned despairingly to Roland. "Are we really bringing that indigo menace and a bunch of nuisancy flapping kittens on a rescue mission?"

"We could leave them, but if they want to come, they'll show up anyway," Roland said.

"And they'll keep the teleporting puppies company," Merlin added.

Carter gave a muffled groan. "They better be housetrained."

They piled into the van and set off, with Roland behind the wheel and Carter giving directions from the passenger seat. Tirzah, her wheelchair buckled in and secured, clutched her laptop, watching the footage.

The faint howls of the puppies made prickles run along Merlin's skin. Somewhere, Ransom was in danger, and he probably didn't even know his team was coming to rescue him. He must feel so alone.

And Merlin had no idea if they'd get there in time.

CHAPTER 28

*R*ansom held tight to the Gabriel Hound's neck, pressing his cheek into her soft fur. He murmured, "I trust you."

Her strong muscles tensed beneath him, and Natalie leaped off the pirate ship. They dropped like a stone. But her wings beat fiercely, sending up a scent like sun-warmed linen. As the ground rose to meet them, they began to veer away, until they were skimming a few feet above the ground. And then up, and up, and up. Up above the tables and chairs, up above the booths, and up toward the sky.

It was glorious. He could sense Natalie's joy at flight without needing any speech, solely by the way she arrowed upward and by the bond they shared. They were together, and in a few more minutes, they'd be safe and free.

His danger sense screamed out a warning.

"Up!" Ransom yelled.

Natalie soared upward, but his weight slowed her. He saw the silvery glint of a tiny projectile hitting her paw.

The next instant, the Gabriel Hound vanished. Natalie was human again, and they both were tumbling through the air.

"Curl!" Natalie shouted.

He had just enough time to obey her, bringing up his knees and curling himself into a ball, before they hit water.

Ransom felt the splash go up as he landed like a cannon ball, and then he was plunging down into cold dark water.

If this isn't deep enough, we'll break every bone in our bodies, he thought.

But he was slowing down, the water cushioning him as he fell. Ransom stretched out his legs, and his feet touched the bottom. He pushed off, and his face broke the surface.

He wiped water out of his eyes, and was immediately reassured by the sight of Natalie bobbing nearby, drenched and, surreally, laughing.

"It's the tomato juice pool," she said unnecessarily; he'd realized as soon as he'd seen the elaborate "tomato vine" waterslide.

"Are you hurt?" he asked, though she didn't look like she was.

"Not really. Something hit my paw—well, my foot now—but it just feels like a splinter."

Ransom immediately *knew* what it was. "You were shot with a tiny fragment of shiftsilver. It'll stop you from shifting until you take it out."

She twisted around in the water, bringing up her foot and pulling it close to peer at the sole. "Maybe I can get it with my fingernails."

A male voice shouted, "Oh, no you don't!"

Norris, the Dunkleosteus shifter, came bolting out from around the water slide and made a flying leap into the pool.

Ransom lunged to push Natalie away, imagining those massive jaws snapping her up in a single bite. But he was slowed by the water, and also by the fact that she'd moved at the same instant to protect him. They were still struggling together when Norris hit the water, still in his human form.

The next instant, the pool was almost completely filled by an enormous armored fish. The water it displaced was pushed out in all directions. The pool overflowed, and Ransom and Natalie were flung up against the side. As the Dunkleosteus tried to maneuver its massive bulk to attack them, Ransom pushed Natalie to solid ground and clambered out himself.

They scrambled backwards, staring at the immense prehistoric fish. Its jaws snapped together with a sound like a gunshot as it thrashed around in the pool, which was barely big enough to contain it.

"It's like an elephant sitting in a wading pool," said Natalie. "And I've actually seen that, so I know."

Ransom would have never imagined he'd be capable of laughing at that moment, but he did.

The Dunkleosteus managed to free a fin and take a swipe at them. They leaped backward, and the fin slammed down into the dirt.

Natalie bent to feel her foot, then straightened up and whispered, "You can help me get the splinter out. Let's go up the water slide. We'll need to jump from a height to take off again."

Ransom could see a whole lot of problems with this plan, but it wasn't as if he had a better one. He whispered, "Follow me."

He grabbed her hand and bolted in the opposite direction, as if he was making for the fence on the other side of Tomato Land. But once they were behind a set of booths, he reversed their direction and made a wide loop, heading for the back of the water slide. With luck, their enemies would waste their time searching for them in all the wrong places.

When they crept back up on the water slide, Ransom could see by the vast silhouette that the Dunkleosteus was still stubbornly wedged in the pool. They couldn't go up the stairs without being seen, but would have to climb the structure of the slide itself, a web of girders, vine-shaped poles, and metal tendrils.

"Easy-peasy," Natalie whispered. "Piece of... tomato."

She, of course, could climb anything. And even for him, it should have been a fun and easy climb. But when he looked up at it now, it seemed daunting. The adrenaline from their fall had worn off, leaving him exhausted and shaky and cold, except for warm patches at his chest and side where either his bandages had come off or he was bleeding through them.

Natalie stepped on to a girder, bringing herself to his eye-level, and kissed his cheek. Her lips were hot as flame. She whispered,

"Take it one hold at a time. I'll be right there with you. I won't let you fall."

He put his foot on a metal leaf and began to climb. Ransom didn't look up or down or to the side, but he could feel her body heat and, often, her small hand giving him a comforting touch on the back, or guiding his hand or foot to a hold.

Once he got so dizzy that he had to stop and lean his head against the cool metal of a girder, trying to hang on even though he could barely feel his hands and feet. Natalie put her arm around him and murmured in his ear, "I've got you. You won't fall. Just rest till you're ready to go on."

He waited till his vision cleared, then went on. One hold at a time, as she'd said. Because he wasn't looking at anything but the part he was climbing, he was startled when he reached the top. Natalie helped him over the edge, and they sat together in a heap atop the platform.

"Thanks," he said quietly. "Let me see your foot."

She gave him a long, worried look, then took off her ballet slipper. He bent over her foot, searching for the dart. He finally had to find it by touch. It was tiny and deeply embedded, like a splinter. He couldn't get his fingers around it, or even his nails.

Natalie twisted herself into a pretzel and tried herself, but she couldn't grasp it either. She muttered, "We need tweezers."

He patted his pockets, but he'd lost his Swiss Army knife. "They're probably at the bottom of the pool."

"If the dinosaur-fish is gone, I could climb down and grab them," Natalie suggested. She peeked over the edge, then ducked back. "Nope. It's still there."

"It's a Dunkleosteus," Ransom said absently.

"Good to know."

She was soaking wet, her already-tight clothes plastered to her body. Her hair looked like she'd gotten herself a pixie cut. In the moonlight, he couldn't see color; she was black and white and shades of gray. If he could have, the tomato-colored water probably made her look like the victim of a chainsaw massacre.

Her warm hands slipped under his jacket, and her eyes widened in alarm. "I thought so. The bandages came off. Sorry, this is going to hurt, but I have to do it."

She pressed hard against his side and chest, but he felt nothing but pressure. "It doesn't hurt."

"That's not good. I think you're going into shock. You need to warm up—You need to stop bleeding—You need to get somewhere safe—"

Her voice was fading out. Everything was fading out. He was sinking into something warm, a very soft bed or maybe a hot bath...

Wake up! His hellhound's snarl made Ransom realize that he was blacking out.

I can't pass out now, he thought. *I'll be leaving Natalie alone.*

Deliberately, he bit down on his lip until he tasted blood. The sharp pain jarred him back into full awareness. He opened his eyes, unnerved to realize that he hadn't even noticed closing them.

"Ransom!" Natalie was whispering urgently, her face dead white. "Ransom, wake—"

"Sorry," he said. "I didn't mean—"

"I know." She leaned in close, pressing her forehead against his. "Just try to stay awake."

A whine startled him. He felt Natalie jump too. Then they both had their laps full of squirming, nuzzling, licking, excited husky puppies.

"Hey, Heidi." Ransom stroked her, and she licked him all over. Much as he wished he could keep her safe, he couldn't help being glad she was here with him now. "I wonder where they went."

"Too bad they can't tell us. Guess we'll never know." She nudged Wally closer to Ransom; Heidi was already cuddled up against his side. "Keep him warm. Good dog."

Wally obediently snuggled in. But even with both of them and Natalie trying to share their warmth, Ransom still felt cold. Every time he blinked, black starbursts flashed across his field of vision. Just staying conscious was a struggle.

"Listen, Natalie, I can't climb back down. But if you go—"

"We've already been through this," she said, so fiercely that it came out in a hiss. "I'm not leaving you."

"I know. I'm not asking you to leave me and save yourself. I'm asking you to do something dangerous to save us both."

She looked vastly relieved. "Oh, good. What?"

He had to swallow before he could speak. That was the woman he loved: utterly fearless.

Our mate, said his hellhound with satisfaction.

"Sneak back into the History of the Tomato exhibit," he said. "Marie Curie had a pair of tweezers. Get the dart out. But sneak back on foot if you can. Our only chance is to take them completely by surprise when we fly out."

She moved his hands to his shoulder and chest. "Keep the pressure on. *Do not* pass out."

"I won't." He was pretty sure he could keep that promise. Worrying about what sort of dangers she might be encountering without him being there to protect her ought to keep him wide awake.

Natalie gave him a quick kiss, then swung over the platform's edge. He watched her swarm down a metal vine, quick and surefooted as a squirrel. At least he didn't need to worry about her falling.

The shadow cast by a tomato leaf below her foot quivered, as if in the wind. But the leaves were solid steel...

"Natalie!" Ransom yelled. "Get back!"

She leaped upward, caught a steel tomato tendril above her head, and swung herself around it. The shadow snatched for her, but fell short. If she'd been like a squirrel going down, she was like lightning coming back up. An instant later, she was catching her breath beside Ransom on the platform, with the puppies barking fiercely.

There were no shadows on the platform itself, which was lit bright as day, but they writhed and pulsed on the structure below it. As they peered down, they saw two figures step into view. One, unsurprisingly, was Elayne. The other was Jager.

"Care to reconsider your choice?" Jager called up. "My offer is still open."

"As is mine," said Elayne. "You can be his lowly lab rat assistant, or you can be my Dark Knight. But if you won't choose either, we'll kill you both."

"Come and get us, then!" Natalie shouted.

Two more figures stepped forward to flank Elayne. One was Costello, in her nightmarish chupacabra form. The other was the skinny woman. Norris was still crammed into the pool, jaws periodically gaping open and snapping shut.

"You haven't met my associate Barnes yet," Elayne said, indicating the skinny woman. "Which explains your delusional belief that you're in a defensible position up there. Barnes!"

Barnes stepped away from the others. In the blink of an eye, she was no longer a woman, but a bird-bat-lizard creature that stood fifteen feet tall. Her immense membraneous wings touched the ground, helping her balance. Her sharp beak alone was as long as a man. She extended it upward, stabbing at the platform. It fell short, banging into a metal vine about ten feet below them.

Natalie flinched, then said, "What is it? I know you know."

"Quetzalcoatlus," Ransom replied. "A type of pterosaur. One of the biggest flying animals of all time."

Loudly, she replied, "But you can still bite her head off, right?"

Raising his own voice, Ransom said, "Absolutely."

But they both knew he didn't have a chance. Barnes could stab his hellhound with her beak before he could get anywhere near close enough to bite her.

"Last chance," called Jager.

"Predator or prey," shouted Elayne. "Choose now!"

Natalie yelled, "I'd rather die now with Ransom than spend a lifetime with you assholes!"

Ransom didn't waste his strength shouting. Once he shifted, he couldn't speak, so he wanted his words to count. He turned to Natalie and said, "I love you too."

With a screech, Barnes rocked back onto her long, skinny legs and extended her wings. Her wingspan was astonishing. She could easily have reached up with her wings and swatted them off the platform—but Ransom could get his teeth into her wings if she tried. Instead, the quetzalcoatlus leaped into the air, beating her immense wings until she soared high above them. Then she dove down, beak outstretched like a spear.

Ransom waited, his heart pounding. If he timed his shift perfectly, he might have a chance to get his teeth around the pterosaur's neck and—

A streak of fire split the night sky.

The phoenix struck the attacking reptile and knocked it clean out of the sky. They went down together with a tremendous crash. The water slide shook. And then the phoenix rose in flames, leaving its enemy in a crumpled heap on the ground. It flew upward, blazing in the night, opened its beak, and let out a ringing cry like a bugle.

"It's beautiful," Natalie whispered. "What is it?"

"It's my boss," said Ransom.

Even as he said the words, he could hardly believe them. The phoenix descended toward them. Ransom flinched back from the intense heat. Then the heat and golden light vanished, and Roland landed on the platform with a thud.

Roland cast a puzzled glance at Natalie. "Hello. I'm Roland Walker."

"Natalie Nash," she said. "Ransom told me about you."

"She's a friend," Ransom said. She was much more than that, but he didn't feel up to long explanations.

Roland frowned down at him. "You look terrible. Are you hurt?"

"He got stabbed," Natalie said, staring hard at Ransom as if daring him to contradict her. "By harpy feathers—they're like flying knives."

"Just hold on," said Roland. "We'll get you down in a moment."

He strode to the edge of the platform and peered down. Ransom, following his gaze, saw that the living shadows had vanished, along with all their enemies. That included the quetzalcoatlus, who had apparently been stunned rather than killed. Even Norris had disappeared from the now mostly empty tomato juice pool.

Roland touched the headset he was wearing and said, "Tirzah? What's our status?" He listened for a moment, then said, "I'm on the top of the water slide with Ransom and a friend of his. He's been stabbed. Are we clear to go down by the steps?" Another pause. "Understood. We're not clear. Over."

He knelt beside Ransom and removed his leather jacket, then took off his own shirt and coat. He used the shirt to pat his skin dry before he applied a pair of emergency bandages from his pockets. Finally, he put his own coat on Ransom and buttoned it up.

As he worked, he said, "Tirzah's in the van, running communications. Dali's guarding her. The others are still clearing the area. We'll stay here and wait for reinforcements. It won't be long."

"But how…" Ransom began. "Why…?"

"Your puppies showed up at your apartment. We put trackers on their collars and told them to go to you." Roland patted Heidi, then turned her collar around to expose the tiny GPS device clipped to it. She licked his hand. "Sorry it took so long. They can only go a couple miles at a time."

"But…" Ransom felt better in the warm overcoat, not to mention the new bandages, but he still couldn't manage to put words to his question.

"Ransom said he left on bad terms," said Natalie.

"Yes. That was on me." Roland put his hand on Ransom's shoulder. "I wish I could take it back. We've all been worried sick about you."

Ransom had imagined his departure as a pebble tossed into a lake: it would cause a brief ripple, and then everything would continue as if it had never been there at all. "You were?"

"Yes," Roland said simply. "All of us. I hope you'll be willing to come back, once you're recovered. No conditions."

"I thought you wouldn't want me back."

They are your pack, said his hellhound. *Of course they want you back.*

"You're part of the team." Roland squeezed his shoulder. "Of course we want you back."

CHAPTER 29

Natalie had imagined Ransom's boss as a caricature of a harsh military officer: a stiff-backed white man with a gray moustache. But once she'd seen the glory of the phoenix, that had gone right out of her head and she'd imagined him as the silhouette of a man, too bright to look at directly, with fiery wings.

Roland didn't match either of those ideas. He was a tall, muscular black man, with short-cropped, silvering hair and beard. Even if she hadn't seen him as the phoenix, he'd have had presence. But his eyes were as kind as his aura was commanding, and when he knelt down, she saw Ransom relax immediately. Whatever had gone down between the two of them, Ransom trusted him.

Natalie too relaxed, as much as she could when she still couldn't shift, Ransom was wounded, and they were stuck atop a water slide and surrounded by enemies. But at least he'd gotten some first aid. And even if she hadn't seen what Roland could do as the phoenix, there was something about him that made you feel like everything would be all right with him by your side.

Something moved in the shadows.

A black lizard-creature the size of a rat, sleek and fanged and clawed, was climbing a metal vine below the platform. Before Natalie could shout out a warning, it was atop the platform and skittering toward the men. It walked on two legs, like a tiny T-rex, and it moved incredibly fast.

But Natalie moved faster. She threw herself in front of Ransom and snatched up the creature, then wound up to hurl it off the platform.

Roland and Ransom started to shout.

And then Natalie was falling in a heap with a man on top of her. She clenched her fists, ready to fight the creepy little reptile shifter to protect her mate—

—and she saw a face almost as familiar to her as her own. It had bright blue eyes and an absolutely astonished expression.

"Natalie!" Merlin exclaimed. "What are you doing here?"

"I'm Ransom's mate. You're a lizard shifter?"

"I'm a velociraptor shifter," said Merlin proudly.

"I thought they were bigger."

"Oh, I can be bigger," he assured her.

Roland's voice boomed like a foghorn. "DON'T."

Only then did Natalie's heart catch up to her mind. Her best friend, her might-as-well-be-brother was there, at last, and now she had no reason to run away from him.

Now she never had to run away from anyone, ever again.

She threw her arms around him, and he hugged her tight. When they let go, they both were laughing, giddy with adrenaline and happiness.

"I was going to throw you like a fastball," Natalie gasped.

"I know, that's why I had to shift so fast," said Merlin. "Sorry about that."

"Don't worry about it. What did you mean, you can be bigger?"

His eyes gleaming, he said, "I can change my size! It's my power and it's *awesome*. I was tiny so I could get up here without anyone seeing me, but I can get bigger. Much bigger!"

"Don't," said Ransom. "At least, not yet."

Merlin peered worriedly at him. "You don't look good. I mean, congratulations on finding your mate! And it's Natalie! That's wonderful. You two will be so happy together. I mean, once we get you off this water slide."

"Carter, Pete, still no sign of anyone?" Roland said into his comm set. After a pause, he said, "Okay, let's wrap it up. Merlin and Ransom and I are at the water slide. Meet us there, and we'll all head back together."

It was only a few minutes before the first of Ransom's teammates appeared, a muscular Latino man with a gun in one hand. He beckoned to them to come down, calling, "Carter's on his way."

"That's Pete," said Ransom to Natalie.

The cave bear, she thought. In fact, there was something about the way he moved that did remind her of a bear, big and strong and capable of startling speed.

"Let's go," said Roland. "I'll carry Ransom."

"You don't need to carry me. Just give me a hand." He gripped Roland's forearm and hauled himself to his feet.

Natalie went around to his other side and put his arm over her shoulders. "We've got you."

Merlin took the lead going down the steps, gazing about alertly with a gun in his hand. Roland too kept a gun in his free hand. Ransom was very pale and kept his arm around her waist, but he walked steadily. The puppies followed at their heels.

"What the hell happened to you?" Pete demanded of Ransom when they reached the bottom of the water slide.

Instinctively, Natalie bristled at his tone. "He got stabbed twice protecting me."

"Who are you?" Pete asked, sounding suspicious.

Merlin broke in. "Natalie Nash! She's my best friend from the circus. She's a trapeze artist and an acrobat and a target girl!"

"So you're the one who's responsible for me having to oil my chest," said another man, walking up. He was a dark-haired white man in an expensive suit and a long black coat. Despite his gun and headset, he looked more like someone on the cover of *GQ* than a bodyguard.

Baffled, Natalie asked, "How did I make you do that? I've never even seen you before!"

Laughing, Merlin said, "You were gone and the circus was short-handed, so Carter had to take your place as target girl."

"Target guy," Carter corrected, looking offended. "Because apparently you and me are the only people who can be strapped to a wheel and spun around without throwing up."

"What's that have to do with you oiling your chest?" Natalie asked.

"They said all target guys had to..." Carter's voice trailed off as the awful truth dawned. "MERLIN!"

But Merlin had gone on ahead, alertly scanning the fairgrounds.

"Stay away from the shadows, everyone," Natalie called. "If Elayne's still lurking somewhere, she can grab you with them."

As they continued on, Pete and Carter fell in beside Ransom.

"And to think that everyone always gets on *my* case for not being around enough," said Carter. "You literally disappeared on us!"

Scowling, Pete said, "You hurt Caro's feelings. You took off without even saying goodbye."

Natalie glanced at Ransom in confusion.

"Pete's daughter. She's thirteen," Ransom clarified. To Pete, he said, "Are you serious? I didn't think she'd even notice I was gone."

"Of course she noticed!" Pete gave a snort. "You help her with her homework and talk to her like she's an intelligent adult. If she flunks chemistry, it's on you."

"I'm—" Ransom began.

Carter chimed in, "I can't believe you'd walk out when I wasn't even there!"

"I'm—" Ransom began again.

Over his shoulder, Merlin said, "I tried to stop you, and you practically threw me into a wall!"

Natalie couldn't take it any more. "What's wrong with you guys? Lay off him! Did you all not hear me when I said he'd been *stabbed*? He needs rest and quiet and medical attention, not a bunch of guys getting on his case!"

"Natalie. It's fine." Ransom squeezed her hand. He didn't look upset, to her relief. His expression was a very familiar one: surprised by happiness.

Roland cleared his throat. "What they're trying to say is that they missed him and they're glad he's back."

The familiar arch of the front gates, wound about by actual living tomato vines, loomed before them. Natalie recognized the ticket booth where they'd gotten their hands stamped with tomatoes. It felt like a lifetime ago.

A shadow blotted out the moon.

Natalie's head jerked up. The quetzalcoatlus flew high above them, flanked by the gargoyle and the harpy.

The men on Ransom's team moved like lightning, aiming their guns at the flying beasts. Natalie flinched, expecting a volley of gunshots. But none came. Instead, the gargoyle let out a triumphant screech as the headsets all fell from the men's heads. They hit the ground and shattered into shiny black fragments, like the wall had when Natalie had knocked out the gargoyle. And like the pieces of the wall, the bits of the headsets dissolved into dust.

"Forget your guns," said Pete. He tossed his to the ground, where it too shattered. "Once something's stone, it stays stone until it breaks, and then it's dust."

"Get to the van," said Roland sharply. "Pete, take Ransom. I can fight in the sky."

Ransom slung his arm around Pete's shoulders. Roland stepped away from them and spread his arms wide. Flames blossomed in the palms of his hands, then raced up his arms.

And went out.

Roland put his hand to his shoulder. "Something hit me. I can't get it out."

"There!" shouted Ransom, pointing. Jager was lurking in the shadows by a booth, with a weird-looking rifle with a sniper-scope on his shoulder. "It shoots shiftsilver darts!"

"Won't hurt me now," said Roland. He charged Jager, moving shockingly fast for a man of his size.

"Watch out!" Natalie called. "He can—"

Roland crashed into the booth as Jager vanished.

"—teleport!"

Roland straightened, rubbing his elbow and wincing. "Everyone! To the van!"

They all turned to run for the gates, but stopped short. The gate was entirely filled by a looming, beak-snapping, fin-twitching Dunkleosteus.

"He can't breathe on land," Ransom said. "Wait a minute, and he'll have to shift back."

With an angry screech, the harpy plummeted from the sky and landed atop the fence. It shifted, becoming a precariously balanced Elayne. She shouted down at the Dunkleosteus, "Stop being that useless fish! Take them out with your vertigo power!"

Norris became a man again. He made a quick gesture, and the world flipped upside down.

Upside down, inside out, spinning and reeling and twirling. It was like being on the world's most intense roller coaster. All around her, everyone was collapsing, even Wally and Heidi.

Everyone, that was, except Carter. He was swaying, his arms stretched out for balance, but he stayed on his feet.

Target guy, she remembered. He and she were the only ones who could stand being strapped to a wheel and spun around. Norris's power was clearly affecting him—it was affecting her too—but it hadn't taken them out. They were the only ones who had a chance of stopping him.

She caught Carter's eye, as much as she could when the world was swinging wildly around her and the ground beneath her feet felt like a treadmill set on Olympic sprint. Together, they rushed Norris at a staggering run.

Instead of trying to fight, he gestured at them again. The spinning feeling increased, making her stumble. But by then she was close, so she hurled herself at him. She crashed into him with no grace whatsover, knocking him off his feet.

A second later, Carter fell on top of them. He tried to punch Norris, missed, swore, then tried again. His fist connected with a solid thud. The vertigo eased as Norris went limp. Carter yanked his arms behind his back and cuffed him with a pair of shiftsilver cuffs.

"Good work," he said to Natalie.

"You too," she replied.

But while Natalie and Carter had been taking out Norris, their enemies had used that time to get into position. Now their way out was blocked by Elayne, the chupacabra that was Costello, the gargoyle, and the quetzalcoatlus. Not to mention the now-unseen Jager, who could shoot them at his leisure.

Even worse, the Defenders hadn't instantly recovered from the vertigo attack. Merlin and Ransom were still down on the ground, while Pete had only made it to his knees. Roland was on his feet, but had his jaw clenched and looked distinctly queasy. Wally and Heidi were curled up into miserable-looking balls.

"Surrender," called Elayne. "As you can see, your position is hopeless."

"Ransom!" Natalie shouted, putting a note of panic into her voice. "Are you all right?!"

She ran to him and knelt at his side. Like the puppies, he was curled up in a ball and was clearly down for the count. She'd expected as much, and was relieved to see that at least the fall didn't seem to have reopened his wounds.

"Pete, Merlin," she said, in her softest whisper. "Don't move." Then, high and shrill, "Talk to me, Ransom!"

"Everything's spinning," he said. Impressively, he was managing to mumble loud enough for Elayne and the others with her to hear him. "I feel sick."

He continued in that vein as Natalie flicked a glance around without moving her head. As she'd aimed for, between her and Pete, the enemies' view of Merlin was blocked.

"Merlin, be a tiny dinosaur," she whispered.

The man vanished, replaced by a velociraptor the size of a gecko. Using her own body to block the view of her foot, Natalie pulled off her shoe. "Get that splinter out of my foot."

The velociraptor was visibly wobby, but he extended his tiny claws. There was a sharp pinch, and then she felt the shiftsilver splinter slide out of her foot.

She replaced her shoe and said loudly, "Lie still, Ransom. Don't move. You'll start bleeding again." Then, very softly, she said, "I'm done."

The next instant, Pete vanished and an immense, shaggy cave bear charged their enemies. His tremendous paws seemed to shake the earth.

Natalie expected him to get shot by a dart and forced into his human form before he reached their enemies. Apparently they thought so too, because rather than run or fight back, they just stood there smirking.

Pete reached the gargoyle, reared up, and swatted him with an enormous paw. The gargoyle shattered into a million pieces of shiny black stone.

The quetzalcoatlus let out a startled screech.

"Jager!" yelled Elayne. "Why didn't you shoot him?!"

"I did!" Jager shouted back. He was now crouched beside a car in the parking lot. "His fur's too thick!"

Pete lunged for the chupacabra, who leaped backward. Now out of his range, she lashed out her tongue at him, aiming for his less thickly-furred face. Pete ducked, and the tongue hit the shaggy fur of his back, writhed like a snake, then withdrew. Carter hurled a picnic chair at the beast, but she leaped aside. Then he was forced to duck that slimy, blood-sucking tongue.

Suddenly, the chupacabra let out an agonized howl. Its tongue began lashing out madly in all directions as it leaped around like it had a hotfoot. Natalie caught a glimpse of a tiny velociraptor clinging to its back, biting it, before the chupacabra threw itself to the ground and rolled. The mini velociraptor leaped free, scuttled away, and vanished from sight.

Pete charged Elayne, roaring, but was turned aside by the quetzalcoatlus. She stabbed her beak at him, but it was bashed aside by Roland, who had charged in swinging a heavy picnic table. She danced aside and screeched with fury, beating her huge wings. The wind they stirred up made even Roland stagger.

Natalie tensed, biting her lip. She wanted to help, but she was afraid to leave Ransom. He'd been able to help her with her ploy to get out the shiftsilver splinter without their enemies knowing, but there was no way he could fight. He hadn't even been able to walk without support, and that was before he'd been hit by vertigo.

But though he was down, he didn't look helpless. He'd rolled on to his belly and was watching the fight with an intensity that made her remember that he'd been a sniper in the Marines. All he needed to complete the picture was a rifle.

His gaze didn't leave the battle, but he reached out a hand to touch her, murmuring, "Wait."

Carter tossed aside his long coat, lunged forward, and grabbed the quetzalcoatlus. He clung tight to a leathery leg that was as tall as he was, making her stagger. Roland hit the great bird-creature again with the picnic table while she was distracted. She let out a frustrated screech, spread her wings, and took to the sky.

To Natalie's horror, Carter didn't let go, but clung tight to her as she vanished into the clouds. Natalie started to leap up to fly after them—she couldn't let Carter fall to his death—but Ransom seized her hand with an iron grip, whispering, "Don't. Carter can take care of himself. You'll see."

Reluctantly, she settled down. An unearthly screaming came from the clouds, mixed with the screech of the quetzalcoatlus. The keen of fury and despair raised the hairs on the back of Natalie's neck. Then the great bird-creature came tumbling down out of the sky, wings flapping madly as she fought…something. The wings of the quetzalcoatlus were so vast that Natalie couldn't get a good look at whatever it was that Carter had become. She saw sharp teeth slashing, a glimpse of a fierce yellow eye, and something lashing out that might have been a tail or a whip or a tentacle.

Together they crashed to the ground. The quetzalcoatlus sprang to her feet, and Carter, naked and barefoot and bleeding, staggered away.

"I'm hit," Carter shouted, yanking his discarded coat back on. "I can't shift!"

Pete and Roland glanced at each other, then Pete again charged the quetzalcoatlus, while Roland hurled the table at Elayne.

Elayne's form melted into that of the harpy, and the table went flying over her head. She sprang aloft, whipping out her wing to send a shower of feather-knives at Roland. He dove out of the way, but when he got up again, blood trickled from his arm. It looked like he'd only been scratched, but what about the next time she tried? They were all sitting ducks for Elayne and her feather-darts.

Ransom squeezed Natalie's arm, whispering, "Wait."

The chupacabra again began to screech and dance. Natalie almost laughed as she saw that Merlin had glommed on to her ankle like a sleek black velociraptor bracelet, biting her with little white fangs. This time she whipped out her tongue, wrapping it around her own ankle.

The velociraptor became man-sized, yanking her forward by her tongue. It whipped back into her mouth as she staggered. He lunged at the chupacabra, fangs gleaming...

...only to become Merlin again.

"Ow!" Merlin yelped, rubbing at his back. He twisted his arm up, trying to reach the area between his shoulderblades, then was forced to dive to avoid another attack from Elayne's feather darts.

"Got it," Ransom murmured. "Natalie, create a distraction. Make sure no one's looking at me. But don't shift until I tell you to."

She'd never in her life been so glad to be given the go-ahead to risk her life. She felt a grin crack her face as she leaped to her feet and screamed, "You think you've stopped me just because I can't shift? Guess what? It's showtime!"

Everyone stopped and stared. Then, moving faster than she had in her life, Natalie began turning cartwheels, flipping end over end as she catapulted herself into the fray.

CHAPTER 30

My mate, Ransom thought, pride swelling his heart.

He'd known he could trust her to create a distraction, but he'd had no idea quite what an amazing one it would be. He would have loved to lie there and watch her. But he had a job to do... if he could manage it.

He hadn't been a sniper for nothing. He knew everything there was to know about angles and velocity and how to find a gunman based on where the bullets hit. Or, in this case, where the shiftsilver darts hit.

At first he'd thought Jager was teleporting from place to place. But he'd been watching the man when Merlin was hit. Jager hadn't moved from his position beside the car. And unless he had the power to bend the path of a projectile in flight, he couldn't have hit Merlin's back from where he was.

Based on where Merlin had been hit, the sniper ought to be hiding in the ticket booth. And... Ransom tilted his head, keeping his eyes mostly closed... he could see a glint of metal from within.

Jager wasn't a teleporter at all. He was an illusion-caster, creating versions of himself that looked and sounded completely real, but disappeared when they were touched. And if Ransom could take him and his shiftsilver rifle out of the game, then Natalie could fight Elayne as a Gabriel Hound.

All Ransom had to do was move a couple yards without anyone noticing he was doing it, get into the ticket booth, and defeat Jager. Considering the number of enemies around, the fact that he had no idea what Jager's shift form was, and that Ransom was unarmed, it would be a daunting task under any circumstances. But right now, Ransom wasn't sure he could even stand up without passing out. He'd fallen hard when the vertigo had struck, and he could feel a spreading wetness across his chest where he was bleeding through the bandages.

You can do it, growled his hellhound.

Heidi, who'd been curled up at his side since the vertigo attack, uncurled herself enough to nuzzle him.

"Stay," he whispered to her and Wally.

The battlefield had erupted into pure chaos. Natalie was moving through it like a whirlwind, an avenging angel, a firecracker with sparkler hair. She was bringing every acrobatic skill she had to bear, tumbling and flying and cartwheeling and leaping.

Dali and even Tirzah had left the van to join the fight, along with Blue and the kittens. Dali was at Merlin's side, swinging a baseball bat at the chupacabra, while Blue pursued it at a leisurely but relentless pace. Tirzah was on the sidelines, operating a drone that harried Elayne while three angry kittens flew at her face. Pete was still a bear, so Jager must be entirely focused on him, waiting for an opportunity to shoot a splinter into the hairless skin of his nose.

Ransom would never get a better distraction.

Gritting his teeth, he began crawling on his belly toward the back of the ticket booth. He'd done that often enough as a sniper—it was much less attention-catching than standing up—but it also required more strength. His own weight felt like an impossible burden. Every time he pulled himself forward, he was sure he'd never be able to do it again. But he kept going, even when his vision grayed out. He had to give Natalie this chance.

His fingers touched something hard. Ransom blinked, concentrating fiercely, until his vision came back into focus. He was at the back of the ticket booth.

He could hear the battle, but not see it. There was a closed door in front of him, and his enemy inside.

Ransom took a deep breath, took hold of the wall, and dragged himself to his feet. Once again, his vision grayed out. He leaned his head against the wall, waiting for the dizziness to pass. While he did, he put his hand on the doorknob and twisted it the tiniest bit to see if it would move.

It didn't. The door was locked from the inside. He'd have to pick the lock with hands that were numb and shaky, without Jager noticing, and then fight him.

A sickening sense of anticipated failure clawed at his heart. How could he possibly fight like this? He could barely stand up.

He'd promised Natalie he'd take out Jager, but had he only given her false hope? Would he be the disappointment she'd feared so much?

You don't have to beat him up or tear his throat out, his hellhound growled. *You just have to make sure he can't shoot Natalie.*

Ransom wasn't sure how he could stop Jager without getting into a physical fight. Unless...

You can show me people's worst moments, Ransom said silently. *Can you be more specific than that? Can you show me their deepest fears?*

His hellhound seemed to think about that, then said, *I can show you the moment when he was most afraid.*

Ransom saw Jager, a little younger than when they'd met, working in a lab, yawning and rubbing his eyes. Clumsy with tiredness, he reached for for a beaker and knocked a jar over. Liquid splashed everywhere, on him and on the table and into the flame of a Bunsen burner. Fire exploded in all directions, burning off his eyebrows and setting the sleeve of his coat aflame. Jager staggered back, terrified, imagining that the entire lab would go up in flames and burn him alive...

And then Ransom was back in his own body, still leaning against the wall. He took a deep breath, then, pitching his voice higher to disguise it, yelled, "Fire! Fire! FIRE!!!!"

The door flew open. Jager stepped out, the shiftsilver rifle dangling from his hand as he looked around wildly.

Ransom snatched the rifle, ducked inside the booth, slammed the door, and locked it. He moved so smoothly and quickly that it was almost a single motion. He was finished by the time Jager let out an outraged yell.

His head swimming, Ransom staggered to the ticket window and shouted, "Natalie! Go!"

He had a perfect view of what happened next. Natalie was just starting a leap, dodging the chupacabra. She transformed in mid-air, becoming the magnificent Gabriel Hound with its moon-bright wings and starlight eyes, and she arrowed straight for the harpy that was Elayne.

Elayne, distracted by the flying kittens and Tirzah's drone, shot feather darts at her, but they went wild. Natalie soared above her and then, to Ransom's shock, became a woman. One hand darted into her shirt as she plummeted toward Elayne, and the other seized the harpy by the throat. Ransom caught the glint of glass and silver as Natalie tossed the remaining contents of the vial of shiftsilver straight into the harpy's beak.

Elayne became an unconscious woman in midair. Natalie, shifting to her winged hound form, closed her jaws around Elayne's coat and brought her down, dropping her in an unceremonious heap when she landed.

Ransom looked around. Costello, back in human form, lay face-down in shiftsilver cuffs. The quetzalcoatlus was fighting Pete, but she was so much bigger than him that it was easy for Ransom to nail her with a dart. The next instant, Barnes was back in her human form, to be pinned down by a cave bear paw and cuffed by a delighted Tirzah.

"Look out!" Roland shouted, pointing.

A huge Siberian tiger was snarling them from the left.

"There!" Dali yelled, pointing at the identical Siberian tiger growling from the right.

"Another one!" Merlin called, pointing at the Siberian tiger crouched in the Viking ship.

They were everywhere, surrounding his team and Natalie, snarling ferociously.

So that's Jager's shift form, Ransom thought. All but one had to be illusions. He could find out which by shooting them all, but he wasn't sure how many darts he had left.

Heidi and Wally sniffed the air. Then both puppies vanished. Heidi materialized behind one of the tigers, and Wally materialized in front of it. Wally barked fiercely as Heidi lunged forward…

…and Ransom fired.

Jager returned to human form, then let out a howl of pain as Heidi sank her teeth into his ankle.

"Good girl," Ransom said.

CHAPTER 31

Natalie called out, "Can someone come handcuff Elayne?"

The instant she saw Carter head over with a pair of shiftsilver cuffs in his hand, she bolted for the ticket booth. She tried the doorknob, then banged on it and shouted, "Ransom? It's Natalie!"

There was no reply.

"I need medical help!" Natalie yelled, snatching her lockpicks out of her bra.

She opened that lock in record time. Ransom was sitting in the ticket-taker's chair, but had fallen forward over the desk. Heidi appeared at his feet, tugging at his pant leg and letting out little anxious growls.

Natalie's fingers trembled as she reached to feel the pulse at his throat.

It was weak but present. Ransom was alive. He'd been willing to give his life to save her—to save everyone—but he hadn't had to.

She was so overwhelmed by sheer relief that dizziness came over her. It felt completely unlike the kind caused by her damaged heart, but was nearly as powerful. Her legs went out from under her, and she sat down on the floor with a thud.

Natalie didn't even try to get up. She leaned her head against the wall and thought about how everything she'd thought was unchangeable had shifted into a new pattern.

Ransom would live.

And so would she.

She imagined dust blowing around her ankles, but this time it was the dust of the open road as she and Ransom walked it hand in hand. And at the end of that road was the home they'd share.

Wally appeared in her lap, plonked his paws on her shoulders, and began chewing on her ear.

Roland and Merlin came running in.

"Merlin, help Natalie," Roland ordered, then went to Ransom and checked him.

Merlin crouched beside her. "Are you hurt?"

She shook her head.

"He doesn't have any new injuries," Roland reported. "Looks like he passed out from blood loss and exhaustion. And over-using his powers, knowing him. I'll take him to the van."

Roland lifted him and carried him out.

"Are you sure you're all right?" Merlin asked. "I mean, you're on the floor."

"I'm fine," she said. "I'm happy. It's just... a lot."

He put his arm around her shoulders. "I know the feeling. Need a hand?"

A month ago, she would have said no. She didn't *need* his help. But she did feel shaky, and some support would be nice. And while she didn't need him to help her walk, she did need his friendship.

"Yes, please," she said, and her inner Gabriel Hound wagged her tail.

"Sorry, buddy," Merlin said to Wally. "You're about to lose your seat."

Natalie had to lift him off. He gave her a reproachful look, then vanished. Merlin helped her to her feet, and kept a steadying arm around her shoulders as they walked out.

She wanted to explain why she'd left. She wanted to tell him how much fun Tomato Land was when you weren't fighting for your life, and that they should all visit it in the daylight. She wanted to ask him what in the world that big blue creature with the tiny wings was. She wanted to apologize for running away without a word, and to promise to never do it again. But there was so much, she didn't know where to start.

"I missed you," she said.

"Me too," said Merlin.

And that felt like enough.

Outside, Carter and Pete were standing guard over the prisoners. Elayne was still out cold, and Natalie hoped she was not enjoying her unexpected visit with her inner harpy. Jager was sprawled in a very uncomfortable position, looking absolutely furious, while Wally stood by his head, growling and barking and occasionally drooling on his ear.

Much as Natalie would have liked to make Jager suffer some more, she wanted to have Wally with her more. "Wally! Come!"

Wally made a sudden rush, bit Jager's nose, and vanished. Jager let out a shriek of shock and pain, and yelled, "By dose!"

"Serves you right!" Natalie shouted at him. Then she bent to pet Wally, now trotting sedately at her heels. "Good boy."

Inside the van, she found Ransom lying on a back seat, wrapped in blankets with a pillow under his head. His eyes were closed, but his color was better and he looked asleep rather than unconscious. Heidi was curled up at his feet, the fluffy blue creature was sitting on the floor and licking his hand, the three flying kittens squeezed in around him, and the two women and Roland were clustered around him.

It warmed Natalie's heart to see so much caring lavished on Ransom. He was clearly in good hands.

She sat down by him and held his hand. Wally appeared beside Heidi, prompting a brief but noisy scuffle between him and the spiky green kitten he'd displaced. It concluded with the kitten jabbing him in the nose with a sharp wingtip, whereupon Wally rolled over and placatingly showed his belly.

Merlin, who had clearly been bursting with the desire to introduce Natalie, indicated the curly-haired woman who used a wheelchair and said, "Natalie, this is Tirzah Lowe, our cybersecurity expert and Pete's mate." Then, in a tone of utter adoration, he laid his hand on the shoulder of the woman with black hair and elegantly arched eyebrows and said, "This is Dali Batiste, our office manager and my mate."

"Oh!" Natalie exclaimed. "Merlin, you have a mate! That's fantastic!"

"*She's* fantastic," said Merlin proudly. "Dali, Tirzah, this is my best friend from when we were kids, the trapeze artist and acrobat and target girl and apparently now a Gabriel Hound—"

Grinning to herself, Natalie thought, *Of course Merlin knows what my shift form is.*

"—and Ransom's mate, Natalie Nash!" Merlin concluded.

"Ohhh," chorused Tirzah and Dali. "We heard about you!"

"You did? Of course, from Merlin."

"Not *just* from Merlin," said Tirzah. "Also from other people at the Fabulous Flying Chameleons. They miss you, you know."

"Yeah," Natalie said, sobered by the reminder. "I know. I'll get back in touch with them."

"Why'd you leave?" Merlin asked. "Why didn't you tell anyone where you were going? And how did you and Ransom find each other?"

"Well…" She glanced out the window, trying to think of a short version, and was startled to see a pair of dragons spiraling down out of the sky. "Dragons!"

"They're friendly," Roland assured her. "I called them myself. They're cops. We can't send dinosaur shifters and wizard-scientists to normal jails."

Sure enough, the blue and silver dragons landed and became a blue-haired woman and a silver-haired man. They spoke briefly with Pete and Carter, who then came to the van.

Carter came in with his coat wrapped tightly around him, went straight to the back of the van with only a brief but very intent pause to check on Ransom, then declared, "Everyone turn your backs! I need to get dressed."

"As if anyone wants to see you naked again," Pete grumbled. He also bent over Ransom, then squeezed Tirzah's shoulder. "Great work with the drone."

"My pleasure," said Tirzah. "Great work with the bat-bird dinosaur."

"Quetzalcoatlus," came a quiet voice. Ransom had woken up, though he looked very tired. "Did I miss anything?"

"I'll catch you up," said Merlin cheerfully. "The dragon cops are collecting the prisoners, Carter's getting naked in the back—"

"Merlin!" Carter yelled.

"Everyone, buckle up." Roland took the driver's seat. Everyone scrambled to find a seat as he pulled out of the Tomato Land parking lot, heading back to Refuge City.

"—and Natalie's about to tell us how you two met," Merlin said, not missing a beat.

She glanced at Ransom, who took a breath like he was bracing himself to fight a quetzalcoatlus and said, "There's something I need to tell you all first."

His teammates all began to talk at once.

"Get some rest now, and tell us later," Pete said.

"Is it something immediately life-threatening?" asked Carter, barging forward barefoot and shirtless. "No? Then save it."

"Natalie didn't lose half the blood in her body, let her explain," suggested Merlin.

Natalie glared at him. That was the worst possible suggestion. Sure enough, Ransom struggled to sit up. "No! I have to tell you myself—"

"Settle down," said Roland, giving him a commanding stare via the rear view mirror. "That's an order."

"No—" Ransom protested. "I have to—"

"Relax," said Dali.

"If it's more than one sentence, it can wait," said Tirzah.

Exasperated, Natalie broke in. "Let him talk, you guys. Can't you see he won't rest till he does?"

At that, they quieted down. She took Ransom's hand. "I'll fill in the details, all right? You can stop me if I say anything that's not true."

He swallowed and nodded. When he spoke, his voice was quiet but steady. "Jager and I worked together. We—I—invented a process for enhancing intuition. I used it on myself." He stopped to catch his breath.

Quickly, Natalie said, "He found out that Jager was going to use it on people without their consent. Ransom tanked his entire career blowing the whistle on him."

He nodded, then went on, "I thought the project was shut down. I didn't know Jager took it to black ops. They made it more powerful. More dangerous. It became the Ultimate Predator Process. And they became Apex."

Carter sucked in a breath, then turned red with fury. "*Now* you tell me?"

Natalie was horrified. She'd been so sure his teammates would understand!

Ransom didn't say a word, but his entire body seemed to sag with resignation. That must be what he'd looked like when he'd been strapped to the lab table, and let the hellhound bite him because he thought he deserved it. Her heart broke for him.

"Jager was *right there!*" Carter went on. "The man who ruined my life! How could you let me get in the van and drive away from him? I would've killed him! For me—for all of us—for you! He stole your invention and twisted it into something evil. Why did you let me go without getting revenge for us both? Roland! Turn this van around!"

Roland kept on driving. Natalie glanced at his face in the rear view mirror, but his expression was unreadable.

Ransom's, on the other hand, was purely astonished. "You're only angry at Jager? What about me?"

"What about you?" Carter snapped. "Roland!"

Without looking back, Roland said, "I'm not turning around so you can attack a prisoner."

"But—" Carter broke off when Natalie grabbed his arm.

"Carter," she said, her patience fraying. "If you don't blame Ransom, tell him so!"

"Of course I don't blame you." Carter sounded annoyed that he had to say so, as if it ought to be self-evident. "If someone gets run over by a reckless driver, that's not on Henry Ford. You should've said something earlier, though. You're, what, a chemist?"

"A biochemist."

"You should've said so sooner. I like talking science. And chemistry's not my field at all, so I could learn a lot from you."

Ransom looked relieved, if a bit bewildered, but hadn't relaxed yet. His gaze slid to Merlin, who waved his hand and said, "I hope you never thought *I'd* blame you. Is that how you always seemed to know when something was going to go down, when we were in the Marines?"

Ransom nodded.

"How cool!" Merlin exclaimed, then chuckled. "Do you remember that time when I think you thought I was coming out to you? I mean as gay? I thought you were a shifter and you could smell bombs or something, and that was why I was trying to tell you it was safe for you to come out to me. I mean as a shifter. Though if I *had* been gay, you would have been a great person to come out to. Or if I'd been a shifter myself, for that—"

Dali nudged Merlin. Hard. He broke off in mid-sentence.

Pete put his hand on Ransom's shoulder. With a surprising gentleness, he said, "I've been inside your mind, remember? I didn't know any of this. But I do know *you*. What Natalie said about you destroying your own career to try to stop Jager—that doesn't surprise me at all. You're not the kind of guy who invents grenades. You're the kind of guy who throws himself on them."

Ransom opened his mouth, as if he was going to argue, then closed it. Natalie felt him try to push himself up—to see Roland in the rear view mirror, she realized.

"Lie down," said Roland. "You know and I know that you're not the one who killed her."

Her? Natalie wondered, then remembered Ransom saying that Roland had never stopped grieving for a woman whose name he didn't know.

"If that's the burden you've been carrying, you can lay it down," he went on. "None of us are asking you to bear it. And I'm sure she wouldn't, either."

Ransom drew in a deep breath. Once again, his gaze drifted around the van, searching for blame that wasn't there.

"Ransom," Natalie asked softly. "What's your hellhound say?"

"He says to lay it down.'" For the first time since she'd met him, he looked truly at peace. His eyes closed, and his breathing settled into the deep rhythm of sleep.

Natalie sat stroking his hair and not paying much attention to anything else while Carter retreated to the back to finish dressing and Tirzah connected her laptop to her drone and Roland made a series of phone calls and Dali petted the puppies and Merlin found a pair of tweezers in a first aid kit and twisted his arms behind his back to remove the shiftsilver splinter. But slowly, what was going on inside the van started registering more with her, especially as the others in the van seemed to decide she'd had enough quiet time.

"Want me to get your splinter out, Carter?" Merlin offered.

Carter emerged, fully dressed but still barefoot. "I was thinking of leaving it in. Permanently."

"Seriously?" Tirzah asked.

He rolled his eyes, then looked away. "Well—Maybe. It's definitely quieter with it in."

Quieter? Natalie thought.

"Not a good idea," Roland called back from the driver's seat. "I just got off the phone with the dragon cops. They strongly advise removing the splinters as soon as possible—they said I should stop at the next rest stop to get mine out."

"What happens if you leave them in?" Carter asked. "You never shift again?"

Natalie couldn't tell if he asked that with dread or with hope. She wondered if his shift form—which, she realized, she still didn't know—talked to him like Ransom's hellhound used to.

"I don't know about that," Ransom replied. "But it's poisonous in large doses, and a splinter of solid metal constitutes a large dose if you leave it in long enough for it to dissolve."

"Oh." Grumpily, Carter said, "Fine, Merlin, take it out."

He took off his black coat, carefully folded it and laid it down on a seat, then pulled up his shirt and tapped his lower back. "Here." A moment later, he added, "Thanks."

Merlin put down the tweezers, became a tiny velociraptor, and leaped from his seat to Carter's.

"Agh!" Carter yelped. "What—"

The small raptor dug his claws into Carter's back, provoking another yelp, and withdrew them clutching a silvery splinter. Still holding it, he jumped back to his seat and returned to human form.

"What did you do that for?" Carter demanded. "Am I bleeding on the shirt I saved specifically *not* to bleed on? You had the tweezers right there!"

"You're not bleeding, you big baby," said Dali. "Merlin was very careful."

"I'm a baby for not wanting to ruin a good shirt?"

"It's easier to use my claws," said Merlin, unruffled. "Also, it's more fun."

Natalie laughed. "You really love your shift form, don't you?"

"It's the best! Do you love yours? You do, don't you? Is it wonderful to fly? Could you take me flying? I mean as a small raptor."

"Yes, yes, and yes. I could take you as a man, actually, if we jumped from a height. I flew with Ransom on my back before I got shot with a splinter and we got dumped into a pool of fake tomato juice." Then, because it was Merlin and he loved a good story, she added, "And then a giant prehistoric fish jumped into the pool."

"You need to tell me *everything*," Merlin said. "The entire story. How you met. How you got the puppies. *Everything.*"

Roland pulled into a truck stop. "Get my splinter out first, Merlin. I'll let you do it as a raptor. As a special treat for you."

Merlin laughed, shifted, and scuttled up front.

"Want some cookies, Natalie?" Tirzah offered.

Natalie was about to say she wasn't hungry when she realized that in fact, she was *starving*. "Yes, please."

Tirzah began pulling little boxes and shrink-wrapped parcels out of her purse. "I have snickerdoodles, chocolate chip cookies, lemon-rosemary shortbread, and Moravian sugar cake. That's not a cookie, it's more like a coffee cake. Gifts from my neighbors. And Merlin. He made the sugar cake."

Natalie's brain stalled out like an out-of-gas car when she tried to decide which sounded best. "Um…"

"She's still in the combat zone, Tirzah. It's not a good time to make decisions." Pete opened a compartment, removed a paper plate, and began opening all of Tirzah's packages and dumping them on to the plate. When he was done and the plate was piled high, he set it down beside her. "There you go."

Natalie grabbed the closest one and stuffed it in her mouth. She'd barely finished swallowing it before she attacked the next. She felt vaguely guilty over using what were undoubtedly delicious cookies as mere fuel, but she needed that fuel.

Roland craned his neck around, making the tiny raptor perched on his bare shoulder give a hiss that probably meant, *"Stop squirming."*

"We can stop at a drive-in," Roland said. "Do you have any special requirements, Natalie?"

"Special requirements?" Natalie asked blankly through a mouthful of buttery lemon-rosemary deliciousness.

"Vegetarian? Kosher? Gluten-free—no, I can see not that one."

She swallowed, then said, "No, nothing like that. But you don't need to stop for me. I can wait."

A chorus of voices went up, as every single person in the van who was conscious and not currently a raptor assured her that they were hungry too and she wouldn't be inconveniencing anyone, then immediately began to squabble over what sort of food they wanted.

"No chain restaurants," said Carter and Merlin, almost simultaneously, then glanced at each other as if they had mixed feelings about being on the same side.

"What's the matter with chains?" Pete inquired in an ominous tone.

Roland started up the van again, an action which Natalie would never have thought of as being expressive but which conveyed a clear sense that they were going to eat whatever was available wherever he drove them to.

So these were Ransom's teammates. She could see why he cared so much about their friendship, and why he'd been so glad to be back on the team. The way they squabbled and looked out for each other reminded her of the circus. Maybe that was why Merlin had been content to leave the Fabulous Flying Chameleons for the Defenders—they were a three-ring show all by themselves.

Merlin noticed her looking at him, and went to sit by her. "I imagined us meeting up again a bunch of times, but I never imagined it would be on top of a tomato vine water slide and you'd nearly chuck me off it because I was a gecko-sized raptor and you thought I was attacking you."

"Me neither," Natalie admitted.

Lowering his voice, Merlin asked, "Why *did* you leave? I've been wondering and wondering."

"It's a long story," she began.

"It's a three-hour drive back to Refuge City."

Natalie had forgotten how persistent he could be. Then again, she no longer had any reason not to tell him. Probably.

You're not dying, said her Gabriel Hound.

Am I completely cured, though? Natalie asked. *Was shifter healing all I ever needed?*

You're not cured, her Gabriel Hound replied, directing her attention to Tirzah's wheelchair and Dali's prosthetic hand. *But you're not dying.*

Merlin flipped his hand in a "go on" gesture.

"Before I start, I want to let you know that I'm all right now. I have a heart condition. But I'm going to live." Natalie heard her own words, which had been so long and hard in coming, and repeated them, just to savor their sound. "I'm going to live."

CHAPTER 32

Ransom awoke in an unfamiliar bed with a gloriously familiar body beside him. Even before he opened his eyes, he knew it was Natalie. He knew her slim legs, her strong shoulders, her breasts the perfect size to cup in his hands. He knew her scent, that bright lemon sharpness with a warm musky tang underneath. He knew the tousled silk of her hair.

He opened his eyes, hoping to catch her asleep. It was a moment in time that he wanted to enjoy, like so many other moments: Natalie sleeping, Natalie waking, Natalie laughing, Natalie flying through the air—with or without wings.

Her head rested on his chest, and her eyes were still closed. Her hair was mussed with sleep, a lock of tomato-red obscuring her shell-pink ear.

I wonder if I'll ever think of anything but tomatoes when I see a shade of red, he thought. A chuckle escaped him at the thought.

And then he got to see Natalie waking up. Her eyelids fluttered, she nestled in closer with a soft sound that went straight to his heart, and then her eyes flew open.

She lifted herself on one arm, peering down at him. "Hey! You're awake!"

He nodded, drawing in a cautious deep breath. It didn't hurt. His chest and side were freshly bandaged, and he wore clean pajama bottoms. "How long have I been out?"

She rolled over to peer at the small clock on a side table. "Looks like a day and a half for both of us. I was exhausted. I vaguely remember taking a shower with Dali knocking on the door every few minutes to make sure I hadn't fallen asleep standing up. I guess I did, because I don't remember going to bed. Whose house did they take us to?"

"No one's. It's the bedroom at Defenders."

Natalie sat up, rubbing her eyes and looking around. "You have a bedroom in your office?"

"We sometimes have witnesses or people we're protecting, who need a safe place to stay..." Ransom realized that he was using 'we' as if he was still on the team, then remembered that he *was* still on the team. Roland had said so. And none of his teammates blamed him or were angry with him. And Natalie would live.

Natalie would live.

"We have time now," he said. "We have all the time in the world."

"Let's start using it." Her eyes gleamed opalescent, catching glints of sea blue and leaf green and storm gray. "If you kiss me now, I won't drop dead."

"How could I resist such a romantic invitation?"

He leaned in, and all playfulness fell away as their mouths met. Her lips were soft and hot, her body molding itself to his. Her small strong fingers clenched on his shoulders as their kiss deepened and lengthened. His head swam with a haze of conflicting desires. He could kiss her forever, and be satisfied. He had to rip off their clothes and bury himself in her, right now.

A yip and a bark made them jerk apart. Heidi and Wally were sitting on the carpet, staring at them soulfully and wagging their tails.

"Just what we want," Natalie said drily. "An audience."

Let me help you, said her Gabriel Hound.

"Go take a walk around the office," Natalie ordered the puppies. "A *long* walk."

A trace of her inner hound's growl was in her voice. The pups vanished.

A silence fell. The air felt charged with electricity, as if before a storm. Ransom imagined that if he touched her now, sparks would fly from the point of contact. And he also knew that if they touched again, they wouldn't stop at kissing.

"It *is* safe now, isn't it?" Ransom asked.

"My hound says it is. And she should know. Apparently I still need some sort of treatment, but…" She shrugged. Even that ordinary up-and-down motion of her shoulders was fluid and beautiful. Entrancing. "If *you're* up to it…"

"I am," he said immediately. "Shifters heal fast."

"Then there's nothing to stop us now."

Ransom swallowed. He could almost hear the air crackling between them. His blood felt as if it had been replaced by a surging electric current. "All that time lying in separate beds. I thought I was going to lose my mind."

"Me too. What did you imagine doing, when we were lying there?"

"Other than everything?"

Natalie's rose-pink lips curved into a smile. Her voice was low, almost a purr. "When you were imagining everything, what did you imagine most?"

An image leaped into his mind, complete with scent and touch and taste. "I—"

She reached out and put the pad of one fingertip to his lips, silencing him. That one little touch sent a jolt straight down his spine. "Show me."

He was relieved not to have to talk. He was hard as steel, his mind swimming with pure need. But even in the midst of the primal drives of body and soul, he was touched by her trust. She was telling him that there was nothing he could do that she wouldn't want. That she wanted him, all of him, everything that he was and anything he might do.

He could see her desire in the brightness of her eyes, hear it in the huskiness of her voice. He could even sense it through the mate bond they shared. But that bond wasn't only of lust, but of absolute acceptance and unconditional love. Ransom, who had never in his life felt that he belonged, knew that wherever Natalie was would always be his home.

They were both wearing the plain black pajamas that the Defenders kept on hand for clients who needed a safe place to stay and hadn't had a chance to pack. Natalie's pair was too big for her; the pants were baggy and the shirt fell low. As his gaze dropped to her cleavage, he saw a flush color her chest, rising upward as if her body was responding to his gaze alone.

"It's like you're touching me already," she murmured.

The tone of her voice made him want to rip her clothes off and have her then and there. But he'd promised to show her what he'd imagined, and it hadn't been that. At least, it hadn't only been that. And after all that long, frustrating time of being so close and yet unable to touch, he wanted to savor the experience to the fullest. And to tease her, just a little bit. She'd teased him often enough.

He unbuttoned her pajama top, taking his time while he listened to her breath catch and watched her flush deepen. Without touching her skin yet, he could feel her heat. Her scent surrounded him, lemon sharpness and a hot feminine musk, going to his head like whiskey.

When the last button was open, he pushed the top off her shoulders. In all that time sharing motel rooms, she'd never undressed in front of him and he'd always been careful not to look. He'd never seen her breasts before. They were small and perfect, pale where the rest of her body was lightly tanned. He thought of white pearls touched with pink, and white roses with pink hearts.

He cupped them in his hands, drawing a gasp from her, then bent his head to kiss them. Her nipples hardened under his tongue, and he felt her breath catch again.

"That's what you imagined?" Her voice was ragged and stuttery.

"That's only the start of it." He felt on the edge of losing control himself. "I want to taste every inch of you."

"Do it."

Taste and scent were intertwined; if you can't smell, you can't taste. Maybe that was why her skin had a tang of salt and lemons. It was unexpected and irresistible, like Natalie herself. It made him want more and more. The more he kissed her, the more he wanted to.

He kissed her breasts and teased at her nipples, then went upward, giving the delicate hollows and graceful arches of her collarbones the attention they deserved. And up to her mouth, where he nearly lost himself in its heat and passion. Then down again, to her strong shoulders and silk-skinned forearms and clever fingers. When he finished kissing her hands, he put each fingertip in his mouth, one by one, and sucked gently.

"No one ever did that before," she said, her voice filled with wonder as well as desire.

He pulled back to ask, "Do you like it?"

But he could see her answer in her body before she gave it to him in words. The flush had spread all over her body. Her eyes were bright as stars, her hair darkening and curling with sweat, shining moss green and ocean blue and old gold. He could see the rapid rise and fall of her chest, and her rose-pink lips were parted.

"I like it," she said, once she caught her breath. "I never knew it could feel so good."

"The hands are an underrated erogenous zone."

Her laugh was a summer breeze on his face. "No, Ransom, I think it's just you."

He caught her by the hand and tugged her to her feet, leading her so she stood with her back against the wall. Then he knelt at her feet.

"Oh," she said in a tone of enlightenment. "Yes, please!"

She stepped neatly out of her pants, kicking them aside. He wanted to take a moment to just look at her, completely nude and beautiful, at her breasts like pearls and her skin like pink silk and at all the lovely lines of her slim, strong body. But her scent was everywhere, driving him wild, and he'd held himself back as long as he could bear.

He bent to her, inhaling her intoxicating scent. She made a soft sound and leaned back, her thighs parting to let him in. The soft curling hair was its natural color, the golden brown of beach sand. He smoothed it aside to reveal her pink folds, wet as roses in rain. She squirmed, her breath coming quick and hard, and her hands came down to grip his shoulders. When he gave her the first exploratory lick, they clenched down hard, and she gasped aloud.

This, *this* was what he wanted: to taste her, to make her tremble, to feel her come under his mouth. He licked at her clit, and felt it swell under his tongue. She tasted and smelled sweet and tangy as lemonade, but that was too innocent an image. There was nothing innocent at all about her wetness, her heat, the pulse of her inner walls, her female musk, the trembling of her inner thighs, her gasps of "Go on, go on, there, there, yes!"

He felt as well as heard it when she came with a short, sharp cry. Her whole body stiffened and trembled, then relaxed, her hands resting lightly on his shoulders rather than gripping for dear life.

"Oops," she said.

"What?"

"Your shoulders."

He twisted his head to see. She'd clenched down so hard on his shoulders that her short-clipped nails had bitten into his skin, leaving tiny half-moon cuts.

"Don't worry about it," he said. "I imagined that, too."

Natalie had come harder than she had in her entire life. But her appetite was more whetted than satisfied. She'd waited so long, she needed more of him. And though he'd obviously enjoyed himself, she wanted to give him some of the same pleasure he'd given her.

She let herself lean on him for a moment, resting her weight on his broad shoulders. She hadn't meant to cut him with her nails—she hadn't realized that was even possible, given how short she kept them—but once she realized he didn't mind, she liked the thought of having marked him.

"It means you're mine," she said.

"Always," he replied, looking up at her. His dark deep eyes now held endless love rather than endless sorrow.

She took him by the hand and tugged. He came easily to his feet. The lean musculature of his chest was heightened by a mist of sweat, and his masculine scent was making her lightheaded. Bandages were still taped to his chest and side, stark white against his skin. He seemed fine, but she didn't want to do anything *too* acrobatic. Luckily, that wasn't what she wanted right now anyway.

"I feel underdressed," she said, startling a laugh from him. "Better take off your pants."

He stepped out of his black pajama pants. For the first time, she saw him completely naked. His body was glorious, a masterpiece of strong lines and firm muscle. He was too tall to be a trapeze artist or acrobat—they tended to be on the shorter side—but he was built like one otherwise, with his long legs and lithe body.

And, looking down, she had absolutely no doubt about exactly how much he wanted her.

"Come on," she said. "Let me show you what *I* imagined."

She led him to bed, and gently pushed him down on his back. A tremor coursed through his body, and his hands fisted in the sheets. She could see how hard it was for him to hold himself back, but he was doing it for her. All that strength and control, and he was giving it to her, offering himself up like a gift. The sight of it made her even more hot and wet than she was already. Desire surged within her, making it impossible to wait and taste and tease him, as he had done to her.

"You always were the patient one," she muttered.

She settled down on top of him, straddling him, taking him within her in one smooth motion. He slid in easily, she was so wet and ready.

"Natalie!" Ransom gasped.

She couldn't speak. The feeling of being filled by him was too intense for words. Pleasure sparked and blazed along every nerve as she began to rock against him, bracing her palms on his shoulders. He grasped her around the upper arms, steadying her as they moved together in perfect sync.

They were joined, not only physically but in the heart and spirit. She could feel the bond between them like a thread bright as sun and strong as steel, a love and a commitment that would never break.

"Mine," he said, in a voice that held a hint of a growl.

"Yes!" Natalie said. "Yes, yes, yes!"

"I love you," Ransom gasped, his eyes opening wide as he gave himself up to ecstasy. "Natalie—"

A wave of pleasure bore her along, higher and higher, as if she was flying. When it finally crashed down, she saw stars.

They fell together, utterly satiated. Natalie slithered down and lay alongside him, and he gathered her into his arms. They lay as if they'd been poured onto the bed, boneless as a pair of cats. She turned her head and lazily kissed the hollow of his throat, tasting the salt of sweat.

"Just think," she murmured. "We could do this every day. We could do it tomorrow!"

"Why wait for tomorrow?" Ransom returned. "We still have tonight."

CHAPTER 33

They took a long, leisurely shower, delighting in each other's bodies and presence. The bright colors of Natalie's hair darkened under the water, scarlet becoming maroon and lemon becoming mustard, then lightened again as Ransom helped her dry her hair.

"I need coffee," she said. "I have a lot of phone calls to make, and I need to be fortified for them."

"To who?"

"The circus. I need to apologize for running out on them, and tell them I'm all right, and I found my awesome sexy mate, and I met up with Merlin, and..." She leaned her head back against his chest, looking up at him. "And I have to tell them I'm not coming back. I guess unless you want to run away to the circus."

"Janet did invite me to join on as a juggler."

"Do you want to?"

Ransom remembered the surprising joy he'd felt performing, and how tempted he'd been to say yes. "I was tempted at the time. But I didn't want to leave my team. And I don't think it would suit me in the long run. But if you want to go back, I'd go with you."

"I'd rather go in with you. Think the Defenders could use an acrobat who can turn into a Gabriel Hound?"

"Absolutely," he said, without even having to think about it. "You fought like you were born to it, you can pick locks and break into buildings, and you always have a story ready. I'd love to work with you. That is, if you were serious."

"I was. We had a lot of time to talk, driving back to Refuge City. I like your team. And hey, I've got a new lease on life. I'd like to try something new."

"Let's talk to Roland. I'm surprised he hasn't asked you already."

The puppies reappeared, then flopped down on the bed and went to sleep. Apparently they'd taken the "long walk" command very seriously.

"Is everyone going to be waiting for us as soon as we leave the room?" Natalie asked. "I'm picturing opening the door and everyone jumps out, yelling, 'Surprise!'"

"It's a bit early in the morning for that. Though I wouldn't put it past them." But once Natalie had put the idea in his mind, he opened the door with caution. To his relief, no one leaped out. The building proved to be inhabited only by Roland, whom they found in his office, prodding at a wilting potted plant.

"If the leaves turn yellow and fall off, does it mean I'm over-watering or under-watering?" Roland asked the room at large, then said, "Don't answer that. I'll Google it."

"Neither," said Ransom. "It needs a bigger pot and more sun. And you don't need to worry, that just came to me. It didn't hurt."

Roland's gaze flickered from him to Natalie, and then he said, "I have some things I wanted to ask both of you about. I could do it separately…" They both shook their heads. "Together, then. Have a seat."

They sat down, their hands clasped over the arms of the two chairs. To save Roland any awkward explanations, Ransom said, "Natalie already knows how I left."

"Yes…" Roland looked them both over, lines of thought creasing his forehead and cheeks.

Once Ransom would have assumed he was being judged or critiqued in some way. Now he thought how lonely Roland's office seemed, with the plants that never seemed to thrive, the big chair where he sat like a solitary king, and the desk that crouched in front of it like a barricade.

"About that ultimatum I gave you," Roland said. "Forget—"

Ransom held out his hand. "Give me the number for the coyote therapist."

Roland hesitated. "I should probably tell you, I was going to say that I was wrong to—"

Natalie held out her hand as well. "I want the trash panda."

Amusement twinkled in Roland's eyes. "Good choices." He rummaged in his desk, produced the slips of paper, and handed them one each.

"Do *you* have someone to talk to?" The question escaped Ransom without planning.

His boss looked taken aback. "You don't need to worry about me. I've got all of you."

Yes, Ransom thought. *But do you ever really* talk *to us?*

But if he'd learned one thing on his road trip, it was that you couldn't *make* someone talk, any more than you could strong-arm them into seeking help. Sometimes you had to sit still, hold out your hand, and wait for them to come to you.

"Last night—or whenever that was—was the last time you'll ever have to pick me up off the floor," he promised. "I've got much better control over my powers now. And my hellhound and I aren't fighting each other anymore. Anyway, I'm doing better."

"I can see," Roland said simply. "Welcome back."

And beneath those words, Ransom heard, *Welcome home.*

"Natalie, I don't know what your plans are," Roland went on. "But I've seen you fight as a woman and as a Gabriel Hound. I've seen that you can take initiative, take orders, and work as part of a team. You're absolutely fearless, you have unique skills, and you could fit into some places the rest of us couldn't."

"Yes, you're all on the large side," said Natalie, nodding seriously.

"Except Merlin, but he's got broad shoulders. I could definitely squeeze through some openings the rest of you would get stuck in."

Roland smiled. "I'll keep that in mind. But I meant in terms of going undercover."

"Like at a nunnery?" Natalie suggested, her eyes gleaming mischievously.

Ransom couldn't help laughing at that. Roland joined him, then said more seriously, "I was thinking more of a girls' school. Or even a regular high school. Any place where you either need to look younger than even Merlin can manage, or where men aren't allowed."

"A sorority," suggested Ransom. "Or a women's self-defense class."

"Or a lesbian bar," said Natalie. "Or Tomato Land 2: No Boys Allowed."

"Or the Flying Broom International Film Festival," said Ransom.

"Is that for real?" Natalie asked.

"Yes, it's held in Ankara, Turkey and—"

Roland held up a hand. "I feel like we're getting a little off-track. Natalie, would you like to join the team?"

"Would I ever! I can't think of anything I'd love more than getting to work with Ransom and Merlin and an office full of flying kittens, and get to wear disguises and pick locks and be a Gabriel Hound and fight crime!" She looked as radiant as Ransom had ever seen her, lit from within by sheer joy. Then, turning to him, she said, "So long as you don't think it would be awkward and unprofessional to date a teammate."

"Nope," he said, echoing her deadpan. "We're good."

"Then absolutely! Thank you so much!"

Natalie practically danced out of Roland's office. The puppies materialized when the door closed, hopefully holding their leashes in their mouths.

"I thought you guys were walked out," Ransom said. "Want some celebratory coffee and gluten, to commemorate your new job?"

"Absolutely. I love your boss. My boss. Our boss. I'll buy him a really special desk plant as a thank-you present."

"Don't get too attached to it."

"Maybe a cactus," she said, after some thought. "All else aside, I could definitely use a paycheck. There's something expensive—probably discounted now, but still expensive—that I have my eye on."

"What?"

"The Mustang. I know it's insured, but we did damage it. I think the rental company would take an offer to buy it."

Ransom thought of all the paychecks that had been piling up in his bank account, both from his work at Defenders and from his time in the Marines, while he spent absolutely nothing on himself because he thought he didn't deserve nice things. And he thought of Natalie's rainbow hair blowing in the wind with the top down, the puppies sticking their heads out the windows, the scent of sea brine, and how for the first time in his life, driving had been a pleasure rather than a necessity.

"Great idea," he said. "We'll fix it up, and we'll give it a good home."

He walked her to Darker Than Black, which he was relieved to see had not only survived, but was bustling. Natalie was very satisfactorily delighted with the décor, and Annabeth the barista was delighted to see Heidi again. Natalie took the puppies outside to claim their table while Ransom paid.

"Gonna be a regular here?" Annabeth asked. "Merlin is."

Ransom hadn't been a regular anywhere in years. A ghost of his old guilt and fear rose up at the thought of being seen, being known. There were many more victims of Apex than the ones he'd personally confessed to.

If any find you, then you will tell them, his hellhound said in his gravelly voice. *Just as you told your pack.*

"Sure," he told Annabeth. "I like the coffee."

He met Natalie at her outside table, and they carefully cut their pastries in half to share them. Glancing up after his first bite of the Coroner's Cake, he caught Natalie watching him with that hound-found-a-squirrel-up-a-tree expression. "What?"

"You don't look surprised," she said.

"Should I be?"

She shook her head, smiling. "No."

As they sipped their coffee, he remembered the last time he'd been there: how his hellhound had dragged him through the worst moments of passersby, and how the moment of peace he'd found drinking coffee in the car with Heidi had felt so fragile and precious.

"It's so peaceful here," he said.

Natalie glanced around, her gaze encompassing six uncooperative dogs dragging a frazzled dog-walker, a bike messenger darting in and out of traffic to a chorus of angry honks, and a person in a lobster suit staging a one-man protest outside of a seafood restaurant. "Yeah. It really is."

He could tell she wasn't being sarcastic. Then again, she'd been raised in a traveling crime circus full of shifters.

Licking a bit of icing off her lips, she said, "You're not getting information thrown at you all the time anymore, are you?"

"No. I get some knowledge without looking for it, but so far it's always been relevant. Merlin and Pete both got their powers under control after they met their mates. They thought the reason the powers were screwed up in the first place was a side effect of the wizard-scientists trying to make sure we couldn't bond with our mates. Once the bond happened, we could learn to use our powers."

"And your hellhound?"

"Also behaving."

You still have a lot to learn about my power, said his hellhound. *Shall I show you?*

Ransom repeated that to Natalie, who nervously asked, "What does he mean?"

"Well, he can do more than show me people's worst moments. I knew to yell 'Fire' because he showed me Jager's greatest fear."

"That's more useful. Though not much fun for you—you still have to experience it too, don't you?"

Ransom nodded, but his mind was already racing ahead. "I always thought 'worst moment' was a bit subjective to make sense as a power. Some people's worst moments were about grief, but others' were about guilt or anger or helplessness. Or fear—that's what gave me the idea that my hellhound could look for a fear, specifically. I don't think his power is about 'worst moments' at all. I think it's to see memories tied up with very strong emotion—any kind of strong emotion."

Natalie leaned forward, excited. "So you could see a person's happiest memory?"

"I think so." He pictured himself stroking his hellhound's soft ears and said, *Go for it.*

The memories opened like flowers. As he saw them, he narrated them to Natalie.

"That bike messenger everyone's honking at is opening an envelope. He got a full scholarship to Yale. He's the first person in his family to ever go to college. He's thinking of how proud his mother will be.

"That woman honking at him loves to travel. Her last birthday, she went to Japan. She was walking along a street in Kyoto on a misty evening, and the only place lit up was a ballet school. The dancers were practicing, and the light and the mist made a golden halo. It was the most beautiful thing she'd ever seen.

"The dog-walker's memory is of the first time she woke up next to the man who would become her husband. She touched his cheek, and he smiled in his sleep. That was when she knew they'd marry.

"The lobster guy… This is interesting. I thought his happiest moment would be scuba diving or something. But he was actually hired by the restaurant. They thought staging a fake protest would attract publicity. The lobster guy's been depressed for a while. When he got asked to do this, it was so ridiculous that it made him laugh. When he did, it was like the storm clouds parted and a little sunlight shone through. It made him realize that the way he felt wouldn't be forever. It made him realize there was hope."

Ransom fell silent. Sitting there with the woman he loved, experiencing the joy of all those people whose names he didn't know and would never know, he felt a hard knot of old pain inside of him starting to crumble away like a sugar lump in a cup of coffee.

"That's beautiful." Natalie sounded choked up.

"When my hellhound showed me everyone's pain, he said he was showing me the truth about the world. But this is the truth too. I just couldn't see it before."

The traffic continued to flow, the lobster guy got in a conversation with a woman wearing a SAVE THE WHALES baseball cap, and people went in and out of Darker Than Black. There were five million people in Refuge City. Every one of them had memories of heartbreak, and every one of them had memories of joy. You just had to know how to look.

CHAPTER 34

THREE MONTHS LATER

Natalie had always thought she hated routine. But she loved the ones she and Ransom had developed. Go to bed together. Wake up together. Shower together. Drink their morning coffee together. Drive to work together. They were ordinary moments, transformed into something beautiful and special with love.

Her pill box, for instance.

Natalie had dreaded seeing another doctor, who she worried would tell her to give up gluten and fun, but Ransom used either his power or Google to find her a cardiologist who specialized in athletes. They went in together, she told the doctor that she was a bodyguard who practiced the trapeze, and he did nothing but order a huge number of tests, then put her on three different medications and told her to practice with a net until she got used to them.

"What's the prognosis?" Natalie asked bluntly.

"Excellent. Take your meds and exercise regularly, and you'll have a completely normal life." Then he'd chuckled, adding, "As much as any trapeze artist bodyguard ever has a normal life."

"You have no idea," said Ransom.

She had no problems with the pills themselves. What she did have an issue with was their container. She had to take one pill twice daily, and two different ones once a day. For a while she had three little orange bottles sitting on a side table, but it was hard to remember if she'd already taken them or not. So she got a pill box marked with days and times, but it was big and ugly and extremely plastic, and she hated having it lurking by her bed among her books.

Ransom had his own pills by then, via a referral from his coyote shifter therapist, but his were antidepressants and he only took them once a day. But he actually seemed to enjoy contemplating his orange bottle. He'd taken the opportunity to study both their medications and how they worked, and for a while half his bedtime conversation was about the chemistry of the brain and heart.

As it turned out, she didn't have to look at the plastic monstrosity for long. A few weeks later, he presented her with a lovely little box carved with a beautifully detailed rendering of a Gabriel Hound. The golden grain running through the dark wood made the hound seem to be flying into the sun. When she opened it, she found tiny compartments with days and times marked on them.

"I asked Pete if he could make you a pill box that you'd actually enjoy using," Ransom explained. "But I didn't tell him what to carve on it. That was all him."

"I love it," Natalie said, running her fingers over the smoothly planed wood. "Now every time I take my meds, I'll gloat over this gorgeous little box, and being able to fly, and having such a thoughtful mate—and an awesome teammate, too."

"You don't know the half of it. He made me one too. I didn't ask him for that. Look." He showed her a box, the same size and shape as hers but made of sand-colored wood with a dark grain. The top of his was carved with a geometric design. "Recognize it?"

She started to shake her head, then remembered the fat textbook he'd been reading for the last month, *The Handbook of Clinical Biochemistry*, which he sometimes referred to when he talked about how their medication worked. "Is it a serotonin molecule?"

Ransom nodded. "I guess I shouldn't be surprised. He *did* get inside my head."

"He deserves the biggest and the best steak," Natalie said. "Though he'll still have to cook it himself if he wants it to come out edible."

Now that she and Ransom had rented a small, cozy house with an actual kitchen, Merlin, Dali, and Pete had offered to teach them to cook. Natalie did intend to take them up on that. Eventually. So far all the attempts had devolved into the cooks in the kitchen doing the actual cooking, and Ransom and Natalie hanging out, chatting and playing with the pets and occasionally chopping things upon command.

Today was no exception. They'd bought the ingredients for the barbecue, but Pete was going to do the cooking.

Ransom stretched. Natalie's heart sped up as she watched his lean muscles flex and lengthen, but now she welcomed the sensation instead of fearing it. Becoming a shifter had healed some of the damage to her heart, and the pills in her lovely little box took care of the rest. She could do and feel all she wanted now. And even months later, she wanted Ransom as much as she had when all they could do was hold hands and hopelessly long for each other.

"Do we have time for a quickie?" she asked.

"You always have time for a quickie," he replied, pulling her down on to the bed. "By definition."

Afterward, they showered and then dressed together. Natalie watched with pleasure as Ransom put on a pair of tight black jeans, an equally tight white T-shirt that showed off his arms and shoulders, and the black leather jacket.

"Best makeover ever," she said.

He looked over her usual leggings and the black top that showed off the rainbow of her newly touched-up hair. "You're gorgeous, like always, but you're missing something."

"I am? What?"

He opened a drawer and removed a tiny box. Not a wooden box, a jewelry box. "A ring."

Her hand flew to her mouth. They'd talked about getting married and had agreed that they wanted to, but they hadn't formally gotten engaged. Her old fear of being disappointed and abandoned flared up.

How awful would it be if she accepted his ring, and then everything fell apart?

Then she looked into Ransom's eyes, and knew that nothing would fall apart. They were the brown of earth, and what could be more solid and reliable than that? He loved her and trusted her, and he always would. She could believe in that.

Open it, said her Gabriel Hound, tail wagging hard enough to stir up a storm. *I want to see!*

She extended her hand. "Will you put it on?"

Ransom opened the box and slipped the ring on her finger. It was set with a small round ruby with a tiny, offset, oval-cut emerald—an unusual and striking ring, much more artistic and interesting than the usual engagement ring.

At least, that was how other people would see it.

"A tomato and a leaf!" Natalie exclaimed. "Oh, Ransom, I love it!"

All the love she felt for him went into their kiss. Then she broke off to exclaim, "Sorry, I forgot to say yes. Yes! Of course."

He smiled—an easy smile, full of love and sensuality and sweetness. "It's okay. I forgot to actually ask you."

A burst of barking alerted them that the guests had started to arrive. On their way to the front door, Natalie paused at the refrigerator to look at her bucket list, which was stuck on with a commemorative Tomato Land magnet in the shape of, unsurprisingly, a tomato.

Touching the very last item, which she'd added the day they'd moved in, she said, "Still my favorite."

"SQUID is my favorite too," Ransom said.

"It's LIVE and you know it," she said, elbowing him, then ran to answer the door.

Tirzah, Pete, his thirteen-year-old daughter Caro, and his mother Lola were first to arrive. Two flying kittens and a miniature pegasus accompanied them. Pete lugged containers of potato salad and cole slaw that he'd made, and also tamales that his mother had made.

"I helped," Caro said proudly. Then she whipped a chemistry test out of her pocket and waved it at Ransom. "Check out that A!"

"Good work," he said.

"I told you she needed you," said Pete. His tone was gruff, but Ransom clearly took it in the spirit in which it had been intended.

Natalie hugged Pete. "Thank you so much for the box. I love it. The old one made me feel like a suburban grandma."

"Nothing wrong with that," said Lola. While Natalie blushed and stammered an apology, Lola winked at her and said proudly, "I saw the box. He's so talented! I'm having him make one for me. Guess what'll be on it?"

Everyone chorused, "A cactus!"

Merlin and Dali arrived next. He carried an absurdly high and teetering set of boxes, while Dali was steadying her grandmother with a hand on her forearm and scolding a hangdog Blue.

"Bad bugbear," Dali said. Blue flopped down on his back, sending up a cloud of bright blue fur, and wagged his tail placatingly. "Oh, get up, you ridiculous creature." To the others, she said, "Merlin went berserk in the kitchen and produced eight different desserts. We brought seven. Blue ate the raspberry cupcakes. No treats for him tonight. He already had his."

Roland arrived late and frazzled, carrying a cake that looked like a sinkhole had opened up in the middle. "I'm not sure what happened. I followed the recipe exactly. But when I took it out to ice it…"

"I'm sure it'll be delicious," Natalie lied. Having tried his valiant attempts at baking before, she was sure of the opposite.

In the backyard, Pete manned the barbecue like a pro with assistance from Caro and backseat barbecuing from Merlin. The pets frisked around the yard, which was shielded from nosy neighbors by a high fence with multicolored morning glories growing all over it—one of the reasons they'd rented the house.

Carter showed up as Pete started handing out the barbecue, marching in with his black coat swirling around his legs and talking into an earpiece.

"She can't cancel the call! Who does she think she is, anyway?" He glanced up at everyone, then irritably said, "Well, make her reschedule it. I'm at a barbecue with my—with some associates."

Removing the earpiece, he said, "Fenella Kim's up to her usual tricks. Or, actually, these are new tricks. Usually she wouldn't miss a chance to get me on the phone to hold her leverage over me and make my life miserable. I'll take that big steak."

"No, you won't," said Natalie. "That's Pete's. He gave me and Ransom a set of absolutely gorgeous little boxes, so he gets the best."

Carter glanced down as she swatted his hand away. "Lovely ruby. Hey, is that an engagement ring?"

Natalie burst out laughing. "It is! I made Ransom promise not to mention it. I wanted to see who'd notice first. My money was on Merlin."

"Mine was on Lola," said Ransom.

Amidst the chorus of congratulations and requests to see the ring, Natalie wondered about Carter, with his sharp eyes and quick mind and mystery shift form. Now that she was on the team, she wished he'd go ahead and admit that he was on it too. But he still wouldn't. And she didn't even know why.

But he did take a different steak, only a bit grudgingly. And she even forgave him for his periodic phone-checking when he produced his own contributions to the barbecue: a bottle of very expensive sipping tequila for the adults and imported French elderflower lemonade for Caro.

"Thanks again for paying for the damages to Tomato Land, Carter," said Natalie. "I think you might've overpaid them, actually. They had a bunch of new animatronics the last time Ransom and I went. You should come with us some time and check them out."

"The way things have been going, I better not," Carter said gloomily. "I'd probably take one look at them, and they'd explode."

"I wouldn't blame yourself for the refrigerator incident," said Merlin. "Things just spontaneously explode sometimes."

"No, they don't!" chorused Carter, Dali, and Tirzah.

When they'd finished eating, Natalie gave a stealthy glance at Ransom. He was sitting on the grass tickling Heidi's belly, loose-limbed and relaxed, the picture of contentment.

"You ever think you'd be throwing a barbecue for your co-workers in your suburban backyard?" Natalie asked.

"If I had, I'd have thought it sounded like a conformist nightmare and the surrender of all my principles, but..." He gave a wave of his hand, encompassing the flock of kittens overhead, Blue creeping up on an oblivious Carter, and Roland trying to saw through his apparently steel-hard cake.

"Who knows?" Natalie said, snuggling in beside him. "A lot of those suburban homes might be surprisingly nonconformist if you ever got a look inside."

He smiled at her, stroking her hair. He looked happy, and unsurprised by it: as if he trusted that good things were real after all.

Laying her head in his lap, she knew she could trust that good things would last.

"Want to shift?" he asked. "I thought we could work up an appetite for Merlin's seven desserts playing with Wally and Heidi."

"Six desserts," she corrected.

The hem of Carter's coat was covered in blue fur, and Blue was slinking away from an empty box on the ground.

"Merlin!" Carter yelled.

"What?"

Natalie and Ransom left them to it. She summoned her inner hound and he summoned his, and a moment later they were chasing each other and the pups around the yard. Without either flight or teleportation, Ransom should have been at a disadvantage in their wild game, but he wasn't; he seemed to just *know* where a puppy would appear or when Natalie would swoop down.

First the kittens joined in, flapping in to swat at the hounds, then dart away. Then Blue, lumbering patiently after the quicksilver kittens and vanishing dogs. Next Caro joined in, with her mini pegasus flying at everyone's faces to distract them so she could tag them. And Merlin, of course, sometimes zipping around in his tiny form, sometimes suddenly growing big to grab at them with his new reach. He too played as a team, paired with Dali, who made up for his lack of flight by occasionally picking him up and tossing him at an aerial attacker.

If Natalie hadn't been a hound, she'd have laughed when she saw how Tirzah and Pete joined the impromptu game. She'd have expected Tirzah to stay in her wheelchair and let Pete chase people to her, as it wasn't easily maneuverable on the grass. Instead, Pete became a cave bear and Tirzah rode him, perched precariously atop his massive shaggy back.

The grandmothers stayed on the sidelines, sipping tequila and watching. Roland stayed with them, either so they didn't feel left out or because he was too comfortable in his lawn chair. Carter also didn't participate, but not because he was having too much fun where he was; in the quick glance that was all Natalie could spare him before she got blindsided by a three-kitten attack, he was pacing around on the sidelines making angry gestures and talking into his earpiece.

At last, the game ended by mutual exhaustion. Everyone who had been playing flopped down on the grass. Ransom didn't shift back immediately, so Natalie got a chance to stroke his soft fur before he became a man, and she found her fingers tangled in his hair.

"Best conformist nightmare of a suburban backyard co-worker barbecue ever," she said.

"Absolutely," said Ransom. Then he straightened up. "Hey—where's Carter?"

EPILOGUE

"*She what?*" Carter demanded.

With what he'd paid for his phone, he ought to get better service than the crackling, indistinct response that came through from Fenella Kim's assistant. "…very important. Where are you? Your reception… Can you go somewhere…"

"It's not my reception, it's your transmission," said Carter.

The shouting inside his head competed with the static as the assistant said, "…call you back in half an hour…. Talk…"

The line went dead. Did Fenella Kim seriously expect him to wander around looking for better reception so she could call him back in half an hour? Apparently so.

On the other hand, he was just as happy for an excuse to flee the happy shifter togetherness of the backyard barbecue.

"I'm taking off. I have a business call," Carter told Roland over his shoulder as he strode out, vainly trying to brush the fur from his coat as he went. Blue's hairs were particularly clingy.

He jumped in his car and peeled out of there, trying to ignore the cacophony of voices in his head. It was like a dungeon full of monsters, all fighting for supremacy. Half the time it was a completely incoherent babble of hisses and snarls and screeches, plus flashes of color that seemed to communicate emotions. Or maybe he'd just lost his mind and was imagining that part.

The actual voices, when he could understand them, were even worse.

Go back to the party, something growled. *I want to play with the dogs.*

I want to fight the dogs, something snarled. *They're our natural enemies!*

I want to fly, something screeched. *Far, high, away!*

Help me, something howled. *Make all these beasts go away! I want you all to myself!*

Help me, something shrieked. *I don't want to be here!*

An unhappy shade of eggplant-purple pulsed across his inner eye, then began rapidly flashing a frustrated bubblegum pink.

"Stop it," he said aloud. "Shut up!"

His inner monsters disliked being yelled at, but sometimes he couldn't help it. Needless to say, that only set them all yammering louder.

Go back!

Go away!

Go home!

Fly!

Run!

[irate maroon]

[ragey teal]

Help!

It was like that all the way to his penthouse. Carter felt like he was losing his mind. It was almost a relief when something slammed into his head from behind, plunging him into merciful oblivion.

He woke up with a splitting headache, in a very uncomfortable position on a very cold floor. His hands were cuffed behind his back.

Great. Just great.

Carter listened for a moment before opening his eyes, in case whoever had kidnapped him wanted to have a discussion with their henchmen in front of the unconscious prisoner, say about the location of the handcuff key. But he heard nothing except the hum of a large engine and some thumping, grunting noises like someone working out.

He opened his eyes a cautious crack, then all the way when he saw that he was in the empty cargo bay of a medium-sized aircraft, and it was empty except for another prisoner.

All he could see of her was a small, black-clad female figure, curled up into a ball with her back to him. Her hands, which had beautifully manicured nails, were cuffed behind her back. She was squirming around and making frustrated grunts, presumably trying to get free.

"Hello?" he said.

The woman uncoiled, as much as she could with her wrists and ankles cuffed, and rolled over. Her black hair was disarrayed, her beautiful face was bruised, and her dark eyes were absolutely furious.

That was before her eyes met his. When they did, he realized that her fury went all the way up to 11.

"You!" gasped Carter.

"You!" snarled Fenella Kim.

A NOTE FROM ZOE CHANT

Thank you for reading *Defender Hellhound!* I hope you enjoyed it. It's the third book of the *Protection, Inc: Defenders* series.

Protection, Inc: Defenders is a spinoff from the seven-book series *Protection, Inc.* The entire series is available now on Amazon. It begins with Bodyguard Bear. If you read the whole series, you'll catch the first appearances of the Defenders characters.

If you enjoy *Protection, Inc.* and *Defenders,* I also write the *Werewolf Marines* series under the pen name of Lia Silver. Both series have hot romances, exciting action, emotional healing, brave heroines who stand up for their men, and strong heroes who protect their mates with their lives.

If you'd like to be emailed when I release my next book, please click here to be added to my mailing list. You can also visit my webpage, or join my VIP Readers Group on Facebook and get sneak previews and free stories!

Please review this book on Amazon, even if you only write a line or two. Hearing from readers like you is what keeps me writing!

ALSO BY ZOE CHANT

Protection, Inc
Bodyguard Bear
Defender Dragon
Protector Panther
Warrior Wolf
Leader Lion
Soldier Snow Leopard
Top Gun Tiger

Protection, Inc: Defenders
Defender Cave Bear
Defender Raptor
Defender Hellhound

See Zoe Chant's complete list of books here!

Made in the USA
Monee, IL
15 October 2020